1921

For Karin and Bharat Parekh,
who introduced me to Bombay

THE WIDOWS OF MALABAR HILL

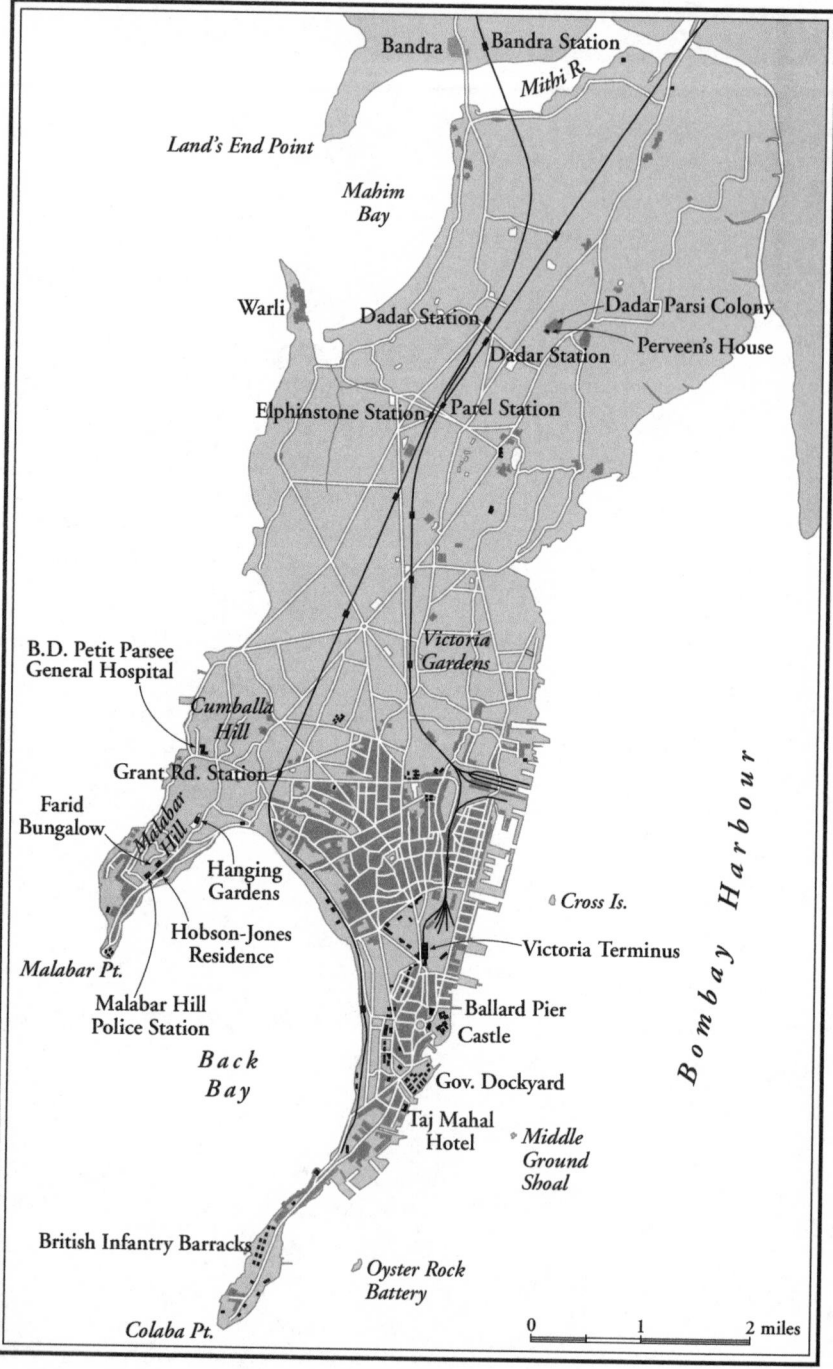

Bandra · Bandra Station
Mithi R.

Land's End Point

*Mahim
Bay*

Warli · Dadar Station · Dadar Parsi Colony
Dadar Station · Perveen's House

Elphinstone Station · Parel Station

*Victoria
Gardens*

B.D. Petit Parsee
General Hospital

*Cumballa
Hill*

Grant Rd. Station

Farid
Bungalow · *Malabar Hill*

Hanging
Gardens

Malabar Pt.

Hobson-Jones
Residence

Malabar Hill
Police Station

*Back
Bay*

Cross Is.

Victoria Terminus

Ballard Pier
Castle

Gov. Dockyard

Taj Mahal
Hotel · *Middle
Ground
Shoal*

Bombay Harbour

British Infantry Barracks

*Oyster Rock
Battery*

Colaba Pt.

0   1   2 miles

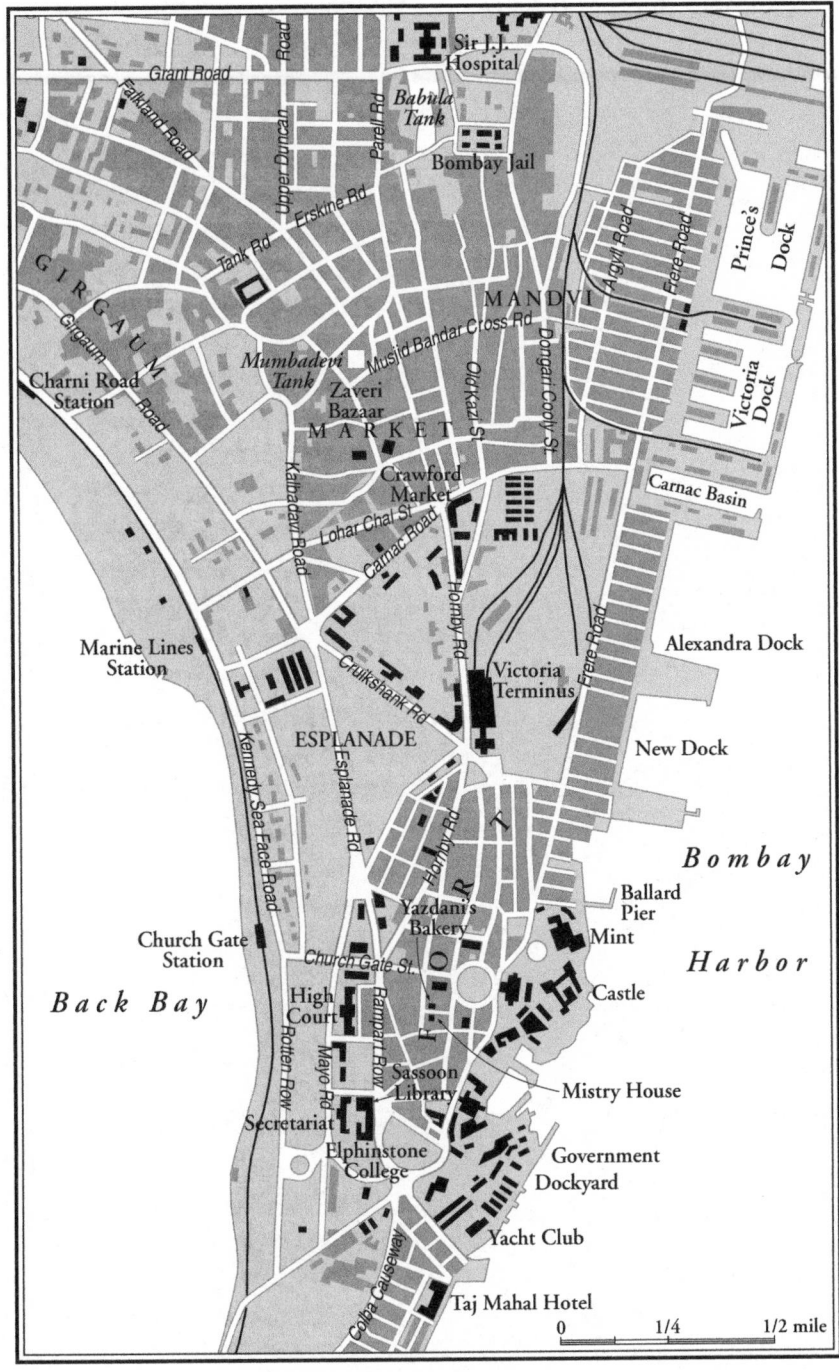

1

A STRANGER'S GAZE
Bombay, February 1921

On the morning Perveen saw the stranger, they'd almost collided. Perveen had come upon him half-hidden in the portico entrance to Mistry House. The unshaven, middle-aged man appeared as if he'd slept for several days and nights in his broadcloth shirt and the grimy cotton dhoti that hung in a thousand creases from his waist to his ankles. His small, squinting eyes were tired, and he exuded a rank odor of sweat mixed with betel nut.

A visitor to Mistry Law this early was rare. The firm was located in Fort, Bombay's first settlement. Although the old wall had been taken down, the district was still a fortress of law and banking, with most openings between nine and ten.

Assuming the man was a sad-sack client, Perveen glanced down, not wanting him to feel overly scrutinized. The idea of a woman solicitor was a shock to many. But when Perveen glanced down, she was disconcerted to see the man wasn't poor at all. His thin legs were covered by black stockings, and his feet were laced into scuffed black leather brogues.

The only place men wore British shoes and stockings with their dhotis was Calcutta, about twelve hundred miles away. Calcutta: the city that would always remind her of Cyrus.

As Perveen looked up, her alarm must have revealed itself. The man scuffled backward.

"Just a minute! Are you seeking Mistry Law?" she called as he rushed across the street.

Feeling perplexed, Perveen rapped on the door, which was opened moments later by Mustafa, the longtime butler in charge of Mistry House. The elderly man touched his heart and forehead in greeting before taking the tiffin box she'd brought with the day's lunch. "Adab, Perveen-memsahib," he said. "And where is your honorable father this morning?"

"He's got Jayanth's trial at the High Court. Mustafa, did you know someone was waiting in our doorway?"

He looked past her into the now-empty portico. "No. Where has he gone?"

"Across the street—he's the man wearing the dhoti." Perveen saw that the man was now standing in the shadow of a building.

Mustafa squinted. "Although dirty, he isn't a beggar. Not with shoes."

"Shoes and stockings," Perveen pointed out.

"Had he knocked, I would have told him to come after ten. You are too busy first thing in the morning for such strangers—although I saw no appointments in the book today?"

Perveen noted the worry in his voice. Mustafa knew that it was a struggle for her to attract clients. "I didn't book any appointments today because an old friend is sailing in from England. I'll meet her when she arrives."

"SS *London*?"

Perveen smiled. "You must have checked today's paper for the listing."

The grizzled old man tilted his head downward, accepting the praise. "Yes, indeed. I'll inform you when the *London* is unloading. And tell me, will your English friend come to Mistry House? I could prepare a small tea."

"I think Alice will go to her parents' home in Malabar Hill first—but perhaps she'll visit soon." Perveen surveyed the marble foyer, which was softly lit by lamps in gilded sconces. She would relish showing the Bombay Gothic building to her friend, Alice Hobson-Jones. The twenty-foot ceilings were a design feature of which Abbas Kayam Mistry, her late grandfather, had been especially proud. It always seemed as if her grandfather were watching from the long portrait guarding the entryway. His eyes, as inky black as his flat-topped fetah, were all knowing but not warm.

"I've got a load of papers to work through upstairs. I hope Pappa's back for lunch because I've brought a very good one today."

"He must win at court, Insha'Allah," Mustafa said piously, "or he won't have an appetite."

"He loses very rarely!" Perveen said, although that morning's case would be a hard one. Both she and Jamshedji had been quiet in the car coming in: he looking over his notes, she gazing out the window, thinking of their young client in jail a few miles away, wondering if this would be the day he was freed.

"Your father wins with his God-given ability to know the thoughts behind people's faces," Mustafa told her. "Mistry-sahib can read the judge's face like a newspaper."

Perveen sighed, wishing she had the same talent. She had no idea if the stranger was a lost soul or harbinger of serious trouble.

Putting the awkward incident aside, she trudged upstairs to address a half-done property contract on her side of the big mahogany partners' desk. Legal paperwork was sometimes numbing, but the subtlety of one word could mean the difference between a client's success and his ruin. Three years of reading law had built her understanding, but a half year working under her father had taught her to inspect each line backward and forward.

As the morning grew sunnier, she switched on the small electric fan that sat in a central window. Mistry House had been the first building on the block to pay for electric service, and due to its high cost, she was supposed to use it sparingly.

Perveen glanced out the window and down to the street. Fort's twenty square miles were once the East India Company's original fortified settlement. Now the district was known for the High Court and the many law offices around it. Nestled alongside the British and Hindu and Muslim law offices were a significant number owned by members of her own religious community, the Indian-born Zoroastrians. Although Parsis accounted for just 6 percent of Bombay's total inhabitants, they constituted one-third of its lawyers.

Iranis—the Zoroastrian immigrants who had come from the nineteenth century onward—prided themselves on running superlative bakeries and cafés serving cuisine influenced by their ancient homeland of Persia. Such was Yazdani's, the bakery-café across the street. The shop drew more than two hundred customers every day. This morning, the customers going in and out were working their way around a solitary obstacle.

It was the Bengali stranger. He'd left the place where she'd seen him earlier and set himself up in the shadow of the restaurant's awning. This allowed him to face Mistry House without roasting in the sun.

Perveen felt a surge of apprehension and then reminded herself that she couldn't be seen inside the second floor of Mistry House. From her perch, she had a bird's-eye view.

In a corner of the office, a tall Godrej cabinet was Perveen's alone. It held umbrellas, extra clothing, and the *Bombay Samachar* article touting her as Bombay's first woman solicitor. She'd wanted to frame the news story and hang it on the downstairs wall along with Jamshedji Mistry's many accolades. Her father had thought it too much to throw in the faces of clients who needed a gentle introduction to the prospect of female representation.

Perveen rummaged in the cabinet until she found her mother-of-pearl opera glasses. Back at the window, she adjusted the focus until the man's sinister face appeared close up. He did not look like anyone she'd ever seen in Fort; nor could she remember seeing him in Calcutta.

Perveen laid down the opera glasses and turned to unopened letters from the previous day. A thick envelope engraved with a return address 22 Sea View Road topped the stack. An existing client was a priority. This client, Mr. Omar Farid, was a textile-mill owner who had succumbed to stomach cancer two months previously.

Perveen read the letter from the appointed estate trustee, Faisal Mukri. Mr. Mukri wanted her to make a change that would disrupt the estate settlement on which she'd been working. Mr. Farid had three widows, all of whom still lived together in his house, and a total of four children—a humble number of offspring for a polygynist, according to Jamshedji.

Mr. Mukri had written that all the widows wanted to give up

their assets as donations to the family's wakf, a charitable trust that provided funds each year to the needy while paying a dividend to specified relatives. While a man or woman certainly could donate wherever he or she desired, wakfs were assiduously monitored by the government in order to prevent fraud, and a sudden infusion of money might be cause for scrutiny. Perveen decided to speak with her father before responding to Mr. Mukri.

Perveen placed the offending letter on Jamshedji's side of the desk as Mustafa came in with a small silver tray holding a cup of tea with two Britannia biscuits perched jauntily on the saucer. After a tiny sip of the hot, milky brew, she asked Mustafa, "Have you been out to the street?"

"I haven't. Why?"

She couldn't express her deep-seated worry, so she only said, "The man who was blocking the doorway has stationed himself across the street."

"Lurking on Bruce Street!" From Mustafa's grim expression, she thought he looked ready to grab his old Punjabi regiment rifle that he kept in a kitchen cabinet. "Shall I toss him to the Esplanade?"

"There's probably no reason to. But if you want a look at him, try these." Perveen went to the window, where she picked up the opera glasses. It took her a few minutes to show the elderly man how to adjust the lenses to his needs.

"Ay, such magical spectacles! One can see all over with these!"

"Aim toward Yazdani's. Do you see him?"

"The man in the white dhoti." Mustafa sighed. "Now I'm remembering he was nearby when I went outside to buy milk."

"How early was that?"

"Usual time—twenty, thirty minutes before your arrival."

This meant the man had been staking out their building for three hours straight.

Legally, he had the right to stand where he wanted. But Bruce Street was Perveen's second home, and she felt anxious to know for whom the out-of-towner was waiting. Trying to sound matter-of-fact, she said, "I'll walk over and ask why he's there."

Mustafa put down the glasses and looked at her with alarm. "You are a young lady alone. I should be the one to send that badmash packing."

Perveen regretted pulling Mustafa into her worries. "Please stay. There are so many people around that nothing could happen."

Still grumbling about danger to young ladies, Mustafa followed her downstairs. He opened the heavy door with great ceremony. Scowling dramatically, he remained on the marble step after she went out.

A bullock cart rolled past, and Perveen took advantage of its cover to cross the street unnoticed. As she came up in front of the Bengali, he acknowledged her arrival with a sharp upward movement of his face. Then he pivoted away, as if meaning to hide himself.

"Good day to you, sahib. Do you work nearby?" Perveen asked politely in Hindi.

"Nah-ah-ah!" his answer came in the form of a raspy cough.

"Sahib, are you waiting for someone on Bruce Street?"

"Nah!" He responded fast this time and glared at her with his bloodshot eyes.

Striving to keep her voice steady, she spoke again: "Do you know Cyrus Sodawalla?"

His mouth opened, revealing crooked, paan-stained teeth. He stood still for a moment—and then he ran.

Perveen stared after him in dismay. She'd hoped he'd say no. She had anticipated a flat denial, not a departure.

"Huzzah!" Mustafa was waving his arms side to side, as if she'd bowled a perfect cricket score.

Perveen felt too shaken to return to Mustafa. She waved back at him and decided to venture inside Yazdani's.

Lily Yazdani was working behind the counter. The fourteen-year-old's long hair was tied up with a traditional mathabana cloth, and she wore a snowy apron over a pretty yellow sari. She beamed at the appearance of Perveen.

"Kem cho, Perveen!" Lily called out a greeting in Gujarati.

"Good morning to you, Lily! And why aren't you in school?"

"A water pipe burst yesterday, so it's closed." Lily drew the corners of her lips down in an exaggerated frown. "I'm missing two tests."

Perveen winced. "I hope Mistry Construction isn't at fault. I believe the company built your school."

"Who cares about the pipe? I'd rather be here baking cakes with my pappa."

Perveen was sorry to hear this. She had a nagging anxiety that Lily would leave high school too early.

Firoze Yazdani emerged from the kitchen, his round face damp from heat. Wiping floury hands on his apron, he said, "What is your pleasure today, my dear Perveen? The dahitan were fried an hour ago and are soaking in sweet rose syrup. And of course, there are the cashew and almond fudges, and the pudding and custard cups."

Because of her inward agitation, Perveen didn't think she could force anything sweet down her throat without gagging. At the same time, she couldn't walk away without a purchase. "I'm welcoming an old friend from England at Ballard Pier later on today, so I'd like you to pack me a small box of your prettiest dahitan."

"Most beautiful and sweet. Just like you!" Firoze's wide grin split his face like a cracked persimmon.

"By the way—did you serve a fellow from outside Bombay this morning?"

Firoze looked puzzled, but Lily spoke up. "We had a dark and grumpy customer with a funny accent. He bought a date-nut cake and some almond fudge. I told him he could sit at a table, but he went outside."

"He stayed outside for a few hours," Perveen said. "I asked him something, and he ran away as if I were a nasty British policeman!"

"Probably he arrived on the overnight train because he seemed quite tired," Lily reflected. "He asked in the funniest accent what time law offices opened up in this area. I said nine o'clock for most firms and half nine if it's the Mistrys."

"What are you doing giving out such information about our esteemed neighbors?" Firoze wagged a reproving finger at his daughter.

Firoze knew things about Perveen that he'd blessedly never disclosed. She could have said the name Cyrus to him, and his eyes would have flared with recognition. But she would not parade her past mistakes in front of his impressionable daughter. "That accent is a Bengali one. Now that Lily's described him, do you recall him?" she asked him.

The baker shook his head. "My cardamom dough needed attention, so I was in back. It's good that you told off that velgard!"

"A wise woman can catch trouble before it starts," Lily said as she tied a fine bow around the box of sweets. "Pappa, would you let me run your business later on, just as Mistry-sahib is doing with Perveen?"

"My father has hardly done that! He'll work for many more years, and I still must prove my worth." Perveen spoke sincerely; it was a heavy responsibility to be the only woman solicitor in Bombay. She couldn't bring shame on Jamshedji Mistry. This was why the stranger's presence bothered her—and the reason she wasn't going to tell her father about it.

2

BEHIND A CURTAIN
Bombay, February 1921

*B*ack at Mistry House, Perveen handed off the sweets to Mustafa for safekeeping and gave a brief summary of the words she'd exchanged with the stranger, not mentioning Cyrus. She didn't want the garrulous Mustafa to ask any more questions. She needed to work.

Upstairs she opened the file cabinets to search for any documents relating to the late Omar Farid. There was plenty to wade through: property deeds, maps of land holdings, contracts with the government for the production of khaki drill cloth. She was startled two hours later when Mustafa knocked on the door to say lunch was served. Her father had just come in and was washing his hands downstairs.

She put the papers aside. "Did my father tell you the outcome?"

"He said he's hungry."

Perveen hurried down to the dining room, where her father was seated at the long rosewood table. Jamshedji Mistry was a trim, good-looking man of fifty with a thick head of graying brown hair. His most dominant feature—which Perveen had inherited in a slightly reduced version—was a beaky nose. Outsiders joked about Parsi noses, but Perveen loved their shared trait.

The two bent their heads and recited their prayers. Then Mustafa served up the lunch sent by John, the Mistrys' Goan cook. John had worked hard preparing lamb koftas, a tamarind chicken curry, a thick yellow dal with mustard greens, and caramelized rice. He'd also sent tangy vegetable pickles, fragrant wheat rotlis, and a tin of almond-honey brittle large enough to last a week.

Mustafa looked disapproving when Perveen requested smaller servings than usual, but her nerves had affected her appetite.

"Pappa. I'm waiting with open ears. Did we win?"

After accepting a large serving of chicken curry, Jamshedji spoke. "Yes, but after a long deliberation. If only you'd seen the opposing counsel smiling, anticipating our ruin!"

"Did he call our client to the stand?" She'd expected it.

"That he did—and the boy was prepared for every question."

The boy was Jayanth, a twenty-year-old stevedore who'd been charged with inciting unrest through the organization of other workers. Taking into consideration the British fear of Communists, Perveen had suggested Jayanth be cast as a hard worker with no political affiliations, just a strong desire for the safety of all the dock-workers. This concern would ultimately aid his employer, she had argued, because fewer accidents and deaths would allow for work without interruption.

"Good," she said, relieved that her coaching had worked. "And what was the content of Judge Thorpe's decision?"

"Innocent on all charges. Judge Thorpe ruled Jayanth must be offered his former position and be paid for every day since his sacking three months ago. That I wasn't expecting."

Perveen clapped. "Splendid! I wish I'd seen you plead the case."

Jamshedji raised a finger, playing teacher. "Ah, but your work as a contract solicitor is what keeps Mistry Law profitable. Without contracts and wills, we could not take on pro bonos like Jayanth."

This was the most praise Perveen had received in the six months she'd been working. She was performing not only the tasks of a solicitor but also those of law clerk, translator, and accountant, but who was she to complain? There was not another law firm in the city that would employ a female solicitor. "Pappa, were you expecting a visitor this morning?"

"Does this have to do with you spying on strangers through opera glasses?"

Perveen scooped rice into her mouth and chewed. Mustafa obviously had mentioned the morning's excitement. She needed to tell the truth, but she also wanted to avoid making her father nervous.

"A Bengali man was lurking across the street for three hours.

Eventually I went across to inquire his reason. He ran off without explaining anything."

Jamshedji shook his head. "Our beloved Fort is becoming over-crowded with all types. But a woman should never approach a man on the street."

Perveen's irritation swelled at her father's judgmental tone. "It was hardly an approach—"

"You crossed the street and sought him out! Tell me, is that a European behavior you learned at Oxford?"

"No—I—" Perveen felt herself reddening. "I first thought he might be waiting for you. Either because he had an appointment or was angry about the outcome of a case."

"I represent clients from all communities but no Bengalis in the last year," Jamshedji said, his voice as grating as Mustafa's serving spoon scraping the porcelain rice bowl. "Don't worry about such matters. Concentrate on pushing forward the contracts."

"Yes. One mustn't lose the title of King of Contracts," Perveen said sarcastically.

"Keep up your efforts, and you might become known as the Queen of Contracts." Jamshedji chuckled.

"Speaking of contracts, we received a request from the Farid household. The cover note was from Mr. Mukri, the family's agent. He wrote that Mr. Farid's three widows want to give up their dowers to donate into the family's wakf." Perveen didn't mask her apprehension that all the women, who no longer had income from a husband, were giving up their only assets to the charitable foundation.

But Jamshedji didn't address the issue of wakfs. Stroking his chin, he said, "It sounds as if you are speaking of mahr."

"Yes, I am." Perveen sighed, knowing she should have used the word for the special two-part dower that Muslim women received from men's families. The first gift symbolized the family's welcome to a bride; the second part, given at either divorce or the husband's death, was a material promise of fair treatment throughout her life.

"Bombay judges have been rather prickly about mahr these days. Let me look at the documents."

After she'd fetched both letters from upstairs, her father pulled out his gold monocle to study the fine sheets of vellum. Then he shook his head. "Worthless!"

Perveen had been perched on the edge of her seat waiting for such a declaration. "Isn't it strange that all three women wish to make a change against their own interests—and that two of the signatures are almost identical? And how convenient for the judge that this letter from the women was written in English. Are they really all fluent in English?"

"I cannot answer the last question because I have never met the ladies. But we must not have immediate prejudices." Jamshedji gave her a reproving look.

Perveen didn't hide her surprise. "Are you telling me you've never spoken to the wives in all the years you represented Mr. Farid?"

"I have not," he said, signaling with his hand for Mustafa to bring tea. "The Farid widows live in strict seclusion. With my late client gone, the only male in the household is the baby son of the second wife."

"Purdahnashins don't speak with men," Mustafa said as he came around with the silver teapot. "My mother and sisters didn't close themselves in—but many of the wealthy do. Especially Hanafi Muslims."

Perveen always appreciated Mustafa's wisdom about areas where she knew little. Now her dismay at the women's situation was being replaced by interest. Secluded, wealthy Muslim women could become a subspecialty for her practice. "Mustafa, I believe 'purdah' means 'veil.' Does 'nashin' mean 'lady'?"

"You are supposed to be studying Urdu," her father interrupted. "'Nashin' means 'sitting' or 'dwelling.' Therefore, 'purdahnashins' means 'those who stay behind the veil.'"

Perveen took a long sip of Mustafa's delicious tea, a mixture of Darjeeling brewed with milk, cardamon, pepper, and plenty of sugar. "What do you think of the household agent, Mr. Mukri?" she asked her father. "I'm supposed to ask him to help sort out details for the estate, but he's not answered many of my letters."

"Mukri was one of Farid's management officers at the fabric mill. He shifted to staying with Farid-sahib during his illness. I saw him when he came in to sign papers relating to his appointment as estate trustee and household agent. A young man—but he was most respectful toward our client."

"As he should have been! But let's talk about the letter he sent that's signed by the widows. I think two of the signatures might come from the same hand."

Jamshedji studied the paper and then handed it back to her. "The names signed by Sakina and Mumtaz do bear a resemblance. Razia's name appears different."

"Excuse me, sahib, but you should say 'begum,'" Mustafa interjected from the corner, where he stood awaiting further command. "To address these married ladies of high birth respectfully, one must add 'begum.'"

After nodding at Mustafa, Perveen said, "I am guessing Razia-begum signed for herself. What if the other two were signed for by someone else, perhaps Mr. Mukri?"

"Conspiracy theory!" Jamshedji said with a chuckle. "We have no way of knowing."

"Shouldn't we ask them?"

Jamshedji put his teacup down so hard it rattled the saucer. "I already mentioned that the ladies live in seclusion. I haven't reviewed the mahr documents since I drafted them all those years ago. Remind me—are these dowers equivalent in value? That's the best case when you've got multiple wives surviving a husband."

"The mahr gifts are wildly different," she answered, relieved that he'd asked the question. "Your client gave the first wife, Razia-begum, a dower of land: four acres in Girangaon, a plot that holds two mill buildings that went up in 1914."

Jamshedji picked up his cup and took a long sip. "That sounds like quite a large gift, but in 1904, it was swampland. Are you saying the mills that made the company's fortune are there now?"

She nodded, feeling pride that she'd caught something her father should have known. "I consulted the map of his holdings we have on file. Part two of the mahr, to be awarded at time of husband's death or divorce, was listed as five thousand rupees." Perveen was glad to have the papers handy so she could keep the details of all the wives' arrangements straight. "Farid-sahib's second wife, Sakina Chivne, received a very different kind of mahr: a diamond and emerald jewelry set comprised of earrings, a necklace, and bangles. Her second mahr payment was also five thousand rupees."

"Mr. Farid was doing well by 1914 when he married his second wife," Jamshedji said. "I don't recall the cost of that jewelry, but we have the insurance papers for many of his valuables."

"Why did Mr. Farid decide to take a second wife?" Perveen asked. Despite what her father had said about the client's good character, she felt squeamish about polygyny, which was still practiced by many Muslims and a smaller number of elite Hindus. In truth, there was surely polygyny in her own parents' family histories. Parsis hadn't made it a crime until 1865.

"The obvious reason." Jamshedji raised his thick salt-and-pepper eyebrows. "Offspring."

"But the first wife, Razia-begum, had borne him a daughter—eleven years old now, I believe," Perveen said evenly. "He had his heir."

"But no son—he needed someone to work inside the mills. His parents were the ones who insisted and found Sakina Chivne. I tell you, it was quite a disappointment when she bore two daughters straightaway. Sakina-begum's son was born a year and a half ago. By then, the complaining parents had both passed."

"Like I said, he got his son." Perveen crossed her arms. "Why did he also need a third wife?"

"He met Mumtaz just last year and married her five months before his death. It was a legal choice freely made by him." Jamshedji shook his head. "Although I considered it rather strange."

Eagerly, Perveen picked up on his language. "What do you mean by that?"

Jamshedji toyed with a few leftover grains of rice. "She was a musician working in the entertainment district on Falkland Road."

"That's the reason for her mahr: two sitars and one veena," Perveen mused. "Did she know he hadn't long to live?"

"Undoubtedly," Jamshedji said. "He was very frail at that time of his life. But those musical instruments are a pittance compared to what the others received. I don't think she did it for money."

"Look at this!" Perveen said, studying Mumtaz's marriage contract with new interest. "Mumtaz signed this document in July 1920 with an X. Yet her name is signed on the new letter. Did she learn to write in the last seven months? I'm interested to ask her about that discrepancy."

Jamshedji blinked. "What do you mean, ask her?"

She'd gotten ahead of herself. Taking a deep breath, she asked, "Might secluded Muslim ladies be willing to meet with a female lawyer?"

He gave her a long look. "There's a chance."

"I'd like to speak to them directly rather than continue my one-way correspondence with Mr. Mukri." Perveen tried to sound detached and professional.

Jamshedji sipped the last dregs of tea and put down his cup. "I'm not certain you're ready to make a personal call to secluded women. You must use caution."

Perveen felt wounded. "I'm always cautious!"

"No," he said with a soft smile, "you are impatient and impetuous. I've overheard you speaking about the government."

Perveen made a face at him. "In private circles only. I know Mistry Construction depends on government contracts."

"You've also said more than most are ready to hear about women's rights."

"Other Parsi women are doing the same. Mamma's groups are always working on women's welfare and education." She felt on firm ground because her father had donated generously to her mother's causes.

"What you say will sound like Latin to these ladies who've been sheltered their whole lives. Your Urdu is less than rudimentary, and you haven't studied enough Mohammedan law."

Were these honest criticisms—or was he just trying to discern how motivated she'd be? Perveen did her best to answer coolly. "I've read Mr. Mulla's *Principles of Mahomedan Law*, which explains everything I need to know. I can speak with the ladies in Hindustani—surely they'll understand me."

"But they've very likely never met a Parsi," Jamshedji objected.

Perveen's frustration spilled over. "Pappa, you own the only law firm in Bombay with an employee who can communicate directly with secluded women. Why not take advantage of the greatly underused asset that is your daughter?"

Jamshedji closed his eyes for a long moment. When he opened them, he gave Perveen a serious look. "If you go, you must carry out the consultations with the same deference you employ with our male clients. Omar Farid would rise from the grave if he knew I didn't serve his family members with respect."

"He is not in the grave anymore. He is in heaven!" Mustafa objected from the corner.

"Mr. Farid will be smiling from the clouds once I've helped his family." Perveen said, leaning over to kiss her father's cheek.

After lunch, Jamshedji strolled off to the Ripon Club. Perveen knew he was headed for one of the Parsi social club's long-armed teak lounge chairs in which certain barristers were infamous for putting up their legs and snoring away. He probably wanted praise from his friends, a glass of port, and then a long nap.

Perveen went back upstairs to the cabinet where client files were stored. As the door swung open, she breathed in the cloying scent of camphor and surveyed stacks of cloth-, leather-, and cardboard folios.

After a few minutes, she located a slim folder of newspaper clippings. Although Omar Farid had died just the past year at the age of forty-five, the coverage of him spanned only the last five years of his life. There was an article from 1915 about Farid Fabrics creating a new section of mills to weave cotton drill cloth for Indian army uniforms. Another report, dated 1917, discussed Mr. Farid's charitable donations to returning military casualties. Finally, she reviewed his December 1920 obituary, which included mention of the mills and his charity. The last line read: *Mr. Farid is survived by his family, including one son.*

The obituary didn't mention his wives and daughters. Had they been left out of the obituary because they were considered unimportant . . . or because the *Times* editor thought the details of a philanthropic Indian businessman's polygyny would cast a negative aspect?

Perveen scrutinized the small photograph accompanying the article about the mill owner's charitable donations. Omar Farid looked serious and respectable. A close-fitting cap drew attention to his narrow face, with hard-looking eyes and a prominent hooked nose. He wore a high-necked kurta and dark sherwani coat. His head was covered with a neat crocheted cap similar to the one that Mustafa wore.

His final marriage had occurred just five months before his death. How shocking this must have been for the existing wives—especially if the woman was a musician who'd once worked on Falkland Road, where sex was as widely available as opium.

Before he'd departed for the Ripon Club, Perveen had asked her father if he thought the last marriage was a sham.

"It is the easiest thing to believe," Jamshedji had told her. "But a dying man does not feel obligated to observe social norms. He needs no one's permission to take what he needs."

From her own experience, Perveen understood.

3

THE SPIRIT OF ECSTASY
Bombay, February 1921

*A*round three o'clock, Mustafa burst into the upstairs office. "The SS *London* has arrived! I saw through the spectacles from our roof over to Ballard Pier."

"Splendid!" Perveen clapped. Alice was just the remedy she needed for her dark mood.

A gust of air blew through the window, ruffling the Farid documents. As Perveen collected them, she thought about the cold, damp winds that had continuously buffeted her and Alice as they trudged from St. Hilda's College to their various lectures. How they had talked and laughed—and shared secrets. This could be her life again, if she chose to open herself to Alice.

Their relationship had started with Perveen serving as Alice's confessor. The Englishwoman's revelation that she'd been expelled at sixteen from Cheltenham Ladies' College for having a girl in her bed had confounded Perveen. It was natural for female relatives and friends to sleep close together. But after Alice explained the longing she still felt for a long-ago classmate, Perveen understood how multifaceted relationships could be.

At St. Hilda's, Alice buried herself in her mathematical studies to push away the loss of her true love. Outside of Perveen, nobody knew her truth—just as Alice was the only one who eventually heard the story of Perveen's own past.

Now she wondered how much Alice had said about their college friendship to her parents. The Hobson-Joneses might be suspicious about any of Alice's female friends, given her past troubles. Perveen decided to be on her best behavior.

Ballard Pier was a twenty-minute walk away, but she didn't want to arrive sweaty or with squashed sweets. It was easier to get a lift

nervously, as if she didn't want to give the impression
nfortable sitting close to Perveen.

oblem," Perveen said with a smile. "I shall enjoy being
ttle silver lady."

ial name of the emblem is the Spirit of Ecstasy," Sir
he's a splendid piece of design, just like the car itself."

's car is right behind us—the Crossley piled up with
hat's why we've got Georgie's Rolls." The governor's
 in a khaki uniform, kept a stone face, as if trying
 indignity of both Alice's words and Perveen's prox-
veen was determined to make the most of the special
e waved at the crowd as they departed.

being an actress. Perveen was a single Indian woman
t in the governor's car, an impossibility that would be
und many of Bombay's cooking fires, verandahs, and
 that evening.

 we, exactly?" Alice asked as the harbor receded.

Sea-Face; but this stretch of curving road along the
mally called the Queen's Necklace because of the way
 the streetlights shine at night," Perveen said, savoring
play the Bombay expert. "Along the Chowpatty Beach
e every sort of person coming out to eat the breeze, as
indi. On the right, many mansion blocks and hotels
 My brother's just breaking ground on an apartment
ight of that white building."

 does your brother work?" Sir David asked.

ned her head to speak directly to Alice's father in the
istry Construction. My brother recently became exec-

was still for a moment, and then laughed. "Good God,
e you were one of *those* Mistrys. Your family's built
bay! In fact, I've got a proposal from Lord Tata on
rding development of Back Bay, with Mistry as the
tractor."

incidence." Perveen felt awkward. She'd only wanted

in Ramchandra's spotlessly maintained rickshaw with its protective sunbonnet.

Ramchandra cycled easily through the streets and out to Ballard Pier, where she could see the impressive bulk of a white Pacific & Oriental steamship rising up behind the high stone walls.

Stepping down from the rickshaw, she paid Ramchandra, who immediately headed toward a beckoning sailor. She unpacked a sign she'd made on the back of an empty folder that said MISS ALICE HOBSON-JONES. Holding up a sign for a newcomer put her in the company of hundreds of male chauffeurs who'd come to meet the ship, but what else could she do?

As she craned her neck, looking for Alice, an Englishman's voice cut into her ear. "Excuse me. Are you Miss Perveen Mistry?"

"Yes, I am." She turned expectantly toward the red-haired gentleman.

"I'm Mr. Martin, secretary to Sir David Hobson-Jones. He and the others are waiting."

Perveen caught a hint of reprimand in the last statement. "Mr. Martin, do you mean that everyone is still waiting for Alice to be ferried in?"

"Miss Hobson-Jones disembarked twenty minutes ago. Her trunks are loaded, and she's already in the car, so come along smartly."

Who did he think he was—a class prefect? Perveen followed the pompous aide through the crowd and to the curb, where he stopped before a long, sparkling silver vehicle.

Perveen gasped outright. "Is that a Silver Ghost?"

She knew for certain it was a Rolls. The shining car's bonnet was topped with an elegantly sculpted silver ornament: a young woman leaning forward as if ready to dive into life, her arms outstretched like wings.

"Yes indeed," Martin said. "It was a gift to the governor from the king of a nearby princely state."

"What a present!" Privately, she wondered what kind of favor the monarch expected in exchange. Or was the gift merely a show of wealth?

"Perveen! You're really here—I hoped you would come." Alice squeezed out of the car's back seat. Within moments, Perveen and her tissue-silk sari were crushed against Alice's warm, peppermint-smelling mass.

Wrapping her arms around Alice's comfortable bulk, Perveen said, "Sorry to have made you wait. I must apologize to your family for having delayed you."

"Stuff and nonsense! I've been off the ship just long enough for Mummy to get her talons into me. You won't believe—"

"What won't I believe?" A very blonde woman who looked barely older than Alice was regarding them from the open-topped touring car. She was sweetly pretty in a lilac-colored frock and a matching cloche trimmed with white silk roses. Perveen looked for a trace of any part of this glamorous creature in Alice but couldn't find anything past their shared hair color.

"Everything!" Alice answered.

From Alice's sarcastic lilt, Perveen realized the mother-daughter relationship wasn't an easy one. And what about Alice's father? Perveen appraised the tall middle-aged gentleman wearing a beige linen lounge suit and a solar topi. Her friend had inherited his height.

As if they were schoolgirls, Alice took her by the hand. "Mummy and Dad, this is my dearest friend of all time, Perveen Mistry. And Perveen, may I introduce my mother, Lady Gwendolyn Hobson-Jones, and my father, Sir David Hobson-Jones?"

"We've heard all about your scrapes at Oxford with Alice!" Sir David said. He had a deeply textured tan that was typical of British who'd stayed a long time in India. When he smiled, his teeth were very white against his skin.

"So you are Perveen." Gwendolyn Hobson-Jones pronounced it slowly, as if it were the name of an exotic place. "In your language, what does that name mean?"

"It means star in three languages: Persian, Arabic, and Urdu. My grandfather chose my name." As Perveen finished, she wondered if she'd said too much.

"Alice says you were the only gi Hilda's, which certainly makes yo delivered his attractive grin again.

"Not at all. Others came before to get a read on whether he was bei

"Perveen, have you any time t house?" he asked. "We're having arrival."

Sir David's invitation seemed t But as Perveen surveyed the car, sl fit. The scowling Mr. Martin woul she didn't see much room in the ba parents.

"That is very kind," Perveen s tion . . ."

"You must come!" Alice said.

"All right, then. If you tell me follow," Perveen said, knowing tha be too difficult for a rickshaw.

"Not a chance," said Sir David.

"But Mr. Martin's with us!" Lad Mr. Martin moved closer to Si veen. "I wished to explain to your young people—"

"Another time," Sir David said to deliver for me at the Secretariat.

"Yes, Sir David," he said. "Shall this afternoon?"

"No. I'll see you tomorrow in walked away despondently, Sir each a wry look. "These young training."

"I know just the school in Switz

"I hope you shan't mind taking three of us in the back, it's a bit cra

smiling rath she felt unc

"It is no close to the

"The off David said.

"My fath my trunks. driver, a Si to ignore t imity. But journey, so

It was li sitting up f discussed a kitchen flo

"Where

"Kenned water is inf it looks whe her chance side, you'll one says in are going u block to the

"For who Perveen back seat. " utive office

Sir Davi I didn't rea modern Bo my desk re proposed c

"What a

Alice's parents to know her brother wasn't a lowly underling working for the British. But now they probably believed she was an Indian currying favor, to use the dreadful cliché.

Perveen returned her gaze to Kennedy Sea-Face. On the beach side, vendors were serving food and tea at dhabbas set up on the sand.

A young Parsi man with curly black hair was standing at one of these outdoor snack shops, talking to the small Hindu cook. The Parsi had a familiar lanky frame and a hooked nose. The Parsi wore an English suit and was leaning slightly on a cane.

Perveen put her hand to her mouth. It was Cyrus Sodawalla. Or, if it wasn't, it looked exactly like the man she'd been trying to forget for the last four years.

Frantically, she reminded herself how many men in Bombay might have fair skin and curly black hair: thousands of Armenians, Anglo-Indians, and Jews. And Cyrus didn't use a cane.

The Silver Ghost was too fast. It sailed past the dhabba. Although Perveen craned her head, in seconds, the man had shrunk into a tiny black speck.

Perveen let out the breath she'd been holding. He was gone. And it was most fortunate that he hadn't seen the car.

"What did we miss, Perveen?" Alice asked. "You look as if you've just seen a demon."

1916

4
THE LAST LESSON
Bombay, August 1916

*R*unning late and praying not to be noticed, Perveen hurried into the Government Law School. A cart had blocked the entrance to Bruce Street where her father needed to be dropped. The delay had caused Perveen to reach Elphinstone College just after nine—and she could only pray the professor hadn't yet taken attendance.

Even though the surname Mistry fell in the middle of the alphabet, the lecturer had assigned Perveen a seat in the back row, ostensibly because she was a "special student" and not enrolled for a law degree. Today, she didn't mind the placement because it made her arrival less noticeable. But after the first few seconds in her seat, she felt something cold and terrible seeping through her sari.

Not again!

The first time, someone had filled the groove in her wooden chair with water. On another occasion, her seat had been filled with black coffee; thankfully, she'd noticed and not sat down. This time, she'd sat down without looking first. She would not know what the fluid was until class was over and she'd reached the sanctuary of the college's ladies' lounge. This particular dampness was sticky. An ominous sign, as bad as the smirking faces of the students sitting nearby.

During the first term, Camellia Mistry had been shocked when Perveen complained to her about the students' pranks. "You must tell the professors! It's outrageous behavior."

Perveen had explained the impossibility of this. "The lecturers don't want me in class, so that won't help. And if the boys learn I told on them, they'll treat me worse."

But life was worsening anyway. Two weeks ago, the results of examinations had been published in the *Times of India*, recognizing Perveen Mistry as the second-highest-scoring student among the first-year candidates for bachelors in law.

The Mistry family had celebrated, John baking her favorite lagan nu custard and Pappa breaking open three bottles of Perrier-Jouët. Neighbors had dropped in all afternoon and evening to share dessert and congratulations.

But her male classmates weren't pleased.

The next time she handed an essay up the row of students to be collected by the proctor, the lecturer never received it and gave her a zero. Another afternoon, a gentleman purporting to be from the school administration left a telephone message at her home about a surprise cancellation of the next day's law classes. Perveen was suspicious and went to check the classroom, reaching her seat just as tests were being handed out.

Today's revenge was a sweet one, judging from the line of ants traveling up the chair. Barely able to absorb Professor Adakar's words, Perveen stared straight ahead. In her mind, the words that he was writing on the board—something about one's right to legal process—were being replaced by the hateful words a boy had hissed in her ear the first week:

You've no right to be here! You'll ruin everything for our batch.

He'd called her a shrewish spoilsport. As if she were the one making life hell and not the wretched lot of them.

"Tamarind chutney," Gulnaz said, wrinkling her nose at the silk sari she held six inches from her nose. "Those pigs must have taken it from their hostel dining room."

"Are you sure it's tamarind?" Perveen was standing in her blouse and petticoat in the college's ladies' lounge. This was the place where female students were supposed to retire between classes. At the moment, Gulnaz Banker and Hema Patel had her sari between them and were valiantly attacking the stains with soap and water taken from the adjacent lavatory.

Hema looked sympathetically at her. "We keep saying, why not read literature like we're doing? We've got four girls together in one class. The men would never dare act against one without fearing all of us would retaliate."

"I can't change my course of study. My father expects me to become the first female solicitor in Bombay."

Gulnaz, who was a year ahead in school but had a rosebud prettiness and tiny size that made her seem younger, spoke up softly. "Perveen, you're the impetuous type. Why not thrash it out with them? You must dream of banging them all over their stupid heads the way you did to Esther Vachha in school."

"I was eight years old, and she'd thrown sand on my lunch!" Perveen was annoyed that Gulnaz remembered this. "I'm more mature now. I keep my eyes on my notebook as much as I can, although that sometimes makes the professor think I'm not listening to him. Then the others laugh, and—oh, it's awful." Perveen felt an unbidden tear slide out.

"Poor girl!" Gulnaz sounded alarmed. "You mustn't cry. Your sari's almost as good as new. We'll just hang it near the window to dry."

Perveen reached out for her sari. "My class on Hindu law starts in twenty minutes. I can't stay waiting for it to dry."

"Mangoes will not ripen if you hurry them," Hema said. "Sit down and take some deep breaths."

Their caring was only making her feel panicked. "If I don't go, I'll miss the test."

"Take it later," Gulnaz advised. "Better not to shame yourself in public."

Perveen took the sari out of their hands. "And what reason will I give the professor for my absence? A spot on my clothes? He'll think I'm a typical silly girl!"

"But the spot is wet. People might think . . ." Gulnaz's voice dropped off. She was also a Parsi brought up with strict standards of hygiene.

"Silk will dry faster in the sun outside than inside this humid hellhole. And I've got an idea about how to wear it!" Perveen explained that if she draped her sari in the Hindu manner, with its pallu hanging over the back, the spot would be obscured. Aradhana, a Hindu girl studying at one of the lounge tables, hurried over to help.

Flanked by Gulnaz and Hema, Perveen went out into Elphinstone's courtyard.

"Look!" Gulnaz pointed. "Esther Vachha is sitting with a man!"

Perveen followed her friend's outraged stare to a wrought iron bench where her primary school nemesis was sitting and laughing. The young man with her was dressed like a Parsi and had thick black curls that tumbled perfectly over his forehead. Esther's companion had an attractive profile with the kind of hooked nose that made Perveen think of portraits of ancient Persian royalty.

"He's not a student here. Who could he be?" Hema asked excitedly.

Perveen had seen plenty of male students at the university, but none as handsome as this one. "I've never seen him before. But he certainly looks like a dandy."

"I don't care. I'd die for my children to have curls like that," Gulnaz said.

"You are far too marriage minded!" Perveen scolded as Hema grabbed each of them by one hand and proceeded toward the bench.

"Hello, Esther," Hema said. "Perveen was asking, who is your special friend?"

Esther smiled smugly. "Isn't he lovely? He's my cousin visiting from Calcutta. Mr. Cyrus Sodawalla."

"Charmed," the young man said, bowing slightly. He glanced over the three of them and then settled his eyes on Perveen. "Don't introductions go both ways?"

"Miss Perveen Mistry is the first woman student at the Government Law School. Actually, she's a third cousin," Esther said with an artificial smile. "Miss Gulnaz Banker and Miss Hema Patel are both reading literature."

"From your name, I'm guessing you're a fizzy one," Hema joked to the young man, making Perveen wince.

Cyrus Sodawalla smiled, displaying perfect white teeth. "When my grandfather came from Persia, his first job was selling bottled drinks. The British census required him to give a surname, and that's what he got. Sodawalla—the soda-selling man."

Perveen noted that his accent was different; it must have been the influence of Calcutta.

"That's how my grandfather got his name," Gulnaz cooed. "And now I'm saddled with the very boring surname of Banker."

"Miss Mistry—are you also Parsi?" Cyrus asked, looking pointedly at the draping of Perveen's sari. While the others all had their heads covered and a swag of fabric across their torsos that tucked gracefully into their saris' waistlines, she did not.

Perveen was flustered. "Yes. I'm just wearing my sari another way."

"Such a shame you lot are already nineteen years old," Esther teased. "Cyrus has come for bride choosing, and his family won't look at a girl unless she's younger than eighteen."

"Is that because you're also very young, Mr. Sodawalla?" Perveen's question was sarcastic. Esther's cousin had five-o'clock shadow blooming on his cheeks and neck.

He gave Perveen a wounded look. "I'm twenty-eight next month."

"He-he! That's old for a bridegroom," Hema cut in. "I shan't accept anyone older than twenty-three."

"The only reason I've held off is our family business. But it's paid off. Soon the Sodawallas of Calcutta will be bottling all the whiskey in Bengal and Orissa. Actually, I've got a sample." He patted a small lump in his jacket pocket.

Gulnaz gasped. "How naughty to be going about our college with a flask!"

Perveen wanted to laugh because Cyrus seemed so different from the pompous prigs in the law classes. Still, she didn't want to be part of a fawning flock. So she smiled briefly and said, "I've no time for cocktails. Please enjoy your time in Bombay, and best of luck finding a wife."

"To walk off just like that is rather rude!" Hema snapped once the three were on their way.

"I've got a test in Hindu Law," Perveen said.

"But you're walking away from the law classrooms," Gulnaz pointed out. "Aren't they on the far side?"

"Damnation—sorry! I must dash." In her haste to get away from Cyrus and Esther, Perveen had passed the place she needed to go.

Stepping inside the building, she paused in the dimness and looked up the stairwell. Not a student was in sight, which meant she'd arrive late for a second time in the same day. Hurrying upstairs, she felt the edge of her sari slip off her shoulder and into the crook of her arm. As she draped the pallu back in place, she realized the folds around her hips were loose.

Just outside the classroom door, Perveen set down her heavy satchel to adjust her sari's unfamiliar folds. What she really needed was to strip the whole thing off and start fresh, but she was too far from the ladies' lounge. As she concentrated on pinching new pleats at her waist, she heard Mr. Joshi saying something about the test. Perveen gave up on her costume and opened the door, the creak of it causing a number of students to turn. All of them were from her earlier class. Raised eyebrows, smirks, snickers, and worst of all, the lecturer's reprimand.

"How good of you to join us, Miss Mistry." Mr. Joshi's voice dripped sarcasm.

Perveen mumbled an apology and kept her gaze low as she hurried to her place. This was a different room than before, and her seat was clean. A mimeographed paper with six questions rested on the desk.

The young men around her were filling their fountain pens and starting in on the exam as Mr. Joshi came down the aisle to address her. "Coming in so late, I'm not sure you're entitled to take this test."

"Entitled" was a word that grated on her. Because she was Jamshedji Mistry's daughter, she was supposedly entitled to read law—even though the law school wasn't yet giving women degrees.

"Everyone's working, and you are not. Did you neglect to bring a pen?" Without waiting for her answer, Mr. Joshi said, "I don't suppose anyone's got a spare pen?"

"There is no need, sir!" Perveen's pen and some pencils were nestled in an embroidered silk pouch she carried inside her satchel. Reaching down, she hefted the heavy bag up onto the surface of her desk. Retrieving the pouch, she was surprised to find the pen missing. But the outside of her satchel showed a spreading black patch. Obviously, her pen had fallen out and was leaking. If she removed it, she'd just make a mess. And Mr. Joshi didn't allow exams to be written in pencil.

As Mr. Joshi went back to the front of the room, Perveen sat in misery, staring at the paper she could not mark.

Forty minutes later, the paper was no longer blank. It was wet with a sprinkling of tears that had fallen fast and hard. As the students to her left began passing their completed tests toward the aisle, she didn't bother putting it in the stack. She stayed in place, ignoring the irritated sounds of the men who had to brush past her to leave the classroom.

Finally, she was alone in the room. That was what she had been waiting for, because she didn't want anyone watching her collect her things.

"What are you doing?" Mr. Joshi called out suddenly, startling her.

"Sorry?" She looked up, taken aback to see the lecturer hadn't departed.

"You just put an examination in your bag—yes, I saw you do it."

Perveen pulled out the damp, slightly crumpled paper. "Here it is. I had some trouble with my pen, so I couldn't write anything."

"But why did you put it in your bag?"

She answered honestly. "I was embarrassed to turn it in. The others would see."

His eyes narrowed. "Stealing an examination is a violation of the honor code. I shall have to report it."

Whispering from behind her informed her that the hall had not completely emptied.

"Sorry, but I was not intending to do anything with the test. As I said—"

"If you were prepared to take an examination, you could have had a pen. You refused one." Mr. Joshi's voice rose. "What game are you playing today—or have you been playing games all along?"

Steadying herself, she said, "It's not a game, sir. Just a mistake."

The lecturer drew himself up; his face was flushed. "I said to the dean that allowing a female in the law school would be a mistake. I will repeat this truth when I write the notice of your honor code violation."

Perveen's whole body felt tight. "An honor code violation? I did nothing."

"You intentionally stole a test that I'm sure you would have filled out at home—perhaps with your father's help."

Now she was furious. "I won't answer to any charges that are unjustified."

He cocked his head to one side and studied her with a cold smile. "It seems you believe your status is exalted enough to hold you above university law. Why is that, Miss Mistry?"

Rising to her feet, she spoke in a trembling voice. "I'm not answering to any such charges because I'll have resigned."

After the words had left her lips, she couldn't believe it. What had she done? The proper behavior would have been to continue apologizing. But Mr. Joshi's formidable expression had told her what was coming. He would have enlisted Mr. Adakar and the other law faculty to ensure she was convicted.

Mr. Joshi looked taken aback. After a moment, he said, "With resignation, there is also a formal process. But first there is my outstanding charge. My statement shall be used by the administration to consider whether to convene a hearing—"

"Have you a brain, or is it sawdust?" The offensive slur flew out before she could stop herself. "I've quit!"

Going down the staircase, she felt as if she were afloat. What was the expression? Yes—a dying man clutches at sea-foam. Like that man, she was moving in a soft, cool cloud that carried her away from the outraged, gesticulating Mr. Joshi. Although the sea-foam was enough to bring her safety, she was still sure to drown.

Emerging from the building, Perveen headed for a dustbin.

Discreetly pulling her handkerchief out of the edge of her blouse, she covered her hand with it and fished out of her satchel the leaking mother-of-pearl Parker pen her mother had given Perveen to celebrate her entrance into law school. It was useless. But then she hesitated. To throw it out would be to discard her mother's generosity and hopes. She wrapped it doubly tight in the handkerchief and returned it to the bag.

"Miss Mistry, is that you?" a pleasant male voice inquired.

Startled, she turned around and saw that Esther's cousin was lounging on the same bench as before near the fountain.

"Hello again." Cyrus Sodawalla raised a hand in greeting. "Esther abandoned me in favor of Chaucer."

Holding her satchel protectively against her drooping sari, Perveen nodded at him. "Kem cho."

Switching to Gujarati, he said, "Sit down. You've the face of one who's drunk cheap oil."

Perveen realized that she did feel faint. She lowered herself onto the bench, being careful to leave several feet of space between them.

"I don't need your whiskey," she said in a warning tone.

Cyrus laughed shortly. "Esther already made it clear that was a poor joke. I'm sorry."

Perveen's faintness was slowly subsiding. "You're forgiven."

"You still look like death," Cyrus said, his expression serious.

"I'll be fine after a cup of tea."

"You also need something to eat." Brightening, he added, "Esther's parents showed me a very good bakery a few streets from here. It's called Yazdani's."

Perveen was impressed that this visitor to Bombay had heard of her favorite bakery-café in the city. But she also knew a decent young woman should not walk with a man unchaperoned. "There's no reason for me to leave campus, Mr. Sodawalla. I can have a cup of tea in the ladies' lounge."

"But I can't go inside there! And the truth is, I've missed a meal."

The little-boy way his mouth turned down was endearing. And she'd rather leave the campus quickly after what had just happened.

Didn't the fact that her family knew the owner of Yazdani's make going there a bit like having a chaperone? Slowly, she said, "That bakery is close to my family's office. I could stop with you on my way there."

Perveen and Cyrus caught the sweet smell from half a block away.

Cyrus sighed. "Cardamom buns are my favorite."

"What kind of cardamom buns?" Perveen asked.

"Meethi papdi. Is there another type?" he said teasingly.

Perveen was amused at how little he knew. "It might be mawa cakes we're smelling, or dahitan, which have cardamom and saffron. Let's find out."

The scent was making Perveen feel stronger. A jolt of sugar and spice would strengthen her for everything yet to come.

Inside the black-and-white-tiled café, Cyrus looked around with pleasure and inhaled deeply. Despite the odd hour, more than half of the tables were filled with a mix of Hindus, Parsis, and Muslims wearing traditional and European dress. Perveen spied only one of her father's colleagues who might recognize her, but he appeared consumed with a business conversation.

Pleased by Cyrus's enthusiasm, she said, "I recommend the chicken berry pulao or kid ghosht for a late lunch."

Firoze Yazdani had been following their exchange from his perch by the cashbox. Coming over to the table, he said, "I will bring those dishes and a bit more. We will discuss pudding and cakes later. Perveen-jaan, which cousin is this?"

The Mistrys were an old Bombay family, so the café owner's assumption was natural. But one of the tenets of her upbringing was honesty. She hesitated, trying to think of what to say.

"I'm the hungry one from Calcutta!" Cyrus said with a big grin before Perveen could come up with a rejoinder.

"Hungry is what we like. Although you will not remain that way for long," Firoze said, beaming.

After Firoze went off and the two of them had gone to the sink in the corner to wash their hands, Perveen addressed Cyrus in a whisper. "Why did you lie?"

He winked. "Esther's your third cousin, isn't she? That gives us some relationship."

"My family and Esther's aren't so closely related. We don't gather for holidays and weddings." She wasn't going to explain their long-time rivalry.

"I had to say it. That bhawa would have tossed me out if he thought I was a masher." Cyrus leaned across the table covered with red-checked oilcloth. "So, what happened at the university that set your hair on fire?"

Reflexively, Perveen's hand went to her temple. Her long, wavy hair was, in fact, slightly disassembled from the braided coronet that her ayah, Jaya, had made hours earlier. "Why should I tell a stranger anything of my life?"

"It's because I'm strange that you can tell me. I don't care about the same things that Bombay people do."

Perveen should have stayed silent, but she was aware that, ever since they'd met, Cyrus had been watching her and listening to her. She sensed that he would be interested, and maybe even sympathetic. In a low voice, she said, "Swear that you won't tell anyone. Not your cousin—not anyone."

He put his hands together in a prayerful position. The familiarity of it made her smile and helped get the next words out of her mouth. "I quit the law school half an hour ago. Though I'm a special student, so I'm not sure if it really counts."

His thick eyebrows rose, and he looked almost admiring. "Congratulations."

"What the hell are you saying? I don't know how I'll tell my parents!"

"You could say you're saving them a pretty penny."

Perveen shut her eyes, remembering the past. "They were so proud when I was admitted to the law school. The only institution that would have pleased them more would have been a college in England. But I didn't want to go so far."

Cyrus nodded sagely. "I wouldn't go to Britain for all the whiskey in London. And colleges and universities are such a waste.

Everything I needed to learn for business I learned on the street side of Presidency College's fence."

Perveen could not imagine one of the young men in her classes ever saying such a thing. She recalled her classmates' self-importance, their comparisons of private high schools and class standings. They would not hang about with flasks of whiskey; they would not talk sincerely with a woman.

Firoze Yazdani was approaching with the tea and their dishes. After he'd spooned out food for the two of them, Cyrus tucked into it with enthusiasm. After half his plate was cleared, he paused. "Such light rice, sweet and spicy all at once. And the mutton is soft and spiced with something I can't recognize. I suppose it is Bombay masala."

"This is the best food outside of home," Perveen said. She wasn't hungry, but she managed to get some rice and meat into her mouth.

"Why did you decide to go for law? Was it even your choice?" Cyrus asked.

For years, Perveen had hung at her father's side at supper, listening to his courtroom dramas. She'd been thrilled by all of it. "Actually, my father encouraged me."

Cyrus finished a mouthful and spoke. "He's a lawyer, then?"

"Yes—in fact, he's at the High Court today. My father's plan was for me to study at the Government Law School, because the law college is bound to grant degrees to women eventually. I'd have my coursework done ahead of time once the bar opens to us."

Cyrus leaned forward, resting his elbows on the table. "What do you make of your law classes? Are they quite interesting?"

"At this point, it's not supposed to be interesting," Perveen said dryly. "But that's not why I'm dropping out. My classmates were the hardest part."

Cyrus rolled his eyes. "Tell me."

Perveen told him about the sticky business in the chair that morning, the lost essay from a previous month, the many attempts to keep her from handing in work and taking tests. As she told her stories, his handsome face moved from compassion to anger.

"Parsi boys behaved like this to you?" he said at the end.

"Parsis and Hindus and Christians! Not every boy in the room is an active player, but at least two-thirds are following with amusement."

He shook his head. "And what has your father done?"

"I haven't told Pappa because I fear his reaction. He's a big man in the legal community. He might try to fix things—and then it would be worse."

"But the fellows who are bothering you are absolute bastards!" Cyrus wiped a napkin across his mouth and tossed it beside his plate. "And they would be the ones you'd have to work with in the courts later on!"

"Yes, most of them will practice here." Perveen hadn't thought about this detail.

"They won't speak to you, although they might very well mock you when speaking to others." His voice was heavy with anger.

Perveen realized she'd confessed too much. Not because he'd tell anyone—but because he was making her think hard thoughts. "I'm not sure I should have told you. I've ruined our tea."

"Perveen, I—" Cyrus stopped, and his fair skin reddened. "Sorry. I should call you Miss Mistry."

"Not if we're cousins," she said archly.

Cyrus cocked a fist at her and laughed. "We're both of us in the fight for our lives, aren't we?"

"What's your fight?" Now she was curious.

"Ensuring the rest of my life isn't dreadful." At her uncomprehending look, he added, "I'm talking about the heartless marriage arrangements driven by parents."

"So you don't wish to marry?" As Perveen said the words, she hoped her emotions wouldn't betray her. She'd been feeling regretful that she'd have only this one meeting with Cyrus, who would very likely be engaged within days.

"I want to be with a woman who suits my taste—not theirs." He looked intently at her. "Can you believe there are just sixteen acceptable Bombay girls that my family was able to arrange meetings with?

I've got to agree to one of them and hope she'll bear two sons or more and keep everyone happy for the next half century."

Perveen giggled.

"What is it?" He sounded irritated.

"I thought there would be a thousand Parsi girls on your interview list. There are so many of us here."

"Not of the proper age, complexion, family. And then we have to think of the proper horoscope!" he added with a grimace.

Perveen looked across the table at the young man who felt himself in a predicament but had achieved the work of his dreams and surely would be matched with a satisfactory woman. "Don't feel sorry for yourself. My parents will arrange my marriage in a few years. It's part of life."

Firoze Yazdani reappeared to coax them to sample the café's baked goods. Cyrus tried a sticky, golden dahitan. Perveen asked for the simpler baked mawa cake. Firoze added a complimentary date-and-almond pastry. Between the sweetness of sugar and the heat of tea, Perveen was beginning to feel renewed.

After Cyrus had forked up the last crumb, he pulled out a gold pocket watch. "Damnation! I was supposed to be at the Taj Mahal Palace twenty minutes ago. I'll call for the bill."

But Firoze wouldn't give it to him. When Cyrus protested, Firoze said warmly, "The Mistrys always pay their bill monthly. Surely they will want to cover the cost of a relative's meal."

Perveen glanced at Firoze, who looked almost stern. She realized his putting the meal on her family's tab was a way that he could remain her father's ally. She might even have to explain if her father asked who had eaten so much with her that the bill was one rupee, three annas.

Sighing, she said, "It's true. We never use money here. Let's go outside, and I'll introduce you to Ramchandra. Grandfather likes him so much he gifted him a cycle rickshaw from Hong Kong. Ramchandra is probably the only cycle-rickshaw driver in all of Bombay."

"Cycle rickshaws are everywhere in Calcutta," Cyrus said,

walking her out the restaurant. Then, he said firmly, "I must see you to home."

"You don't!" Perveen gestured toward Mistry House. "I'm just going across there."

For a long moment, Cyrus gazed at the vast Gothic stone mansion. "That big place?"

"My grandfather built it in 1875. He's still there, staying in some rooms on the first floor now that his legs are weak."

"Not at home with you?" Cyrus sounded confused.

"We'd like him to stay with us, but he won't leave. He vowed he will enjoy the house he built until the angels call him to their home."

"But it looks like a fortress!"

Perveen felt the familiar mix of pride and embarrassment over her family's ancestral home. "I suppose so. But it was really built as a kind of exhibition piece."

"What do you mean?"

"My grandfather wished to show all of Bombay the artistry and quality he could offer. He hired James Fuller to draw the plans—he's the English architect who built the High Court," Perveen added. "All the furniture is imported from Hong Kong or crafted by graduates of Sir Jeejeebhoy's School of Art. It's a bit much to live in, but it's nice to use as a law office. My father's practice is on the first floor."

At last, a look of understanding passed over his face. "Your father and grandfather are together every day. That's very good."

"I think so. And while my grandfather might seem like a show-off, he's still got a laborer's head. I've seen him glance at a perfect-looking pillar and know without even touching it if the wood inside is rotten."

"He sounds like an intelligent man," Cyrus said approvingly. "Will you show me more of Bombay tomorrow?"

Perveen looked at him incredulously. "How can you sightsee when you've got all the bridal meetings stacked up?"

"My mother is a late sleeper, so my mornings are free."

"You'll ruin your chances, and I'll ruin my reputation!" But inside, she couldn't help feeling regretful that the only young man who'd ever asked her opinion of anything was passing so swiftly through her world.

"Perhaps Esther or one of your friends could come with us?" he suggested casually.

"But it's a Wednesday. We—I mean, they—must attend classes."

"Then suggest what I should do. I'd like to get a full view of the Arabian Sea. We have a big port in Calcutta, but it's crowded with ships and buildings. We've no swimming beaches."

Perveen thought of Land's End. It offered breathtaking views of the sea. However, it was north of the city and probably too far for him to find on his own. "Chowpatty Beach is easy enough. Any rickshaw-wallah will know the way."

"All right, I'll go. But what will you do starting tomorrow, now that you're not studying?" Cyrus's warm hazel eyes were fixed on her.

Perveen considered the question. She couldn't stay home with a feigned illness for more than a day or two. Yet she didn't feel ready to say she'd quit—her father would go straight to the dean and send her back to classes.

No. For the time being, it was wise to behave as if she were still studying and use the time to organize a plan.

"But we must meet again!" Cyrus said.

Perveen hesitated. "I'm in enough trouble. But if you want to say hello, I'll be inside the Sassoon Library, which is just next to Elphinstone. I shall ride into town every morning with my father, just like always."

His smile was glorious. "I shall bring my own book, and I promise not to ruin your reputation."

Watching Cyrus Sodawalla leave the café and head toward the rickshaw stand, Perveen felt slightly dazed.

She'd started out the morning hating all young men. Then she'd become so angry with her law professor that she'd quit school. Finally, she'd gone to eat rice with a man she didn't know. But Cyrus Sodawalla's perspective had lifted her mood and helped her understand what was needed to be true to herself.

Cyrus was really something. She had never met anyone who was both handsome and frank talking. After their heartfelt conversation, she doubted any arranged marriage candidates could hold a candle to him.

Perveen reminded herself of Esther's words. Cyrus Sodawalla was in Bombay to look exclusively for Parsi women under the age of eighteen. He couldn't have eyes for anyone who wasn't on his parents' list.

5
LAND'S END
Bombay, August 1916

*S*itting in the ladies' car on the Western line, Perveen ruminated on the various rules she was breaking. She was riding a train alone, which she'd never done before. She'd only ever ridden one in the company of chaperoning relatives or teachers. But this was hardly anything compared to her misdeeds of the past week.

She'd met Cyrus Sodawalla in the Sassoon Library garden three times. Then he had managed to have Esther Vachha invite her to join a chaperoned group of young people for a cinema matinee. Somehow, Cyrus had wound up seated next to her at the show. The whole time, she felt energy radiating out from his arm lying on the rest. He didn't touch her, but she could not stop thinking about what that might feel like.

Today's was the boldest rebellion. Cyrus had repeated his desire to go to the beach before his family left Bombay. She hadn't asked him whether anyone else would come. She sensed that he wished to be alone with her to tell her the outcome of his marital interviews. Hearing about such dismal news at a place called Land's End seemed fitting.

Stepping out of the darkness of Bandra station, Perveen saw Cyrus waiting. He was holding his fetah in one hand and had unbuttoned the neck of his jacket, giving him a comfortable look. He seemed a part of Bombay now. The crowds moved around him, not giving a second glance to the confident young businessman.

"Finally!" he said happily as he greeted her. "I've been worrying for the last half hour about why it would take so long for you to travel one stop from Dadar to here."

"Sorry. I left from Churchgate station, not Dadar." She was still going to Elphinstone every morning, keeping her parents clueless.

"I've been here since nine-thirty, but that's given me time to find a suitable tonga. The driver said the best views are at the Bandra bandstand. What do you think?"

"Let's go!"

Perveen made small talk about Bandra's history in the tonga, feeling nervous the driver might deduce that they weren't married and either scold them or refuse to drive them any farther. She was relieved that Cyrus did not say anything personal. Instead, he brought up the news of the Sodawallas' new contract to send bottled raspberry sodas to a restaurant in Bombay.

"It's very surprising, because there are plenty of soda factories in Bombay," he said. "But we've got the better price."

"Even with the cost of transportation added?"

"They'll have that cost split up in many small parts when they are billed," he said with a wink. "In any case, the contract's signed."

"Might you stay in Bombay to expand the business?"

"Not a chance. I've got to take over the operation in Calcutta when my father retires, which will very likely be in the next ten years."

"Won't you tell me about your family?" It was a question she loved to ask. She knew all about the Yazdanis' dreams for young Lily, Gulnaz's mother's health problems, and Hema's competitive relationship with a perfect older sister.

"There's Nived, my elder brother. He's well married and settled in Bihar with a son and a daughter already."

"How nice. But your mother must miss her grandchildren."

"She does miss them," he said, smiling at the children playing alongside the road. "Nived had to leave when we bought a bottling plant in Bihar. My father sent him there to set up the business. He was the only one my father trusted to go—I was too young and about to start at Presidency College."

"Then you are the only two children?" Perveen was intrigued by the similarities between her life and Cyrus's.

Cyrus looked straight ahead as he spoke. "I had a younger sister, Azara, but she died at fourteen. It was the worst thing that ever happened to our family. It was another reason I didn't marry at the typical age."

"What happened to her?"

At her question, Cyrus stiffened, making her realize she was intruding on too much pain.

"Cholera," he muttered. "It was during monsoon. It's common to fall sick when streets flood and filth is floating everywhere."

"I'm so sorry. I can only imagine what it's like to lose a sibling. And so terribly young." Without realizing it, Perveen had put her hand atop Cyrus's tight fist. He looked at her gratefully, relaxing his fingers so they could weave into hers.

Perveen felt light-headed: exultant yet terrified of this act committed so daringly in public. The tonga driver had his back to them, so he wouldn't suspect, but when she glanced at the cart driver on their right, he glowered and curled his lip as if he considered her a harlot. Instead of averting her eyes, as she would have in the law classroom, she glared at the driver until he looked away.

"We're all right now but very careful about cleanliness, especially during rainy season," Cyrus said soberly. "So many times I've tried to convince my parents to move somewhere less congested, but they would never move from Saklat Place because of the fire temple being close by."

"Are your parents quite observant?"

He nodded. "After losing Azara, they found great comfort in the old prayers."

"Azara is such a lovely name. I don't know anyone called that."

"It's from Persian and means red. Just like the color of those roses along the roadside. Bandra is quite beautiful!" He sounded as if he was trying to divert her from the sad topic.

The tonga had been slowly, steadily climbing up Hill Road, passing pastel-painted, tiled-roof bungalows built in the Portuguese fashion. After they passed St. Andrew's Church, the sea spread out before them. What a picture it made—the vast, shimmering stretch of blue edged by sharp black rocks. Seagulls wheeled overhead as if dancing on the winds.

"Would you ask the driver to stop here?" Perveen suggested, prudently releasing his hand from hers. "We're very near the bandstand, where the best view is."

He laughed. "Fair lady, your wish is my command."

As Cyrus paid the bill, Perveen strained to hear the music from the bandstand. Happily, she said, "It sounds like a military band. Let's see how many players there are."

"I don't know if we should. They're always looking for men to join up!" Cyrus said with a laugh as they walked in step with the music.

"Have you thought about enlisting?" Perveen asked.

Cyrus snorted. "Even if I were demented enough, my father wouldn't allow it. There's no Parsi regiment."

"Or perhaps he'd rather not lose his son."

"I've seen enough of your bandstand," Cyrus said. "Let's get our feet wet in the sea."

"I've been here with my family, but we've never walked down to the water," Perveen said, looking warily at the steep, rocky landscape. "Straight from here, it looks too difficult. But I've heard about people walking down through the watchtower ruins."

When they reached the blackened arch in a fragment of broken wall, they found they could get down close to the water by traversing steep, uneven land punctuated by rocks. Perveen was wearing sandals, so she had a more precarious journey than Cyrus, who was wearing sturdy laced brogues. At the edge of the water, both of them took off their shoes and held them, letting the cool seawater creep up past their ankles. A light current swirled, and she realized that if she kept going deeper, the water could probably pull her into its luscious, cool embrace.

"What are you thinking?" Cyrus asked.

"A dying man clutches at sea-foam," she said. "Do you know that saying?"

Shaking his head, he said, "I don't."

"It means a desperate man clutches at any straw."

"I never learned to swim, given the hazardous nature of Calcutta's Hooghly River." He turned to smile at her. "Make me stop talking about what we can't do. We must enjoy this day."

Looking into Cyrus's eyes, Perveen felt as if she were sinking into something deeper than water. His words were true. Although he would be gone in three days' time, she would always have the memory of their secret excursion.

They walked about a mile along the sea's edge, investigating the tiny crabs crawling around the rocks and naming the storks, egrets, and pigeons. All the birds hunting for a meal reminded Perveen it was after lunchtime, and she thought of saying something to Cyrus about going back up to buy a bhel poori snack before returning to Bandra station. She wasn't especially hungry, but she was nervous being so far from the city. And she didn't want to cause complications for Cyrus, who surely would need to be back in South Bombay by midafternoon, as he usually did.

It was two-thirty, but Cyrus didn't seem ready to leave. Perveen thought this might be an indication that his parents had settled on a bride.

The strong breeze ruffled Cyrus's curly black hair. Privately, she admired this—as well as his noble profile. Cyrus, the ancient Persian king, had looked like this in the paintings she'd seen.

"Let's sit down," Cyrus suggested. "Look, that's a nice place."

The wide, flat rock was behind an outcropping of higher stone that shielded them from view of everyone at the bandstand, as well as the few fishermen with nets on the sand. Sitting down, Perveen felt the warmth of the stone underneath her, all along her thighs and that private place that sometimes pulsed when she thought about Cyrus at night.

He gave a long, relaxed sigh. "Perveen, thank you for bringing me. I've always wanted to face the Arabian Sea. This endless blue is what my grandfather saw when he was coming to India. I wanted to see it for myself."

"I wish I knew my family's migration story as well as you know yours," Perveen said wistfully. "Nobody knows exactly when we came, but it might have been five to seven hundred years ago. And then, in the seventeenth century, the British called on Parsis to leave Gujarat to travel here and build up an old, ruined Portuguese fort into a modern walled city."

Cyrus shifted closer so the sides of their bodies were touching. "Why did your father shift away from building to law?"

The feeling was electric. Perveen spoke rapidly, trying to seem unaffected. "My father was the youngest of three sons, and the other two had joined Mistry Construction already. He pointed out that a construction company needed legal protection and, if he became a solicitor, he could provide it for them free of charge. Because my grandfather saw this as a way to show status, he sent Pappa to Oxford for his studies. Fortunately, he got a top-notch education. Pappa thought Rustom might follow his pattern, but he was a chip off the old block and went into Mistry Construction."

Cyrus snorted. "So your brother's defection forced you to continue your father's business."

"I hated law school," she said with a shudder. "However, working as a solicitor would be thrilling. I'll admit to that."

"I suppose so," he said with a shrug. "But if women lawyers can't yet appear in court, I don't see the point of your studying law."

"That's not exactly true. Solicitors don't have to argue in court. And most legal business is routine—contracts and wills. My father expects me to help him straight after finishing the law course," she added, feeling the familiar guilt weigh on her.

Sounding sympathetic, he said, "My parents sent me to college to study what was most important to them: commerce. But the teachers at Presidency were fools! Everything I know about business I learned on the outside. And look at how well things are going now. My father's never been prouder."

"That's grand." Perveen sighed, leaning forward to put her chin in her hands. "I wish law worked like business."

He looked keenly at her. "Our ancestors weren't supposed to leave Persia, but they did. They took a chance on a better future." As he spoke, his arm crept up and gently cradled her back.

Perveen whipped her head around, looking to see if the fishermen had noticed or if anyone else was coming down along the rocks. They were still alone.

"I want to ask you something." Cyrus's voice was quiet, so she had to strain toward him to hear.

"What?" she asked breathlessly.

"If you are able to give up law, I'll give up something, too."

Her eyes widened. "What is it?"

"I want to tell my parents I won't marry the stupid girl they chose for me two days ago. I am so lonely. I will be only lonelier if forced to be with someone I don't love."

Perveen put a hand to his lips. "Don't say such things. If a marriage is set, it must go forward. And please know that I never meant to divert you from that purpose. It would be wrong."

"My darling." He kissed her hand.

Pulling it away, she said, "You mustn't call me by endearments!" She did not want memories of him promising her the moon to haunt the rest of her life. Better to cut things short.

"Don't fight it, Perveen. Just think how your life is opening— as wide as the sea," he said, taking up her hand again. "Now that you've left law school, you are free to be with me!"

She let him hold her hand, but she would not look at him. "I'm not. You're going more than a thousand miles away."

"Stop talking for just one moment." Cyrus's voice rose. "I'm telling you clean that I want you to be my bride."

He had proposed. She was overwhelmed with happiness that was quickly followed by pain. Turning to look at him, she said, "But your marriage—your marriage is already—"

"They chose, but I haven't agreed. Now they are pressing me to explain why." Cyrus gazed deep into her eyes. "I haven't said anything about how we've been meeting. But I told them that Esther introduced me to a friend of hers at college who's better than all the other girls."

His words gave her an idea: if he could stay a few weeks longer in Bombay, they could become acquainted under proper chaperonage. Hesitantly, she said, "Perhaps my parents would consider a long engagement. But I must earn some kind of degree first! I'm supposed to be an example for the rest of the community."

"My parents won't wait, and yours won't think I'm good enough! They would rather match you with Bombay old money: a Tata or a Readymoney." Cyrus picked up a stone and threw it toward the sea.

Perveen watched the stone bounce off another rock. Sadly, she said, "I don't know whom they'll suggest. But having met you, I don't know how I can marry another man and be happy."

"Perveen, do you realize what's happened? We chanced to meet and fall in love!" Cyrus spoke breathlessly. "Our parents will be surprised that we found each other without their guidance, but we can tell them that God did the arranging."

Perveen nodded, thinking they had many similarities. Cyrus was full of energy and had an impetuous nature. He looked at things in a fresh way and took risks. He was the match fated for her. She almost felt that he was a yazata: an angel sent to bring her happiness. And now it would end.

"Tell me. Am I wrong to have been so bold?"

Perveen felt tears starting at the corners of her eyes. "No. I am glad for these days we've had. I won't ever forget them."

Cyrus took Perveen's face in his hands and leaned in until their lips touched.

She should have pushed him away, but she felt riveted by expectation. Finally, the thing she'd dreamed about was happening. She might miss him the rest of her life, but she would have this moment.

Cyrus's lips were smooth, warm, and insistent. He kissed her until she understood that her mouth could part, and then she could taste him: his lips, his tongue, and a delicate, inward essence that tasted of fennel and alcohol.

Her excitement rising, Perveen kissed him back. She could not get enough.

The rock was hot as he pressed her down on it, covering her with his own body. His kisses moved from her mouth to her neck, and she felt something blooming. Was this love?

Yes, she decided. True romantic love must be an overpowering desire to meld two essences into one.

Cyrus's hands slipped underneath both her blouse and the gossamer white lace sudreh. This hidden stretch of her body was prickling with sensations. He touched her breast, and she gasped from the pleasure of it.

While reading a novel, she'd once come across the phrase "wanton woman." It had sounded awful. She had traveled to Bandra fearful that Cyrus might take liberties. Now she reveled in them. She was taking her own liberties with him. Was this liberation? Abruptly, Cyrus lifted himself, and she felt desolate. Wrapping her arms around herself, she came up to a sitting position.

"I'm so sorry," he panted. "I shouldn't have done such things to a girl like you before marriage. But I want every bit of you so much. And now we know that we are meant for each other. Our marriage will be blessed with this—passion."

Perveen was trembling. She wanted him to crush up against her again—to never stop touching her.

"I've fallen for you, Perveen," Cyrus said, stroking her hair away from her face. "Now I know what love is."

Perveen's breathing slowed. The excitement she'd felt was transforming into serenity. A person had only one soul mate. Who was she to disregard this truth? Looking at him, she whispered, "It's been fast. But I think I fell in love, too."

"Please accept my proposal. I'll throw myself into the sea if you don't."

Perveen stared at the Arabian Sea. Cyrus was daring her to follow her heart—to venture on her own journey just as their ancestors had, risking all for a golden dream.

She turned back to Cyrus and put her hands in his. "Yes. I would like to marry you. I don't know that our parents will ever agree—but it's my heartfelt wish."

"My family will adore you," Cyrus said, stroking away the hair that had fallen on her face. Kissing her brow, he said, "My mother has been missing having a daughter so much. Once she meets you, she'll not want to let you go."

As he pulled her close again for a dizzying kiss, the crash of waves that followed sounded like applause.

1921

6
HOUSES OF POWER
Bombay, February 1921

*P*eople were clapping.

Perveen jerked herself out of her memories. A pair of well-dressed Indian guards along the road were bowing and applauding the governor's car as it passed. What sycophants! But then again, she was riding in the car and could hardly cast a stone.

"Father, I daresay they think you're Georgie," crowed Alice.

"I suppose that with a solar topi shielding us, we all look the same," Sir David said.

"Who knows, darling?" Lady Hobson-Jones laughed lightly. "You may very well be the next governor of the presidency."

"Would you really like that?" Alice sounded shocked.

There was a long pause. "I'll do whatever the government wants," Sir David said. "But I hardly expect it."

From the measured sound of his words, it seemed that rising to that post was certainly something he wished for. It felt almost treacherous to be in the car with such a man, because Perveen had been to gatherings with Indians seeking self-rule. In Oxford and London, she and Alice had attended a few such lectures together.

Eventually the car pulled up at a very tall gate that was overshadowed by a giant vanilla-colored bungalow. Four guards rushed forward, a pair saluting the car while the other two opened the gate.

"This seems very secure," Perveen said, thinking of the contrast with the gate at her house that was guarded by a fellow who sometimes fell asleep at his post.

"The presidency has provided us with more than enough help," Sir David said.

"We've leased it ever since it was built last year," Lady Hobson-Jones told Perveen. "Being the first family in the place means no breadcrumbs in drawers or stains in the bath. I absolutely adore it. We wanted a home big enough for Alice to knock around in."

"Actually, it reminds me of St. John's Wood," Alice said flatly.

"Why do you say that?" Lady Hobson-Jones sounded taken aback.

"It's so neo-Georgian. Not like our old home in Madras. That was a real Indian bungalow."

The India Alice was referring to was from fifteen years past, an era when Alice's father had been less important than now. Perveen was almost sorry for Lady Hobson-Jones, who seemed flattened by Alice's reaction.

"In a sense, neo-Georgian architecture fits Bombay," Perveen said. "Bombay emerged from Fort George. This bungalow is new, but its style is a testament to endurance."

"Hear, hear," said Lady Hobson-Jones, giving Perveen a faint smile.

Realizing that she'd scored a point with Alice's difficult mother, Perveen opened her own car door and stepped down from the running board. Sir David went straight inside while Lady Hobson-Jones fussed with her cloche, which the wind had put askew.

Perveen followed Alice, who'd rushed into the garden to gaze at a hedge of orange and pink hibiscus flowers. Perveen raised her eyebrows in the universal are-you-all-right? expression. Alice rolled her eyes. And then Perveen understood that Alice was embarrassed by the car and the house and the ambitious parents.

"We can still find the real India: it has so many different kinds of people and customs, you'll never be bored," Perveen said. "I want you to come to my home for a real Parsi supper as soon as possible."

Alice's eyes shone. "Don't leave out the spices."

"Sweet and spicy is the key. I have brought some Parsi sweets for you today." Perveen brandished the box.

"Yazdani," Alice said reading it. "Is that the type of sweets?"

"It's the café's name—"

"Alice!" her mother shouted from the distance. "Come meet the staff."

An impressive line of servants had emerged through the portico and stood at attention. Perveen counted eight servants wearing uniforms and four dusty, ragged men and boys who were likely gardeners.

Alice was asking names, and the staff's answers came rapidly and in a variety of accents. Alice had a strong memory; Perveen thought her friend would be able to recall most of them.

Alice's mother didn't ask her daughter's opinion of the home's interior, perhaps because she couldn't bear further criticism. Perveen was surprised that the furnishings were simple modern pieces: low settees and chairs covered in creamy, soft colors, punctuated by the occasional tall mirrors or paintings of old Englishmen. All together, the effect was an interesting harmony.

Gwendolyn Hobson-Jones led the girls straight up a flight of mahogany stairs that curved gently as they rose. Upstairs, closed doors flanked both sides of a long hallway. She opened the door to the one in the very center. "Presenting your new bedroom, Alice. Rather a change from college digs."

Alice's vast bedroom was papered in pale pink and fitted out with fashionable rattan furniture. But the stunning thing was that the room was the shape of a half moon. Through five tall bay windows, Perveen was dazzled by a view all the way down to the pale blue water sparkling with pinpoints of light.

"What a view," Alice said after a pause. "But it's so large! I don't need so much space for myself. And I'm not exactly the pink type."

"You deserve it," her mother said. "You've got the sea on one side, and in the other direction are the residences of Malabar Hill."

Alice sighed, moving from one window to the next. "If I had opera glasses, I could see the people walking on the paths below. Perveen, do you still have yours?"

"Yes. I used them today." Perveen wondered whether there would be a chance to tell Alice her worries. But should she? Her friend had just arrived and was surely exhausted.

"Mummy, do you know who lives next door?" Alice was grimacing at a giant bungalow that could have been a twin to the

Hobson-Joneses' place. It was also so close to their bungalow that there was little more than a hibiscus hedge between the properties.

"Edward Lipstye, general manager of White Star Line's India shipping operations." Lady Hobson-Jones was standing so close behind them that Perveen could smell her floral perfume. "He has two unmarried sons. The younger boy is reading economics at Cambridge, and the elder is here working inside the company. You must meet him. He's a friend of Mr. Martin's."

Ignoring the bait, Alice asked, "Who lives in the smaller bungalow down the hill? It looks more Indian than the other bungalows."

Before the car had turned onto Mount Pleasant Road, a long stucco wall had caught Perveen's notice because of the sharp glass shards embedded along its top. Now she saw this wall surrounded a sprawling Indo-Saracenic bungalow with gardens on its north and south sides and a central garden courtyard with a long, rectangular pool.

"That low cream-colored house that's going to ruin?" Lady Hobson-Jones sounded distracted. "I heard it belongs to a Muslim nawab—there are so many royals around here. He died in December, but the property's still occupied, I assume by his wives and children."

"Lady Hobson-Jones, do you know the name of that street?" Perveen asked. An odd feeling had sprung up in her at the mention of the unseen women and children.

"Sea View Road," Lady Hobson-Jones said. "Although that bungalow really doesn't have a sea view because of the other houses."

"Please don't tell me they also have eligible sons," Alice drawled.

"Don't be silly!" chided her mother. "I think the children are quite young from the shrieks and cries I hear every day. But I don't know the family. Muslims keep to themselves. Isn't that true, Perveen?"

"It depends on the family," Perveen said, feeling certain this must be the Farid bungalow. "Some Muslim females live in purdah, but not the girls I went to school with."

"Last month Lady Lloyd arranged the most beautiful purdah party," Lady Hobson-Jones said as she fussed with the curtains.

"The passageway in Government House was shielded to allow for privacy, and the room had only lady servants in attendance. Lady Lloyd did so much to make it perfect, but only two ladies out of the twenty invited came."

"That must have been quite a disappointment," Perveen commented.

"I suppose it's to be expected. I wouldn't like such a secluded life, but I suppose these ladies have eunuchs to keep them company." Lady Hobson Jones's lips stretched into a knowing smile.

Perveen longed to take her handkerchief and wipe off both Lady Hobson-Jones's smirk and her coral lipstick. Instead, she murmured, "Eunuchs are mostly found in palaces."

Alice lingered at the window. "I quite like the place. It reminds me of a miniature ivory palace."

"You're too far to see the patches of mildew on the walls. The stucco's peeling, and the glass spikes along the top are so primitive." Lady Hobson-Jones shuddered. "I'll leave you to look at the eyesore. I'm going downstairs to see about tea."

"By the way, I've brought sweets. They might be nice with the tea." Perveen offered the box that she'd been holding for the last hour.

"How considerate." Lady Hobson-Jones smiled uncertainly as she took the box.

As her mother's heels clicked down the marble stairs, Alice turned to Perveen. "I'm awfully sorry. I hadn't seen her in three years, and she's become worse."

Perveen decided to be magnanimous. "Well, not many British people would invite an Indian up to their veranda—let alone into a family bedroom."

Alice pressed her lips together. "Do you realize what their giving me this excessive bedroom means?"

"They want you to be happy and relaxed?"

She shook her head violently. "My parents expect me to live with them for the long term. I thought I was coming on holiday with a return ticket for April, but they just bought me one-way passage."

"Why is staying in Bombay so dreadful? You told me you wanted to come!" Perveen was perplexed.

"I want to be here." Alice's words were measured. "But I also know they want me under their thumb because they didn't approve of my London activities."

Perveen exhaled, thinking of Alice's many controversial causes. "The Communist meetings or the marches for women's suffrage?"

"It's worse." Lowering her voice, Alice said, "Father wrote a letter to say someone had seen me at the Fitzroy Tavern. He was concerned."

"My father would also take issue with my drinking at a public house. Never mind that Parsi ladies can tipple to their hearts' content at parties and weddings!"

Alice walked to the bank of windows that faced the sea. Looking out, she said, "It's more a matter of the Fitzroy Tavern being known for queers."

"Oh dear." It had been a long time since they'd spoken about Alice's clandestine social life.

Alice spoke, her voice still low but vibrating with anger. "After that nightmare at Cheltenham, I was only allowed out of the sanatorium and into Oxford because I pretended I was cured. But now that lie's come home to roost. I'm twenty-three and still unmarried, so they've brought me here to change things."

Perveen went to Alice and put a gentle hand on her rigid back. "It's 1921. Your parents can't force you into marriage."

"But they can heckle me endlessly! My mother didn't think twice about setting me up with a chinless wonder like Mr. Martin. And now she's dangling the wealthy neighbor. Can you imagine being called Alice Lipstye? It sounds like a dermatologic condition!" As Alice ranted, her body swayed slightly.

Perveen grabbed her friend's elbow. "Are you all right?"

"Let's sit down. It feels like I'm still on the ship."

Perveen settled down next to Alice on the pink chenille bedspread covering the four-poster.

"Interesting, isn't it, that neither you nor I can marry?" Alice said.

"Look at the two of us in the mirror over there. A perfect image of young spinsters."

"It's one of the things that links us." Perveen wasn't exactly a spinster, but there was no reason to hammer the point when Alice was melancholic.

"But you got through it. You work hard and are rewarded with money and society's appreciation, while I've had to give up my teaching in London and go on idle."

"You can work again, Alice," Perveen protested. "This country needs skilled mathematics lecturers. So many high schools and colleges here would be delighted to have someone from Oxford."

"My mother worried all the while I was studying that I'd become a bluestocking," Alice grumbled. "Of course, I have done just that. I'm even wearing blue."

Perveen regarded herself and Alice in the round mirror on the modish dressing table across from them. With them seated side by side, the top of Perveen's wavy black pompadour hairstyle came to just above Alice's shoulder. Because of their nine-inch difference in height, they'd always looked comical together. But now Perveen's large hazel eyes looked more tired than merry. Perhaps it came from legal reading—or the shock she'd experienced that day. Perveen decided her face made her appear a touch older than twenty-three: fine for working with clients but injuring to her vanity.

Alice also looked changed. Her aquamarine cotton frock was heavily creased and stained as if she'd worn it more than once without laundering. The dishevelment could have been due to traveling or Alice's discomfort with a warm climate. What was more concerning to Perveen was that Alice's round, sunburned face showed a tension that hadn't existed when they'd said goodbye a year ago in England. Not in Alice's clear blue eyes, but around her mouth, which was unsmiling.

"What is it?" Alice asked, catching sight of the covert inspection.

"Blue suits you," Perveen said hurriedly. Just as their intense college friendship had suited Perveen, a vulnerable young woman trying to forget her past.

Alice had made England tolerable and had also made it easier to stop thinking of the threat of Cyrus. But one evening, a drunk fresher had lobbed a bottle across the quadrangle when they were passing Balliol College. Perveen had screamed and run off into the dark. Alice had followed and uncovered the truth about why the sound of breaking bottles had sent Perveen back into the past.

Perveen had been grateful that Alice didn't pity or judge her. She'd helped set her back on her feet, thinking about something other than a wall of glistening bottles falling—

Perveen caught herself with a shudder.

"Tell me. Something's wrong!" Alice demanded.

Perveen longed to tell her about the possible reappearance of Cyrus. However, her thoughts about Alice's likely exhaustion deterred her, as did the knowledge that the inquisitive Gwendolyn Hobson-Jones could walk through the door at any moment. If the woman sensed any trouble in Perveen's life, she might think it too dangerous for Alice to spend time with her.

She said, "Just feeling a chill."

7

A BIRD TAKES WING
Bombay, February 1921

After indulging with Alice and her parents in a rabbit-sized tea—a small plate of sandwiches, plain sponge cake, and papaya slices—Perveen made her apologies and said she needed to start for home.

"You should have put out more of Perveen's dahitan," Alice said to her mother. "They were the best part."

"Sweets in moderation. You look as if you've consumed plenty since I last saw you," Lady Hobson-Jones sniped.

"I'll never be thin like you. Why keep pushing?" Alice retorted.

"Miss Mistry, wouldn't you like another ride in the Silver Ghost?" interrupted Sir David. "Sirjit can take you home."

"That's very generous of you, sir, but Dadar Parsi Colony is out of the way."

"May I come along?" Alice said. "A colony of Parsis sounds fascinating."

Lady Hobson-Jones shook her head. "Darling, you've been at sea for two weeks. How can you meet Perveen's family without having a proper bath?"

"I'm free tomorrow after work," Perveen said. "Could you come to my house for tea?"

"Mr. Martin is taking Alice to a welcome party," Alice's mother swiftly rejoined. "However, you could certainly make a date for the future."

"Ring me. We have a telephone set at home and also in the office. That's where I am most days from eight to six." Perveen opened her purse and extracted her card case. She handed Alice a card, which her parents studied in turn.

"Is this your father's business card?" Sir David asked with raised brows.

"It's mine. I use my initials only for business—P. J. Mistry. It's easier to attract new clients if they don't know my gender."

"So you're actually working as a solicitor!" He looked from the engraved card to her face with surprise.

"Father, we talked about it in the car already," Alice said.

"There's a difference between training in the law and practicing it. I haven't seen any woman lawyers in British or Indian courts," Sir David told Alice.

"Working as a solicitor doesn't require going to court," Perveen said. "I do the discovery work on court cases and write contracts for our clientele. My father appears in court, and we hire barristers to present our cases."

"My goodness," Lady Hobson-Jones said, pouring a glass of sherry. "I find your set quite inspiring."

Alice sprang on the comment. "Mother, I'm glad to hear you believe in women working. Apparently there are plenty of teaching opportunities in Bombay."

"But you worked so hard at that dirty grammar school in North London! Don't you want a small holiday?"

Perveen sensed that a storm was brewing. Placing her silver fork across her empty cake plate, she said, "Sir David and Lady Hobson-Jones, please excuse me. It shall soon be dark, so I'll just walk down the hill to the rickshaw stand."

"As I said, you must ride in the Silver Ghost!" Sir David huffed. "I review crime reports. Over the last year, a number of women traveling in cars and rickshaws have vanished."

Who was she to turn down what she needed? Perveen smiled and said, "That's most kind. However, I have a quick stop to make to see a client in the vicinity. Would your driver mind terribly?"

The Silver Ghost departed the Hobson-Joneses' bungalow gate and reached the entrance to 22 Sea View within two minutes. This time, Perveen waited for the Hobson-Joneses' driver to open her door and signify authority to whoever might be watching.

Perveen approached the gate, a fresh business card already in hand. A broad-shouldered durwan wearing a worn green uniform hastened past her toward the Rolls's other side.

"There's no one else," Perveen called after realizing the guard assumed such a grand car would contain a man.

He returned with a disappointed air. When Perveen told him she was there to speak to the Farid wives, his head shook vigorously, as did his fez's limp tassel. "The begums are in mourning, not seeing anyone."

"I received word from Mukri-sahib that they requested consultation." This was stretching the truth just a little bit.

The man stood in silence, as straight and thick and unrelenting as the columns on either side of the property gate.

Perveen decided to wait out the durwan. She knew that the Silver Ghost had drawn the attention of the watchmen guarding other nearby houses. If she remained in place, these men would notice the rudeness of the Farids' employee toward a woman who might have been sent by the governor.

Looking regretful, the watchman opened the gate and kept his head down, as if not wishing to see her go through. Perveen thanked him and moved confidently ahead on a stone path, passing a small family of peacocks who seemed to look after her with suspicion. The grass was high and uneven, as if a gardener hadn't cut it over the last month.

Standing in front of the house, she noticed the stucco was deteriorating, and greenish mildew had bloomed in places. Gwendolyn Hobson-Jones was correct in her assumption the house wasn't properly kept up.

The door creaked open on its heavy, rusted hinges. A young boy stood before Perveen wearing just a shabby vest and pantaloons. She couldn't help noticing the giant black birthmark obscuring most of one of his cheeks: the kind of mark that many people still believed was a devil's curse.

Perveen smiled encouragingly at the bearer, who couldn't have been more than ten years old. "I'm Perveen Mistry, the family solicitor. I've come to see Mukri-sahib. Will you please give him my card?"

"Yes, memsahib." The child took what she gave him and padded silently out of the reception room.

Removing her kidskin sandals, Perveen brought them to a carved camphorwood shelf where she saw some men's European shoes and Indian chappals. She wondered if there were no feminine sandals because the family's women didn't go out. Perhaps they even had their own door leading to a zenana, a section of the house meant for wives and small children.

Perveen gazed around, taking the measure of the beautiful old bungalow. The diamond patterns of the blue and orange floor tiles were replayed in marble lintels that ran along the tops of the high walls, which had been painted a soft cerulean. The reception room had grand columns with inset panels depicting twisting vines and flowers made from semiprecious stones. She guessed the house was built in the 1880s, just a little bit later than Mistry House.

Perveen settled herself on a low divan and leaned back against a bolster. It was elegant indeed, although the velvet was almost worn through.

She straightened when she heard the slap of slippers on tiles. A well-built man in his midtwenties wearing a silk kurta pajama was proceeding from the passage toward her.

Perveen performed the adab greeting gesture Mustafa had taught her, touching her fingers lightly to her heart and then her forehead. The man didn't reciprocate.

"Are you from Mistry Law?" he demanded.

Noticing the rudeness, she countered, "Are you Mr. Mukri?"

"Yes. Why didn't Mistry-sahib come himself?" His voice was heavy with irritation.

Perveen's back went up. "He sent me. I am P. J. Mistry—the firm's other solicitor."

His frown drew down the curled, waxed corners of his mustache. "I don't want a change in representation."

She sensed a subtle threat behind his words. "There is no change. We are a family firm working together to serve you best. My father dispatched me because, as a female, I can address the begums directly. I'd very much like to speak with them about the letter."

Mr. Mukri waved his hand as if shooing away an insect. "There is no need for conversation. I have sent your father a letter with their signatures. That has always been enough."

Her father hadn't done a thorough enough job; that was why she'd taken over. But she could hardly tell this man that. "We have carefully reviewed the document, but there are some issues about the mahr—"

"They all wish to put their mahr in the wakf," he said flatly. "Truly, what they receive isn't much: one thousand and one rupees a year. This renowned wakf—the Farid Family Foundation—needs every bit of revenue. Funds are especially needed because the wakf shall now support a boys' madrassa."

"Oh? That's a change!" Perveen was startled.

"It was Farid-sahib's dying wish."

She had never seen any mention of a religious school for boys in Mr. Farid's papers; she'd have to ask the widows about this dying wish. However, Mr. Mukri controlled access to them. She needed to proceed carefully. "Sahib, you are taking care of the estate very well. But there are clear rules guarding the contracts already written for the ladies' mahr and the settlement of the estate. We must be careful to operate within the strictures of Mohammedan law."

"Yes." Mr. Mukri seated himself in the chair farthest away, as if establishing a boundary. "First one must pay funeral expenses and the remaining doctors' bills. All that has been covered."

"Thank you for paying those bills." Perveen's smile stretched thin, because it had taken forever for him to forward evidence of those payments. She took out her notebook and her old Parker pen from her briefcase. "The next responsibility is to make sure all other debts are cleared. Have you had time to read the letters I've sent asking for the names of various creditors?"

"I have seen them, but do not worry. Those bills are paid. Farid-sahib appointed me because he knew I would take care of such matters."

Perveen scrutinized him. She saw shrewd eyes set in a once-handsome face puffed from too much food. His relaxed clothing almost gave the impression he was living inside this household. Obviously, this was a luxurious world he didn't want to lose. "I agree with you, sahib. However, it would be best if the merchants who regularly supply the household—tailors, grocers, builders, and the like—could provide evidence of paid accounts. I can gather this information, if I only have the names."

"Yes, yes," he said, twisting the ends of his mustache as if he was nervous. "I am doing it. But we need to fix the situation with the widows' donations to the wakf."

"You included a letter signed by all three begums," Perveen acknowledged. "However, any judge considering the matter will certainly question whether anyone witnessed each woman signing her own name."

His eyes narrowed. "You have a paper showing that they certainly signed their names."

Perveen's pulse began to race, because she intended to challenge him. "A judge would not believe this without anyone witnessing their signatures."

"But they are forbidden to be in the same room as men. It is iddat, the mourning period for widows, which lasts four months and ten days."

Here was her opening. "Of course you would not wish to violate religious custom. This is the reason I have come. It is quite simple for me to meet with each woman individually. If she states to me her wish to donate her mahr, I will then draft a special contract for her saying this."

"Must all this extra truly be done? We plan for the madrassa to open this July. Builders need to be paid, and we require money for books, and the teachers must have their salaries."

"Unfortunately, it cannot be avoided—and because this is the first I've heard of the madrassa, can you tell me its name and address?" As Perveen wrote notes on her pad, she saw Mr. Mukri's face tighten.

"It shall be called the Farid Institution. It's in the neighborhood where most Muslims stay."

"I see," Perveen answered, having realized he was building a wall against her as sharp as the glass-topped one outside the bungalow.

"How fast can you get the money for the school?" Mukri asked.

What she was going to say wouldn't please him, but it was the truth. "Changing established agreements means we must file for approval in several different courts. Given the slowness of bureaucracy, I'm afraid we are speaking of at least three months."

Grimacing, he said, "We are coming close to the hour of evening prayer, so you cannot see the women tonight. You may call on them tomorrow."

Perveen didn't mind the delay. It would give her a chance to gather the mahr documents to bring to the women and do a little more research at the office. Smiling gratefully, she asked, "Mukri-sahib, what is the best time tomorrow?"

"I'll be at the mill for most of the day, but you may come to see the women anytime before four o'clock—late afternoon prayers."

"I'll come at two. And thank you very much for speaking with me today. Let me assure you, our interest is serving the honorable Mr. Farid in the manner he wished."

Rising from his chair, he pointed a finger at her. "I expect your best effort on this, or I will surely report to your father!"

Mr. Mukri did not stay to see her out the door. This was another rudeness. Feeling irritated, Perveen bent to take her sandals from the shelf where she'd placed them. As she looked down toward it, she noticed something. The wall behind it was a jali made of marble with many geometric perforations. Through these small teardrop spaces, she saw a dark shape. As she stared, the dark shape moved to one side and slipped away.

The presence of jali walls and windows allowed a household's women to observe the action from which they were excluded. It was an intentional part of Muslim architecture, a way of including those who sat behind the screens.

Perveen couldn't tell if the shape had been a lady, child, or servant. All she could guess was the individual hadn't wanted to be seen.

It was barely a half hour to Dadar Parsi Colony, but the journey seemed to take forever. Perveen was anxious to talk things over with her father. She hoped she hadn't given Mr. Mukri the impression that she'd influence the women to make changes he didn't want. Having observed his dictatorial nature, though, she felt emphatic that the women needed to know about all their rights.

"My house is the large yellow one on the right with two doors," Perveen said to Sirjit when he turned into Dinshaw Master Road.

As the driver halted before the Mistrys' two-year-old stucco duplex, the neighbor boys who'd been playing in the park nearby laid down their cricket bats and rushed over to caress the car.

"Don't touch! Can't you idiots see it's the governor's car?" Sirjit barked at them.

"What has Perveen done—eaten him up?" a boy shot back.

Amid peals of laughter, the boys kept circling the car. Perveen wished Sirjit hadn't been so specific.

"Get going before I turn your faces to cauliflower mash!"

Perveen looked up to see Rustom. Her older brother and Gulnaz were leaning over the curly wrought iron railings of the second-story balcony that ran along their bedroom and parlor. Both of them wore dressing gowns, and Gulnaz's long, lustrous hair was not only loose but also uncovered.

Perveen felt a flash of irritation. Napping at six o'clock on a Monday! It was as if the two of them were still newlyweds and not married two years.

"What's this about, Perveen?" Rustom called out.

"My friend sent me home in a borrowed car. If you were decent, you could come down and have a look."

Now the car had attracted a few young men. Perveen saw Rahan Mehta and a couple of non-Parsi companions, all of whom were wearing Congress Party caps. Her father sarcastically called them the Freedom Brigade.

"What is this? Why are you riding in a car with government seals on the door? It must belong to someone very high up," Rahan accused.

"Sir David Hobson-Jones is the governor's special councillor," Sirjit answered with obvious pride. "Governor Lloyd has given his car for his use."

"An official government car!" Rahan said, staring Perveen up and down. "You must be really close to Georgie."

"Eat sugar," Perveen retorted, thinking that the ride, which had started out like a dream, was turning into an embarrassment. "Sirjit, thank you. Please tell them how much I appreciated your service."

After Sirjit drove away, Rahan continued his slurs. "English lover! It's no surprise that your family's building that ludicrous royal gate."

He was referring to the involvement of Mistry Construction in the Gateway of India construction at Apollo Bunder. Perveen glanced up and, even at a distance, could see her brother's face reddening. She shook her head at him. She was on the ground and fully dressed. She'd take care of it.

Perveen marched up to Rahan and his friends until they were inches apart. "I'd be pleased to speak to your group about the activism of Indians throughout Europe, including Madame Bhikaiji Cama, who was jailed after speaking about Indian independence to India's overseas soldiers."

The young men murmured uncertainly.

"Madame Cama's speaking cost her greatly; she's not allowed to come back to India," Perveen said, looking them over with contempt. "You should think about her example and whether freedom might be won not by insults but rather by mixing with people outside one's community."

"You caused quite a stir tonight," Rustom said as the Mistrys all sat down to dinner that evening in the parents' dining room.

"I didn't mean to. Alice's father insisted I ride in that car. Rustom, I thought you might have liked to inspect it." She paused a beat. "But you weren't properly dressed."

"Your tongue is like scissors right after the sharpening." Rustom gave her a killing look.

"Why does your friend's father have use of Governor Lloyd's car?" Jamshedji asked as he buttered a puri.

"Sir David Hobson-Jones works for the governor. They took me in the car from the pier to their bungalow in Malabar Hill, and of course, they wanted to ensure my safe return."

Rustom hooted. "Sir David Hobson-Jones is the governor's special councillor overseeing the development of Back Bay!"

"I heard something along those lines." Favoring her brother with a smile, Perveen added, "He knows of Mistry Construction."

"As well he should!" Camellia opined. "Tell us all about Alice's home."

Perveen rolled her eyes. "It's one of those monstrous places Grandfather Mistry used to say would be the death of Malabar Hill. But it was interesting inside, with very modern furniture."

"How clever of you to make friends with Sir Hobson-Jones's daughter!" Gulnaz said enthusiastically.

"Sir David," Rustom said, patting Gulnaz's hand. "Just like our governor must be called Sir George, in the event one needs to address him. And now, thanks to Perveen, we might very well have invitations to the Secretariat."

Laughter rippled around the table, and Perveen had to hit her glass with a fork to get back their attention. "Enough! I've known Alice for almost four years, and I would never use her for gain. Our friendship stands apart from family politics, business, and everything else."

"But we are talking about a family interest," Gulnaz said. "That is entirely different. Your friend should be our friend, shouldn't she?"

Perveen and Gulnaz's casual relationship had changed now that they were sisters-in-law. It was loving, but not entirely comfortable. Carefully, Perveen said, "There's a misconception that Parsis support the British unconditionally. We have to do better."

"If that's your aim, how do you explain lounging in the governor's car?" Rustom demanded.

"I really had no choice in the matter. And I thought you'd like seeing the car, not rip me up about it!"

"Oh dear!" Gulnaz's anxious gaze turned from one sibling to the other. "I didn't wish to cause an argument."

"There's no argument here, darling," Camellia said. "It is only brother-sister blustering."

Jamshedji looked down the table and spoke in a mock-scolding tone. "I think it's extraordinary that nobody's asked a question about my day. It just happens that I won a very big case."

"Oh, Jamshedji-pappa, do tell everything!" Gulnaz said, going into sycophantic daughter-in-law mode.

Jamshedji reminded everyone of the case's particulars and then went into full reportage: "And Judge said . . ." followed by "I'd coached my barrister to respond . . ." and "Then the boy, Jayanth, took the stand . . ."

As everyone else listened raptly, Perveen saw no place in her father's golden evening to tell him her worries that Cyrus Sodawalla and an associate might be in town. Besides, if he became nervous, he might not let her go out to the Farid bungalow the next day. And she had to speak to those women.

After dinner, Perveen climbed the stairs to her room. In her hands she held a small tin bowl containing half a banana and some leftover cooked cauliflower. After slipping into her nightgown, she opened the French doors to her own balcony overlooking the quiet green garden. Inside her brass cage, Lillian was sleeping with head under wing but came quickly awake.

"Ahoy there, matey!" Lillian squawked, hopping off her perch.

"Ahoy there, Lillian," Perveen answered, smiling at the Alexandrian parrot.

"God save the Queen," cackled Lillian, catching sight of the bowl of food.

Perveen's late grandfather had been Lillian's first owner, and he'd taught his bird the toast during Victoria's reign. The bird had been unwilling to change her allegiance to Edward VII or George V, no matter how hard Grandfather Mistry had tried to get her to do so.

Perveen had taught Lillian to recite one line from "Vande Mataram," the freedom poem, but she only chirped a random "mataram" after a particularly tasty treat.

Perveen opened the cage door. The bird exited in a gorgeous rush of pale green feathers. She made some fast-flapping circles over the garden before returning to the arm of the lounge chair where Perveen had placed her supper bowl. Lillian ate delicately and then began a series of brief forays into the garden, where she screamed at the other birds as if they had no right to the territory.

Sometimes Lillian stayed outside for hours, sipping water from the birdbath and monitoring the garden for avian intruders. But when mosquitoes descended, Perveen would leave the balcony to read in her bedroom, in the comfort of a netted bed.

Losing Lillian wasn't a worry. She was part of the Mistry family, and like a prodigal daughter, she always returned.

8

FINE PRINT
Bombay, February 1921

The Principles of Mohammedan Law had been written in English, which should have made understanding it easy. But the more closely Perveen read the book, the more it seemed like a minefield.

Muslim marital law stated that a widow's claim for dower was a debt chargeable against a husband's estate. It had to be paid out before legacies and inheritance distribution. But the word "claim" bothered her. One might interpret that to mean that if a widow wished *not* to take her mahr, the inheritance distribution and legacy donations could go forward without making any subtractions. Probably, this was what Mr. Mukri believed.

Perveen rubbed her eyes. Two hours of reading a legal treatise was exhausting. She wanted to ask her father about the issue, but he had gone to Kemps Corner to see a client. She wrote down the question in her notebook and shifted to another pressing job: writing out a Hindustani translation of Mr. Mukri's letter, which had been written in English. She finished at twelve and went across the street to see a notary public at another firm to have the translation certified.

Stepping into the busy atmosphere of Bruce Street reminded her of the stranger she'd recently seen, and Cyrus. She inspected the fronts of every business, including Yazdani's on the corner, before going back upstairs to read more Muslim law.

At a quarter to one, Mustafa announced that Jayanth had arrived to see her. Glad for the distraction, she hurried down.

Jayanth pressed his hands together in a namaste greeting at the sight of her. He looked so much better than when he'd been in the Bombay jail. He was bathed and freshly dressed in a clean lungi and vest. His back was straight, and his face seemed fuller; it was as if all his heavy anxiety had lifted.

"Good morning to you, Jayanth!" Perveen said. "I'm very sorry for not being in the audience yesterday and seeing your grand victory."

"I missed you, too. I came to give thanks." From behind his back, he brought out a small, tender-looking green parcel. "My mother made you sweet coconut rice. It is a Koli specialty."

Kolis were a local population, many of whom worked the water. Perveen thought it was ironic Koli sounded a lot like "coolie," the Anglo-Indian word for Indian loaders, which was Jayanth's trade down at Ballard Pier. It was punishing work—most men were finished by the age of forty due to injuries.

"Coconut rice—my favorite!" she said, taking the banana-leaf wrapped delicacy into her hands. "How did you know I get hungry around this time every afternoon? This is much nicer than biscuits. But tell me—why are you here at this time? Have you been able to start work?"

"Since five o'clock today. Old Ravi's face was sour as tamarind, but he let me in. And my friends are grateful that we all will have a daily break now. I used this break to come to see you. I know it was your hard work that won the case."

"I can't take responsibility," she demurred. "My father was the one who spoke so convincingly to the judge."

"Using the things you wrote down!" Jayanth said emphatically. "I may have no money—but whatever you need at the docks, I can get. Tell me if you need to know about any particular person, or company, or ship. Also, if you wish for goods at a special bargain—"

Hastily, she said, "That is so kind. Our accounting for your case is closed." The last thing she needed was for him to be arrested for stealing.

After Jayanth departed, Perveen took the package of coconut rice to her desk. It was vulgar to eat and work, but she had so little time. She'd just finished the last morsel when she heard her father coming in downstairs. Quickly, she threw away the banana leaf and wiped her desk blotter clean with a handkerchief.

"Goodness, Pappa, you look warm!" she said, noticing the sheen of sweat on her father's bald spot.

"I asked Arman to drop me at the Ripon Club for a spell, and I walked from there. Spring must be coming early this year."

"Sit, and I'll bring you water." Perveen tipped cool water from the silver pitcher on the stand into a fresh tumbler and added a sprig from the mint plant by the window.

"Mustafa should be doing this, not you," he said as he settled into his chair with a soft groan.

"Today I asked Mustafa to go out and buy something for me." She'd wanted Mustafa to ask around the street about whether a Bengali stranger or any curly-haired Parsi had been seen that day.

"He is always happy to go out," her father said, taking a long, pleasurable drink. "Somehow, the heat does not bother him, despite his age."

"He always says heat gives strength." Perveen picked up *The Principles of Mohammedan Law.* "May I ask you about Section One Eight-Four, 'Nature of Widow's Claim for Dower'?"

"Go on," he said, taking another draft of water.

Perveen asked whether deferred dower always needed to be paid at the time of a marriage's dissolution through death or divorce. "Could such a payout be overlooked if a wife wishes not to take the gift?"

"At the time of marriage, this community tends to demand the prompt dower. But later on, there is no requirement of prepossession," Jamshedji answered easily. "However, the judge would be happier if the solicitor could testify that the women have received what is due. Then they can donate it. It makes the situation clean."

"Some of the mahr should be on hand. I'm almost certain Sakina-begum would have possession of her jewelry and Mumtaz her musical instruments—but I'll ask each of them." Perveen picked up the Farid folder and flipped through it again. "Proving Razia-begum's possession of the four acres will be harder, because amongst all these papers, I haven't seen a deed for land in her name. Is it filed elsewhere?"

"No," Jamshedji said, setting his glass down. "After the wedding, I asked Farid-sahib if he wished me to put through the ownership change in court. He declined. I didn't press him because a solicitor isn't required to make such a change. Such a filing could be done at any time, given the commitment made by the mahr contract."

Perveen was annoyed by her father's decision to be so passive. "I hope the deed can still be switched into Razia-begum's name."

"Her husband's intent to transfer it to her is stated in the contract. We can do the work, or it could be executed by Mr. Mukri."

Perveen was fairly confident he'd have no interest in doing that—unless the land gift was going toward the wakf. But what would that mean? "Land wouldn't enrich the wakf, unless the land is sold. And how could Razia-begum sell it now that the mills are on it?"

Jamshedji sat still for a moment and then shook his head. "The fabric mills could stay, but the land underneath could become part of a family trust, and that trust could be paid rent by the company. But it involves more legal work than you are experienced enough to do. When I gave you this yesterday, I didn't know this was an issue."

"Who knows? Razia-begum might not wish to give up those acres once I've explained everything."

Jamshedji held up a cautionary finger. "Remember, Razia-begum is the one we think had the genuine signature on the relinquishment letter. She may be all for giving them up to the wakf."

"I suppose so," Perveen said, feeling doubtful.

"Now, what about lunch? Now that my throat isn't so dry, I hear my stomach's call."

"I wish I could eat with you, but I must be at the Farid bungalow by two. May I use the car?" She looked at him entreatingly.

"Certainly. It's too far for a horse to pull a tonga from here all the way up Malabar Hill. And I've just realized the other reason you won't eat lunch with me," he added in a sly tone.

She was confounded. "Why?"

He pointed to the iron wastebasket that was now circled by a few flies. "It is a lowly habit to take anything more than tea and biscuits in the office. Your grandfather would weep."

The ride from Fort to Malabar Hill took less than a half hour. Still, Perveen was sweating when she arrived. It wasn't just the warm February day. She was nervous about explaining things to the widows correctly, and also because she intended to learn what they thought of Faisal Mukri. If he was as unpleasant and controlling with them as he'd tried to be with her, she imagined they would be an anxious group.

At 22 Sea View, the same belligerent durwan was on guard. When he looked into the Daimler and saw Perveen, his face reddened. He jabbed a finger at Arman and barked that he was in the wrong place.

"Memsahib?" Arman turned to look questioningly at Perveen.

Perveen spoke to the guard in a controlled tone. "Actually, you admitted me here yesterday. I'm the family lawyer and was given permission to return by Mukri-sahib."

"Yes, yes!" the durwan said shortly. "But to see the wives, you must go to the zenana entrance. That is the second gate. I opened it already."

Now she felt foolish. Arman drove a few more feet and turned into the second gate. The brick driveway led to the house's north side, which had a long, copper-roofed porte cochere at the door. She imagined that this extra structure offered privacy to women getting in and out of carriages or cars.

Perveen stepped out and surveyed the garden. This side of the property was thick with tall trees. Weeds had grown high on the neglected lawn, although a border of rose bushes had been tended and looked healthy.

When Perveen rapped at the door, she was met with silence. She called out a greeting through the holes of the marble jali window, and a minute or so later, a small girl in a worn cotton salwar kameez opened the door.

"Adab," Perveen said, noting the girl appeared to be the same age as the boy she'd seen the day before. "My name is Perveen Mistry. I've come to see the begums."

"They know about you. Please come inside." The girl kept her head down, as if Perveen's presence made her shy.

"Yesterday, a boy answered the door on the main side of the house," Perveen said as she stepped out of her sandals.

"My twin brother, Zeid. A good boy," the girl added, turning to look at Perveen. The similarity in the small heart-shaped faces was apparent, although the girl didn't have the birthmark.

"Zeid was most helpful to me. What is your name, my dear? And are your parents working here?" Child servants were a fact of life in the city, but Perveen felt concerned for ones who'd come alone from the villages to work in big houses.

"My name is Fatima. Our father is the house's durwan; he is called Mohsen. Our mother, may Allah keep her, went to paradise when we were born. We were too much for her."

"I'm very sorry." Perveen wanted to say more, but the young maid interrupted her.

"Memsahib, kindly wait here. I'll fetch them."

After Fatima hurried up the staircase, Perveen toured the reception room, which was approximately the same size as the room where she'd met Mr. Mukri. This room's decor was different, with a floor of aged gray and white marble tiles covered in areas by ornate Agra rugs. She smelled the delicious scent of roses in a vase on a central table.

Seeing an opening off to the room's west side, Perveen went a few steps and found herself in a small room about eight feet square that was dominated by a six-foot-high, ceramic-tiled niche. The niche was fitted out with hundreds of tiny mosaic tiles that formed pictures of flowers and curving arabesques in shades of blue and violet with touches of yellow. Gazing into it, she was overcome by a sense of an old, elegant culture that seemed somehow familiar. Zoroastrians had ruled Persia before the Arab conquest in the middle of the seventh century, and a shared aesthetic came through in the ornate floral tiles.

A soft swishing sound made her quickly turn.

"Do you wish to pray?" A thin girl who looked about twelve was regarding Perveen with curiosity. The girl's salwar kameez didn't fit well, but it was of a fine embroidered silk that made it clear she wasn't another servant.

"Amina!" A petite woman with luxuriant black hair coiled into a top-knot rushed up behind the girl. "Don't say such things. The lady is not Muslim."

Perveen was embarrassed to be caught wandering. She made a quick adab gesture to the woman, who had long-lashed, beautiful eyes and an unearthly fair complexion that was evidence of life lived indoors. The lady who appeared close to Perveen's age was dressed in a borderless black sari, which should have been grim but was elegant due to its silk chiffon.

Feeling flustered, she said, "I didn't know this was a holy place. I'm sorry."

"No need for apology," the lady said in a markedly sweeter tone. "The mihrab is our central point for worship. You are Miss Mistry, aren't you? I am Sakina."

Her courteous response eased Perveen's tension. "Adab, Sakina-begum. My name is Perveen. I'd like to offer a very belated condolence on the passing of your husband. My father said he was such an honorable man, always treating everyone kindly."

Sakina nodded soberly. "Your condolence is gratefully received, and it is not late at all, for we are observing the mourning period." As she spoke, two other women in black arrived, their beaded slippers making light sounds on the marble. "May I introduce Razia and Mumtaz? We will do whatever you wish."

Perveen repeated her adab gesture, and both ladies reciprocated. The tall, slender woman with gray streaks running through black hair pulled into a tight bun must have been Razia. Although the papers at the office revealed her to be thirty, Perveen thought she looked slightly older due to long frown lines running between her nose and mouth.

Mumtaz, the third wife, was quite brown: natural for someone who'd not been sheltered her whole life. She was not as alluring as Perveen had expected. Her hair was scraped into a messy braid, and her face was puffy and tired looking. Another difference between her and the other wives was her dress. All the wives wore borderless black saris. But while Sakina wore silk chiffon and Razia tussah silk, Mumtaz wore a baggy sari of cheaply dyed black cotton—a fabric more likely to be worn by a poor woman than a rich one.

"Thank you for coming. I am Razia, the mother of Amina, who was the first of us to greet you." The senior wife's voice was lower-pitched than Sakina's and had a reassuring gravity. "She has been very excited about your arrival since Mukri-sahib alerted us yesterday evening."

Perveen was distracted by the sound of small feet running. Within seconds, two young girls in white, lace-edged frocks had appeared.

"It's time for playing music with Mumtaz-khala!" the older of the girls sang out. She looked about six years old and was likely Sakina's first-born daughter.

"Nasreen, you are interrupting Perveen-bibi, who is our guest," Sakina said, tapping Nasreen on the head. "And Mumtaz-khala cannot play music with you and Shireen today. She is busy."

Five-year-old Shireen hopped up and down. "Who is our guest? Where does she come from?"

"None of you girls should be downstairs. This is time for grown-ups talking. Go to Ayah." Razia's tone was reproving.

Perveen sensed the widows were anxious about her presence, and this feeling would pass to the children. There was no need for it. Smiling at the children, she said, "Might we all say hello to each other? The judge will ask whether I've seen the children and if they are in good health and spirits."

"All right, then," Razia said with a nod. "You girls are lucky to have this chance."

She crouched to get on eye level with the two younger girls. "I'm Perveen; call me Auntie or Khala if you like. I live in Dadar Parsi Colony, and I work with my father in an area called Fort. We are lawyers, which means we help people keep what belongs to them.

We promised your father we would watch over your family to make sure you were fine."

After Perveen spoke the word "father," Amina rushed forward and put a protective hand on each of the other daughters. "Don't say that."

"I'm sorry—" Perveen felt alarmed.

"Abba is still watching us," Amina said reprovingly. "From heaven."

Parsis and Muslims both believed in heaven and hell. This was a major difference from Hindus, who believed in reincarnation. "You must miss him very much."

Amina nodded. "I do. He talked to me every day, even when he was sick. Shireen and Nasreen don't remember him so well, because they didn't go in the sickroom."

"Abba is happier in heaven, Ammi says." Nasreen reached out a finger to eagerly stroke the border of Perveen's sari. "Your sari is very pretty. Not black like theirs."

For a moment Perveen was confused, but then she remembered "Ammi" was the Urdu word for mother. "I don't think they will always wear black, but it is the custom now."

"We mourn for four months and ten days," Razia said flatly. "After that, we dress as we like—but there really is no reason for festivity."

Perveen had the sense Razia was heavily grieving her husband. Perhaps she felt the burden of the whole household upon her in addition to the emotional loss. Mumtaz and Sakina both looked somber. It made Perveen wonder about how Omar Farid's relationship with each woman had been, whether he had shown a different side of himself to each one, or if he had loved one more intensely than the others.

"Why have you arranged your sari so strangely?" Shireen chirped, interrupting Perveen's thoughts. "It's not correct."

"Shireen!" Sakina reprimanded her with a soft laugh. "Please excuse my daughter's rudeness."

"It's a good question!" Perveen said. "I am a Parsi, and it is our custom to wear saris this way."

"May I please?" said Nasreen, stretching out her fingers to touch the embroidery.

"Of course." Perveen stood like a mannequin, feeling the way she had when the women in her family had rushed around draping her sari for her wedding.

"What is a Parsi?" asked Amina in slow, studied English.

"A Zoroastrian born in India." Seeing Amina's small brows drawn together in a questioning way, Perveen elaborated. "We worship God, but we call him Ahura Mazda rather than Allah. My people came on boats from Persia a very long time ago. Other Persian Zoroastrians have come in the last hundred years. They call themselves Iranis, because that is the country's name in Persian. "

"Ah. It is like British calling us Mohammedans. We are Muslims." Amina's gaze was bright. "My ancestors came from Arabia. Also on very long boats."

"Amina, are you studying English?" Perveen was surprised both by the girl's swift logic and the fact that she kept answering Perveen's Hindi words in English.

"We were learning until our English governess went. May I properly say to you: 'Good afternoon, Miss Mistry'?" Amina put out a slender hand for Perveen to shake.

"I am very pleased to meet you," Perveen said, shaking Amina's hand and thinking that all three girls had a sparkling energy. She turned to Shireen and Nasreen and spoke in Hindi. "The only one missing is your brother. I'd like to meet him, too."

"He's napping upstairs. Now that all have been acquainted, shall we sit down?" Sakina suggested with the air of a comfortable hostess. "Fatima, go to Iqbal and ask him to make a pitcher of falooda."

The young maid nodded and hurried out the door.

The hospitality was enticing, but Perveen couldn't allow her consultations to become a family affair. Gesturing at her briefcase, she said, "I am very much looking forward to talking with all of you, but I should speak with each lady alone."

"In the zenana, there are no secrets. We are all sisters!" Sakina said with a friendly laugh that revealed a mouthful of sparkling teeth. How was it that Sakina looked so well when Razia and Mumtaz did not?

"I understand that. However, the judge requires a different letter from each wife. It is just as your late husband made an individual marriage and mahr contract with each of you." Perveen regarded each widow as she spoke. Both Razia and Sakina appeared startled; Mumtaz's expression didn't change. She looked as if she were accustomed to being told what to do.

"Can't we stay?" Amina asked. "It sounds very interesting."

Perveen paused, thinking how rare it must have been for the children to have a visitor. "I've an idea. If the children wish to play music with Mumtaz-begum, there's no reason not to do that now. I will come for a performance before I have my visit with her."

"We can certainly do that," Mumtaz agreed, giving the children a tired smile. "Let's practice to make a lovely concert."

"But the falooda!" Nasreen whimpered.

"You may have a small glass after you've practiced nicely." Sakina gave her an indulgent look. "Perveen-bibi, I will speak to you first in my private quarters upstairs."

"Bibi" was the proper honorific to use with Perveen, who was a young single woman.

But this was a very unusual household if the second wife decided to speak before the first.

9

PIERCED WALLS
Bombay, February 1921

*P*erveen followed Sakina up the wide marble staircase into the Farid widows' private world. Here every window was shaded with a marble jali screen, casting dotted bits of light everywhere. It was beautiful but dim, reminding Perveen of what it was like to try to read on her balcony after the sun had set.

The zenana hallways upstairs were in the shape of an *L*. Sakina led her through a long hallway and into a shorter one that ended with a metal jali screen. Drawing closer, Perveen noticed that the delicately tooled metalwork was made to resemble a trellis covered with clusters of grapes and their vines.

"Such lovely metalwork; it reminds me of the doors of a cabinet in our office. I wonder if your cabinet was made by the same metalsmith." As Perveen moved closer, she saw that the golden jali appeared to be locked on the other side and had a wide slot in the middle with a hinged covering. "What's this?"

Sakina smiled at the compliment before answering. "This jali makes a border between our zenana and the main house. The opening is a place where we may pass papers and other small things. It is a relic from the old days, but now that Mukri-sahib is here, we find it convenient to use it again."

"Is this the place where you sit when you converse with Mukri-sahib?" Perveen regarded a small bench covered in pink velvet.

"Yes. There's a seat on the other side for any gentleman who has been approved to come into the bungalow and needs to speak with us."

Perveen wanted a sense of how many personal connections the women had. "Besides Mukri-sahib, who has come recently?"

"Many mourners came in December. Two weeks ago, a military

officer came to discuss some matters of the wakf with Razia, but he could not enter the house because of our mourning period."

Sakina had referred to the household's senior wife by her first name only—an act that did not show the respect that adding "begum" would have provided. Perveen wondered what Mustafa would think. "How often do your own relatives visit?"

"My family is from Poona; therefore, visits aren't frequent." Sakina had straightened slightly, as if she were less comfortable. "But I'm not lonely. As you can see, we have a very lively home, and we can sit outside in our gardens when the weather is fine."

Perveen didn't entirely believe her. "What about telephoning—can you ever chat?"

The widow's long-lashed eyes flared. "Telephone calls are expensive. And the telephone set is in the main section. It is for business matters only."

"Do you visit friends elsewhere in Malabar Hill or Bombay?" Perveen was worried that Sakina was putting up a brave front.

"A few acquaintances." Sakina gave Perveen a level glance. "I hope you don't consider us poor, trapped females because we observe purdah? It is entirely by choice."

"I understand you've chosen to live this way." But Perveen remained concerned about how little contact they had with others—and not even a telephone for emergencies.

"I thank Allah daily that we are not on the streets surrounded by dangerous types and that our daughters are growing like roses in a walled garden. This is a special, peaceful life. If only we can keep together and stay in this home, I will have no worries."

"Of course, we will try to ensure that, Sakina-begum." Feeling chastised, Perveen followed Sakina through the doorway that was closest to the golden jali. Inside was a sumptuously decorated bedroom dominated by a big four-poster dressed in pink silk. The drapery color was exactly the same as that of the roses in the blue-and-pink mosaic tiled borders around the windows and doors.

"What a charming room. And it looks like another room is attached." Lowering her voice, Perveen said, "Is your baby son sleeping there?"

"All the children stay in the nursery with Ayah. Jum-Jum is always sleeping this time of day—he's just turned one. I use the other room for taking tea with visiting relatives or friends, for simply enjoying some rest," Sakina said with the gracious smile that Perveen realized was her hallmark. "Let's go in together."

"How many servants work in the house?" Perveen asked, settling down on a purple velvet settee while Sakina took a matching wing chair. A black lacquered curio cabinet was filled with English and French china figurines, and a grand mahogany commode was topped by an arrangement of lilies and tuberose in a bowl. There was a feeling of luxury and peace in the room. "Did you make the lovely flower arrangements?"

"Yes," Sakina said, looking a bit startled. "I must take care of the flowers now. I go very early in the morning, when the sun is not strong. We did have a gardener, but to conserve funds, we let him go, as well as the governess Amina mentioned, the cook's assistant, and our head bearer."

"You are very talented at it," Perveen said, realizing that Sakina seemed ashamed to be performing an art that many other ladies would have prided themselves in. "If so many staff are gone, do Fatima and Zeid take care of the cleaning?"

"Yes. Their father, Mohsen, is our durwan. We still have Iqbal—our cook—and Taiba-ayah, who has been with the family since my late husband's childhood."

Fatima came in, awkwardly carrying a silver tray weighed down with two tall crystal goblets brimming with a pale pink beverage. The fruit-and-milk punch was room temperature, not chilled, and Perveen realized the house didn't have an icebox.

"Delicious," she said after sipping. "And is Mukri-sahib staying in the house or visiting when needed?"

"He has taken a room in the main section of the house. Having a responsible man inside the house was my husband's wish; it keeps us safe. We hope he will continue living here, although it is certainly an imposition for him."

Because of Mukri's casual clothing the day before, Perveen had guessed he lived in the home. But it certainly was unconventional for a man who wasn't their blood relative. She wondered if he had anyone to keep him company on the other side of the house. "Has he a wife and children?"

"No. That is the reason my husband thought he would be able to dedicate himself to helping us." Sakina carefully set down her own glass of falooda on an embroidered cloth on the table before them. "Perveen-bibi, were you going to explain about the necessary papers?"

"Sorry," Perveen said, realizing she'd strayed too far into the personal. "I'd like to start by reviewing the mahr papers your husband signed in 1913."

Perveen opened her briefcase and presented the Urdu version of Sakina's mahr agreement. Sakina's eyes ran slowly over the lines. "I understand. The paper describes the jewelry set that I'm planning to give to the wakf."

"I assume such valuable jewelry is in a vault at a bank?" Perveen said, taking a legal pad out to begin her notes.

"No bank," she said dismissively. "My father-in-law built safes in all the bedrooms, and that is where I've always kept my jewelry."

"Oh! It's right here, then."

"Would you like to see it? I haven't looked at it since before my husband's illness."

"Certainly." Perveen was pleased that verification would be so simple.

Sakina rose gracefully from her seat and went to the wall, where she shifted aside a small painting of orchids. Behind it was a brass plate with two round dials. After a few seconds' work, the door sprang open, and she pulled out a drawer with boxes. Sakina returned to Perveen and set down a series of velvet boxes on the table between them.

"What beautiful pieces," Perveen said as Sakina brought forward a gleaming necklace of emeralds, diamonds, and delicate gold links.

She opened a smaller box, showing the matching bangles and yet another one with fine emerald drop earrings. The size and clarity of the gems was astounding. Perveen was not the same kind of jewelry connoisseur as her sister-in-law. She suddenly wished Gulnaz was with her.

"The earrings and the pendant all are made with four-carat emeralds from Burma and two-carat diamonds from India. The bangles are studded with five single-carat emeralds and five single-carat diamonds each." Sakina's eyes glowed as she looked up at Perveen.

Perveen still couldn't guess how much wealth was lying in front of them. "Have you had an appraisal done?"

"Never. As a young bride, I saw how much my husband valued me with this gift. But now he is gone, and there is no use for such extravagant jewelry. It's better to gift it all to the wakf."

Perveen nodded, taking note of what Sakina thought about her late husband's feelings. Perhaps Perveen's earlier thoughts of love between the husband and his three wives had been too sentimental. She wrote in her notebook, *Consented.* "Now, what about the five thousand rupees that are coming to you as the second half of the mahr payment?"

"That can go to the wakf. All of us are giving it up; we've agreed."

Perhaps Sakina's attitude was natural in a joint family with multiple wives and children. Everything was shared. But Perveen sensed the widow didn't understand the implications of giving up such an asset. "How much have you heard about the rules of Muslim charitable trusts?"

Sakina gave an apologetic smile. "Razia is the one who concerned herself with it—she doesn't speak much of it to me."

"I suppose the best thing is for you to read it. I brought the official document explaining the wakf's purpose, including the shares distributed to your family. It's in English, though."

Smiling again, she said, "Just explain it to me, then."

Perveen summarized the wakf's purpose of contributing fifteen thousand rupees each year toward necessities and continuing care for wounded army veterans. As she'd discussed with Mr. Mukri, the wakf paid each of the Farid wives one thousand and one rupees per year. The same allotment would be granted to each of the Farid children from the age of eighteen onward.

At the end of the complicated report, Sakina sighed. "Fifteen thousand is a lot, isn't it? When my husband was alive, he donated to the wakf every year! Perhaps he was too generous. The trouble is how to keep funding the wakf with his income gone."

"There will still be income flowing to you; he didn't sell the company," Perveen explained, surprised she hadn't known that. "Did Mukri-sahib mention a plan for the wakf to start a madrassa?"

"Yes. He spoke of it when we met at the jali screen last month. It is a sensible thing to do, since the war is over. Also, so many poor Muslim boys cannot afford schooling."

Perveen looked at Sakina's open, sweet face and wondered whether her own schooling had ended at age fifteen, when she'd married, or even earlier. Gently, Perveen said, "Literacy is valuable for both boys and girls. Did you know the literacy rate for Muslim girls in India is less than two percent?"

"My girls will read well!" she retorted. "They must learn the important prayers and to converse politely in Hindustani and Urdu. They also learn stitching and fine needlepoint from me."

"Amina is learning different things," Perveen said, watching her for a reaction.

Sakina smiled. "It's her mother's choice—and she had the advantage of a governess for more years of study. After the estate is settled and we know our financial situation, Mukri-sahib can seek a new governess—but in the meantime, Razia and I can give them their religious training."

Perveen realized Sakina could not picture a life for girls different than what she knew in her home. "I understand you trust Mukri-sahib greatly. However, there's a problem with his desire to use the wakf to fund a school. The law is written so that a wakf cannot change its charitable purpose. Because the wakf was defined as a foundation to benefit injured veterans, only a judge can allow the funds to go elsewhere."

Sakina was silent for a moment. Then she looked at Perveen. "Does this mean a lawyer could help us—you could do that?" Perveen shifted uncomfortably on the settee. How could she answer? Of course, she was there to do all she could to help the family. However, she couldn't go against the law. "Such work would be done in steps. Firstly, the plan to change a beneficiary for a wakf must be ordered by the mutawalli—the person who is the wakf administrator. And then comes the decision to hire a lawyer."

"Mukri-sahib has already done the first part, by speaking to you, hasn't he?" Sakina queried.

Perveen saw that Sakina was missing the obvious point. "Actually, he's not in charge. Razia-begum has always been the wakf's mutawalli."

Sakina looked as if she'd been punched. Taking a shaky breath, she said, "What do you mean? Razia helps with the wakf—but it was my husband's foundation. And now Mukri-sahib has naturally taken it over."

"No. Her name is listed in the paper as the mutawalli—the administrator in charge of everything."

Sakina still looked disbelieving. "A woman can do that?"

"Mohammedan law allows for a mutawalli to be any religion or gender. I shall ask Razia-begum about whether she thinks both missions can be accomplished. I imagine that if she looks at the accounting, she might realize two projects could deplete the wakf's funding."

Sakina's look toward Perveen was pleading. "What should we do, then?"

Perveen felt awkward because she could not steer Sakina, and her confused, unhappy state was clearly the result of the new information. "One thing at a time. Do you still wish to give up all of your mahr to the wakf?"

"I don't know." Her voice was shaky, as if she were about to cry.

"I'm terribly sorry to have surprised you like this, Sakina-begum." Perveen was belatedly realizing her explanation of Razia's status could become the start of a family feud. "I thought this was something you already knew."

Sakina wiped a tear from her face. "Now I understand why you wanted to speak to each of us alone! Two of us have bad news and only one person good."

Perveen felt apprehensive. "What does that mean?"

Looking down, Sakina murmured, "I thought our late husband had treated all of us well—but if he gave Razia the wakf, it means she was his favorite. And how can she decide sensibly on matters when she knows even less about the world than Mumtaz and I do?"

Mumtaz had surely experienced hard times if she'd had to support herself as a musician. She had to be street-smart, although her illiteracy would prohibit her from being able to perform the tasks of a mutawalli. But Perveen couldn't understand why Sakina felt so righteous about her own powers. "Sakina-begum, weren't you raised inside a zenana?"

"Yes—but our compound in Poona was large and always filled with relatives coming and going. It was a happy place. I learned everything from my father, my brothers, and cousins—" She broke off, her face pinkening.

Sakina probably was embarrassed to give the impression she was brought up with more freedom than she had now. Trying to sound understanding, Perveen said, "That must have been a happy time for you."

Softly, she said, "Children are happiest if they grow up playing with many sisters and brothers. For this reason, I want my daughters and son to live with Amina and their aunts. That is why the wakf must stay strong. It keeps us together. No one of us wives should have power over the others."

Perveen put her hand over Sakina's, thinking she now understood why the second wife had referred to the senior wife by first name only—although, as a lawyer in service to the family, she herself could not. "We can't change your husband's decision to give guardianship of the wakf to Razia-begum. I urge you to speak with her about whether there's any change in her intentions for the wakf.

Take time to decide whether to sign over your assets. If you don't give your jewelry and money to the mahr, they could be financial security for you, or an inheritance for your daughters."

Sakina flicked off Perveen's hand to take up the emerald necklace. She turned the elaborate piece this way and that so its stones flashed in the soft light coming through the jali. To Perveen, it didn't look as if Sakina wanted to lose it. But she'd already made the point about choice—and the choice was the widow's.

Perveen withdrew one of her business cards from her briefcase and laid it on the silver tray next to the glass of falooda that Sakina hadn't touched. "My card has telephone numbers for my house and office and also my mailing address. I'm able to come back, if you'd rather speak in person."

Sakina shook her head.

As Perveen took hold of her briefcase and stood to take her leave, she studied the woman, who'd stopped putting her jewelry away. Sakina was running her emerald necklace gently through her hands, as if weighing something a good deal heavier than twenty-four carats.

10

SECRETS BETWEEN WIVES
Bombay, February 1921

*O*pening the bedroom door into the hall, Perveen almost tumbled over Amina.

Razia's daughter was sitting against the wall and looked up with an innocent expression. "I shall walk you to my mother's room. Won't you please speak more English with me?"

"You couldn't understand my Hindi just now?" Perveen asked, challenging her to deny the eavesdropping.

"Yes. But I want to learn English."

Perveen was intrigued by the girl's attitude. "Why is that?"

Amina paused. "Ammi went to a school. The teachers spoke English. Maybe one day I'll also go to school."

Razia must have been listening for them, because after they rounded the corner into the next hallway, she appeared in an arched doorway. "Please come in, Perveen-bibi. I've had a pot of tea brought up."

Perveen knew that turning down a drink offered by any of the wives would be a slight. "How kind of you. Just a small cup, please."

"I shall pour," Amina said, hurrying to a tea table set with gold-banded Minton china.

Razia's room was slightly smaller than Sakina's but had the advantage of being on a corner, with windows on two sides cross-ventilating it. Its aged plaster walls were covered with framed sketches and tinted photographs of the Taj Mahal and some significant Bombay buildings: Victoria Terminus, the Secretariat, and the Haji Ali Dargah mosque.

While Sakina's centerpiece had been her large, elegant bed, Razia's room held twin beds covered by cotton patchwork quilts. The room's piece of pride appeared to be a large mahogany partners' desk with a Queen Anne style chair on each side. One side of the desk was covered with children's books and colored wax pencils and pieces of chalk. The other had a stack of ledgers on a blotter and a stack of stationery and a line of old-fashioned fountain pens and ink bottles. Perveen could imagine the mother and daughter working together, the same way she and her father did in the law office.

Amina carefully carried two cups of tea over to a wide teak swing that hung from the ceiling by silk-covered cords. The swing was wide enough to seat at least four people. It hung close to the veranda, which was enclosed by a cast-iron jali that offered a hint of the blue sky and green trees outside.

Perveen had more to discuss with Razia than anyone, but she was determined not to rush. As she seated herself on the swing next to Razia, she decided to speak in Hindi, to be certain all she said was understood. "I appreciate your agreeing to speak with me. But wouldn't Amina like to join the other children for the music lesson?"

"It's a simple song. I know it already!" Amina stamped her feet as she made her way to the desk and sat down with her cup of tea. She kept her eyes on her mother.

Razia looked shyly at Perveen. "I don't mind if she's here. Amina helps me with my papers and knows all that I do. And it's her legacy we will talk about."

Perveen sipped the tea, which was blisteringly hot and sweet. Trying not to wince, she realized she could not go against a client's wish when she was trying to make a reassuring impression. "Very well. But Amina, I am going to teach you a word in English. It is 'confidential.'"

"Con-fi-den-tial," Amina repeated back slowly. "The meaning?"

Looking intently at the girl, Perveen said, "The word 'confide' is a verb that means trusting another person enough to tell them something one doesn't like telling many others. The lawyer that you share such talk with does not tell others, unless you've given permission. And that is how this conversation should be, for your mother's sake."

"It's secret," Amina said in English. "Why not say that?"

Perveen drank again to allow herself a moment to think of a sensible explanation. "Secrets are often about bad things. We are not trying to hide something bad. And it seems to me that secrets almost always wind up being told."

"Agreed. There are few secrets inside a zenana," Razia said with a weary half smile.

Perveen considered saying to Razia that she'd been very good at withholding the information that she ran the wakf from Sakina—but it wouldn't have been a tactful way to start their conversation. "Thank you for granting me this time. It must be a very difficult time, since your husband's passing."

Razia shrugged her thin shoulders. "Actually, it's not different than the last two years."

This surprised Perveen, who'd painted a picture in her head of Razia as the most devoted wife. "Tell me about the last two years."

"After Dr. Ibrahim diagnosed cancer, my husband began going in the evenings to Falkland Road. Mukri-sahib brought him. There he found relief of some sort." Razia leaned back and started the swing slowly rocking. "He no longer stayed with me much. Then he brought a musician who worked there home. This was Mumtaz. He began to stay in her room only. So we could not see much of him."

Perveen was astounded Razia had spoken in front of Amina about Falkland Road, an area known not only for music but prostitution and drugs. But the Farid females lived in seclusion, so Razia might not have understood. "Not seeing your husband during that time must have pained your heart."

Razia looked thoughtful. "I'd lost him once before—when Sakina came," she said quietly. "That was the time when he appointed me mutawalli of the wakf. I think he wanted me to be busy, to have something. And it has been worthwhile work. But it seemed terribly wrong that I devoted myself to getting good care for wounded men all over India, but my husband didn't want my care."

Perveen looked over at the desk where Amina was fiddling with the items before her: pens, pencils, a letter opener. She wasn't looking at her mother, but Perveen thought she was listening closely.

Razia brought her heels down on the floor, stopping the swing. "Perveen-bibi, do you wish me to sign a new paper? Mukri-sahib said the document we signed was not enough."

"Certainly," Perveen said, picking up her briefcase. "Are you the one who had the idea of shifting all the wives' mahr into the wakf?"

She shook her head. "Mukri-sahib spoke of it to me last week, explaining the financial duress we are under, and said we should give more to the wakf. As our guardian, he suggested we all put our mahr into the wakf. I thought it was a sensible idea, because we can do good for others yet not worry we will lose our home."

"What is the current endowment?"

"Come. I'll show you." Razia stood and walked to the partners' desk. Pulling out a large book, she opened it and showed Perveen columns of withdrawals.

"It looks like there are one hundred seven thousand rupees, and the last addition to the endowment was two years ago."

"My husband was very set on building the endowment during the war years, when our mills were running day and night. We are losing ground because every year fifteen thousand flows to the veterans and three thousand to us wives. The family payout will rise to seven thousand rupees per year after the children come of age."

Razia understood the mathematics. But how far into the future had she thought? "At the rate you're giving, the endowment could all be gone in a few years," Perveen said.

Razia's expression was grave. "I know."

There were so many things Perveen had to share with Razia—but first in her mind was what would happen if even more than fifteen thousand flowed out per year. "Have you estimated the extra expense of building the madrassa?"

Razia's eyes widened. "Madrassa? What do you mean?"

Perveen had a sinking feeling she was spilling another secret. But this one needed to be known by the wakf's mutawalli. "Mukri-sahib told me the wakf funds will build a madrassa for boy students. He plans to hire teachers soon and open this year."

Razia was silent for a long moment. When her words came, they were spoken in a grim undertone. "I—I am shocked. He did not speak of any madrassa when he gathered us to ask for signatures for the wakf donations."

Sakina had known. Was it because Mr. Mukri had told her, perhaps favoring her as the leader of the wives?

"Mukri-sahib told me," Perveen said, trying not to reveal the unease she felt. "It was the reason he wished everyone's mahr to be transferred quickly."

"I suppose that if we gave *all* the mahr we had, there might be enough money to support two projects for a short time." Razia's voice was grave. "But truly, our wakf is for helping wounded veterans."

Perveen needed to know more. "It sounds as if the foundation's mission is still important to you. How did it come about?"

"It began with the war," Razia said, shifting her feet so the swing rocked back and forth again. "In 1915, the government requested that Farid Fabrics produce thousands of bolts of khaki cotton drill cloth. For my husband, it was good business. But in my mind, we were dressing men so that they could fight—and very likely be wounded or killed. I didn't like that."

"It's sad to die!" Amina commented in her know-it-all tone from her post at the desk. "So sad for the people you leave behind. Although if one leads a righteous life, he goes to heaven."

"I was haunted by the thought that men wouldn't have been able to go into battle without our uniforms." Razia was rocking the swing steadily now. "We can do nothing for the poor souls who died, more than seventy thousand from India alone. But the least we should do is give clothing, wheelchairs, and other necessary supplies to the wounded—and extend help to their families, since military pensions aren't sufficient for living."

Razia's words reminded Perveen of how she and Alice had seen the condition of some wounded veterans who were housed in some of Oxford's halls. It had been horrifying to see their injuries. "What are some of the ways you have provided aid to Muslim veterans?"

"We help all the Indian Army soldiers, regardless of religion.

The soldier only needs a commanding officer or hospital worker or chaplain to ask. I know one—Captain Aarif Ali—who has made it possible to help many of his troops and others beside. May I show you some of his letters?" Razia went to a tall bookcase and brought back a heavy album with a letter pasted to each page. As Perveen leafed through, she saw the letters were written in a variety of scripts—Urdu, Hindi, Punjabi, English, and Tamil. Captain Ali had written many letters of his own, too—in English, likely because everything he wrote was subject to review by a commanding officer.

Your kind transfer of 100 rupees of May 1918 was most appreciated. I was able to purchase clothing for five veterans, 10 walking sticks, and three wheelchairs. Per your suggestion, I am continuing to provide men returning home with a gift of 100 rupees to spend as they see fit at home, and encouraging family members with special needs to submit claims with specific details.

Perveen turned the page and read another letter from Captain Ali.

Your payment for the schooling of Private Bhatia's son and daughter was received with heartfelt tears from Mr. Bhatia. His wife has sent a heartfelt letter to you that I am including with this. Mrs. Farid, your continuing questions to me about the needs of family members are no trouble at all for me. They have given me a greater understanding of the character of my men and how much they gave up to serve the government.

"After the war ended, Captain Ali came to this house to pay his respects to my husband and me and explain about the ongoing need. Even though the war is over, soldiers are still coming out of hospital and have needs for equipment and physical therapy that are beyond what the army can give."

"Captain Ali came to talk to Ammi a few weeks ago, but

Mukri-sahib did not allow it," Amina said, repeating the story Perveen had heard from Sakina.

"It is iddat," Razia said crisply to her daughter.

"I saw the captain through the jali, Ammi. He is handsome as a king."

"Amina!" her mother reproved.

Perveen thought the women deserved to talk through the jali with men who had legitimate household business. But that was tangential to the matter at hand. "Razia-begum, because you are the mutawalli, all decisions about the wakf are yours. In any matter, the court will likely be hesitant to change the recipient of the wakf's monies. I'm advising you based on previous cases decided by the court."

Razia looked almost angrily at her. "You speak as if it's a simple matter. How can I push my wishes on Mukri-sahib?"

"Don't think of it in such terms," Perveen said gently. "Your husband appointed him to serve the family."

"Mukri-sahib is the agent for the household—which means he stands as the man of the house. He manages everything. If he doesn't like my behavior, what might he do the next time he goes to the bank to withdraw funds for us? The bankers allow him full privileges."

Perveen was suddenly uneasy. She'd seen Razia's ledger—but it was a handwritten account. Mr. Mukri could already be withdrawing money without Razia knowing it.

"What could happen with the allowances for food and clothing if he's unhappy?" Razia's voice rose. "Will there be money to pay for electric lighting in the house, for the fans to run? Already the children lost their governess."

"What are you thinking, Miss Mistry? Your face is so angry. Are you upset with Ammi?" Amina's voice was anxious.

"No, I'm not angry. These situations happen all the time with household agents." Perveen tried to relax her jaw. Her thoughts had turned to the possibility of the widows filing a suit for the removal of Faisal Mukri. The best chance of success would be if all of them agreed to participate, and they had hard evidence of malfeasance.

It would take at least a month to prepare, and such a case could take months to reach court. And what would their living situation be like in the meantime?

"There are so many things you can do," she continued, picking up the mahr contract that had not yet been discussed. "We should discuss the issue of the dower that was promised to you when you married."

"A small amount of swampland near the mill district," Razia said dismissively. "I don't think it's worth much."

"Actually, it is. The land was filled in, and two company mills stand on it."

Razia's shoulders jerked in surprise. She looked hard at Perveen, as if trying to figure out if the words were true.

"Does this mean Ammi owns the factories herself?" Amina asked, her voice rising in excitement.

"A court would decide," Perveen said, looking at Razia, who was still speechless. "The promise is in the mahr letter; however, your husband didn't ever change the title on the land. But it can be done. You would have to instruct me, or another lawyer, to go forward."

Razia was silent for a while longer and then took a long, shuddering breath. "I don't know if that's a good idea. My husband was using the land for the company, which benefits all of us in the family. Why should there be concern?"

Her words gave Perveen the spark of an idea that could protect the wakf. Leaning forward, she said, "If the land is not titled to you, you cannot donate it."

Razia gave her an incredulous glare. "Sakina has her jewelry gift and Mumtaz the instruments. They are giving up these things— how will it look if I give nothing?"

Listening to her, Perveen realized that perhaps the widows were close enough that they all used first names. Such a relationship might make Razia feel especially bad about having more. "For each of you, it's an individual decision. And knowing what you do, would you want to give up this land to the mahr—or would you like to retain it as an asset for the protection of your daughter and yourself?"

Razia hesitated again before speaking. "Sakina will be very jealous to know that I have land with factories. And what about Mumtaz? She takes joy in her musical instruments, but they are worth little next to what I have. I wish to be confidential about the factories on the land."

"It seems there are a great number of confidences that are being kept in this house. Sakina-begum didn't even know you were the wakf's mutawalli."

"If she had asked, I would have told her!" Razia sounded almost flippant. "But she had no interest. She enjoyed a rich life with my husband for many years. She never knew what it felt like to be ignored until Mumtaz came."

Perveen winced, realizing her earlier assumption of closeness had been naïve. Jealousy and resentment were the running themes in this household of women. "Razia-begum, it seems that you are chained to some people and a large old house that you cannot fully enjoy."

Razia looked warily at Perveen. "Is that not the meaning of family?"

A shiver ran through Perveen. A few years earlier, she had felt exactly the same. Pushing away that memory, she said, "You three have the right to sell this house and share the proceeds. This would enable you all to live at ease wherever you might choose. Perhaps you would like to see your natal family again, or you could rent one of the new flats with seaside views right here in Malabar Hill."

Razia gave her a withering look. "A woman like you could live without protection—but I have no experience in the world. I have to worry about Amina's safety, and the danger to me, too. This is all so difficult. I don't know what to do about the mahr, and what you've told me about the wakf is distressing!"

"Tell Mr. Mukri that he needs to speak with me. I'll explain the needful," Perveen said, handing her a business card. "I shall leave the translated copy of the mahr document for you to keep. Write to me if you wish to talk again—although I hear you have a telephone on the other side of the house. Both my telephone numbers are listed on the card."

Razia studied the card and put it in the central drawer on her side of the partners' desk. "So now you are going to Mumtaz."

Packing up her briefcase, Perveen said, "What is your relationship like with her, now that she's no longer caring for your husband?"

"It's all right," Razia said with a shrug. "She nursed my husband without complaint, and she has been a good help with our girls."

"Mumtaz-khala is my favorite aunt," Amina said. "She says I'm very good on the veena."

"You must not say such things about favorites! We are one family," Razia chided.

Amina set her mouth in a firm line.

Wanting to cut off an argument, Perveen gestured to the jali. "I hear beautiful music playing outside. I wonder whether that is Mumtaz-begum or the little ones."

"Mumtaz-khala, of course! May I bring you there?" Amina asked eagerly.

Perveen smiled at her. "I'd be grateful for your guidance."

"Is it really safe for women to live outside?" Amina asked after they'd left the zenana's second floor and were going down the stairs.

"I've been fine." *More or less*, she thought.

"May I ask you another thing, Perveen-khala?"

"Of course."

"Will you . . . be confidential with me?"

Stopping her progression down the stairs, Perveen looked at Amina. "I will—unless it's something your mother must know to care for you better."

Amina looked at her intently. "I love my whole family very much. But . . ."

"But what?" Perveen prodded gently.

"I would like to go and live somewhere else, like you said."

Perveen asked, "Do you wish to see the outside world? Everything in the pictures on your walls?"

The child hung her head. In a whisper, she said, "I don't want to live here because of Mukri-sahib."

Fear rose up around Perveen like a chilly wall. "Why? Has he—has he ever laid a hand on you?"

Amina shook her head but remained silent.

Perveen had to figure it out. "Does he speak cruelly—threaten you in any way?"

"He speaks terribly to my mother and me. But don't tell him we said this, or things will be worse." Amina started walking quickly, as if she regretted starting the conversation.

Perveen followed her down the rest of the stairs. "Amina, does your mother feel as troubled about this as you do?"

"I'm not troubled—I wish death upon him. Ammi is too good, too quiet. She is afraid."

Razia's response to the idea of challenging Mr. Mukri on the wakf had already proven that. But perhaps there was more—something that could be used in a case against him. "What has he done to make your mother afraid?"

"I can't say now. It is confidential. Nasreen and Shireen are here."

Amina had run ahead into the garden, holding out her arms for the younger two to rush forward into them. She embraced her half sisters, laughing as if her short, disturbing confession had never taken place.

11

CONCERT IN THE GARDEN
Bombay, February 1921

*P*utting on a calm face, Perveen followed Amina and her half sisters to the thin carpet spread out in a stone pavilion, where several instruments were arranged. Perveen seated herself on a stone bench and watched Amina take a teacher's place to the side of the two little girls. While Amina played with confident dexterity, Nasreen and Shireen were too small for their hands to range very far across the long wooden instruments. The girls plucked randomly.

Perveen let her thoughts wander. At that moment, she had no request from Razia or Sakina to donate their mahr. Their explanations made it seem that Mukri was intent on both controlling and altering the wakf. There was a case for removing Mukri as the household agent; but it would have to be done very carefully, so as not to cause trouble for the widows.

The girls finished with a wild twanging sound, and Perveen hastily applauded. "Beautiful singing and playing. Mumtaz-begum has taught you well. But where is she?"

"She went under the almond tree to sleep." Shireen pointed to a grouping of trees.

Perveen didn't see Mumtaz, so she stood. "I'll look for her."

She shouldn't have felt anxious—but she did. Quickly, Perveen moved toward the grove of fruit frees. Just past them, she saw a bit of gray.

Mumtaz was lying slumped against a stone step on the other side of the garden, close to a marble jali.

Perveen's stomach lurched. Calling out, she asked Amina to bring a glass of water from the house. Nasreen and Shireen launched into their next song, seeming utterly unconcerned.

Perveen went swiftly to the woman and crouched down to gently touch her shoulder. "My dear, are you all right?"

Mumtaz groaned and slowly turned her head. "I was just resting. But I feel ill."

"You must go inside." Perveen let out the breath she'd been holding, relieved that the widow was strong enough to speak. She'd thought the worst when she'd seen the gray heap.

"No, no, it is my time to play music with the girls. I was only taking a rest for a moment."

With Perveen's help, Mumtaz struggled to a sitting position.

"Amina is bringing water to you," Perveen said. "Would you like some sweets?"

"No, no, but—you? You are our honored guest," Mumtaz croaked. "You must have refreshment . . ."

Perveen was too worried to continue the etiquette dance. "I'm already full with tea and falooda—there's no need for anything more. It doesn't seem that you are well enough to talk with me. We can do that later."

Mumtaz peered at her through half-open eyes. "I must speak with you and—and fix things."

The words she'd chosen sounded strange. Perveen asked, "What do you know about the situation?"

"If I give the wakf my money, it will let me keep living in this bungalow."

"Who told you that?"

"Sakina-begum says if we give the wakf our money, it will keep us living in the bungalow forever." Mumtaz lowered her voice. "Isn't that true?"

"Not exactly." Perveen paused. "Did you read the paper that was sent to me by Mukri-sahib and sign your name?"

Her eyelids fluttered. "Why do you ask?"

"You signed an X on your mahr agreement seven months ago." Perveen was careful not to mention this was what illiterate people did. "But your name was spelled out on a paper that he sent me."

"I did the X for mahr because my writing is poor. Sakina-begum signed the other paper because it would look better."

The court accepted documents signed with fingerprints and X

markings, but that was irrelevant to bring up. As Perveen understood it, Mr. Mukri had told Sakina to get the authorization from Mumtaz. But had Sakina explained everything so that Mumtaz realized what she was giving up?

"If you feel well enough, I'd like to talk to you about what was in the letter," Perveen said as Amina arrived and crouched down to give Mumtaz a brass tumbler of water.

"Thank you, sweet Amina," Mumtaz said with a sigh.

Amina settled down next to them. In a whisper, she said, "Perveen-khala and Mumtaz-khala, you should know—"

"Amina, please tell me later, when I've finished this talk. Will you go listen to the girls?" Although Razia had allowed her daughter to be present during her consultation, Perveen was determined not to compromise Mumtaz's privacy. After Amina had slunk off, shooting her a look of annoyance, Perveen began. "The document Sakina signed for you said that you wished to give up your musical instruments and five thousand rupees for the family's wakf, which is a charitable foundation—"

"Lose my musical instruments? She didn't say!" Mumtaz's mouth fell open in an *O* of surprise.

"Don't worry," Perveen said, responding in her most soothing tone to the stunned young woman. "If any wife wants to give up her mahr, she must write her own letter saying that. You haven't done so yet."

"Music was what calmed my husband. He could only fall asleep when I played." Mumtaz closed her eyes, as if to summon back those nights. "The sitars and veena are as dear to me as Amina, Nasreen, Shireen, and Jum-Jum are to their mothers."

"That's fine," Perveen said, glad that the decision had been easy. "I'll make sure you won't relinquish any musical instruments."

"I don't mind about the five thousand rupees." Mumtaz pinched her mouth into a pious expression. "Whatever little bit I receive from the wakf is enough."

Perveen was curious about the words she'd chosen to describe her wakf dividend. "That charitable fund pays each of you wives one thousand and one rupees a year to use as wished, for savings or personal expenses. Did you receive that sum last year?"

"No. Razia-begum said five hundred and one was the proper amount for being married only one-half of the year. Isn't that true?" Mumtaz pushed the hair back from her face as if she wanted to get a better look at Perveen. She had high cheekbones and a face shape slightly similar to Razia's. Perhaps Mr. Farid had loved her for this similarity as well as the music.

"Razia-begum is correct in her accounting because you married him last July." Perveen thought the senior wife's decision was stingy, but she didn't share this opinion. "You will also receive some inheritance from the estate, but I won't know the amount for several more weeks."

Mumtaz nodded. "But what about the five thousand? Mukri-sahib said because I can't save money, it is better for me not to take it but to put it in the wakf."

Perveen wasn't surprised by Mukri's recommendation, but she was wondering if it was true Mumtaz was bad with money. "What is this about you not saving?"

Holding up her palms, Mumtaz smiled ruefully. "Money is like sand running through my fingers. From the wakf money I received in December, I've less than one hundred rupees left."

This struck Perveen as suspicious. "But you live inside a house—going nowhere. Were you charged for food or household expenses?"

"The special foods I like that are expensive—pomegranates and fresh dates. I've bought new strings for my instruments, too, and some saris and caftans. A lady tailor came around, and her materials were so fine—more expensive than I realized. That is why my mourning saris are so plain."

Nodding, Perveen realized that the water was doing the trick—it was giving Mumtaz the strength to speak with her.

"I also ordered some furniture from a carpenter who comes through the street every month," Mumtaz continued in a whispery tone. "I wanted my room to look just a little bit like Sakina-begum's. My room is not a sickroom anymore. If I spend the rest of my life here, why shouldn't my room be pretty?"

"I agree." Perveen had not realized that a person's illness could saturate a room so much. But, she reflected, she should know. She thought of the rank odor of the little room upstairs at the Sodawalla house, and her head started to ache. Quickly, she changed the subject. "Are you happy here? Are the other begums friendly to you?"

"What wife would welcome a woman of my background coming in as the new wife?" Mumtaz said in a low voice. "Sakina-begum was jealous, even though my arrival meant she didn't have to nurse her sick husband at all! And Razia-begum is her senior—thinking she is better than both of us and so clever with all her letter writing."

Perveen could have soothed Mumtaz and said that things might get better with time. But looking at the twenty-year-old girl with such fragile ties to the other wives and little more than three instruments to her name, she did not feel like saying that. "Mum-taz-begum, would you be happier living here or somewhere else?"

"Do you mean—go away?" Mumtaz's voice broke. "Even though I'm a wife?"

"You would still be a respected widow—but think of all the pos-sibilities," Perveen said gently. "You could use the second part of your mahr to pay for a small bungalow or house, and you'll also have your inheritance. If the neighborhood is a good one, you could also use your residence as a music school. And—"

"Stop your scheming!"

Instinctively, Perveen turned her head, looking for the origin of the harsh male voice that had interrupted.

Nobody was visible, but Mumtaz was staring with a stricken expression at the house wall just fifteen feet away. On the other side of the garden, the girls stopped playing music.

"Mukri-sahib, are you there?" Perveen called out to him while she looked at the thick wall she guessed was attached to the house's main wing. There were no windows. From where was he listening?

"I trusted you to carry out work for me, and you have abused that by feeding the widows falsehoods. You are a devil!"

"On the contrary, it's my duty to ensure this family's welfare." Perveen was shaking slightly from the shock of realizing he'd overheard her.

"Telling a foolish woman not to sign a paper that would secure this household's future is against the welfare of the widows. I am hereby severing your representation—"

"Excuse me, Mukri-sahib." Perveen enunciated every word to the utmost. "You should not shout at me. I shall come into the main house and speak with you."

Perveen tried to still her trembling and went from the garden into the zenana entrance, where she came upon Amina and the girls huddled together.

"He's angry at me, not you. I must talk to him to make my responsibility clear." Perveen put on her sandals with shaky fingers. This was a terrible outcome of the confidential interviews.

"I tried to say to you that he'd come home"—Amina's voice was choked—"but you made me go away."

"I regret I did not listen," Perveen said grimly. "Where are the other begums? Did he question them?"

A tear slid down Amina's cheek. "I don't know. I was doing as you said, just listening to Nasreen and Shireen playing. Are you going home now?"

"Not until I have a discussion with him and make sure that your mother and aunt are all right."

Perveen strode outdoors and under the porte cochere, where Arman was lounging against the car, spinning his chauffeur's cap idly in his hands.

"Ready to go, memsahib?" His neutral expression told her he'd heard none of what had happened.

"I'll just go over to the other side to speak to Mr. Mukri. Bring the car around to the main entrance. I shan't be long."

The main door was closed. When she knocked, it was opened by Zeid. He looked as anxious as the little girls had been.

"I've come to see Mukri-sahib." She did not bother to take off her

shoes but stood in the entrance of the reception room. She wanted
to remain near the exit, because she couldn't be sure of the extent of
the guardian's anger.

As Zeid crept out of the reception room, Mr. Mukri came bar-
reling in. He wore a European suit, likely because he'd come from
the office. That's where he'd told her he would be.

"We've some matters to clear up, Mukri-sahib. I believed myself
to be having a private consultation with the begum. I'm willing to
address—"

"Shameless!" His eyes narrowed. "You disregarded my directive
as the operating household trustee. And what stupid advice. These
women can't leave home. They wouldn't know what to do!"

"I am not trying to cause trouble. It is my duty to give them a
full understanding of their assets and how the law works to protect
them." Perveen delivered her words loudly, realizing that Razia and
Sakina might be listening. "You cannot decide what happens with
the wakf. You are not in charge of it."

"How dare you speak of being in charge?" Mukri's voice was contemptuous. "You are not even accredited by the Bombay Bar. You
have no power in the court."

Perveen realized he must have looked into her background and
had prepared to fight. His insulting declaration was intended to
scare the begums into thinking she couldn't defend them. Drawing
herself up to her full five feet three inches, Perveen said, "The
women on the other side of the jali are not weak. They hold more
power in their six hands than you have in two. I have it in mind
to terminate your association with this household, based on your
attempts to manipulate their assets."

He advanced toward her. "I am the only one who can do sacking.
I have power of attorney to decide the household's course. Leave
this place at once, and do not return. I will telephone your father
and tell him that Mistry Law has been terminated. When you arrive
home, prepare yourself for a proper beating!"

"A beating?" Perveen defiantly met his gaze. "My father is a good
man, so that is not a fear of mine."

"Is that so?" He walked up very close to her and raised a flattened palm.

In that awful instant, she knew he was going to hit her. He meant to prove that he was stronger than her words, that he had rights over her as well as the others. He would hit her again and again. Pain flashed through her, and suddenly she wasn't in Malabar Hill but a bottling plant more than a thousand miles away.

Just as suddenly, she was back. The surly durwan had appeared at the door. Loudly, he said, "Sahib, excuse me!"

Mukri snarled, "What is this?"

The durwan was a godsend. Perveen used that moment of distraction to slide out the door. The car was under the porte cochere, and Arman was anxiously motioning her to get in.

"Memsahib, it is not my custom to ask about your business matters," Arman said after they'd turned the corner past Alice's house and were going down the hill. "But that was a terrible fight!"

"I never expected that man to be listening!" Perveen put a hand to her chest, which was still vibrating with fear.

"He was very angry. I heard the shouting and called out to the durwan. He said that man is crazy. Did he touch you? Your father won't forgive me for my lack of protection." Arman's voice broke.

Perveen hesitated, still feeling jumbled. Her back ached as if she'd been hit with a series of blows. How could that be? She knew Mr. Mukri had been in front of her. What he had done was break through to memory.

"What did he do, memsahib?" Arman was looking anxiously in the rearview mirror.

"He shouted, and then he tried to get me to cower. Some men use fear to get what they want, and I'm sorry to say that he raised enough worry in me to make me run away."

"It is not running away—it is self-defense!"

"I meant to check on the begums—I left without doing it. Now I won't know if he approached them and forced them to say what I'd told them." A lump rose in her throat. "I didn't keep my word."

"Sometimes Mistry-sahib's clients have been angry with him. Usually it is after losing at court."

"Thankfully, that doesn't happen often." Perveen sighed, because Mr. Mukri had been right in guessing that her father would be upset. In less than two hours, she'd turned a straightforward series of private consultations with women who'd never met a lawyer into a dramatic conflict. Perhaps Mr. Mukri really could fire Mistry Law, and then she'd never have access to speak to the begums again.

As they turned off Malabar Hill and onto the Queen's Necklace, Perveen's thoughts became even more miserable. What if it really was true that Faisal Mukri had power of attorney? She'd seen a paper certifying him as the family's agent, but not granting him power of attorney, which was significantly stronger. Had she missed it? What kind of a solicitor was she not to have taken this into account? Perveen reached beside her for her briefcase, but felt nothing.

"Damnation!" she cried.

"What is it, Perveen-memsahib?"

"I left my briefcase behind."

"The fancy London briefcase? It must be worth a lot."

"It's what's inside that matters," Perveen said, sickened by this additional evidence of her carelessness. "All those documents. I must go back."

Arman sucked air through his teeth. "I don't know. The gentleman was so angry! Shouldn't you ask your father to return for the briefcase, for safety's sake?"

"We cannot wait, because the papers inside my briefcase could be stolen or destroyed. It would be terrible for my clients. You must turn around, Arman."

"But memsahib—"

"I am ordering you!" Perveen's voice cracked.

Arman didn't answer, but his shoulders rose as if Perveen's harsh words had affected him deeply.

They were already a mile down the seafront. Arman slowed, crossing the road sharply in front of a bus that sounded its horn. He turned around on the rough ground of a construction site and started back for Malabar Hill.

Perveen checked her watch. They'd left Malabar Hill twenty

minutes earlier; it would be twenty more minutes before they got back, at least. As they went back up the incline, past the beautiful mansions surrounded by tall trees, every twisting road increased Perveen's feeling of dread. It would be wonderful luck if her brief-case was still in the zenana garden. But she had no idea of the safety of the women. Did she dare to stop to check on them, too?

She had to. It would mean a visit longer than five minutes, but she would be negligent if she didn't make sure they knew she could help them get away from Faisal Mukri. "I want you to go past the bungalow," Perveen said to Arman when they approached Sea View Road.

"Why?" Arman sounded uneasy.

"I don't want us to have to ask the durwan for admission into the property. I will go inside on foot through the second gate, which is the one we used for reaching the zenana. Mohsen can't guard more than one gate; he's always been at the one to the main house."

"But if it's the second gate you want, he will see you passing by in this car."

"I've thought of that. After you have dropped me off past his line of vision, I'd then like you to drive back and create a distraction by stopping at the main gate. Then I'll walk in through the second gate—"

"If it's open!"

"That's a good point. If it is open, I shall go in, and when I'm finished, I'll walk back to the same place you dropped me."

"It sounds very complicated. And what will I say to distract him?"

"Try to find out whatever you can about Mukri from him. I'm sure he's got something to say."

To her surprise, Mohsen wasn't even in sight when the car rolled past. Out of caution, Perveen told Arman to stop around the bend of the road. He didn't look happy, but he could not refuse an employer's command.

The second gate had not been locked, so it was easy for Perveen to slip inside, although the durwan at a bungalow on the opposite side of the road gave her a curious glance. She made an effort to stroll in looking like a relaxed, respectable person: the opposite of how she felt.

Though she was on the property, she could not access the zenana garden, which was shielded by a high wall. She'd have to enter the garden the same way as before: through arched doors at the back of the zenana's wide reception room. Perveen knocked at the zenana door very lightly. There was no response, and she thought it too risky to call through the window as she'd done before.

Tentatively, she put her hand on the knob, and it turned. She guessed that there had been too much commotion after her departure for Fatima to remember to lock up.

Nobody was in the reception room, so she went silently into the garden, walking along the house's edge to avoid being seen by anyone looking out a window. The garden was deserted. Her briefcase wasn't where she'd sat in the pavilion and watched the little girls playing music. Nor was it where the musical instruments still lay on the rug. Perveen rushed to the spot where she'd spoken with Mumtaz; no briefcase was there.

She realized that she couldn't recall when she'd stopped carrying the case. She was almost certain that she'd brought it out of Razia's room, but she wasn't completely certain. Another possibility was that Mumtaz or Amina had spotted the briefcase after she'd left and taken it for safekeeping.

At the zenana entrance, Perveen peeked through a gap in the curtains. The room was still empty. She went in, keeping her sandals in one hand, and eyed the staircase. It was empty, too, though she could hear the muffled sound of voices upstairs. She heard women talking and a young child bawling. Perhaps it was Jum-Jum, the baby she hadn't yet seen.

Perveen went up. At the edge of the first hallway, she stood, adjusting her awareness to sound.

In Razia's room, she could hear a rumble of conversation, but the door was closed tightly enough that she could not distinguish anything except the fact there were three voices. Knowing that the three widows were together made it possible for her to check the other rooms before asking them about the briefcase. She passed the nursery, where Jum-Jum's wails were subsiding just as Shireen's and Nasreen's voices were rising. "Why can't we . . . ?" Shireen was saying.

Perveen heard an older woman answer reprovingly, "It's not for you!"

Sakina's bedroom suite door was open. Inside, everything was as orderly as before; even the silver tray was gone. Perveen looked under the bed and in drawers and then lifted aside the picture to look at the locked safe door. The safe was certainly wide enough to accommodate the briefcase—but perhaps not deep enough.

Being in Sakina's room alone made Perveen feel almost like a thief. She put her head out of the door, checking in the hallway for new sounds. Perhaps five minutes had passed since she had entered the room. It was too bad she didn't know which room was Mumtaz's.

Perveen glanced toward the brass jali that Sakina had said was the conversation place between the zenana and main house. If Mr. Mukri chose to eavesdrop, he could only do so from there; that was the likely reason the wives were speaking in Razia's faraway bedchamber rather than Sakina's closer quarters. As Perveen studied the patterned brass border, a smear of red caught her eyes.

A dash of red, reminding her of the kumkum Hindu and Parsi women used to make a decorative marking between the eyes. But this red marking was slashed across the brass metalwork, and there were droplets and smudges on the floor. It could not be vermilion powder. With a growing sense of worry, Perveen stepped out of the doorway, taking care not to touch any of the red droplets as she approached the screen. Squatting, she could make out a shadowy mass just below the document slot.

Although she knew it was improper, Perveen lifted the long, wide brass lid that covered the slot. Her last calm thought was that this lid was about the same weight and size as the one on the mail slot in the door of Alice's ancestral London townhouse.

Then she felt sick.

On the other side, Mr. Mukri lay collapsed, arms and legs skewed wildly, as if he'd tried to escape but failed. Half under him was the edge of her Swaine Adeney bridle-leather document case. Blood covered the back of his head and collar and ran in thick rivulets down his black suit jacket. Something long and silver protruded from his neck. Was it a knife? She didn't care. She couldn't bear to look any longer.

Perveen put her hand to her mouth and stepped back. If she hadn't looked through the slot, she wouldn't have known he was dead. Now it was too late: she was aware of this death and the responsibility that would follow.

1916

12

BOTTLING PROMISES
Bombay, August 1916

*I*t was as if Cyrus had died and left her bereft.

After they had spoken their hearts to each other in Bandra, Perveen didn't hear from him at all. She remained at the family bungalow, imagining one bad scenario after another.

Cyrus must have told his parents about her and received a flat refusal. The Sodawallas could have been angry enough to take him back to Calcutta. Believing that was easier than contemplating the more obvious possibility: that Cyrus had not kept his word. His romantic declaration could have been a ruse to allow him to take his pleasure with her. Or perhaps he'd thought things through and decided the girl his parents wanted him to marry was the better choice.

The other reason she was stuck at home was because of her parents' anger. At the Ripon Club on Friday afternoon, Jamshedji had awoken from his nap to overhear two lawyers gossiping about whether the Government Law School's first female student had been expelled or dropped out.

That evening, she'd been called into the parlor to face him and her mother. Unable to look at them, Perveen had muttered, "I meant to explain that day. I just couldn't think of the proper words."

"So you mounted a deception! You went into the city carrying books every day and were dropped at the college. What were you doing all those hours if you were not in class? Spending money, going to films, eating in restaurants?" Jamshedji railed. "You won't be going outside for a while, I'll tell you."

"I was in the library." Perveen's voice shook. "I couldn't spend another day with the students and professors in the law school."

"Can't bear the law school?" Now her father looked perplexed. "But you were a top student."

"Nobody wanted me there—and they did all manner of things to make it hard for me to attend class," Perveen said.

"It's true," Camellia interjected. "The students made life hard for her. She's mentioned some tricks they played. But that could have been addressed—"

Perveen was grateful for her mother's words, but she didn't want to create the impression that she wished to act against her classmates. "It was more than tricks, and something happened every day. They killed my desire to study law. I'm sorry, Pappa."

"But . . ." Jamshedji's tense expression was replaced by a look of confusion. "What then? What do you want to be?"

"Why do I have to be something? Can't I simply be myself?" She couldn't declare the truth: *I want to run away from here and become Cyrus's wife.* She wasn't about to hit them with another scandalous confession, especially if it turned out the man she loved had vanished.

But two days later, everything changed. It started with a phone call on Sunday evening from Grandfather Mistry. Perveen was the one who picked up, and when she heard his familiar, gravelly voice, she braced herself. He typically called to complain about some trouble: his arthritis, a missed delivery from a tradesman, Mustafa's inadequate service.

"A Parsi family from Calcutta came to Mistry House and insisted on seeing your father. I told them he was out, and they left a letter. What nonsense could it be?" he growled. "The ghelsappas said they are not looking for a lawyer."

Perveen felt the hairs on her arms standing up. "Bapawa, how many of them were there?"

"Husband, wife, and a grown son. Mustafa admitted them. He said the son was most persuasive. I told him never to do such a thing again."

"I'm glad he did. They are very important people!" Perveen relaxed into happiness, although she didn't understand why the Sodawallas had gone to Mistry House. She'd told Cyrus her home address. Perhaps the family had thought it important to pay respects to her grandfather first. "Did you tell them to come here?"

"Why should I send strangers to bother your father?" her grandfather answered crossly.

"I'll come for the letter, then."

"You shall not travel about in the evenings. But I shall come to you with the letter, if you like." He paused. "What is John making for dinner?"

"Prawn curry. Please come. I'm sure there's enough!" Perveen suspected that he'd mainly called about the letter because he'd wanted to see them. Well and good. He'd get what he wanted—and maybe she would, too.

Perveen greeted her grandfather when he arrived in the hallway, asking him to reserve the letter for her father until after dinner. She knew that a hungry person was more likely to be feisty, and if her father and grandfather ate well and had a few drinks with dinner, their reactions might be better.

After the last bit of pudding was finished, Perveen asked everyone to come into the parlor. She said, "Bapawa has brought an important letter. I have not read it, but I hear it concerns me."

"Goodness!" Camellia said, brightening. "Maybe it's from the law school, and there's some hope—"

"Till the hen gets teeth," said Grandfather Mistry. "This letter is from some Calcutta Parsis."

Jamshedji opened the letter and put his monocle to his eye to read it. After he finished, he looked at the assembled family and shook his head. "It's very odd. This is a request for a meeting at the Taj Mahal Hotel tomorrow afternoon to discuss a possible union for Perveen."

"With whom?" Rustom, who'd been sitting restlessly next to Grandfather Mistry, looked up.

"They're called the Sodawallas," Jamshedji said. "A common enough name, but I can't think who these people are."

"I know them." Perveen delivered a heavily abridged account of meeting Cyrus at Elphinstone and Sassoon Library and his presence at the group outing to the pictures.

Camellia looked hard at her. "Is that all? I heard a rumor you were seen walking out of Bandra station with a young man. I said it couldn't possibly be, that you don't go about with men."

"It was the day he proposed," Perveen admitted with embarrassment. "He couldn't very well propose to me with a chaperone there."

"This boy sounds loose at the drawstrings!" Jamshedji's mouth pursed as if he'd bitten into a spoiled papaya.

"He's hardly immoral if he's looking for a bride," Perveen protested. Her father's swift disapproval was exactly what she'd feared.

"I'm supposed to marry first—and that's not happening for two years, isn't it?" Rustom looked for confirmation from his parents.

"An older sibling should go first," Jamshedji assured him, all the while looking at Perveen through narrowed eyes. "We shan't rush. It is better for you to have a higher position in the company before we look."

Grandfather Mistry cleared his throat and said, "If a younger sister marries before an older brother, people will believe she had to marry for reasons of pregnancy. Every bead of her reputation will be sold."

"We aren't like that." Perveen struggled to keep her voice level. "And what else can I do with myself now that I'm not a student, except get married?"

"The one who digs a hole falls into it," Grandfather Mistry replied dourly, and Rustom snorted.

Camellia pressed her manicured hands together as if she was nervous. "You were always such a dear, agreeable daughter. You appreciated what you were given, not like some others in town. How can you do this to us?"

"I didn't do anything to you! His parents have asked for a meeting. Won't you at least give them the respect they deserve by going?" she pleaded. "Wouldn't you rather have us marry within our society's embrace?"

"What is the alternative—elopement?" Rustom snapped. "I'll never get a bride if you shame us like that!"

"I don't mean to hurt you." Perveen knew he had a point. "But everyone should know that I am prepared to step away if I must. And so is Cyrus."

"See how you like living on the street!" cracked Grandfather Mistry. "Then tell us what you think of disownment."

Camellia spoke quickly. "We would never do such a cruel thing. It's because we love you very much that we supported your schooling—our love is the reason we wish to keep you with us for a few more years, rather than marrying you off too early."

Her mother's gentle declaration began to undo Perveen's resolve. She really didn't want to live her married life without a chance of ever seeing them again. Choking up slightly, she said, "You have done everything for me. I love you, too."

Jamshedji gave her a long look. "We shall go to the hotel and meet these Sodawallas. It does not mean I am saying yes. But I will give them a fair chance."

"That is your business, then. I'm not going." Grandfather Mistry folded his arms disapprovingly.

This was distressing, but at least she had her father. Perveen looked gratefully at Jamshedji. "One short meeting is all I ask. Thank you, Pappa."

They went to the Taj the next afternoon. As they proceeded through the stately hotel lobby, Jamshedji spoke in an undertone. "Just as important as the boy is the family. And there's been no time for checking. That is a real shame."

"What would you do, employ one of your detectives?" Perveen sniffed. She had a low opinion of the streetwise detectives her father hired to unearth infidelity and other minor crimes.

"I would have. All I know is what your mother learned from her friends: Mrs. Sodawalla is Homi Vachha's second cousin. The Vachhas barely know them."

"Esther likes Cyrus."

"What kind of endorsement is that, with your eye-to-eye hatred of Esther Vachha?" Jamshedji grumbled.

"Don't be such a lawyer, Pappa. Promise not to grill them!" Through gritted teeth, Perveen smiled at the familiar faces in the lobby. The Mistrys knew a lot of people who worked at and frequented the Taj. Grandfather Mistry had even known its founder, Mr. Jamsetji Tata, who had been a pillar of the Parsi community.

"Enough, you two," Camellia said. "Let's find these people."

In the dining room, the maître d' led them through a sea of white-covered tables open to the general public to a table in the corner.

"We are so very glad to see you!" said Cyrus, who looked handsome in a high-collared white suit. Rising to greet them, he murmured, "Mr. and Mrs. Mistry, may I present my parents?"

Mr. Bahram Framji Sodawalla had Cyrus's good features but had put on the weight of middle age, which softened them. Gray hair escaped the edges of his black fetah. Behnoush Sodawalla also was gray but had a young-looking, rounded face. Perveen noted evidence of wealth in the woman's gara silk sari, which was covered with lavish embroidery. Behnoush's sari was grander than Perveen's—a blue-silk satin with a pettipoint border—and grander still than the understated yellow chiffon with zari embroidery worn by Camellia.

Greetings were made in formal Gujarati. Like Cyrus, his parents spoke with a slight accent. It charmed Perveen and made her think about how her own voice might change if she were lucky enough to marry and move to Bengal.

"Please sit down," Bahram said heartily. "I've already ordered whiskey—I hope you don't mind."

"A small one, on the rocks," Jamshedji said with a nod. A waiter standing nearby moved forward to pour for him from the cut-glass bottle on the table, and then for Bahram and Cyrus.

"My daughter and I will take tea," Camellia said with a ladylike air that made Perveen cringe. "Darjeeling, milk and sugar on the side."

This was the English manner in which tea was usually served at the

Taj, and not the way they drank tea at home. It seemed as if Camellia didn't wish to allow herself and Perveen to feel comfortable.

"I am usually a teetotaler, but my husband convinced me to take a little whiskey over ice. I am all nerves!" Mrs. Sodawalla giggled— an unexpectedly girlish sound.

"I'm very nervous, too," Perveen blurted out. "But I am grateful you acknowledged Cyrus's wish to consider me."

"Apparently our niece Esther introduced the two them," Bahram said cheerfully. "Our apologies for being so forward. Cyrus said you are not yet seeking a groom."

"We hadn't been looking due to the fact she is a student," Camellia said, declining to take anything from the bearer who was handing around silver bowls of nuts and biscuits.

"I *was* a student," Perveen corrected. "But I am no longer at the Government Law School."

"Cyrus said that. But he's not sure how old you are. Can you imagine?" Mrs. Sodawalla laughed lightly, scrutinizing Perveen's face, chest, and every other part of her above the table. Perveen didn't like it; but she knew anyone considering her as a daughter-in-law would do the same.

"I'm nineteen." Perveen guessed that Cyrus hadn't told them because it might have meant they'd refuse the meeting.

"At your age, I already had two sons. Our oldest, Nived, is married and living in Bihar. Now the only one at home is Cyrus. The house is much too quiet!" Mrs. Sodawalla looked questioning at Jamshedji and Camellia. "We visited your ancestral house in Fort. But why aren't you staying there?"

"Mistry House is where I see my clients," Jamshedji said, allowing Mr. Sodawalla to pour another two inches in his glass. "My wife preferred to shift to the suburbs for the good air and less crowding. I soon came to realize I like the tranquility."

"Yes, but old city districts hold memories of so many people and events; you can feel them in the bricks and stones!" Perveen didn't want the Sodawallas to think she wouldn't like living in the heart of an old city neighborhood like their own.

"What about lunch?" said Mr. Sodawalla, looking around the table. "Shall we eat a bite together? My invitation."

"I'm not sure if time permits," Jamshedji said.

"Of course we've eaten here many times over the last few weeks," Bahram Sodawalla said, as if to remind everyone they had met plenty of prospective brides. "I like the veal escalopes."

"Perveen is a pretty thing, isn't she?" said Mrs. Sodawalla, giving her a warm smile. "Such thick, dark hair. She must require two maids to brush it every morning and evening."

"I do it myself." Perveen blushed. She didn't like being called a pretty thing, but at least it meant Mrs. Sodawalla's inspection had been positive.

"Cyrus, tell us something about yourself." Jamshedji had a forced note in his voice. "All I have heard is your family business is bottling."

"Empire Soda Limited, the firm started by our grandfather, is the third-largest in Bengal and the biggest in Bihar, where my brother is handling matters. We've just acquired a plant in Howrah, across the river from our home. I won't be traveling much, so I can show Perveen Calcutta. Have you been there, sir?" Cyrus asked eagerly.

Jamshedji shrugged noncommittally. He was playing hard to get.

"India's biggest and best city," pronounced Bahram. "People from all over the world come to see Calcutta."

"And also to study," Perveen added for her parents' ears. "Mrs. Sodawalla, is it true there are several women's colleges in Calcutta?"

"Yes. And there are also many ladies' clubs that do good works for the community," Mrs. Sodawalla said, looking pointedly at Camellia. "We pray at an agiary very close to our home. What has your daughter's religious training been, Mrs. Mistry?"

Camellia took a sip of tea before answering. "Perveen celebrated her navjote at Seth Banaji Limji Agiary. It's where my husband's ancestors have worshipped since the seventeen hundreds."

"And what is her religious activity since her navjote?" Mrs. Sodawalla asked.

Perveen exchanged glances with Cyrus, who was looking at her with a beseeching expression. She hadn't been prepared for such questions.

Her mother answered. "We attend agiary during religious holidays and ceremonies involving family and friends. But the way our family practices our religion every day is through our actions."

"My grandfather is an agiary trustee," Perveen added, wishing he hadn't refused to come. He would have been more comfortable with the old-fashioned Sodawallas than her parents seemed to be.

"I told you: she's top-drawer!" Cyrus said, beaming at her.

Mrs. Sodawalla nodded. "That is good. My late father was a priest."

Mr. Sodawalla drained his whiskey and signaled the waiter to pour more. "We are large supporters of our local agiary because there are few Parsis in Bengal; right now, it's doubtful that we number five thousand. Not enough people to build big housing communities and schools and such—not like you have here."

"We may have these institutions in time. Our agiary ladies' committee endeavors to raise funds for a Parsi primary school; but of course, we need more Parsi children to fill such a place." Behnoush gave Camellia an appraising look. "The Vachhas say that you are particularly expert at such charitable work, Mrs. Mistry. You've started up six schools and two hospitals, isn't it?"

"Not by myself," Camellia demurred, but from her expression, Perveen could see that she was flattered to have been recognized for her work. "Bombay is growing in numbers, with poor coming from all over the region, and we must respond."

"It is always up to our community to open up our pockets for these things. And to think, Britishers are the ones sitting at the top with the really big money!" said Mr. Sodawalla.

"That is true. But they don't have the benefit of the Parsi standard: good thoughts, good words, good deeds," Perveen said.

"Your daughter speaks from the book!" Cyrus's mother laughed happily and reached across the table to pat Perveen's hand. The touch was warm, reminding Perveen of Cyrus, at whom she'd been trying hard not to smile.

"Yes, Mrs. Sodawalla, she enjoys studying," Camellia said. "In fact, we remain concerned of the need for her to have further, wider knowledge, as she's not mature."

"A woman has a lifetime for reading. A whole week every month!" Mrs. Sodawalla said.

Perveen didn't quite know what she meant by that, but she smiled and nodded. "That sounds very good to me."

"If we're permitted to marry, I pledge my life to making Perveen happy," Cyrus said. "I understand that our suggesting the marriage to you may seem disrespectful. But when two people are especially suited, they might meet first and know this so strongly, they can't help but share the truth."

Softly, Perveen offered another religious phrase. "Truth is best of all that is good."

"Spoken first by our prophet!" said Mr. Sodawalla with delight. "Listen, I am sincere in saying that Mrs. Sodawalla and I have not seen such a fine one as your daughter."

After this proclamation, Perveen felt as if she were melting into a warm pool of happiness. The Sodawalla parents wanted her for a bride. But what of her parents?

She glanced at them. While Camellia's expression had softened, Jamshedji looked the way he did when he came home after losing a case. Under the tablecloth, Perveen slipped her hand into his. She squeezed it firmly. In the touch, she tried to say what she couldn't. *Yes. I want this.*

Jamshedji let her hand stay in his. "Before coming here today, I resolved that this meeting would not be a khastegari."

"It certainly is not!" said Mr. Sodawalla showing a flare of temper. "We had not met the girl yet. We had our own judgment to make."

"Our children chose each other without our assistance," Jamshedji said grimly. "They ignored the fact that marriage is the most serious contract that can be undertaken. Such a union should not come about without investigation. My wife and I expected we would be well acquainted with a groom and his family."

Perveen pulled her hand out of her father's. Despite the amiable conversation going around the table, she sensed he was going to deliver a negative pronouncement. She had seen him do this in court before—build a case, seeking agreement, until everyone had come to see his point as reasonable.

"I know your expectation," Bahram Sodawalla said, who had sat back in his chair and was looking more at ease. "We first searched for a bride from a family in our city. But as I said, the Parsi community in Calcutta numbers fewer than five thousand. We could not find the right type for Cyrus. That is why I'm pleased his cousin introduced him to a girl from a good family."

Her prospective father-in-law was meeting might with right. Perveen appreciated it—and she could not bear to keep silent in the face of his humility and her father's rigidity. Leaning forward, she said, "Mr. and Mrs. Sodawalla, I am so glad that your family came to meet us. I only wish my parents would realize that your son is the best groom they could ever find."

"Hush, Perveen!" Camellia said, her face flushing. "It is not decided."

Looking directly at Jamshedji, Mr. Sodawalla said dryly, "You might think we seek financial gain through our son's marriage. But we have no need for any kind of gift or promise."

Jamshedji nodded and took a sip of whiskey. What did that mean? Was he going to listen? The Sodawallas were offering everything possible to get her family to agree.

"Perhaps they did fall in love at first sight," suggested Behnoush Sodawalla with a demure smile. "It is hardly proper before the wedding. But who are we to keep two Parsi children of good families from making an auspicious union?"

"I would like to hear my wife's thoughts," Jamshedji said, turning his head to look Camellia in the face.

He always asked his wife's opinion on serious household and family matters. Perveen held her breath.

"Perveen can be strongheaded—but she is intelligent." Camellia looked down at her plate, still glossy and untouched. "I appreciate that she consulted us and that your son also spoke with you. This is a modern age, and some young Indians are even marrying outside of their religious communities. These two are staying inside our faith."

Perveen exhaled, giving her mother a thankful look.

After a long pause, Jamshedji said, "Yes, it is good the children asked our blessing. Therefore, if Camellia agrees, I shall consent to an extended engagement so both parties might become acquainted."

"Father! Thank you!" Perveen turned to embrace him, moving so fast that she knocked her cup of tea between them on its side. Camellia reached over to right it and accepted Perveen's kisses.

"Nine months to a year should be sufficient time for further chaperoned meetings," Jamshedji said, offering a faint smile. "And in this time, Perveen can revise her college field of study."

Perveen nodded happily. She had suggested this timeline to Cyrus when he'd proposed to her at Bandra. It had seemed entirely reasonable. Not only would there be time to see each other, but they'd also be able to plan the most spectacular nuptials.

Cyrus bowed his head, and when his face came up, there were tears in his eyes. "Sir—I am so very thrilled to have your consent. Even though we've spent such a short time together, I love your daughter with all my heart. But there is a problem with the engagement you propose."

"Oh?" Jamshedji put his drink down hard.

Perveen stared at Cyrus, wondering what was to come.

Glancing sorrowfully at Perveen, Cyrus said, "Calcutta and Bombay are more than a thousand miles apart. I'm not able to travel back and forth frequently between them. Will you forgive me?"

"Of course," Perveen said quickly. "An engagement is a matter of months, but a marriage is forever! We shall do what's necessary for the marriage to take place."

"Perveen, you're putting the cart before the horse," Jamshedji reproved. "If a marriage is forever, what's wrong with delaying its onset to a mutually convenient time?"

"Very sorry, sir, but my boy is correct," said Mr. Sodawalla, sounding unapologetic. "We increase production for the winter holidays—our busiest season for sales of bottled alcohol. We have no time for weddings from October through next March, and then the weather becomes too unpleasant, and we are pushed to full capacity for soda bottling."

"So you are saying my daughter is just another bottle on the belt?" Jamshedji said sharply.

Bahram Sodawalla chuckled. "Ha-ha, that is funny!"

Mrs. Sodawalla turned to her husband. "Now that we have had the joy of finding a bride, can we stay in Bombay a few more days? That would allow time for some chaperoned visits."

Camellia spoke softly. "That would be fine."

"I've just had another idea," Behnoush said, looking from her husband to the Mistrys. "The wedding could be held later on this year, if it's held in Calcutta. Then there is less time away from the bottling plant."

"I don't know about that," Camellia said quickly.

Perveen's mind was spinning. She would be delighted to marry Cyrus soon—but not having their wedding in Bombay would be a shock. She'd grown up attending dozens of relatives' weddings and wasn't sure if these people would be able to travel to Calcutta. And how strange it would be not to have the wedding in the Taj Mahal Palace's ballroom—her grandfather expected it to be there, given his relationship with the hotel's founder.

"We are paying for the wedding. It should be here in the Taj Mahal Palace," Jamshedji said heavily.

"But Pappa!" Perveen couldn't bear to say the rest: *If you don't go along with them, I could lose Cyrus.*

"This hotel is pleasant, but there are places like it in Calcutta," opined Mrs. Sodawalla.

Perveen wondered if Mrs. Sodawalla didn't know they were sitting in the most expensive hotel in Bombay. But a favorite hotel wasn't the point; Cyrus was. Perveen murmured, "I'm happy to marry in Calcutta. It's not the wedding that matters; it's the husband and family."

"If there is any difficulty with bookings, you must allow us to help," Mrs. Sodawalla said, patting Perveen's hand. "There are many fewer Parsis in Calcutta, which means the agiary should be ready for us when we need it."

The warmth of Mrs. Sodawalla's smile made Perveen glow inside, knowing she was wanted.

"Shall we order lunch, Mr. Mistry?" Mr. Sodawalla asked eagerly.

"Very well." From the way Jamshedji spoke, Perveen knew he had resigned himself to the situation. "Let us not be overly hasty with our luncheon. We need time for these ideas to digest."

After ordering, Perveen made an apology and slipped out to the ladies' cloakroom.

Cyrus caught up with her in the marble corridor. Looking straight into her eyes, he said, "How dearly I love and admire you. You were magnificent with them—I never dreamed you could bring both sides to a compromise."

"I could not risk losing you," Perveen said. "That's why the words came."

They certainly could not kiss or hold hands; that would have disgraced their parents. But they could stare at each other for just a few minutes, promising with their eyes all the things that couldn't be said.

13

RICE AND ROSES
Calcutta, September 1916

*A*ll that stood between them was a sheet.

Perveen sat rigidly on a small velvet chair on one side of the length of pristine linen being held up by Rustom and Cyrus's brother Nived. In accordance with custom, her gaze remained downcast. Her lap was filled with a bouquet of red roses, a gift from Behnoush Sodawalla that signified fertility and love. Their scent rose up, blending with the rich frankincense already in the air. Perveen felt light-headed knowing that within a few minutes she'd be married.

Cyrus was on the other side of the sheet, so close that she could hear his breathing. It reminded her of how close they'd been at Land's End. Here they were, surrounded by family, living out the dream that had seemed impossible a month earlier.

Cyrus had appeared a vision of strength and grace when he'd entered the wedding hall in his dagli, the high-collared white suit worn for religious events. The stiff pagri he wore atop his head made him look much taller than he really was, and his face was very closely shaven.

She was similarly prepared to look her best. After the morning's ritual bath, Camellia had spent more than an hour draping Perveen's wedding sari. She was wearing a nine-yard length of Chantilly lace made even more dazzling by seed pearl embroidery over its flowers. Her wrists were stiff with bangles: heavy gold ones from her own family and ivory bangles inset with rubies from the Sodawallas, which harmonized perfectly with her diamond-and-ruby engagement ring. Around her neck hung a gold-and-ruby necklace that had been her mother's and the heavy white-and-red rose bridal garland.

Perveen continued studying the bouquet in her lap, resisting the temptation to pull the flowers close to her for a long, heady inhalation. Her hands lay open, as the priests had instructed. This allowed for a priest to drop dry rice grains into her left palm—the rice she'd be allowed to throw very soon per the ritual.

As the group of priests chanted, one of them reached under the sheet to move her right hand into Cyrus's. This was the hand-fastening. She imagined how frightening such a touch would feel to a couple that didn't know each other. Cyrus's hand was reassuring, familiar; she squeezed it.

Prayers continued as the senior priest wrapped a soft string around their clasped hands seven times, symbolizing the divine heptad of God and his six archangels. Two priests kept the sheet steady as he wound the same string around their chairs. It was a symbol of union: the tying of two individuals into marriage. She'd seen marriage rites like this so many times, but it felt thrilling to be tied into traditions which went back thousands of years.

Finally the seventh circle was completed. Suddenly, many female voices broke the solemnity, shrieking for either Cyrus or Perveen to be first to throw rice.

A small shower of rice hit the top of her head before she could raise her own left hand. Laughter and applause erupted, and the sheet was dropped. She saw Cyrus grinning. Because he had hit her first, he would be the one to rule the family, according to the proverb. Perveen knew this would please the in-laws, but it meant nothing to the two of them, as they were bound together in a relationship like no one else's.

After the noise died down, the chairs were shifted so Perveen and Cyrus were seated next to each other, rather than opposite, with their families behind them.

"May Ahura Mazda grant you sons and grandsons, plenty of means to provide for yourselves, heartfelt camaraderie, physical strength, long life, and an existence of one hundred fifty years," a priest intoned.

Perveen thought she'd be quite happy to live half that long, if only Cyrus was with her.

Her smile lasted all the way to the reception line, even though the wedding photographer implored her to look properly serious. But she couldn't hide her joy that the impossible had actually come to be. She was a new woman: no longer Perveen Jamshedji Mistry but Perveen Cyrus Sodawalla, with a gold ring on her finger to prove it.

Aside from her immediate family and ten relatives, there were only forty other guests who'd come the distance from Bombay to see her wed. The worst part about it was Grandfather Mistry's absence. His heart had been beating overly fast, so his doctor hadn't allowed such a lengthy trip. But Perveen remembered what he'd been like when the formal khastegari had taken place a few days after the Taj meeting. He'd said very little but afterward had told Perveen she had done wrong to select a groom for herself when her parents knew better.

It had been an irrelevant comment, because her parents had consented. Trying to create a link between her grandfather and Cyrus, Perveen had told Grandfather Mistry that her fiancé was a straightforward businessman who, like him, wasn't afraid to speak his mind. But the family's patriarch had looked off in the distance, as if he already wanted her gone.

Perveen shook off the sore memory as the maître d' motioned her and Cyrus toward the head table, where the wedding feast had already been placed.

The Sodawallas had invited 220 guests, and they all seemed to be enjoying the meal. The menu contained the requisite succession of Parsi wedding dishes: steamed fish, fried chicken, egg curry, lamb curry, sago crisps, carrot-and-raisin pickle, and an extravagantly seasoned mutton pulao. Dessert was kulfi and lagan nu custard, but Perveen was too full to manage more than a few spoonfuls of each creamy dessert.

"A small wedding is good, isn't it?" Cyrus whispered in Perveen's ear as she gave up on attempting to finish. "I'm so glad we are already home rather than in Bombay."

"The wedding isn't so small. I doubt I'll remember half the people's names."

"And I thought your memory was magnificent!" Cyrus teased. "You've been quoting our prophet ever since our engagement."

She gave him a mischievous look. "Only because it charms your parents."

Cyrus murmured, "The wedding's gone like clockwork, except for the string breaking. I tell you, my mother almost cursed!"

"What do you mean?" Perveen craned her head to look at the Sodawalla parents, who sat happily feasting a few feet down the table.

"It took the priests such a long time to tie our chairs," Cyrus said. "I think it was because the string broke. They had to crowd together to fix it before all the guests saw."

She shrugged, relieved it had been nothing serious. "Funny little accidents happen at weddings. They become the best stories to tell later."

Cyrus lowered his voice. "But that string is supposed to bind us together in our lives and eternity. And my mother's superstitious."

"She's having as much fun as us," Perveen said, glancing again at Behnoush, who was chatting with gusto with a relative.

"She is overjoyed," he whispered in her ear. "She's grieved my sister for so many years—and now she has a new daughter."

It wasn't that simple to replace people. Perveen knew she would find it hard to call Behnoush "Mamma." Just as her own mother would have a hard time giving up overseeing her life.

Days before the wedding, the Mistrys had been invited to the Sodawallas' large old bungalow. They were shown some downstairs rooms and the wing where Cyrus and Perveen would stay, and Camellia had been concerned with some crumbling plaster, mildew, and a rank smell. Jamshedji had gone to the heart of the matter and offered to pay for renovations to the newlyweds' quarters.

"Bengali house painters don't get far. They're always dreaming of making masterpieces on the easel rather than doing work on other people's houses," Behnoush had said with a laugh. "And what can one do about these bathrooms when the sewers outside are clogged?"

"Teakwood and gold will never become old," Perveen had

said—it was one of her grandfather's favorite proverbs—to prove she didn't mind the aged interior. Behnoush had bestowed a doting smile that confirmed she'd said the right thing.

Perveen pulled herself back to the present. She was at the head table at her own wedding with the most attractive and understanding man in the world. As long as she had Cyrus, nothing else mattered.

Shortly after one in the morning, two cars traveled the short distance from the Great Eastern Hotel to Saklat Place. Perveen rode with the Sodawallas in the family's Buick, its black body gleaming with wax and festooned with jasmine garlands. Perveen's parents and Rustom followed in a smaller car driven by one of the hotel's chauffeurs.

The long windows of the Sodawallas' bungalow were lit, and the house servants quickly emerged to pay their respects and offer ginger-lemongrass tea and the tray of kumkum for Behnoush to use in her final, formal welcoming of Perveen.

Perveen held her breath as her mother-in-law dipped her finger in the kumkum and touched Perveen's forehead. Behnoush recited a long prayer in Avestan, adding at the end: "May Ahura Mazda guide you, and may you perform your duties as a good daughter."

Behnoush had anointed Perveen with kumkum right before the wedding, but this time her mother-in-law's touch felt different. It seemed to sear. Just as the priests had bound Perveen and Cyrus together, this was a formal bonding. To her mother-in-law and everyone else in the community, she was now Bhabhi—a brother's wife.

Perveen saw her parents standing just behind Behnoush. Jamshedji's arm was around his wife, as if she needed some kind of support, but it was his eyes that had the glaze of tears. *Don't cry*, she thought, looking imploringly at him. *If you cry, I will, too.*

"That's done!" Behnoush said, after she'd taken her finger away and was wiping it on the cloth a servant girl had handed her. "Perveen must be very tired. Poor thing—so much heavy food and too many people. You are home now and must take a rest."

Cyrus flashed a look at Perveen and said, "Yes, she can hardly keep her eyes open. Gita must bring her upstairs to unpack."

Perveen would have liked to linger downstairs with Cyrus, who was happily accepting his father's proposal of a whiskey nightcap. But the Sodawallas thought she shouldn't, so who was she to challenge things moments after arrival? Besides, her parents were already making motions to leave, as it was so late, and their train would depart in just seven hours.

"You must write. I am already beginning a letter." Camellia's voice was choked as she opened her arms for a farewell embrace.

Perveen kissed her mother on both cheeks. "I'll write every day. Show my letters to Pappa, if he has the time to read them."

Jamshedji muttered, "No legal brief could be more important than a letter from you."

"Oh, Pappa! I will miss you every day."

And now the tears were running from Perveen's eyes. For years he'd spoken about the importance of strong writing skills for lawyers. And she'd given up the plan to become Bombay's first woman lawyer, ending his dreams.

"Good night, my dear, sweet daughter!" Behnoush beckoned her to come close, offering her powdered cheek for a kiss. "And don't feel you must rush out of bed tomorrow morning. Gita will bring your bed tea whenever you like it, and we breakfast at ten."

The young maid named Gita kept peeking at Perveen and giggling as she carried Perveen's valise upstairs. Perveen paused at the door of her marital bedroom, where an embroidered toran curtain hung across the top. It hadn't been present before: nor had the beautiful chalk decorations made from powdered limestone on the threshold.

"What a pretty entrance," Perveen said. "Who made it?"

"Your mamma. Now look!" Gita flung the door open, displaying a place unlike what had existed five days earlier.

A new, high-posted mahogany bed dressed in a rose silk quilt sat in the room's center under a modern electric ceiling fan. Silver lanterns glowed from matching carved camphorwood tables on either side of the bed. Happily dazed, Perveen crossed the soft pink-and-red carpet patterned with flowers and prancing deer toward the archway leading into the adjacent room.

The lounge room was another revelation. Candles shone from well-polished brass sconces, illuminating the pair of green velvet chairs that faced a mahogany tea table. An ornamental chest stood against one wall, and along the other, there was a set of glass-doored bookcases.

"The bathroom will be fixed next week," Gita chirped. "New toilet with flush and a bathtub. First-class modern for Bhabhi."

The marital suite was beautiful—but terrifying. How had it come about? If her parents had overstepped, she would have to apologize—maybe even send things back. But it was ever so much more pleasant now. In her heart, she wanted all of it.

Perveen turned at the sound of soft footsteps. Cyrus was no longer in the formal white wedding suit but wearing only a sudreh and the white trousers that had been part of his wedding costume. Walking slowly toward her, he asked, "How do you like our honeymoon suite?"

"It's the loveliest place imaginable." She hesitated, afraid of having her suspicions confirmed. "I'm only worried my parents overstepped and made your family spend on something they didn't want."

He stood before her, his face filled with pride. "I ordered everything. It's for the two of us."

He was truly a man of swift action—and deep commitment. If he'd done this to surprise her, what other delightful moments lay in store? Slipping her arms around his neck, she murmured, "You are the cleverest, dearest man. It's so romantic. I am utterly overwhelmed. It's the best wedding present I can imagine."

"We couldn't take a honeymoon, so I had that money to spend. And you can't believe how pleasing it is for me to have my creaky old bed replaced with something so big and new."

Gita began giggling, and Cyrus looked at her with irritation. "Go on! We don't need the likes of you on our wedding night!"

"I am your servant," Gita said demurely, fixing her gaze on Perveen. "What else shall I do?"

"Please get some rest," Perveen said, feeling exultant. "And don't come to us too early tomorrow."

When they were alone, Perveen tilted her face up toward Cyrus, who gave her a long kiss that was sweet with whiskey and desire. When they parted, Perveen looked past him to the tall, luxuriously draped bed. She imagined herself beckoning him toward it, but that would be too fast.

She walked into the lounge, knowing he would follow. Filled with a sense of power mingled with delight, she murmured, "What a haven you've made for us. I can't believe you managed this in just a few days. How did you do it?"

"Remember, I didn't come along when my parents were taking you here and there. I'll confess that Sahar chose the textiles and furniture. It was also no coincidence that she crossed paths with your mother inside Whiteaway Laidlaw."

Laughter bubbled up inside her. "It's all very fresh and soft and comfortable. And I can hardly wait to fill the bookcases with novels and my *Encyclopaedia Britannica*. My parents will send it. I'll tell them—"

"Tomorrow," he said firmly.

Perveen caught her breath as Cyrus took her by the hand and led her back into the bedchamber. She'd been anticipating this for months—but now it was a little scary. What if she was no good at marital congress? How could anyone be good the first time? And she wanted to please him.

"Aren't we supposed to bathe?" she ventured, playing for time. Camellia had told her taking a bath both before and after the act was customary and might even relax her a bit.

"Who's watching?" Cyrus said, lifting the lace sari away from her face. "Oh, Perveen. How long I've waited for you."

"It's been just two months—"

"Two months too long," Cyrus said, slowly unwrapping the length of lace from around her. "I wanted to touch you that very moment we met. I've thought so long about what you'd look like, how you'd feel . . ."

The ethereal sari fell to the carpet, but she could hardly take time to pick it up. Cyrus was holding her close, tempting her to do the things she had half-imagined. With trembling fingers, she unhooked the long lace blouse that matched the sari, and Cyrus pulled off his own sudreh and trousers. He stood before her in only his drawers. He was broad chested and strong as any young man who worked the Bombay docks, although he was much more fair skinned. The only darkness on him was the mat of curly hair that covered his chest, running in a narrow line down to a place she'd long imagined.

"Oh!" Perveen turned her head away, shocked by the feelings that had come with looking at him.

"What is it?" Cyrus asked, smiling.

Awkwardly, she said, "You've removed your kusti already."

"A sacred cord should never be worn during congress," he said, pronouncing "congress" as if the word were entirely natural. Then he laughed. "Mrs. Sodawalla, where is your kusti?"

"You'll have to find out—" And then she lost her breath because he had pressed himself against her so she fell backward, and his whole naked, warm length was atop her on the soft bed.

Slowly, he began unbuttoning the tiny pearl buttons that closed the front of her silk sari blouse. In moments, her muslin sudrah was gone, and he had clasped his hands on her breasts, sending little shocks through the skin and to her core.

This was like Bandra—only it would not stop. It would keep going to a place she'd always wanted to travel, the heaven where they were meant to be.

"I love you," Perveen whispered, her fingers trembling as she began to unknot the sacred cord at her waist.

"My beautiful wife," he breathed, "don't be afraid."

"I'm not," Perveen said, reaching up to pull him closer.

14

A WIFE'S PLACE
Calcutta, October 1916

*C*yrus held out his arms toward Perveen as she slipped a gold cuff link into his starched white cotton shirt. "I can barely stand being away so long today."

"I feel the same." Perveen sighed, accepting the fact that this would be another day when he was gone twelve hours or longer. Cyrus was dressing very well that day because he had an appointment with the food and beverage manager of a European social club in Barasol. If all went well, the Sodawallas would get the contract for all domestic hard liquor. Perveen said, "I wish I could come along with you and boast about the world-class bottling plant you've got in Sealdah. The only trouble is I haven't seen it yet."

"Nothing to show off, really. It's just an ordinary bottling plant: crowded, and such a din from the sound of glass bottles moving along the belt—one hundred every five minutes."

"Goodness! I'd love to see a place like that." She had a vision of herself moving down the line, seeing ways to make it even better; after all, this was her family business now.

"And what's on for you today?" he murmured, ducking his head to kiss her.

"Another day in Behnoush-mummy's cooking school. Today she's teaching me sali boti." Perveen kept her tone light. She didn't understand why it was so necessary for her to learn all of Behnoush's favorite dishes when the household had a perfectly capable cook. But if a little cooking was the price of life with Cyrus, Perveen would gladly pay.

"When I saw you just a few months ago in Bombay, I said to myself, there's a girl who can make sali boti with the best of them."

"Don't lie!" she said, putting a finger to his lips. "What you saw was someone who appeared serious but, underneath, had the drive to stay up all night with you. Someone with more passion than sense."

Cyrus gave the low, rolling laugh that never failed to thrill her. "If I'm not too late, let's go out tonight. You've not yet seen the Victoria Memorial, and we can have kulfi afterward."

"Really?" Perveen's spirits rose, because in the two weeks since the wedding, she'd been outside the house with Cyrus only a few times. "Is there time to take the car into North Calcutta?"

He frowned. "That's a bit far. Why go there?"

Slipping a cravat around Cyrus's neck, Perveen said, "I heard from a friend whose sister studied in Calcutta that there's a very lively coffeehouse in the College Street area."

"That place is full of Bengalis in training to be radicals," Cyrus said with a chuckle. "Not many Parsis in the bunch."

"I'd love to see what a Bengali radical looks like!" Perveen said, tying the silk in a French knot. "The servants have taught me some Bengali already. We might make friends. Bethune College must be nearby."

"Yes, you mentioned your interest in that college." Cyrus stepped away from her, looking in the mirror to adjust his tie slightly. "Let's drive there on Saturday and see a picture afterward."

"I'd love that," Perveen said, coming up from behind to wrap her arms around her handsome husband's bulk. "And as for today: you'll do your job, and I shall do mine."

"Don't let my mother drive you mad in the kitchen," Cyrus murmured.

"Nobody can drive me mad except you."

Two hours later, though, Perveen wasn't so sure. Cooking was hard. After a long slog of onion chopping, her eyes stung. She blinked furiously as she worked at slicing potatoes thin as matchsticks. Nobody else's eyes seemed to be hurting. She'd look a wreck, with such red eyes, when Cyrus came back.

"Is this enough?" Perveen asked when a small white pyramid of potatoes rested on the wooden board before her.

Behnoush tilted her head and looked down at the pile. "A little thinner next time, but it's good enough for a beginner. Now soak them in cold water with salt—half an hour."

"Shall I fetch my watch?" Perveen had been instructed to wear no jewelry and a simple sari. It turned out that much of her trousseau was too luxurious for kitchen training, so Behnoush had taken her to Hogg Market to buy a stack of practical cotton saris. The cost of five of these rough saris had been less than the cost of one of Perveen's everyday silk saris. Behnoush had dressed ostentatiously throughout her time in Bombay and given Perveen beautiful clothes for the wedding, so Perveen was surprised to learn her mother-in-law had a frugal side.

"Are those eyes or marbles?" Behnoush chided. "There is a clock over the table."

The six-by-ten-foot kitchen was packed with pots and pans hanging from the ceiling, a two-burner hob, a griddle for breads, a curry stone for spice grinding, and a wide stone sink. Perveen hadn't noticed the clock.

"Never soak potatoes in water from the sink tap—it's full of germs. Use filtered drinking water from the crock," Behnoush said, pointing to it.

"Yes, Behnoush-mummy." Perveen was glad to put some distance between herself and the third person in the kitchen: Pushpa, the kitchen servant, who was also Gita's mother. Pushpa had been kind enough to teach Perveen many Bengali words, but she also had the annoying habit of calling out to Behnoush whenever she thought Perveen was in error.

"Bhabhi's not using salt!" Pushpa sang out just as Perveen put the potatoes into the water.

"It would seem you've never been inside a kitchen, Perveen!" Behnoush-mummy said, her stern words softened by a smile.

"The last time was when I was thirteen," Perveen admitted, hoping to play on her mother-in-law's sympathy. "I wanted our cook to teach me how to make trifle. My mother interrupted and told me to get back to my Latin. She said there would always be someone who could cook for me—but never somebody who could study for me. After that, I didn't dare go back."

"A deprivation!" Behnoush shook her head. "In my house, there was only one servant who came for a few hours a day. So of course, I learned all the cooking and cleaning."

"I'm glad to learn," Perveen said, because the sweaty, tedious labor had been her first exposure of what life was really like for household servants. "Last week, bottling up all those sour mango pickles was good fun. I can only hope they turn out well enough that Cyrus will like them."

"Making pickles is no game; if it's done incorrectly, it can result in poisoning." Behnoush drew her lips into a tight line. "Did you know?"

"I didn't—"

"Now you do. And right now, we still need the masala," she said, tapping her spoon against the edge of an empty bowl. "Pushpa measured all the necessary ingredients while you've been telling your Bombay stories. Perhaps your mother's servants cooked with prepared powders, but here we grind on the curry stone every morning!"

Perveen didn't answer but settled down near the heavy black granite slab that Pushpa had toweled clean for her use. Reaching forward, she rolled the heavy black stone pin over the salt crystals, ignoring the slight pulling in her belly. Her period had surprised her by starting shortly after breakfast. She'd learned from her mother that two aspirin and moving around relieved the symptoms. She hadn't mentioned it to Behnoush because she didn't want any old-fashioned advice. Her condition was a matter between herself, Cyrus, and Gita, who had brought the necessary bucket to the lavatory. It had been the same with her maid at home, who had delivered the unmentionables to a washerwoman.

Rolling the spice pods into powder, Perveen hoped that the stern mother-in-law business would end soon. In a recent letter from Bihar, her sister-in-law had written: *Truly, she's a dear. But you must show her that you're respectful. Remember, she's the one who's losing something.*

And that something was Cyrus. Perveen thought about how mournful Behnoush looked when Cyrus came home and barely spoke to her before urging Perveen to come up with him to their rooms. How much fun the two of them had in their getaway; sharing gin and tonics and amusing stories on the veranda, and then bath and bed.

Perveen had not thought much about her body before. But she thrilled to journey with Cyrus in different, daring directions that always seemed to end at the same mountain peak where sensation mixed with breathlessness.

How do you know how to make me feel this? she'd once asked. He had not answered her with words.

Perveen scooped up the finished masala powder and put it into the proper brass bowl. She hoped the mixture would meet her mother-in-law's specifications.

Behnoush instructed her to smear the squares of lamb shoulder meat and set them to rest. The hob's burner was taken up with a pot of lamb's livers, heart, and lungs, Behnoush's special recipe that Perveen felt loath to taste.

Frying a batch of matchstick potatoes would be a delightful respite from blood and bone. Mohit, the household cook, carried away the simmering lamb, making space for a new pot, into which Perveen carefully poured groundnut oil. She'd checked the clock, so she knew a half hour had passed, and she could drain and dry the potatoes.

"Don't add potatoes until it's hot enough," Behnoush advised, dropping a bit of water in the hot oil. As it sizzled, she looked impatiently at Perveen. "What are you waiting for? It's ready!"

Perveen dropped spoonfuls of potatoes into the golden oil. She jumped back in surprise as they crackled, sending a mist of oil upward.

"Dud-wallah has come," Gita called to Behnoush from the entrance to the kitchen. "He has milk and cream today."

"He should have come hours ago, so I have words for him." Calling over her shoulder, Behnoush added, "Don't burn the potatoes. Lift them a half minute before you think they're done, and let them drain on paper."

Perveen nodded, her attention concentrated on the potatoes. She would get it right, because she knew how sali boti potatoes should look. As she saw the first flush of color, she reached for the metal strainer and suddenly remembered Behnoush's advice.

"Can you get paper?" Perveen asked Pushpa.

"Paper?" Pushpa began rummaging in a cupboard.

So quickly, the potatoes were transforming from pale yellow to gold. Pushpa still hadn't found the paper.

Perveen had a flash of memory; she'd seen the *Statesman* lying on the hall table.

Perveen dashed out, grabbed the newspaper, and came back, spreading it two layers thick on a cutting board. Then she dipped the hand sieve into the oil, bringing up a crunchy group of potatoes, which she deposited on the newspaper. Once the pot was clear, she added a little more oil and then the remaining raw potatoes.

Behnoush returned, bearing a heavy glass jar of cream. Cheerfully, she said, "We'll make that custard cake you dreamed of. Now, how about the potatoes?"

"They're right here," Perveen said.

Behnoush gaped at the perfectly fried potatoes. "Chhee! You used newspaper?"

"Yes, I—"

"Newspaper with ink! Just look!" Behnoush jerked the newspaper, revealing that the undersides of all the glorious matchstick potatoes were smudged with black.

Horror swept through Perveen. "Oh dear. I was in a rush—I didn't think the ink would spread—"

"How stupid of you. The waste!" Behnoush continued her tirade, making Perveen dizzy with shame. "How could anyone—especially a rich girl like you—think of putting good fried food on such dirty paper? Five large potatoes were wasted, and the oil."

"I'll make the potatoes again," Perveen said. "If it turns out there is correct paper for draining. None was in the kitchen—"

"There are no more potatoes in the house. I must send Mohit to the market." Behnoush swung around and began shouting in Bengali at Mohit, who'd been taken off duty during the cooking lesson.

"I'm sorry," Perveen apologized, feeling an utter fool. She couldn't possibly serve such potatoes to Cyrus or anyone. But how many more hours in the hot, tense kitchen would it take to remedy her error?

As if sensing Perveen's anguish, Behnoush said, "Just forget it. Mohit can make the sali later. Do you remember how to sort dal?"

"Of course." The inspection of dried yellow split peas was a tedious, slavish job she'd done four times in the last five days. She'd grown to suspect that the dal-wallah added in small stones the same color and size as his peas: a nightmare for anyone trying to prepare a satisfactory meal.

The rest of the morning passed horribly and was followed by lunch at one. Perveen could barely get down the fibrous spiced offal, which was served with plain rice and the dal. At least there were no stones in the dal on her plate. She and her mother-in-law ate together in silence.

At the end of the meal, when Mohit filled their cups with too-gingery tea, Perveen thought about what course her father would recommend. He handled his own missteps with grace, apologizing to clients, inviting the opposing council and judges to supper or cocktails.

"I wish I could be a better daughter-in-law," Perveen said.

Silence followed, and she did not break it. Her father had taught her that speaking rapidly, and not allowing breaks, confused others and made one appear rattled.

At last, a heavy sigh. Perveen looked up from her plate and saw Behnoush looking appraisingly at her.

"You have good manners," Behnoush said. "You are very well bred. Your mother may not have taught you cooking, but she did teach you to speak well. I do not expect you to cook all the time. That is not why my son married you. He married to have a good mother for his children, someone who will take her place in the community."

He married me to please himself, Perveen thought. *To have nights full of passion and a close friend to joke with, and share troubles with, too.* But that was not what Behnoush wanted to hear. In a low voice, Perveen said, "Your cooking is so excellent, I won't ever match it."

"A man always loves his mother's cooking best; it is true. But do not worry; you can improve." Behnoush leaned back in her chair and let out a hearty burp. "I became overwrought, so I will take rest after lunch. Along with the sali, Mohit shall make the vegetable curry for this evening. And also the custard cake you enjoy."

"Shall I learn it from him?" Perveen thought that the quiet cook would be easier to spend time with than Behnoush.

"No, no, he cannot instruct you properly. It will be my duty, another time."

Two o'clock. How still the house was when Behnoush slept. Perveen had been sitting at the desk, willing herself to finish a letter to her parents. But it felt odd writing to them about how wonderful things were in Calcutta after the events of the morning.

Her mother's last letter had included a question about whether she'd visited Bethune and Loreto Colleges, two institutions where Perveen might earn a bachelor's degree in some liberal arts subject such as English literature or teaching. Camellia had written, *Your strength is words. Why not turn to this?*

Perveen had initially bristled at Camellia's intrusion into her life plans, but after the tedium of household life with Behnoush, she'd realized college would give her a valid reason to leave Saklat Place during the day. Her parents had set up a bank account for her at Grindlays, so she wouldn't need to ask anyone for money. It was an unusual arrangement, but it meant she'd never have to ask her in-laws for anything. It turned out that Cyrus was paid an allowance, not a salary. He hadn't minded her having the security of more money for them in her account.

Even though they'd discussed it that morning, Cyrus's plan to visit Bethune with her seemed so far off. He also had a charming, but infuriating, way of getting interested in other activities. Because

Cyrus was usually working, she'd agreed to whatever he wanted. But today she had the gift of a little time to herself. Since Behnoush had given her a free afternoon, she would visit the college in North Calcutta by herself.

Perveen went to her bookshelves and pulled out the Calcutta pocket guide her parents had left. A section detailed tram routes and fares, with maps of the city's central and outlying areas. Bethune College was on Cornwallis Street, a north-south artery. It would be a long walk to Cornwallis, but once she was there, she could catch a tram for the rest of the journey.

Perveen went into the lavatory to bathe and dress in one of her own good everyday saris, a blue-and-cream patterned silk. Picking up a cream parasol and a straw shopping bag, she put the envelope containing her college and high school transcripts inside. She also took twenty-five rupees, in case the college required a deposit.

As she came downstairs and headed toward the front door, Gita came awake on the mat where she'd been napping. "Memsahib, where are you going?"

"Sightseeing," Perveen said. "If Behnoush-mummy awakens before I return, please tell her I'll be home by teatime."

Calcutta was like Bombay—and not. From the wooden seat in the first-class car, Perveen gazed hungrily at her new hometown. The men were intriguing, several of them wearing traditional Indian clothes along with proper English shoes, spats, and gartered stockings. She imagined they worked at the many British businesses she saw along the route. Ladies also traveled freely, just like in Bombay. As the tram rattled its way north, Perveen saw knots of young men building colorful, sparkling shrines right on the streets. Cyrus and his father had been talking about big party orders for the Bengali Hindu holiday honoring Durga, their exalted mother of the universe. Perveen drank in the splendid gilded pandals, remembering what a Hindu classmate had once said about the sword in Durga's right hand symbolizing the power of knowledge.

Seeing so many visions of Durga on the way to Bethune College seemed an auspicious sign. Giving up law didn't mean she couldn't keep learning things; she would become a student of literature, perhaps studying Bengali language and literature. *Yes!* Perveen decided with new energy. Though her mother had suggested English, this was the right choice, now that she was a Calcuttan. And if she fell pregnant, she could use the quiet hours for reading and writing—it would be an easier field of study than law.

Bethune College was much smaller than Bombay's Elphinstone College. She stared at the elegant building with Grecian columns, thinking it looked more like an old bungalow than an educational institution. But she was sure of being in the right place when she saw young women passing through the doors with heavy satchels just like she'd carried a few months before.

Perveen was surprised to feel herself envying the girls their satchels. It had been easy to leave the law school, but she missed the camaraderie of the Elphinstone campus and all her female friends. Getting to be with Cyrus in Calcutta had consumed her thoughts for the months leading up to the wedding, but now, just two weeks into married life, she longed for something to do in the daytime.

The bearer guarding the entrance brought Perveen inside and to a high-ceilinged office, where she introduced herself to an elderly Bengali lady and expressed her interest in applying for an academic transfer. She spoke English, because this would show the receptionist her qualifications instantly.

The woman had an unpleasant, narrow face that seemed to grow longer at Perveen's request. She answered in Bengali. "Many young ladies are inquiring these days—and the school year is already underway."

Perveen nodded. She understood the rebuff.

"We are taking applications for next year, and they must be completed in writing." Giving Perveen a smug smile, the lady went to a file cabinet and took out a thick packet of papers. "You may have this application, but only if you will use it. We must not waste."

Perveen hadn't come all the way just to be sent packing. Her Bengali wasn't strong enough for her to converse in it yet, so she shifted into Hindi. "I'm interested in learning more about the courses before I apply. Whom may I ask?"

The receptionist shrugged. "Our headmistress is giving a speech to the second-year students at the moment; and after that she has a conference with the teachers."

Perveen sensed the two of them had entered a contest rather like when her father parried with opposing counsel. "Is there a commons room where I might be able to meet some of the students?"

"Those areas are closed to the public." The woman licked her dry lips. "Actually, Mrs. Kamini Roy is in the office today. But she might be too busy to speak with you."

Perveen gaped. "The famous poet and social worker?"

The receptionist gave her a faint look of approval. "Mrs. Roy was one of Bethune's first graduates. She teaches in literature and Sanskrit."

"If she's here, would you please tell her I was formerly enrolled at the Government Law School in Bombay?" Feeling desperate, Perveen babbled on. "I completed most of the requirements for a first year of college. With regards to the Oxford examinations, I've passed Latin, French, and first year literature. It's all in the papers I've brought—"

The clerk held up a finger. "Give me those papers you brought. In the meantime, you may sit in the parlor. The student prospectus is on the table."

As she waited, Perveen could hardly bear the suspense—and for the first time in ages, she wished her mother could be with her.

Camellia Mistry was one of Kamini Roy's great admirers and had convinced the teachers at Perveen's high school to add her poetry to the curriculum. She could hardly wait to tell her mother Kamini Roy taught at Bethune College. It would be a more interesting letter than the last one she'd written, about cooking dhansak.

A Bengali woman wearing gold-rimmed glasses and a simple white sari walked swiftly into the room. In a cut-glass English accent, she said, "Mrs. Sodawalla, how good of you to visit us."

"Mrs. Roy! I read all your poems in school." Perveen was blushing from excitement. "Thank you for seeing me."

"Certainly. It is rare to see a potential student come without her parents and from so far away," she said, her eyebrows raised in an unspoken question.

"Yes, I can imagine! I'm from Bombay but am now living in Calcutta with my husband and his family."

Kamini Roy looked thoughtful. "Ah. That explains your departure from the Government Law School. Although it must have been a shame to leave—I wasn't aware females could study law in India."

"A special provision was made for me to attend classes and sit exams—it was not a formal change in admission rules," Perveen said. Kamini Roy still looked questioning, so Perveen added, "My father is a lawyer who wished me to join his practice. But at the law school, I discovered it wasn't the right vocation. I've always loved reading and literature, so that's why I've come to Bethune."

"Your Oxford examination result was very strong in languages and writing." The lady adjusted her spectacles as she read Perveen's transcript. "Didn't you think of applying to Oxford or Cambridge?"

"We talked about it then, but I didn't want to be far from my family. And I prefer a new field of study." As she spoke, Perveen knew it was only a half-truth. She still longed to practice alongside her father—but there was no way that could be.

Mrs. Roy smiled warmly at her. "There may be an opening. But before offering admission, the committee must be sure you've got the necessary support."

"I understand." Perveen's hand touched her purse. "My parents have provided the funds. I don't need to ask for a scholarship and have enough for a deposit today—"

"No need. I'm asking what your husband and his parents think about your idea of studying here."

Perveen hadn't expected the question. "My husband already knows of my interest. In fact, when he was trying to convince me to marry him, he told me about all the educational opportunities in Calcutta."

"That is a good sign," Kamini Roy said, her face relaxing. "Our application must be cosigned by a responsible, employed family member. Our principal must meet your husband and possibly his father."

"But why? I've got my own money. That seems—"

"Unfair?" Mrs. Roy gave her a wry smile. "I agree with you, Mrs. Sodawalla. I'd like to change the rules to allow women more control, but I am not a trustee with such powers. I suggest you prepare the application and bring it to the interview along with your father-in-law and husband. I anticipate seeing you in class very soon."

Feeling both irritated and heartened, Perveen said goodbye.

She was thrilled to have met Kamini Roy and guessed that the poet would advocate for admission on her behalf. But now she had to ask Cyrus and Bahram to take time away from the factories to pay their respects at Bethune College. She sensed this wouldn't be easy.

It was teatime when she arrived back at Saklat Place. Even before the door opened, the smell of simmering meat reached her nose. After being in the fresh air for a few hours, she found the aromas sickeningly heavy.

There was a low murmur of voices, and then she heard Behnoush-mummy's giggle. Perveen stepped carefully over the stenciled chalk border in the entryway, noticing an unfamiliar pair of ladies' chappals nearby.

"Who has come?" Perveen asked Gita.

Gita whispered, "Her best friend, Mrs. Ghandy. But Behnoush-mummy is upset."

Perveen felt torn between paying her respects and going straight upstairs to begin the Bethune application. Duty won out, and she approached the parlor. Drawing closer, she heard an unfamiliar, high-pitched voice that must have been Mrs. Ghandy.

"And she just went out? You must be worried!"

Behnoush's answer sounded irritable. "Yes, not knowing anything about the streets, the bad types, and so on."

"A Bombay girl always wants to shop!" pronounced Mrs. Ghandy. "But why would she go out without a family member?"

Perveen felt awkward to be listening at the door. Walking straight in, she said, "Behnoush-mummy, I'm sorry not to have told you I was going out. You were still taking a rest, and I didn't want to wake you."

Behnoush batted her eyes rapidly at the sight of her. Rising from her chair, she began waving her hands as if shooing her away. In a low voice, she said, "Go."

"You wish me to go away?" Perveen couldn't understand the look of intense embarrassment on her mother-in-law's face. Mrs. Ghandy was studying the carpet, as if she couldn't bear to see Perveen.

"Upstairs," Behnoush hissed. "I'll come later."

Trailed by Gita, Perveen climbed the steps to the second floor. Behnoush might have guessed she'd overheard the gossip and felt she needed to behave sternly in front of Mrs. Ghandy. Perveen felt steam rising from her body—the heat of shame at having acted so impulsively and entered the room, ripping up the fragile bond with her mother-in-law.

"Should I have waited for an introduction?" she asked Gita. "What did I do wrong now?"

Instead of explaining, Gita said, "This way. You must follow me."

Perveen halted in surprise. The three-story house was built in a square with an open-air courtyard in the middle; Gita was taking her to the side that was farthest away, with doors she'd never opened.

"What do you mean?" Perveen asked. "I'm going to my room now to take a bath."

Nervously, Gita said, "Your Behnoush-mummy doesn't want you to."

"What nonsense!" Perveen said, her irritation rising. "If she wants to speak with me, she can find me in my quarters."

Gita winced. "But memsahib, you cannot do that there. Not now."

Perveen put her hands on her hips and addressed her ayah in slow

Bengali. "I must bathe. I've been outside, and it's my monthly time as well."

Gita's eyes flared. "That is the reason why! Behnoush-mummy knows what happened—that it started today. She says you must go to that room."

"What room?"

"Here." Gita opened a metal door that was just slightly taller than Perveen. The cloying smell of urine hit her first. Was it a latrine?

Perveen held her nose, trying to adjust her eyes to the dark room, which she saw had one long window shielded by a patterned iron screen. Gita covered her hand with a cloth before pulling the string for the light in the room's center.

Perveen blinked, trying to make sense of the place. It was a small room, about twelve by eight feet, with the same red-oxide flooring as the rest of the home. The room held a narrow iron cot; there were two sheets folded at the bottom and a worn-looking pillow in a yellowed case at the top. The only other pieces of furniture were a straight-backed chair and small table, both made of iron.

On the table were three small piles. One contained folded rough cotton saris; another, clean but worn-looking menstrual cloths; and the last, a few stained towels. There were also a few moldering Gujarati novels. A door in the back led to a small space with a toilet.

These quarters were too bleak for even the lowest servant. Feeling indignant, Perveen asked, "Whose room is this?"

Gita was standing at the door's edge, looking nervous. "It's the place for Parsi women's resting during binamazi. Don't you know it from home?"

Perveen swallowed hard. The literal meaning of binamazi was "being without prayer." It was the term used for menstruation. Parsi women were not supposed to wear their religious garments nor pray at the agiary during binamazi. But those were the only rules Perveen had been taught by her mother.

"Gita—I don't understand. Does this room have something to do with menstruation?"

"Yes, you must stay here because of that." Gita shot her a sympathetic look. "The tall pitcher is water in case you need a drink—you can ring the bell anytime, and I'll come to the door and bring more water and your daily meals. The smaller pitcher contains taro. I think you know what to do with it."

"Taro," she repeated. She knew the urine from a white bull was collected for use as an antiseptic, a Zoroastrian tradition dating from the faith's origins in Persia. Was that what made the room smell so fiercely?

"Mummy says it's for cleaning yourself."

"It makes no sense not to wash one's body with water when it's very much needed. I didn't see a sink or bath in the back. I shall be coming out for that—"

"No, you must not," Gita said anxiously. "She believes everyone should stay three paces from a bleeding woman, so do not get too close to the door."

"How many hours must I stay here? Just the first day, surely?"

"No. It's the whole time and one extra day past the time you stop bleeding." Gita shifted uneasily in the doorway. "That is how she did it."

"Do you mean Behnoush-mummy?"

Gita lowered her voice. "Yes, before her bleeding ceased. But Azara was in binamazi before she died."

Perveen shivered at the mention of the lost family member, whom she'd tried to speak about with Cyrus a few more times to no avail. To think that a child had had to stay in such conditions made her sick. "When she had cholera, they still told her to stay here?"

"Not cholera." Gita shook her head.

Looking at Gita's anxious face, Perveen realized she shouldn't keep interrogating the poor servant. Perveen needed to make a compromise with Behnoush—perhaps staying away from the kitchen, prayer room, and so on.

Gita closed the door, and her footsteps faded down the hall.

Now that Perveen was alone in the little room, she realized the full horror of it. This was a stinking prison; she would not tolerate it. As she stepped toward the threshold and opened the door, it smashed back into her face, sending her a few steps back.

"What? Who's there?" Perveen called out crossly. "You hit my nose!"

"Don't come out!" Behnoush shouted.

Perveen tried to recall everything she had said since coming upstairs. How much might Behnoush have overheard? She didn't want her mother-in-law to know the extent of her annoyance.

"Oh, sorry! Is your guest still here?" Perveen asked, striving to sound conversational.

"No!" Behnoush maintained her angry tone. "I sent her off straightaway, for fear of illness."

"But—but I'm not ill," Perveen protested.

"It is your time. You will bring disease if you come into contact with others. Gita, tell her! Are you allowed to come to work when you are bleeding?"

"No," Gita mumbled dutifully from somewhere along the hallway. "I cannot come. And I shall wash carefully after having been near Bhabhi."

Perveen knew this was going to be a serious argument—a litigator's opening statement. She swallowed hard. "Behnoush-mummy, people practiced seclusion a very long time ago. But the Parsis are the most progressive people in Asia. My mother didn't seclude herself, nor did any of my aunts and cousins."

A silence fell. Behnoush was on the other side of the door, so Perveen could not see her face. She had no idea if Behnoush was listening thoughtfully or spinning into the kind of anger she'd shown in the kitchen.

When she finally spoke, her voice was choked. "This is your house now. And I love my son enough to wish him to stay in good health. Don't you understand about your dirty condition?"

"It is called menstruation," Perveen answered, using the English word. "I don't enjoy it. But it is natural and my own business. That's why I'd like you to allow me to return to my room."

Behnoush's voice was low and fearful-sounding when she spoke.

"I don't know that word you use. Your body is shedding the dirtiest blood and dead eggs. This attracts Ahriman."

Perveen's heart felt like it was jumping out of her chest. "Good Zoroastrians live on a path—we choose the direction of good or evil through our thoughts, words, and actions. That is why I don't fear the devil."

From the other side of the door, Behnoush snapped, "I'm telling you. If you leave this room—you leave this house forever."

Perveen was alarmed. "Mamma, no! I don't wish to go away. I dearly love Cyrus, and he loves me."

"I know you want this marriage. You will do the necessary and remain here while you are in bleeding." Behnoush's voice softened. "And just think, if you fall pregnant, you will have plenty of time outside of this room."

Behnoush's voice was so intimate that Perveen thought her mother-in-law was about to come inside to console her.

But she only shoved the door more firmly so that it latched.

1917

15

A MATTER OF TESTING
Calcutta, January 1917

*M*y dearest Perveen,
My very best love to you and the Sodawalla family. How is the weather in Calcutta in January? You must be looking forward to your first Nowruz celebration there!

We are all well here in Bombay. Your father has taken on three new clients who are keeping him busy. Rustom is over the moon to learn that Mistry Construction has approval to build several office blocks in Ballard Estate, a neighborhood coming up between Fort and Ballard Pier. With luck, the project will be underway by your visit this May.

It's a shame your in-laws did not agree to your enrolling at Bethune. However, the college is located in the north, and if nobody can escort you, they would naturally worry. Also, if you'd have to miss a week every month, you would hardly make progress. My suggestion to you is to investigate Loreto College, which is closer, and inquire whether you might be allowed to do classwork from home five days per month. You might learn of other orthodox female students in similar situations.

I'm sorry that the Sodawallas are insisting on the practice of your monthly seclusion. They should have mentioned their commitment to this antiquated custom when we met in Bombay. I'm enclosing an edition of the Gujarati women's magazine Stree Bodh *that contains a good article explaining the folly of feminine seclusion. I suggest you give Behnoush-mummy the entire magazine in order for her to discover this gem of knowledge herself, rather than to feel you are challenging her any more than you already have.*

I continue to urge caution in your behavior. The

*mother-daughter bond is a delicate one that can be ruined
with hasty action. Have you spoken to a doctor? Perhaps one
could recommend that it is better for you to avoid this practice.
A doctor is a more acceptable figure of authority than a daughter-in-law.*

*I have not told you this before, because I never wanted you
to think ill of your father's parents. When I entered Mistry
House as a young bride in 1890, there was a seclusion room.
Both Grandfather and Grandmother Mistry believed it was
essential for the household's health that I confine myself to this
tiny room on the third floor for the heaviest part of my cycle.
I didn't enjoy it, but I used the time to read and sleep. After
giving birth to you, I convinced your father to move out of Mistry
House to Byculla, where people were building modern bungalows without those dreadful little rooms.*

*In the event that you and Cyrus decide to move to your own
home in Calcutta, we are very happy to help with the purchase.*

I remain,
Your ever-loving Mamma

Perveen folded the letter and put it into the desk. This was startling information about her family's life inside Mistry House. A
barrier had risen between her and Grandfather Mistry ever since
his avoidance of all her engagement and wedding activities. Because
she now understood he'd enforced her own mother's seclusion, her
discomfort with him had turned to anger.

Staring out of the lounge's long windows onto the street, Perveen
thought about her parents' generous offer to fund a new home. Her
mother was trying to cheer her up, just as Cyrus did on the twenty
days each month that she lived freely. But Cyrus had just finished
paying for their suite's modern porcelain bath, toilet, and sink. Furthermore, he was the only Sodawalla child living in Calcutta. If he
left his parents alone, it would seem uncaring—especially as they
were heading into old age.

Cyrus had come several times to the door of the little room when she was secluded, knocking only in the early hours of the morning when he was sure his parents were asleep. Perveen had rushed up to open the door to him, maintaining three feet distance between them after his twitching nose had revealed to her that she'd acquired a stench. It couldn't really be that he believed she was tainted and capable of transmitting disease.

Cyrus had explained that it wasn't Bahram who cared for tradition as much as Behnoush, who'd been born in a priestly family. "They were poor, so this is her only point of pride. It is why she takes you with her to agiary so often. You must see her customs as a matter of faith, not any kind of dominance."

"But I don't think God wants women to lie in filth," Perveen insisted. "And I'm your wife, Cyrus, not hers—can't you be the one who insists on my well-being?"

He sighed heavily, exuding a whiff of sweet bourbon. "I've tried, but they don't listen. And better not come out to the hall again! She knows you did earlier this week."

Perveen was indignant. "I needed water. I had to call out for one of the servants—"

"Yes, yes. She was worried if you had too much water, you'd break the rule and use it for cleaning yourself."

Perveen was on the verge of telling Cyrus she had done just that when there was a banging sound down the hallway.

"Someone's up," Cyrus whispered, putting a finger to his lips.

Panic mixed with defiance. "Now's the time. Take me back to our room, and I'll take a bath. It will all be over if we stand up to her. I'm not going back in!"

"Soon enough, you will be pregnant." His voice sounded almost merry. "I must go!"

Cyrus pressed her hand one last time and swayed off toward their bedroom.

Remembering this, Perveen thought that asking for a new home would make her parents-in-law think of her as even more of a spoiled, wealthy girl. However—if she were carrying a baby, safety for the baby's health could be used as the reason. She wouldn't mention the death of Azara, because it was painful for Cyrus and his parents. But surely they would realize that moving to Alipore's fresh air made sense for a baby.

Then again, having a baby would quash any chance of her studying. And that filled her with regret. She'd so enjoyed meeting Kamini Roy and had written her a letter of thanks, which had been answered by one from the scholar herself, asking whether Perveen's family was amenable to coming in for the interview.

Which did she want more—a life of the mind or one devoted to heartfelt caring? It was frustrating to have neither choice assert itself. After four months of married life, she had not conceived. Perhaps it was anxiety. Whenever Cyrus lifted her nightgown, all she could think about was whether that night would be the start of her salvation. As the thought remained in mind, her other body parts lost their sensitivity, and she now couldn't always reach the thrilling peaks. Her body was losing its powers, just as her spirit was.

Not long after, Behnoush suggested Perveen see a doctor.

"Dr. Bhattacharya is highly respected. He is a specialist in women's health; many ladies from the agiary have sent their daughters-in-law. Although he is a Bengali, he's familiar with our culture."

"What happens in an examination?" Perveen knew seeing a doctor was exactly what Camellia had recommended, but she still felt nervous about the prospect of a physician looking at her private parts.

"I've never had one," Behnoush said, patting Perveen's hand. "I hear from my friends' daughters that it is embarrassing, but there should not be pain. Nothing like childbirth."

Dr. Bhattacharya's office was on the second floor of a stately white building on Theater Road. The waiting room did not have the typical wooden benches crowded with the ill but plush velvet chairs and couches, so the waiting patients could separate themselves. Several other flat-stomached women were waiting with older women she guessed were their mothers-in-law. One pregnant woman was seated on a small sofa, reading a book, while her husband looked around the room smiling. Perveen nodded approvingly at the man, thinking this would be the ideal way for Cyrus to be, accompanying her and giving loving care throughout pregnancy.

Behnoush pinched Perveen's arm. "Don't look at another woman's husband!"

"I didn't." Perveen flushed at her mother-in-law's supposition. She wished she'd thought to bring a book to read. She had paper and pen, but she could hardly write a letter complaining about Behnoush when the woman was right beside her.

After almost an hour's wait, a nurse called for Perveen to come along and meet the doctor.

"No, madam," the nurse said when Behnoush rose to accompany Perveen in. "I'm sorry, but Doctor prefers only the patient in the examination room. He shall speak with you afterward."

Perveen was relieved for a few moments, but when she entered the examination room, she felt faint. A table draped with a sheet stood before her, and on a tray table nearby lay an array of long metal instruments and a mirror. There were glass vials and syringes and so much more she could not identify. She felt dread and almost wished Behnoush were with her.

"The first thing is obtaining a specimen." Dr. Bhattacharya, a man about Perveen's father's age, had silver hair and thick glasses. He spoke English with a heavy Bengali accent. "This allows us to know if you are with child."

Could she be?

Perveen supposed there was a chance. She went into the modern lavatory and managed to urinate a tiny stream into the little cup. When she came out, she marveled at the nurse taking the cup in her gloved hand, behaving as if this was absolutely natural and not an abominable task.

The nurse instructed her to remove her clothing below the waist, including her petticoat and pantalettes. A rough sheet was given as covering after these clothes were gone.

Perveen stared at the ceiling, thinking of Cyrus. She'd asked him to come on the doctor's visit, but he'd joked that it was not his body under examination. She wondered what he was doing at the factory. Perhaps he was making rounds of the workers—or sampling the wares. Whiskey was always on his breath when he came home every evening; the only comfort she had was a chauffeur was driving.

The doctor and nurse came in together. The doctor asked Perveen the date of her marriage and the estimated number of times of marital congress. Had the frequency fallen off since the marriage?

"Yes," she said, seizing the opportunity he'd given her. "My in-laws have insisted that I seclude myself eight days per month. I have to stay one day longer than the first day there's no blood. It's a very long time."

"Orthodox Parsis observe this custom of menstrual seclusion," he said with a nod. "It would be quite unlikely for you to conceive during that time."

"But the seclusion and not being allowed to bathe can't be healthy," Perveen said. "It's not the way I was raised."

"Even though you are Parsi?"

"Yes, from a modern family in Bombay." In a rush, she said, "Actually, seclusion has been very hard for me. I dread it the entire month. It's begun to affect my sleep and mood."

"How so?" Giving her a sharper look, he picked up his pen and began writing notes.

"I have terrible nightmares that I'm in that little room, even when I'm away from it," she said, remembering the dreams of the prior week. "I have a feeling of sadness and hopelessness. It's made me angry with my husband. He won't defend me against his parents, even though he thinks it's old-fashioned."

"Every young bride, regardless of religion, struggles with adjusting to the in-laws' house. It will improve." The doctor's voice was dismissive. "I am concerned with your relationship with your husband. What is the frequency of congress?"

"Between four and six times."

"A month?" he asked, not looking up.

"Every week," she said, blushing. It did sound like quite a lot—but it was the one thing Cyrus still had time for.

"Healthy newlyweds." For the first time, the doctor sounded approving. "Now we shall commence the examination."

Talking with him had helped keep her mind off his hands and instruments. Now the long double-sided metal tool went inside; Perveen gasped at the pain. As her body stiffened, she wondered whether the examination could be dangerous if she was indeed pregnant.

"Sorry. It is always hard," Dr. Bhattacharya said, putting his metal tool down on a tray. "Now, I have a few questions."

"Yes," Perveen said, struggling up to a sitting position so she could see his face.

"Have you had congress or any sexual activity with another man?"

Perveen was shocked that he'd think such a thing of her. Swiftly, she said, "No. Only my husband—"

"You are certain of this? No fathers-in-law, uncles, brothers-in-law—"

"Of course I haven't. I do not come from that kind of family!" Perveen's voice shook at the indignity. Ever since she'd arrived in Calcutta, all kinds of sly comments had been made about decadent, rich Parsis of Bombay. Any question about her family made her react violently.

The doctor steepled his fingers and leaned forward, studying her. "You would be surprised what happens in the best of houses—Hindu houses, Parsi, Muslim. And even among the English."

Perveen felt her pulse pick up. In a low voice, she said, "Are you asking me this because you see signs of a sickness? Is this the reason I haven't conceived?"

"I cannot answer those two questions for certain at the moment. There are signs of change in your body: some lesions, and a cloudy discharge."

Perveen's pulse was now racing. She had noticed some discharge in the last weeks and had carefully rinsed her underthings before leaving them for Gita to give the dhobi. She did not want any further reasons to be sent into seclusion.

"Maladies affecting the reproductive organs are called venereal diseases. I have taken a sampling from your body for our laboratory. Within several days, I will have an answer."

"What is that word—'venereal'?" she asked, hearing the sharpness in her voice. She felt angry not to understand what was wrong with her.

"Originally it is from Latin. Venereus means pertaining to sexual love or intercourse." He spoke drily, as if giving a college lecture.

"Oh!" She blushed again, wishing she hadn't asked. The visit was becoming more embarrassing by the minute.

Sounding stern, he said, "There are several of these diseases. They cause discomfort and can gravely endanger the people who have them."

Fearing the worst, she ventured, "Do you mean that I could die?"

Dr. Bhattacharya picked up a fountain pen and filled it carefully before answering. "In the case of a woman, we worry first about the health of any fetus being carried. This testing will inform us whether you are pregnant."

"I don't think I am. I had my monthly two weeks ago. If I'm ill, might I—never be able to conceive?" In the space of a few minutes, her life as a married woman seemed to be collapsing.

"Don't leap to conclusions," the doctor said, not looking at her as he wrote fluidly on the paper in front of him. "You must return for an appointment to learn the results of the cultures, and then all will be known. In the meantime, refrain from intimate contact. And next time, you must bring your husband."

Just like the lady in the waiting room with her spouse. But how could Cyrus beam proudly if they were awaiting a diagnosis of life and death? Perveen wished she could read the truth that the doctor had surely already written down. Trying not to cry, she said, "I don't know if he'll come. He's very busy with his bottling plants. He usually is gone by nine every morning and sometimes isn't home until ten or eleven at night."

"I should not release your diagnosis and treatment plan without the presence of a husband."

Just as she could not enroll in college without the signature of a male relative. Suddenly, all the anger she'd been closing inside herself broke out. "Why must I bring him? Don't you realize that he may want to divorce me when he hears this news? And if my mother-in-law learns about it—"

The doctor's voice was unemotional. "They have no reason to fault you."

"But from what you're saying, I've got a terrible illness. Of course they will blame me."

Dr. Bhattacharya shook his head. "Venereal diseases pass from one person to another. And since you've only had relations with your husband, you surely know the culprit."

16
BROKEN DESIGNS
Calcutta, March 1917

*S*quatting on the tiled floor of the foyer, Perveen arranged the tin stencil box and picked up the shaker of lime powder. Carefully, she shook chalk inside the stencil and watched it flow through to the floor.

The week before, she had made a special design for Behnoush's birthday. Today it was back to normal: the swastika pattern that represented the revolving sun's life-giving force.

Stenciling chalk designs was something she'd enjoyed doing occasionally in Bombay. Her mother had explained that in olden times the limestone chalk had trapped dirt and disinfected the feet of people entering the home. The custom endured as a way of showing welcome—and also the accomplishments of the household's women.

These days, crouching down to decorate the Sodawallas' house was nothing but a chore. It felt like making an elegant frame to go around the ugly picture that her life had become. If Perveen had permission to pick out the chalk's color, it would have been a blackish gray like the ashes from dirty fires on the Calcutta streets.

Just down the hallway, a pure sandalwood flame burned on a table in the parlor. The house would soon be overpowered with sandalwood when the Persian New Year was celebrated over thirteen days. Behnoush, Perveen, Gita, and Pushpa had cleaned for three weeks, making everything fresh for the relatives and visitors who'd come by.

Perveen was highly conscious of how many days of the month she had until she went into the little room. She had calculated that her menstrual cycle would send her into seclusion midway through the holidays, and it would be about eight days until she could leave.

The previous time she'd been in the room, she'd stared at a pattern of smudges on the wall until she realized they were more than dirt. They formed a kind of calendar, with patterns of seven or eight filling a space running from just over the top of the cot down to the baseboard. She wondered if Behnoush had marked off her days. Or had it been Azara?

Perveen had used a pencil to add her own marks, detailing the approximately forty-three days she had been confined over her six months in the bungalow. But she hadn't been able to recall the exact length of each stay. Everything ran together.

On that stay, the spring heat had made the room stifling, and she'd smelled her own sweat and the blood more than before. She could imagine what summer would be like. As her mother had suggested, she passed as much of her time in the room as she could reading or sleeping.

Although she feared her dreams.

Sometimes her dreams were terrifying. She was happily pregnant but then delivered a blind baby. In another dream, Cyrus was plotting with a beautiful woman to throw her off Howrah Bridge. More than once, she'd dreamed she was fourteen-year-old Azara, sick with fever, rolling off the same hard cot.

The hardest dreams were the ones about being back in Bombay. In these nighttime escapes, she was still a college student lounging in a chair on her bedroom balcony. Then she'd wake, realize where she was, and begin to weep.

Nothing had been the same since the visit to the doctor.

Perveen had told Cyrus that the doctor thought she might be ill—but nothing more. She hadn't had the courage to tell him any sickness was likely his fault. She didn't like how brusque Dr. Bhattacharya had been. He didn't know Cyrus, and the diagnosis was not yet certain.

In the doctor's private office, Cyrus had been all smiles and encouragement until Dr. Bhattacharya told him that both of them needed to be treated for gonorrhea. Cyrus's face had gone pale, but he'd agreed to provide a culture for the doctor, who'd then discussed treatment with a modern drug, Paragol. Dr. Bhattacharya said that because Perveen wasn't yet pregnant, they did not have to worry about a baby being born blind.

Later that evening, when they were alone on their balcony, she asked Cyrus how he'd caught the infection.

Cyrus shook his head, looking helpless. "I don't know. But for my sixteenth birthday, my father took me to Sonagachi. He had done the same for my brother. It was his way of teaching me how to be a man. Many fathers and uncles bring boys. We cannot fight it."

She thought about her gruff, quiet father-in-law and could hardly imagine him going to such a place. But it must have been true. "Your sixteenth birthday was twelve years ago. Did you have symptoms then?"

"What kind of question is that? I feel like I'm in court facing a prosecutor."

"Hush. I'm your wife, and I deserve to know."

Cyrus shrugged. "I knew nothing. Remember that the doctor said that some men can be ill for years without knowing. "

She'd believed that Cyrus's skill as a lover was a gift and that he brought her to such heights due to their fated connection. But now she could not stop brooding over the idea he'd had sex with other women. Hesitantly, she asked, "After that birthday, were there other times?"

"No!" Giving her a horrified look, Cyrus launched himself up from the teak chair where he'd been sitting. "I won't stay here if you continue such insults."

"I'm sorry," Perveen said, feeling desperate. "I didn't mean to cause offense. I'm just so worried."

As Cyrus grudgingly returned to his place, she looked at him critically. At twenty-eight, he was so handsome and assured, she thought it might be possible that he had dallied with other women. She had met a few other young Parsi women in the small community—some of them were quite pretty. What if one of them had longed for him, but wound up married to someone else? Cyrus and such a woman might harbor a secret love. *No*, she told herself. He loved only her.

"Has Mamma asked you about the appointment?" Cyrus asked. "I put her off."

Perveen pressed her lips together and nodded. "Yes. I told her the doctor requires us to visit together several more times for treatments to encourage conception. It's not quite a lie, is it? We really can't have a baby until we are free."

"Do you still want a baby?" He tilted his head to one side, as if trying to get a better read on her.

"Yes, but it's safer not to try this year," Perveen said, feeling a gray shawl of sorrow wrap around her. So many possibilities were vanishing.

"You'd forego trying for a baby? Even though you hate going into that room every month?" Cyrus sounded incredulous.

Perveen had agreed about wanting a baby because it was the right thing to say. But the prospect had become terrifying, given the uncertainty of the baby's health, and also knowing Behnoush-mamma would control the way the child was brought up. She couldn't say that to Cyrus because it would create a new argument. He clearly was upset about the upcoming months of celibacy. Clearing her throat, she said, "I must finish that medicine. But if your mother discovers my bottle of Paragol, she'll think I must be confined."

"You mustn't worry about everything! It's turning you into a crone."

Bristling, she shot back, "And what might Mummy do if she learned you were ill? Would she lock you in a little room to keep you from spreading the germs?"

"That's not funny," Cyrus said, finishing his bourbon. "You were different in Bombay—so sweet and agreeable. But since marrying, you've become shrewish."

"I'm not like that!" Perveen protested, thinking of how many times she'd kept back an opinion and how hard she worked to be pleasant to Bahram and Behnoush.

"Just listen to yourself." Cyrus gave her a reproving look before rising and going inside.

Perveen did not go after him. She'd been full of righteous indignation—and somehow he'd managed to turn the tables on her. They'd had a small argument about her applying to Bethune or Loreto College, which he'd won by telling her it was the worst time to agitate his parents. She had a lifetime to study, and the degree would take less than three years. This was true—but now she knew that her finishing college might threaten him.

The information had emerged when Bahram was scolding his son at supper for not having read through a particular contract carefully. "I can't sack you for neglect like they did at Presidency!" he'd bellowed, and Cyrus had delivered a blistering look of rage.

As she continued chalking the hallway, Perveen thought sadly about what she'd given up back in Bombay. The design she was crafting reminded her of the patterned moldings that bordered the ceilings of the hearing rooms within the High Court. As a child, she'd sat in court with Grandfather Mistry, who sometimes stopped in to see his son's performance.

Perveen had been too young to understand the long words being used. She'd only loved the building, with so many wolves, monkeys, and birds carved into it, and the graceful gothic arches that made her feel like a princess in a castle. Here was a place where teakwood and gold never would become old.

The High Court was a place she'd likely never see again. Perveen raised a hand to wipe her eyes and felt the unexpected smarting from the limestone dust.

"Oh, how nice it looks. You are getting better with chalk."

Perveen turned to see her mother-in-law standing over her.

"The ladies are coming soon; we have some weaving," Behnoush said.

Perveen tried to blink the powder out of her eyes so she could get a clear look at Behnoush's expression. It seemed kind.

"Are you making kustis?" Perveen asked.

"Yes, my dear. But don't be disappointed you won't be allowed to weave."

"Why?" Perveen didn't know whether to be relieved or offended.

"The weaving can only be done by ladies of the priestly families. My late father was a priest, and Mrs. Banaji's husband is one— remember, he ministered at your wedding."

Perveen nodded, not remembering that at all.

"Mrs. Banaji's daughter and daughter-in-law are coming today. Everyone is working hard to have new kustis ready for their families at Nowruz."

"I'll greet them." Perveen kept on meeting with every one of Behnoush's friends' daughters, hoping that somehow she would find a true friend. The girls were pleasant, but they did not make invitations for excursions or to their homes. Was it her depression that they sensed or just that she was a spoiled girl from far away?

Smiling through her nerves, Perveen presented cups of ginger-lemongrass tea to Mrs. Banaji and her daughter, Sayeh, and daughter-in-law, Touran, who each sat before a small wooden loom.

"This tea needs more sugar. Bring it!" Behnoush said after a sip.

Perveen found a sugar bowl and little spoons and went around to everyone before sitting in the room's smallest chair.

"I will tell you about kustis," Mrs. Banaji said, judgment in her eyes as she looked at Perveen. "Seventy-six strands of extremely fine wool must come together. It is very tight and strong; it cannot be broken."

"It looks like nice work to do, but I've heard I'm not the right social class." Perveen felt she'd better defend herself for not helping.

Sayeh giggled and said to the group, "Of course she wouldn't want to weave! Perveen is a real-estate heiress."

"That's not true." Perveen frowned at the smirking girl.

"She is being too modest," Behnoush said with a benevolent smile. "Mr. Mistry is a lawyer, but his father built up half of Bombay. I've seen their ancestral house."

How odd that the family affluence that Behnoush always criticized was now being exaggerated. Feeling annoyed, Perveen said, "Our ancestral house was a hut in Gujarat. Not that it could still be standing, after all these centuries."

Ignoring her comment, Sayeh Banaji said, "If the British paid your grandfather to build so much of Bombay, your family must be very rich indeed."

"A number of Indian contractors got work from the British. Grandfather was just one of them, and he was busiest in the 1870s," Perveen said. "My only close family member in the company today is my brother."

"A brother?" Mrs. Banaji's eyes lit up. "How old is he?"

"Twenty-one." Perveen could anticipate the next question.

"Married?"

"No. He must have a higher position in the firm before my parents will let him."

"Aha! Perhaps your brother will build the Sodawallas' next bottling plant and meet one of our girls. Wouldn't that be fine?"

"Oh, I'd adore it if he could come for a long visit. But Mistry Construction is only in Bombay. Imagine the difficulty in transporting cement and such—"

"Yes, yes." Mrs. Banaji's three chins nodded. "But even if they can't come, they can pay for it."

"Of course!" Behnoush smoothly slipped wool over her fingers. "The in-laws are so generous. We tell them we need nothing, but they only give more."

Perveen went rigid. "What are you talking about?"

"The new bottling plant," Behnoush said, tightening the fibers on her loom.

Perveen hadn't known about this. Behnoush's statement was likely an exaggeration. But it created a new, awful thought that the Sodawallas expected a return for their son's love match.

"What is it, Perveen? You aren't watching the weaving anymore," chided Mrs. Banaji.

"Daydreaming of her handsome husband!" Tourna giggled.

"Behnoush-mummy, have you or Bahram-pappa written to my parents about this matter of this new bottling plant?" As the words left her mouth, Perveen realized how direct they were. Everyone looked up from the looms.

Behnoush's eyes sparkled with irritation. "Let's not talk of men's business. This is a time to make friends and learn about our religious traditions."

Enough had been said, though, that Perveen finally understood. The Sodawallas had allowed Cyrus to marry her not because they recognized his love—but because of her family's money.

Now she felt frantic. Had Cyrus gone after her in the first place because Esther Vachha had dropped a comment about the Mistrys' money? She recalled the way he'd gazed up at Mistry House after they'd come out of Yazdani's. And he had brought his parents there, rather than to her family's modern duplex in Dadar Parsi Colony.

But she and Cyrus had had a love for the ages. They had connected so beautifully, with both understanding and passion.

But now what did she have to show for the marriage? A husband who thought she was shrewish. The gonorrhea infection. One quarter of every month spent in stinking solitude.

Perveen stared at her mother-in-law's loom and thought about the unseen threads that had spun around her, creating an unbreakable trap.

"Good evening, Bahram-pappa. Where is Cyrus this evening?" Perveen asked her father-in-law at seven when he came into the house alone. She was desperate to see Cyrus and clarify her fears.

"He is staying late tonight," Bahram said, taking off his fetah. Perveen put it on the high hat rack in the hallway and followed him into the parlor.

Mohit had already set a whiskey-and-soda for Bahram on the little table next to his easy chair and was winding up the gramophone. Every evening, it was her father-in-law's custom to drink his highball while listening to Beethoven. Perveen knew he preferred to enjoy this routine alone, but that night she felt a sense of urgency. She had to find out about the funding for the bottling plant.

"What is it?" Her father-in-law looked distracted.

"Bahram-daddy, excuse me, but I'm a bit nervous." Perveen

perched gingerly on the settee across from him. "I must ask you something."

Giving her an indulgent smile, he said, "Yes, my dear. But it is time for my music and drink."

"I'll be quick. When I became engaged to Cyrus, he mentioned you had taken over an existing factory."

"You are speaking of the place across the river in Howrah."

"Are you trying to build another factory?"

"Yes, in Orissa. Why so curious?"

"I wonder if you and my father chatted about building the Orissa factory."

His answer was gruff. "I'm sure we did."

Her suspicion was growing. "Did you ask my father to finance it? Or are you going to ask?"

"Ah, you would like to help," Bahram said, smiling knowingly. "Leave the business dealings and talking to me. Your work is with Mummy, isn't it? Nowruz is in a few days, and she says so much is left to do. She is too tired, and here you are chattering to me. She is the one needing your help."

"Yes, Daddy." Out of rote courtesy, she had mumbled her assent. But inside, she was boiling. She had no intention of going into the kitchen and begging Behnoush's permission to help cook. Perveen would find Cyrus.

Everyone knew it was dangerous to take a rickshaw or tonga when you were a lady on your own. One might be cheated by the driver or set upon by street criminals. But Perveen had seen the proud-looking elderly Sikh tonga-wallah several times. Saklat Place was his station; he was obviously reputable.

He had noticed her, too.

"You are the Sodawallas' new daughter-in-law," he said after she'd requested that he drive her to Howrah.

"Yes. I want to go to the bottling plant."

His expression was grave. "Your family wishes you to travel alone?"

She realized how suspicious such a journey might look. "It's only because I'm bringing something my husband needs. "

After a pause, he nodded. "I shall take you, then. When one or the other of them is away with the car, I've taken the other in my tonga. I know the place."

It was just after seven, and the moon was rising. Its pale light and flickering street lamps were the only illumination as the tonga moved steadily out of central Calcutta.

After they had crossed the bridge into Howrah, the rough, dark roads were brightened only by roadside fires. Figures were gathered outside ramshackle shelters made of cardboard and cloth.

She wasn't surprised to see a chawl established next to the Sodawallas' bottling plant. Perhaps only a few men had jobs inside, but plenty of people would seize discarded bottles for their own purposes. In fact, as the tonga passed, someone was standing on the edge of the rubble selling dark brown liquid in what she recognized as Empire raspberry soda bottles. It was probably toddy, the poor man's homemade alcohol.

The plant was a long, dark box of a building with several lit windows. Their golden glow reassured her that Cyrus very likely was at work. Although she'd flown the house on wings of anger and fear, she was beginning to calm. She'd be able to explain to Cyrus her anxiety about her parents being pressured, and he would do something about it.

The driver stopped so Perveen could address the two uniformed durwans guarding the entrance. The pair waved her through, though she imagined from their desultory air they would have allowed entry to almost anyone. She resolved to warn Cyrus about this.

The massive main door was bolted shut. Perveen banged several times, paused, and saw through the glass window an elderly servant dressed in a vest and dhoti coming forward. He unlocked the door, looking frightened as he stood before her in the scuffed wooden hall.

She realized her jaw was clenched. Now she relaxed it. "I'm here to see my husband. Mr. Cyrus Sodawalla."

"Not here!" he said, nervously bobbing his head.

Perhaps he hadn't understood her accented Bengali. Patiently, she said, "He is working late."

"Nah, nah." He shook his head with the jerky movements of a puppet.

She heard a rumble of voices through a half-open door down the hall. Ignoring the man's mutterings, she walked toward it and pushed the door open all the way.

She was inside a neat waiting room with chairs and a vacant secretary's table. A framed portrait of Cyrus smiling and holding a bottle of raspberry soda hung on the wall. A second door marked OPERATIONS MANAGER was closed.

She heard Cyrus's laugh through the door, as well as the rumble of another man's voice.

Perveen knocked sharply.

"Finally you're here!" Cyrus bellowed. The door swung open so quickly she almost fell forward. Righting herself, she stepped into Cyrus's office, moving her eyes from her jovial, rumpled husband to the rest of the room.

How different it was from her father's office. Bookcases along the walls were filled with bottles: a display of all the sodas, fruit drinks, hard liquors, beers, and medicinal drinks sold by the Sodawallas' company. Even the big desk had bottles standing on it, as well as glasses.

A typewriter stood on a desk in the corner, but surely the young woman tipped back in the chair near it could not have been anyone's secretary. She was bronze colored, about sixteen, with long hair that flowed over her filmy pink sari. Realizing she had Perveen's attention, the girl turned her head sharply, hiding her face. As the young woman shifted, she revealed the curves of a bare breast.

"My God," Perveen said. She closed her eyes for a moment, willing it not to be true. But when she looked again, the half-dressed woman was still there, along with two other people. She recognized one man slumped in a lounge chair as Cyrus's close friend Dexter Davar. The other was a Hindu named Bipin Dutta she'd briefly met at the wedding.

Bipin jumped to his feet, looking horrified, but Dexter reclined farther in his chair, drunkenly grinning.

"Perveen—what is this?" Cyrus gripped her arm with a hand like iron.

"That is my question for you." She struggled to keep her voice even. "When you opened the door to me, whom did you expect?"

"Our dinner delivery!" he said, his hot breath filling her nose with the fumes of bourbon. "Not you!"

"A delivery of food—or another woman?" Perveen had guessed that the long-haired girl came from the nearby chawl. Perhaps she was often with him in the evenings. Maybe the only reason the durwans had let Perveen through the gate was they had caught a glimpse of her and thought she was invited to the sordid gathering.

"What I do is my own affair," Cyrus slurred. "You've no right to be here or to meddle."

Still sprawled in his chair, Dexter hiccupped and said, "Oh, this is bad luck!"

"I only came because—" Perveen stopped her explanation. There was no point in addressing anything but the present. Snarling, she said, "It seems you've been selling me a lot of stories about why you're staying late at work."

"You know nothing." Cyrus's hazel eyes were on her, but they held contempt, not love.

Perveen broke their mutual gaze to inspect the female stranger, whose face was crumpled in terror. "Is she the one who gifted you with venereal disease? Or did you invite her for the first time tonight, which means you'll soon infect her?"

His eyes shone with rage. "May you die."

"Mrs. Sodawalla, please calm yourself," Bipin interjected. "This person came on her own. Your husband did not request her—"

"Don't lie for him." Perveen turned back toward Cyrus, thinking she'd never been angrier in her life. Inside, she was truly boiling; not just with rage but humiliation.

Cyrus's face was flushed a deep red, and his words were menacing. "You should have kept your mouth shut."

Out of the corner of her eye, Perveen noticed the young woman had left her chair and was sidling toward the door. Sharply, Perveen called out, "Get to a doctor before it's—"

Too late, she would have said, but she was knocked backward with a blow from Cyrus.

He had bashed her across the nose and cheekbones. Perveen staggered back a few paces. But there was no time to recover; in the next moment, Cyrus leaned in and punched her in the eye.

Pain exploded in her brow as she collapsed against a bookcase, which rocked hard. The display bottles began falling, and she felt them crashing into her back like rocks as she lay on the floor, the sharpness of breaking glass followed by the cool of spilled alcohol. As she shielded her wounded face with her arm from the tumbling bottles, she was dimly aware of shouting and the sounds of a scuffle. Bipin Dutta was trying to pull Cyrus away from her.

"Don't do it, man—you're insane," Bipin said. "Her father's a lawyer—"

"She's my wife," Cyrus roared. "I'll do what's needed."

She was throbbing with hurt. She struggled up to a sitting position, and as she put her hands on the floor, broken glass sliced into them.

"You bastard!" she screamed, unleashing all her rage at Cyrus. "You never loved me, did you? It was all about money."

She felt a tug on her arm and realized that the drunken other friend, Dexter, was pulling her up. In Gujarati, he said, "You shouldn't have come. Please go now—"

Cyrus broke free from Bipin's hold and was coming for her again. Dexter reached out to delay him. As the three men grappled, Perveen moved from a kneeling position up to standing. Her sari had come loose in the fall. She pulled the silk around her, trying to protect some modesty as she limped out.

The tonga-wallah sprang to his feet when he saw her coming slowly out of the building. "Memsahib! What has happened? I must send those durwans to call for the constables!"

"Please don't call anyone." Her voice came out like a croak. "Just take me back."

"To home, then?"

Coughing, she said, "Yes. As quickly as you can."

As the driver cracked the whip on the horse's back, she flinched, reliving the pain of Cyrus's attack. He'd kissed her goodbye that morning. She knew now that it had been the last time.

As they rode past the chawl, she wondered if the young prostitute had run back to her home—or the man who'd sent her out. If she hadn't gotten the pay from Cyrus tonight, she might get it tomorrow. Perveen didn't care what happened between the two of them; she would never speak to Cyrus again.

"It's not safe for women at night," the tonga driver muttered. "Not safe anywhere! Your husband and father must catch the villain who did this. Did you see his face?"

She was too spent to tell the driver anything. And she wouldn't tell Bahram or Behnoush either. Like tree, like fruit. They had made their son into a weak, corrupt man.

Perveen asked the driver to wait for her a few doors down from the Sodawallas' home while she went in to get money. "Don't return to your station because we're going to drive again. I just need to go inside for a quick stop."

"Will we go to the hospital?" he asked anxiously.

"No. Sealdah station." She paused, thinking of the many things that could go wrong. "If I'm not out in five minutes, knock on the door and ask for me. Tell the bearer it's an emergency."

"An emergency." Slowly, the driver repeated the English word she'd just taught him.

Gita opened the door just as Perveen approached. The maid's hands flew to her mouth at the sight of Perveen's injuries. Ignoring her, Perveen walked straight into the hallway and toward the stairs.

Behnoush must have heard the door opening because she rose to her feet and came out into the hall from the parlor.

"Arre marere!" she exclaimed. "What is this?"

Perveen didn't answer because she was intent on getting what she needed and escaping before Cyrus arrived. He had the car—he could be back any minute.

As Perveen rushed past, a few blood drops spattered the floor. Catching sight of this, Behnoush moaned. "You are soiled! What happened?"

"I'm sorry," Perveen said stiffly. She realized that if the truth of the evening's circumstances came out, Behnoush might never be able to convince another family to provide a replacement bride.

Behnoush began weeping. "Why, why? Why do you go out like that? Why are you leaking blood everywhere? You know the rules!"

Was she mad?

Bahram's voice called from the dining room. "What is that racket?"

Perveen wanted the two of them together and away from her. Clearing her throat, she said, "I'm not well. I must go upstairs."

"Yes, but clean yourself. And it's better if you go to the little room."

Behnoush probably thought a stranger had raped Perveen. Stifling her desire to scream out that the cuts and bruises were Cyrus's work, she answered obediently. "Of course I will go there. I'm only stopping in my room for my diary."

"All right. I will send Gita later with food."

Perveen went straight up to her room. But instead of just reaching for her notebook, she grabbed a shawl from the almirah and wrapped it around her shoulders. She pulled out a small valise from underneath the almirah and stuffed in all her spending money and her jewelry—all the treasures her parents had given her and the wedding bangles from the Sodawallas.

Thinking again, she opened it and removed the ivory bangles, laying them out on the bureau. She would let her in-laws keep the expensive shackles.

She snapped the valise closed and came downstairs, not wanting to be seen.

Bahram's loud voice on the telephone could be overheard. "You saw her tonight? She did—what?"

She was just stepping into her sandals when Behnoush rushed out and saw her. "What is this? You cannot go out. You are dripping blood! What will people think?"

"You don't need to worry about those things anymore," Perveen said evenly. "Tell Cyrus I've gone back to Bombay—and not to bother me again."

As she left, Perveen stepped firmly into the stenciled chalk border, smearing her delicate powdered designs into dust.

1921

17

BLACK FINGERPRINTS
Bombay, February 1921

At the Farid bungalow, Perveen sat on a rosewood chair and watched Sub-Inspector K. J. Singh shake black powder across the floor.

The dark powder, late afternoon heat, and the stench of blood had brought up memories of the Sodawallas' home: both the horrible little room and the foyer where she had stenciled for hours over the months.

What was going on now felt like a nightmare. And although Perveen might avert her eyes from Faisal Mukri's body, she felt a duty to remain.

Knowing her father would expect her to report on every detail of the situation, Perveen had asked to stay. It was a nervy thing to do, and Perveen had been surprised that the sub-inspector had allowed her to linger. As the fingerprinting continued, she realized her presence gave the sub-inspector a chance to show off. After all, his boss hadn't yet arrived, and she was the first female lawyer he'd ever met.

Sub-Inspector Singh had swiftly dispersed the thick black powder over everything: the marble floor, the walls, and the furniture. He was making a mess of this elegant old house, but she supposed it couldn't be avoided. She studied the junior police officer, who wore a neatly trimmed beard and had an impressively large dark-green turban. Unlike ordinary Indian constables, who wore blue tunics with pantaloons, the sub-inspector wore the crisp white uniform of jacket and trousers of the Imperial Police.

The golden-brown bridle-leather briefcase, which had originally been underneath Mr. Mukri's body, now lay blackened with powder. She eyed it, wondering how she'd be able to convince the sub-inspector to return it. As one of very few Indians in police administration, he would probably not want to give the impression he would cut another Indian a favor.

"Are you finding many impressions?" Perveen asked in a friendly tone.

He gave her a supercilious look. "I was trained in Calcutta in the Henry Fingerprint Classification System. I don't suppose you know that fingerprinting science began in India?"

"I didn't know," she said honestly. "About how many fingerprints are on file in Bombay?"

"Over forty-five thousand," he said with pride. "In these times, whenever a man is arrested, his fingerprints are taken."

"Are there only criminals' fingerprints on record?"

"Not exactly. Almost every sweeper and guard is requested to let us take impressions. We saw no guard at the gate. That is already suspicious. My inspector, Mr. R. H. Vaughan, will certainly pursue him."

Feeling jittery, Perveen tried not to concentrate on her private suppositions that at least one of the women on the other side of the screen might have been involved with Mukri's death. She was supposed to defend them, not throw them to the wolves.

Perveen studied the hallway, wondering if she might notice something important. She surveyed everything: the floral mosaics on the walls that bore splatters of the blood, the velvet stool that was knocked over, and the open door to a bedroom.

Perhaps this was where Mr. Mukri had slept. As Sub-Inspector Singh kept dusting, she got up and entered the room. The handsome bed was neatly made with a red silk quilt; on marble-topped tables on either side, there were crystal goblets.

A slight hissing sound caught her attention. She followed it to a closed door, which she pushed open to discover that behind it was a bathroom with a marble tub. She'd heard the faint noise of taps not closed all the way, judging from the moisture beading up on a long rust stain inside the tub.

"Where have you gone?" Sub-Inspector Singh's voice was sharp and close behind her.

Perveen felt like a child in trouble. "I'm sorry. I did not know this was off-limits."

"Touching the door ruins fingerprints! There may be evidence here."

Perveen looked at the trickling tap. She could have pointed it out to him. However, she was not legally obligated to assist; and if she became involved in the defense of anyone within the household, tipping the detective about anything could have disastrous implications. Still, she wanted to foster a good relationship; there were many things a lawyer could learn from the police. This was why her father—the next person she'd telephoned after she'd rung the police—was downstairs with the two constables.

"My inspector will want to know what was taken," Sub-Inspector Singh said. "This will be difficult indeed, since the three widows live on the other side. What can they tell us?"

Perveen was pleased to have a way to redeem herself. "Our law firm has a written record of some of the household's most important assets. I believe we can share such information to assist in your investigation."

Singh looked appraisingly at her. "When can you give it?"

"Perhaps tomorrow. But I'll need my briefcase. It's the one lying against the wall—"

"You own a man's briefcase?" He looked disbelievingly from her to the case.

"It's mine!" she bleated, feeling desperate. "I can tell you that it was manufactured by Swaine Adeney of England and has my initials stamped on it. PJM."

He shuffled over to the briefcase and lifted it up for inspection. "Why would your briefcase be with the deceased?"

Perveen took a deep breath. If she wasn't careful, she could turn his suspicion on herself. "I misplaced it when I was visiting earlier today. I'd come on a routine visit that dealt with the estate settlement. The late Omar Farid was originally my father's client, and now I'm helping, because the wives will speak to me."

Sub-Inspector Singh handed her the case. "You may have it, then. But will you tell me if anything's missing?"

"Thank you. I'll look right now."

Perveen shook off her worries about being considered culpable along with the black dust covering the case. Her notebook, a Bombay street guide, three pens, twenty rupees, and some odd paisa coins were still inside. The mahr and wakf papers showed signs of rifling. Mr. Mukri had looked. Not that it mattered anymore.

"Nothing's been taken. Not even the small amount of money I always carry," she said.

"Any thief would have taken the case. It looks expensive—" He broke off at the sound of Jamshedji's voice booming from downstairs.

"My apologies, madam, but this area is not open for visitation! It is under police protection."

"Is that so?" drawled a recognizable female voice. "Then what about your presence, sir? You're too nattily dressed to be a constable."

Sub-Inspector Singh gave Perveen a comradely glance and muttered, "Those Angrez. Everywhere they should not be."

"It sounds like my father needs help." Briefcase in hand, Perveen hurried down the main staircase.

Alice was dressed in a white linen frock that was not only creased but also stained with red dust. She goggled at the sight of Perveen. "Perveen! How did you get here?"

"I'll ask the same of you!" She laughed, trying to sound amused—although she wasn't. It was an inconvenient time for Alice to blunder in.

"I was coming back from sightseeing on Elephanta Island when I saw the hubbub. The whole street's up in arms."

"Even so, that is no reason to enter another person's property," Jamshedji said icily.

"Pappa, she is my closest college friend, Alice Hobson-Jones," Perveen interjected because as annoyed as she was about the interruption, she didn't want Alice to feel rejected. "She lives just around the corner."

"So you're the famous Jamshedji Mistry, Esquire!" Alice beamed as if she was intent on ignoring his unfriendly reception. "Perveen has told me loads about you. Actually, I only came because of the commotion. Our guards said a police cart went by—the kind that is used to carry bodies."

"I regret to say that the information is correct," Jamshedji said stiffly as he shook Alice's outstretched hand. "A gentleman from this house has passed away."

Alice gasped. "But I thought the nawab died some time ago!"

Father and daughter exchanged glances. At Jamshedji's nod of permission, Perveen spoke. "Alice, you are correct that the householder, Mr. Omar Farid, died last month—although he was a businessman, not a nawab. The gentleman who died today was the family's household agent and guardian."

"How ghastly," Alice said. "Was he killed defending the widows and children? What a hero he must have been!"

"We don't know specifics," Jamshedji said in the patient voice he employed with foreigners. "That is a matter for police deduction. And now, Miss Hobson-Jones, if you don't mind—"

"But Mr. Mistry, can you tell me, were the ladies and children harmed?" Alice persisted.

"They're fine," Perveen said. "I've been inside the zenana section to check on them." Although there hadn't been time to talk.

"Perveen, perhaps you and Miss Hobson-Jones could visit with each other later?"

Jamshedji's discomfort was obvious to Perveen. The sudden interloper was a social superior who could cause all manner of trouble. Perveen would put him at ease later; for now, she'd do as he asked.

Perveen walked out to the garden with Alice.

"Why didn't you tell me that you already knew my mysterious neighbors?" Alice grumbled. "We looked down at the garden together, and you didn't say a word!"

"I didn't know you were such close neighbors until I visited your parents' house, and I'm duty bound to protect my clients' privacy," Perveen said, putting an arm through one of Alice's. "My father only said as much as he did because you'd arrived and there seemed no way to keep it hidden. But do be quiet about it to others."

Alice rolled her eyes heavenward. "I shall. But does this gag order preclude me from telling you what I think?"

"Speak, but in a lower voice," Perveen whispered. "There are open ears on the other side of the wall."

Alice regarded the high property wall with its spiked glass topping and winced. "All right. Mother says that whenever there's a murder in India, one can count on the evildoer being a disgruntled servant."

Mohsen was still missing from his station; however, Perveen refused to engage in typical prejudices and didn't want Alice to absorb them. "Here's what I think. Because there are so many more poor people in India than rich people, they receive most of the convictions. Their fate is decided by judges who come from the elite."

"I hadn't thought of that," Alice said, looking a bit shamefaced. "Whoever it was, I hope that he or she is caught. Do you see how fair-minded I can be?"

"I do."

"Will you come to the bungalow after you're finished here?"

"Your mother said yesterday you'd be busy tonight."

"I've got that thing where your legs are still rolling the day after you've been at sea. I tripped in the caves; that's why I look such a mess."

Perveen hesitated because, although she would have liked to talk about everything with Alice, it would be difficult to resist saying too much. "I'll have to see what my father thinks."

"It was his suggestion!" Alice said heatedly.

Perhaps. But her father had no idea how hard Alice was likely to press her about the case's details. And after all the truth telling that she and Alice had gone through over the years, Perveen wasn't sure how much she could deny her.

18

THE SOUND OF MURDER
Bombay, February 1921

*P*erveen bid a restrained goodbye to Alice at the gate, where one constable was holding back a cluster of neighbors and tradesmen who had come to inquire about the presence of the police car. As Perveen began a quick walk back to the bungalow, the Farids' young maid ran after her, calling out her name.

Perveen stopped. "What is it, Fatima?"

"Can you tell the police to bring back my Abba?" she said between sobs. "The policemen took him."

Perveen was staggered by this new information. "But—I didn't see him when he arrived. And the sub-inspector was still taking fingerprints."

"Others came. A white man. I think he's the one who ordered the constables to take him. But it's all my fault!"

Perveen felt a mix of emotions. First was great relief that a perpetrator had been caught, which meant the widows would be safe. But Fatima's tear-stained face moved her, and the haste of the arrest made her skeptical.

"Tell me what happened."

"They came to me and grabbed my hands. They pushed them into black ink. I washed and washed, and I cannot get rid of the marks."

Examining the girl's stained fingertips, Perveen said, "They might have fingerprinted because you're the only one who goes on both sides of the house. They must distinguish you from the person who attacked Mr. Mukri. It doesn't mean you are considered guilty."

"I would rather have them take me than take Abba," she wailed. "Who will take care of Zeid?"

"Please try to calm yourself. What did the constables ask you?"

"They asked if I saw Abba go into the house, and I said yes—remember, he came to save you when Mukri-sahib was shouting. But then he was gone. He only just came back and they surrounded him and wouldn't let me near. Then they took him!"

"I need to know more. In the last hour, did you hear anything unusual?"

"They asked that, too. I told them the truth: I couldn't hear anything but Jum-Jum crying. He is getting a tooth." She shifted from one small bare foot to the other. "Could you please come back to the zenana? The begums are terribly upset. The nasty white policeman is still here."

It dawned on Perveen that the man was likely Sub-Inspector Singh's boss—Inspector Vaughan. Perveen told Fatima to go to her brother. Then she walked to the doorway of the zenana, where she found a short Englishman in his late twenties at the closed door. He was hammering it with his fists.

"Namaste!" he shouted in a manner that had little to do with the word's meaning. It was also a Hindu greeting not used with Muslims.

"Good afternoon, sir!" Perveen said in English. "I'm afraid—"

The man whirled around and gaped at her. "Farid-begum?"

Holding out her hand, she said, "My name is Perveen Mistry."

He didn't take her hand, but he peered accusingly at her with bulging blue eyes. "Do you have any association with the Parsi gentleman who's bothering my constables?"

Coolly, Perveen said, "I'm the daughter of Mr. Jamshedji Abbas Mistry, and we practice together at Mistry Law. Are you Inspector Vaughan?"

"Chief Inspector Vaughan." He squinted at her suspiciously. "I didn't know lady vakils existed."

"I'm a solicitor, not a vakil." Taking out her handkerchief to dry off her palms, Perveen tried to sound pleasanter. "I don't know if my father mentioned that the widows who live here are pur-dahnashins. They would feel violated if they had to face you in an interview. They have very limited contact with men."

"One would think they'd wish to relax the rules to capture a murder suspect," he grumbled.

"Typically the custom is for men with a valid need to speak with them through a screen," she said crisply.

"I've been hammering this door for ten minutes and am on the verge of breaking it down. I won't have to do it if you'd convince them to speak with me."

Perveen paused, reading the anxiety in the detective's red face. Since Mohsen had been taken into custody, it was unlikely that Vaughan thought one of the widows had killed Mr. Mukri. However, they were all potential witnesses, given that they had been on the scene. And it would be safer for them if she met privately with them first.

"I'd be very glad to help, Inspector Vaughan, but I can tell you that they will be more candid if I talk to them alone. Would you like me to ask what they might have seen or heard?"

"Naturally," he said, sounding slightly mollified. "Do you know where Faisal Mukri's family lives?"

She shook her head. "Sorry. Mr. Mukri was a bachelor and employed at Farid Fabrics, so management may have a family record."

"And there's the matter of the watchman. The little maidservant told Singh that he was briefly in the house and then went on an errand. But she's his daughter, so he could have made her lie for him. I can't see a reason for a bungalow watchman to leave his post to run errands," he added with a snort.

"I'll do my best with the ladies," Perveen reassured him. "Will you be on the other side of the house?"

Vaughan blinked, as if she'd startled him. Perhaps he wasn't used to being questioned by Indians. "Yes. I'll be at the death scene with the coroner."

Fans whirred quietly on the ceiling of the downstairs great room where Sakina sat against the bolsters. The second widow's head was bent over the embroidery piece she was working on. Razia's daughter, Amina, appeared to be reading a book.

Soft chanting could be heard from the small side room.

"Razia is praying," Sakina said, tilting her head toward the room where Perveen had admired the mihrab. "I have prayed already with my daughters. Razia wished for Amina to pray, but she has not done it."

Amina's lips were pressed together, and her eyes had a dull look. Perveen longed to embrace her but knew better. She'd learned about the power structure of the zenana and didn't want to usurp Sakina's role.

"Sakina-begum, shall we go upstairs to talk?" Perveen asked.

Sakina looked up, revealing reddened eyes. "I want to stay near my children. They are just outside in the garden now, with Taiba-ayah. After what happened, I want to be near them."

For all Sakina's concerns about her children, Perveen wondered at the widow's decision to sit inside and leave the ayah caring for them. She suspected this was the custom, just as Sakina chose not to have the little ones stay with her in her elegant private bedroom. Perveen hadn't even seen Jum-Jum yet. Clearing her throat, she said, "I'm so sorry this happened. I wonder, if I'd stayed with you this afternoon, it might have deterred whoever did it."

"We shall never know," Sakina said, wiping at her eyes. "I keep thinking, what would my husband say if he knew the man he appointed guardian died protecting me and all the others?"

"My poor father," Amina said in a whisper.

"They will be in heaven together." Sakina reached out to stroke the girl's hair. A loving gesture, but Amina moved away.

Perveen told Sakina about Mr. Vaughan's arrival and how he wished to know if she'd heard or seen anything unusual.

Sakina gave her a rueful look. "What could we possibly see when we are on the secluded side of the bungalow? And we can't hear much except for what's right under our windows."

"It's possible to see into the main reception room," Perveen said, remembering the shape she'd spotted before.

"The girls sometimes take turns peeking from the shoe cabinet," Sakina said. "But neither they nor I were downstairs after you departed us."

"Mohsen wasn't at his post. Do you've any idea why?"

"After you departed, I had such a bad headache that I asked Fatima to see if he could go to the market and fetch some attar for me." Sakina touched her hand to the side of her head. Perveen noted the widow had loosened her hair from the elegant topknot she'd worn before, and her long inky-black hair was wet and hung straight down to her waist. "I went to lie down. Do you think Mohsen's absence led to this crime?"

"Of course!" Amina said emphatically. "If nobody is guarding the gate, anyone could come in. And you are always sending him on this errand and that. We hardly have a guard at all."

"Don't be insolent!" Sakina scolded.

"It's nobody's fault," Perveen said hastily, because Sakina's hand had come up as if ready to slap the girl. "The police will surely need to know that Mohsen was away on official business, so thank you, Sakina-begum. Amina, it would be most helpful if you could tell me anything you heard outside of the ordinary. I promised the police I'd ask."

"I'm sure I heard a scream," Amina's answer came readily.

"When?" Perveen was eager to hear more.

"About a half hour after you left. I was in the garden with the other two, putting away Mumtaz-khala's musical instruments because she was feeling poorly. I heard this scream. I didn't know who it was."

"There is plenty of yelling on the street when merchants come through selling their wares," Sakina said. "Perhaps it was one of them."

"I think I knew it was a man's voice—but the shout didn't sound like selling," Amina said. "It sounded scary. But the others were chattering, so they didn't notice it."

Sakina's expression tightened, as if Amina's description had worried her. "I heard nothing because I was resting in my room. You are a good girl, Amina, to help Perveen-bibi."

"I shall tell the police what you've said, and they may want to know more." Perveen saw the tension on Sakina's face. "What is it?"

She shook her head. "This is such a terrible shock. I just can't imagine how we are going to manage life by ourselves. And we haven't got our money yet from the estate. That is your job, isn't it?"

"I'm sorry for the delay," Perveen apologized, knowing that she had worked intermittently on the papers since December. "I was waiting for Mukri-sahib to provide me with creditors' names. I'll do it without him." She paused, not knowing how the next part could come out without offending the child. "Amina, I beg your pardon, but I need to speak privately with Sakina-begum for a few moments."

Amina gave the two of them a look that was almost venomous. "And why can't I be part of it? A man died. Do you think I won't notice?"

"There are things that are too much for someone your age," Perveen said gently.

"Very well then," Amina said. "I'm going upstairs. There's something I need to see."

"Your mother wouldn't like to know you're behaving like this," Sakina told the girl.

Perveen watched Amina tread the stairs up to the second floor, imagining the child would fit herself into some hidey-hole to keep listening. Turning back to Sakina, Perveen lowered her voice. "I heard your voice coming from Razia-begum's room a few hours ago. What were you talking about?"

Sakina's eyes flashed with surprise. "You went upstairs on your own, without us knowing?"

Her question made Perveen realize that her own behavior could look suspicious. Trying not to sound defensive, she said, "I was looking for my briefcase; that was all."

There was a rustle of silk, and Perveen looked up to find Razia had come from her prayers. Her face was drawn into long lines of exhaustion, and her eyes seemed sunken and despairing.

"My condolences to you, Razia-begum." Perveen felt awkward uttering the rote phrase. Faisal Mukri had come into Razia's life and made it awful. The sympathy Perveen offered was a response to the shock Razia had suffered—and the fear of violence she would perhaps live with for the rest of her life.

"I can answer the question about our conversation," Razia said soberly. "This afternoon, Amina looked through the slot in the jali and saw a man lying in blood. She came running to tell Sakina because her room was closest. She told Sakina that the dead man was Mukri-sahib. Sakina told me and I called Mumtaz to join us."

Perveen wasn't surprised that Amina knew what Mr. Mukri looked like. The girl had surely peeked through the jali at him. She had probably been the one watching Perveen through the shoe case the previous day. But if Amina had spied Mr. Mukri's corpse, why hadn't she mentioned this to Perveen? Amina had spoken of hearing a scream—but not encountering a horrific sight.

"I was shocked and thought Amina could have been wrong," Sakina said, cutting into Perveen's thoughts. "Just because the man was dressed in an English suit, it didn't mean he was our household agent. He could have been some enemy from the outside. To answer any doubts, I said we should have Fatima look. She has served him before, so she would know his appearance."

Razia sat down, giving the second wife a reproving look. "I didn't agree with that. Amina was very upset, and I said that no other child in the house should see such a bloody death. I suggested Mohsen should go to look because he is a man accustomed to the hardness of the world. Sakina said he could not go because she'd sent him shopping."

Perveen noted the contempt in Razia's voice, although Sakina did not visibly react. Perveen asked, "Did you consider calling the police and asking them to make the identification?"

"To make that telephone call, we would have had to go downstairs and into the main house." Razia dropped her gaze to her lap. "That was frightening because we did not know if the murderer was still on the property."

"We did the first thing that came to my mind: taking our children into our private rooms and locking the doors," Sakina said, shivering as she spoke. "We stayed until we heard the sounds of police arriving. Did you call them?"

"I did," Perveen acknowledged. "Now, I'm wondering something:

Do you have any knowledge of trouble between Mohsen and Mr. Mukri?"

"I have not heard of any trouble," Razia said. "Mohsen used to work for Farid Fabrics on the docks, but my husband shifted him to this job at the house when his wife died, because this was a safer place for children without a mother to grow up. We could direct them, as could Taiba-ayah. In the six years we've had Mohsen, I've spoken to him through the jali just a few times. Usually Fatima is the go-between."

"Perhaps you should ask Mumtaz. She was acquainted with Mukri-sahib when he went with our husband to see her on Falkland Road." As Sakina mentioned the name of the entertainment district, she raised her eyebrows, as if to remind both of the third wife's unsavory past.

Mumtaz's absence from their conference seemed to be another example of how she lived on the edge of the family's framework. Perveen said, "Before I speak with Mumtaz, tell me which relative you'd like to come and stay."

Sakina was silent for a long moment and then shook her head. "My brothers are doing business in Poona, so it is impossible. I don't believe I can suggest anyone."

"Really?" Perveen was surprised because Sakina had such a dominant role in the house. "I am speaking of any relatives who could give company and also assist with needs you have. Or perhaps a good friend?"

Looking tiredly at Perveen, Razia said, "The situation is a bit difficult because of Mumtaz."

"How so?" Perveen asked.

"Our families look down on women who go about the world—and even more so on those who have entertained men," Sakina said bluntly. "They believe to stay in the same bungalow with her would soil them. That is why we've had very few social callers in the last year. Our husband made a choice that has affected this house forever."

If this was the way both women felt, Perveen wondered if they had ever tried to convince Mumtaz to leave.

Razia's raspy voice interrupted Perveen's thoughts. "Allah must be looking kindly on her for the care she gave our husband. She has nothing to do anymore. That's why I suggested she teach the children to play music."

"Do you have a suggestion for the next household agent?" Perveen asked Razia.

"My people are even farther than Sakina's. They have an agricultural estate in Oudh. Amina enjoys them very much—we last visited two years ago. But it just isn't possible for anyone to shift here."

"Are there friends in Bombay who could come?" The two remained silent. "If you can't think of anyone, I'll ask Mumtaz-begum for a suggestion."

Razia's eyes widened, and Sakina gave a small exclamation of dismay.

"Yes," Perveen said. "Please think some more about who you'd like to have visit."

Maintaining a hard silence, Sakina guided Perveen upstairs to Mumtaz's room.

It took several knocks before Mumtaz responded. The room was dark, with curtains drawn across the jalis, and the air held a thick, musty odor.

"Please turn on a light," Mumtaz whispered from the rumpled bed where she lay.

"I see you're still not feeling well," Perveen said, moving to the bed to take Mumtaz's hand. "Shall I call a doctor?"

"No need. I was feeling better," Mumtaz murmured. "This will pass in some hours."

"I heard from the others that Mukri-sahib's body was discovered before I came to the house and called for the police. Apparently the three of you talked about there being a body on the other side."

Mumtaz pulled the sheet closer around her body, as if shielding herself from Perveen. "Sakina-begum wanted me to look through the jali, because I'm the only one who's seen his face. But I wouldn't."

"Why not?"

"To look on a dead man would bring the worst misfortune to future generations!" Mumtaz said vehemently. "I would not risk it!"

If the belief was true, Perveen thought it just as well she'd been the one to see Mukri. She would never bear any children. "What did you do after Mukri-sahib interrupted us in the garden?"

She shuddered and said, "It was just dreadful. I was so frightened I ran to my quarters and then went to take a bath."

"A bath?" Perveen found that hard to believe. It seemed like an indulgent act, in the midst of a storm. But both Sakina and Razia had retreated to their rooms.

"While I'm in the bathroom, nobody will bother me. It is too far from the hallway," she added.

"I'll tell the police where you were. However, can you recall any kind of noise or commotion in the time before the other wives called you for the discussion?"

"No. The bathroom is close to the outside garden. I hear only birds from that place and sometimes people in the street."

Perveen caught an inconsistency. "How did you hear the other widows call you for the discussion, then?"

"Amina came into my room and knocked on the bathroom door."

"Thank you for your explanation." Perveen considered her next words carefully. "Can you think of anyone trustworthy to come here as a household guardian?"

"Must we have a new man staying here?" Mumtaz sounded alarmed. "Who will choose him so we don't have such a terrible time again?"

"It doesn't have to be a man. However, unless one of you decide to give up purdah, you will require someone to get money from the bank and deal with merchants and other officials. I will help as best I can, but I regret to say I cannot stay here as a household guardian."

After a pause, Mumtaz said, "I have a sister who is married; her husband is a good man who makes his living building sitars and veenas. I think they would gladly come. But the other wives would never allow it."

"A lady with a husband sounds like a good idea," Perveen

reassured her. "And neither Sakina-begum nor Razia-begum have made suggestions yet, so I will bring this to them."

Shyly, Mumtaz said, "If they are willing, I would like to speak to my sister Tanvier. Can you send word to her to come?"

"If you give me her name and address, I'll send a messenger."

Mumtaz gave her an address, which she duly wrote down. Then Mumtaz said, "It's all so frightening, to have had this happen. I can't think how someone could have entered the bungalow without Mohsen stopping him."

"Mohsen was away from the gate running an errand for Sakina-begum," Perveen said.

"He does that for us," Mumtaz said, nodding. "Always keeps a bit of the money for himself—the service fee. But what choice do we have?"

The widows had lived a life at the mercy of men who were supposed to serve them, Perveen thought as she left Mumtaz and emerged into the dappled light of the zenana hallway. She walked slowly down the hall and descended the stairs. Fatima was there, apparently waiting for her.

"What is it?" Perveen asked. "Is your brother all right?"

Looking about as if to make sure no one was watching, Fatima whispered, "Yes, I told him you would help us. Razia-begum wants to speak to you alone."

The timing wasn't good; Perveen wanted to tell Vaughan the brief reports she'd received from all of the women. "I shall be back to speak with her in just a bit—"

"But Razia-begum must see you now. She's waiting in your car."

"Inside my car?" Perveen was stunned. Did Razia want to leave the bungalow—and if so, would she take Amina?

"I suggested the car to her because it's parked so very close to the zenana entrance."

"But my driver doesn't know about the customs of ladies in purdah!"

"He's not there," Fatima said quickly. "I went out to that driver and said your father needed to speak with him. He went in the bungalow. When he returns, I shall tell him you are inside and ask him to stay away until called for."

"How clever," Perveen said, patting Fatima's small shoulder. Despite her youth, she was a master of subterfuge. But then again, such a talent could prove suspicious.

Razia was in the back seat of the Daimler with the window rolled up. Perveen peered in from the other side of the passenger row, watching the widow's bent head and her moving lips. Her eyes were closed, and it looked as if she was whispering a prayer. A veil covered much of her head and face. Perveen supposed it was for protection against the gaze of Arman and any other men who might come by.

Perveen tapped on the glass, not wanting to startle her by suddenly opening a door. "It's only me. Shall I come in?"

Razia turned toward the window and nodded.

Perveen opened the car door and spoke in a whisper. "This car is very warm. May I roll down my window? Nobody else is nearby."

"Are you certain?"

Perveen turned all the way around to survey the scene. Arman had come out of the main house but was sitting on the step, too far away to see or hear them. "It's all right. Tell me, did you come out to my car because you want me to take you and Amina away?"

"No. I've something to tell you that I didn't before."

Razia's face was drenched in perspiration—either from the warmth of the car or her emotion. Perveen's suspicion of some connection between her and Mukri's death was growing.

Looking sick, Razia murmured, "I've come because I want to confess. Tell the police not to question anyone else about Mukri-sahib's killing. I am the one who did it."

19

THE GUARDIAN'S SCHEME
Bombay, February 1921

Perveen took a deep breath, allowing herself time to respond to Razia's shocking announcement. Razia certainly had motivation to want the household agent dead—but it seemed unbelievable that she'd have had the strength and skill to carry out the heinous act.

"To whom did you tell this?" Perveen asked, hoping against hope she hadn't spilled to Amina.

"Nobody."

"All right, then." Perveen tried to sound calm as she opened up her briefcase and took out her notebook. She was sitting in her own car with a confessed killer; this was something many lawyers had experienced. "Let's make a timeline together. It was about three-thirty when Mukri-sahib interrupted my consultation with Mumtaz-begum. Where were you?"

Her words tumbled out. "I was with Amina on our veranda. We overheard what he yelled at you through the jali into the garden."

"He was quite put out," Perveen said, giving her a half smile. "After departing the zenana, I went to the main entrance and told Zeid I had come to speak with Mukri-sahib."

Razia's eyes widened. "But weren't you afraid?"

"I wasn't thinking about myself. I was quite worried he might take out his anger on the three of you. I tried to remind him it was my duty to your husband to explain your assets to you, and also the way that mahr and the wakf operate. But my words did not calm him, so I left." She would not tell Razia that Mukri had almost struck her. That would make her seem vulnerable when she needed to appear strong.

"So, it must have been very soon after you left that Mukri-sahib rang the bell on the second floor." At Perveen's puzzled expression, Razia explained, "There's a bell on either side of the jali; it's a way to tell someone to come there to speak."

"How would you know who was being called?"

"Fatima's job is to go and hear whom he is requesting. I heard the bell, but I stayed inside my rooms praying he wasn't calling for me. But Fatima came and told me I'd been chosen." She swallowed hard and then added, "I was sick with fear. The jali screen is really a door with a lock, and I was sure he had the key."

Perveen felt a cold finger of dread at this knowledge. "Had he ever gone through?"

She shrugged. "Not that I know of. In the old days, the jali stayed closed but was not locked. Our husband walked through, and we also went to the other side if there were no other gentlemen visiting the house."

"I understand. What happened next?" Perveen settled deep into the car seat, getting herself in the right position to observe any changes in Razia's expression.

"When I came to the screen, I could see the shadow of his figure on the other side. He asked why I'd changed my position about donating my mahr to the wakf. I dared not say what I really felt—that I didn't want him using our wakf funds." Razia sucked in air, as if she needed it to go on. "That man told me that I had proved myself incapable and said I must write a letter resigning from being a mutawalli. I was to write that I'd lost my ability to think well following my husband's death."

Mukri had landed on insanity, one of the few reasons a mutawalli could be taken from their job. Even if Razia didn't sign such a statement, he could solicit accounts from others defaming her. "How did you respond?"

"I said I needed to think, and that such a letter would take time to write. Then he warned me if the paper wasn't ready within the hour, he would . . ." Razia shook her head. "I can't even say it!"

"Tell me.'"

In a wavering voice, the widow continued. "He said if I didn't give him the paper, he would go straight to Falkland Road and find a husband for Amina."

The prospect was horrifying, but it was within Mr. Mukri's rights as the household agent to arrange marriages for any of the females in the family—the daughters as well as the widows. Shaking her head, Perveen said, "What a dreadful threat."

"And while I was standing there—feeling so dead inside—he told me he was through with talking to me. He wanted me to bring Mumtaz to speak with him. Surely he had some terrible plan in store for her, too." Razia moistened her lips and looked nervously at Perveen. "She was lying asleep in her bed. I spoke several times, but she would not get up. I left, thinking that I had enough to worry about."

Mukri could have told the illiterate Mumtaz to draw an X on a statement about Razia's mental infirmity. Perveen wouldn't have put anything past him. The only question nagging at her was why someone as intelligent as Mr. Farid would have hired such a loathsome man to care for his family. But she wouldn't interrupt Razia, who was now speaking freely.

"I went out, and as I turned into the next hallway, I saw my daughter. She'd heard everything Mukri-sahib had said to me and was terrified at the prospect of being taken for marriage. She wouldn't let me near her—she rushed out to the garden in tears." Razia wiped her own eyes as she spoke. "I went to my desk. All I had to do was write a simple statement giving up duties as the mutawalli. I didn't want to do it, but I realized that if I angered him, he might seek revenge."

"That is correct. He could still have married off Amina, and he might have even had you committed to an asylum." It was a shocking, terrifying prospect. Perveen thought back to her recent conversation with Amina and wondered why the child hadn't mentioned this as well.

"So I had an idea." Razia looked steadily at her. "It was an immoral idea but the only way to save Amina and all of us. I decided to deceive him into believing that I had prepared the statement for him. And when I opened the pass-through slot to give him the document, I would instead shoot something sharp through and catch him in the throat."

Perveen sat silently, trying to imagine it. "But the pass-through slot is only about three feet from the ground!" she said after a moment.

"We sit facing the slot when we speak," Razia explained. "Then the slot is just below the level of each person's face."

Perveen nodded, recalling the bench Sakina had shown her. However, Perveen couldn't remember whether she'd seen a chair or bench in the area where the detective had been taking prints. Unless it was the rosewood chair she'd sat on. The thought of this made her grimace.

"He was waiting when I arrived. From his shadow behind the jali, I saw that he was standing. That would not work with my plan." Razia took a deep breath. "I requested that he please sit down to receive the papers. He did so. And when I opened the slot, I shot my letter opener through it hard. He cried out, just as Amina said she heard."

"Your letter opener!" Now Perveen realized why the object in the man's neck had looked familiar. She'd seen Amina toying with it at Razia's desk.

Razia closed her mouth and looked expectantly at Perveen.

Perveen thought that parts of Razia's story had seemed very believable, but the method of murder did not. "Can you tell me more about the death? Was there a struggle?"

Razia fell silent and looked as if she was thinking hard. At last, she said, "Do you know how, after awakening from a dream, you can't remember the whole thing?"

"It happens." Perveen had awoken in a sweat after a bad dream about Cyrus the previous night.

"I don't remember more than pushing the letter opener through the slot. I must have dealt a mortal blow. After that, I went back to my room, washed my hands, and prayed."

The perpetrator had to have been very close to Mukri to make the many stab wounds on his body. Blood was splattered all over the main house's second floor hallway. Yet there was no blood on Razia's sari. "What happened after you prayed in your room?"

"I drank water." She pressed her lips together. "Why are you looking at me that way?"

"I don't feel like I'm hearing the whole story." Perveen chose her words carefully, not wanting to accuse Razia of lying. "May I ask how you managed to make multiple stab wounds through a small space?"

Razia's tired eyes blinked. "I said before, it was all like a dream. I cannot recall."

"And how could you carry out such an assault without getting any blood on your sari?"

Razia looked down, and a single tear fell on the black silk.

"Of course, one might wear different clothes to commit a crime, and then change back to the other clothes again. Can you show me the clothes you wore to commit the killing?"

Wiping her eyes, Razia shook her head.

"You said you came here to confess," Perveen said.

Razia was studying the car's metal door handle.

"Might you be taking the blame because you're trying to protect someone from conviction?" When Razia didn't answer, Perveen said, "Are you trying to protect Amina?"

Razia shook her head again, but still didn't look at Perveen.

"Amina confided her great distrust of Mukri-sahib to me. Surely her fingerprints will be on the letter opener she played with at your desk. But that is hardly enough to send her to prison."

"How can you be sure?" Razia asked anxiously.

"For a start, such a small girl is no physical match for a big man like Mukri-sahib. Also, she told me she was in the garden when she heard him cry out. She never mentioned to me that she discovered the body."

Razia looked at her again. "Actually, Sakina said Amina was the one who told her about the death. I can't bear to ask Amina. I thought the less we spoke about it, the safer."

"I doubt the police will suspect her. But others in this house were aggrieved by him. And we don't yet know if he had enemies at work or amongst his acquaintances and relatives."

"That's right," Razia said, her voice catching. "We don't know."

"As the senior wife, you naturally take on the responsibility for the family." Perveen put a hand over Razia's, which was strikingly cold despite the car's heat. "But you cannot lie! In fact, lying in court is a chargeable crime."

Razia looked anxiously at her. "You speak as if I shall go to court."

"I've every intention of keeping you out of court." Perveen kept her hand on Razia's as she continued. "If you'd like, I can be your lawyer. This is different than my father representing your late husband. It is a separate, clearly defined agreement. Anything you say—including what you've already told me—would be confidential."

"I'd like that, but what if someone else needs you more than I do? What happens to her?" Razia's voice wavered.

"Don't worry. If another person needs representation, I will help find suitable counsel."

"Would this second lawyer be a man?"

"Yes. Sadly, I'm the only woman solicitor in Bombay. I shall ask my father if he thinks he can help another family member without there being a conflict of interest." Perveen saw from Razia's face that this offer hadn't done much to soothe her. "Do you wish to stay here tonight? I could take you and Amina to stay elsewhere."

Her eyes widened. "Do you mean go to my family's house in Oudh?"

"The police wouldn't like you being so far away," Perveen said. "You could stay with my family. My father has brought home clients before."

Razia put her hand to her mouth. "But you are Parsis."

"Don't worry about it. We worship differently, but we are not so far apart in our hearts, don't you think? And being with us might be a helpful distraction for Amina."

Razia looked as if she was deliberating. At last, she shook her head. "She's rarely been away from Sakina's children. Now she is needed by them more than ever."

Perveen didn't think that any of the family should remain inside the house. If the killer was a stranger who'd come in from the outside, he'd know of the house's riches and perhaps want more of them. And if the murderer came from within, she was likely a woman with her own unspoken agenda.

"Now that there is no longer a man in the house, would you ever walk through to the other side?" Perveen was intent on helping Razia establish an escape plan.

"I suppose so. As I've said, we observed a limited form of purdah when my husband was alive. We didn't go out in public, but at home we only secluded ourselves when businessmen and my late husband's friends called."

"Will you ring the police or me if you've any worries?" Perveen looked intently at her, trying to communicate how bold she might need to be.

"Yes. Perveen-bibi, you've been so good to counsel me like this. For the first time in hours, I feel as if I can breathe again." Razia opened the car door. Pulling her sari over her face, she slipped back into her secluded world.

Wiping away the sweat that now covered her whole face and arms, Perveen returned to the main house. The constables confirmed that Bombay's coroner, Dr. Horace Cartwright, had arrived. Dr. Cartwright had declared Mr. Mukri dead and had overseen the removal of his body to the police morgue.

"Where have you been?" Jamshedji asked. Her father looked disheveled, as if he'd also absorbed the true meaning of the afternoon. A family they'd promised to protect was in crisis. Helping the Farids now was a great deal more than figuring out the financial payouts from the estate.

"I was holding a consultation inside our Daimler." At his raised eyebrows, she said, "We must talk. Razia-begum has some concerns."

"Is she safe?"

Perveen sighed heavily. "As safe as any of them can be. I really think—"

"Let's speak of it when we're home tonight," he said in a low voice. "I'm on my way to the Farid Fabrics office to inform management about Mr. Mukri's passing."

"Please try to get his parents' names and an address." Perveen imagined his parents would fall into a deep grief. No matter how unpleasant a person might be, there would always be those who'd raised him and saw a different aspect of him.

Sub-Inspector Singh carefully trod down the staircase, his heavy box of fingerprinting equipment in one hand. "Miss Mistry, have you finished speaking to the widows?"

"Yes. I am ready to speak with you and your inspector." She did her best to sound civil.

"It shall be me alone," he said with a hint of pride. "Inspector Vaughan has already left."

Perveen was upset with herself for not moving faster to share the information she had gained. "I've heard your men took Mohsen into custody. It turns out that Sakina-begum confirmed to me that he was sent on an errand—"

"A widow may have given him an order," Singh said in the same superior tone he'd used with her when she'd chatted with him about fingerprinting, "but how can she know if he went straight out or lingered inside the main house? His own daughter admitted Mohsen went to the house to break up a quarrel between you and Mr. Mukri."

She realized that if he knew about the argument, she could join a cast of suspects. "I can certainly address the quarrel. But that doesn't take away my concern that with Mohsen gone, nobody is here to guard the widows and children."

Jamshedji spoke up. "A good point. But my daughter and I have a genuine concern that by taking Mohsen away, you are leaving a family of women and children unprotected."

"I'm sure they'll have some family members come to stay," Mr. Singh said.

Perveen's back went up. "I asked them about that, and they could not agree on who they'd like to come. In any case, nobody will be here tonight!"

"Inspector, what do you think about the idea of having some constables remain stationed outside the bungalow and perhaps on the first floor?" Jamshedji asked in a collegial tone.

"To take men off regular duty for personal guarding is outside our purview," Singh said, looking uneasily at Jamshedji.

"If the Malabar Hill Station can't spare men, perhaps the commissioner would send someone from central headquarters. This is rather an important district, and the residents are anxious about the possibility of burglaries." Jamshedji gave Perveen a serious look, and she nodded back. She wished to God that she could operate as smoothly with the police as he did.

"I'll speak to my inspector about it," the junior detective answered, sounding slightly more agreeable. "But that hall area should be cleaned before any constables come in for duty."

"Is all your evidence collected, then?" Perveen asked.

"Yes. So cleaning can be done by the servants," Singh said. "It's rather a mess upstairs, I'm afraid."

It seemed to Perveen that he was asking the impossible. "Sub-Inspector Singh, despite this house's size, cleaning is done by two child-servants. For them, cleaning a murder scene would be upsetting, perhaps even cause nightmares—"

"Isn't there an ayah?" Jamshedji interjected. "She can do it. Ayahs deal with every sort of mess."

Perveen hadn't met Taiba-ayah yet, but she could imagine how any children's ayah would feel about mopping up a dead man's blood and a thick layer of black powder. Warily, Perveen said, "I'll ask her, but she might refuse."

"Speak to her, and then let's go," Jamshedji said decisively. "I shall drop you home before I go on to the mills."

"But I can't go home. Alice is expecting me."

He raised his eyebrows. "That's right. You have a date with the English chatterbox. I shall have Arman drop you at her family bungalow, and he will return for me. What is the address?"

"Twenty-two Mount Pleasant," Perveen said. "The very new, big white bungalow."

The sub-inspector's eyebrows rose. "Isn't that some government bigwig's place?"

"Yes. It's the home of Sir David Hobson-Jones, who works for the governor," Perveen said, deciding to needle him a little for the sarcastic comment he'd made upon hearing Alice's voice.

But it didn't cow him. Singh merely snorted and said, "Just what I need: a councillor living around the corner from my investigation. Everything will have to be done twice as fast."

Perveen didn't think a murder investigation could be fast-paced. She felt as if she'd just boarded a long-distance train. Who else would come on, and where the journey would end, was far from certain.

1917

20

SWEETNESS OF HOME
Bombay, March 1917

ARRIVING ON BOMBAY MAIL STOP
VICT TERMINUS 10 AM SAT MARCH 20 STOP
YOUR LOVING PERVEEN.

*P*erveen had paid to have her tersely worded telegram sent from Nagpur, one of the stops on a journey that was supposed to take forty hours but that, due to a locomotive change, had stretched to forty-four. As she emerged on the platform at Victoria Terminus, she wondered if anyone would come.

Looking across the platform, she saw families dressed in white flitting through the crowds and remembered it was the Persian New Year. She had been so distraught that she'd not realized her journey would bring her home on the first day of Nowruz, when Parsis filled the city's fire temples and then one another's homes at celebratory parties.

Her family would have plans today. Her throat was tight as she looked around the platform and searched the hundreds of figures for anyone she might recognize. Perhaps her father would have thought to send Mustafa. She couldn't imagine Grandfather Mistry would come. He was the one who'd never warmed to the idea of her marrying Cyrus. And now she'd done the unthinkable and become a runaway wife. She was sure her grandfather would say that every bead of the family's reputation was lost.

"Ay, Perveen!"

Spinning around, she peered through the crowds to see her father dressed in the crisp white suit he always wore to the agiary. Right behind him were Rustom and Camellia, also bedecked in holiday finery.

"What a surprise!" Jamshedji waved, looking at her with a cautiously hopeful expression.

Camellia's smile faded as she came close enough to see the yellowed bruises on Perveen's face. "Darling! What happened?"

"Perveen, did you fall off the bunk on the train?" Rustom teased. "Where's your luggage?"

"I have no suitcase, just this bag." Perveen realized that her voice sounded dry from two days of not talking to anyone. People had kept a wide berth from her, even after she'd cleaned the blood from her face and back in the lavatory.

"But why?" Rustom demanded. "What the hell happened?"

"She will tell us later." Camellia held out her arms, and Perveen collapsed into them.

Because it was Nowruz, Jamshedji and Rustom had to represent the family at Uncle Gustav's New Year's lunch. Perveen was too tired to go, and Camellia said she'd stay.

Once the men left, Camellia drew a bath for Perveen and told John to prepare poached eggs on stir-fried fenugreek greens for a meal afterward. Perveen drank five cups of water boiled with mint, which tasted so much better than the Calcutta water she'd drunk for the last six months. And then she went to bed and fell into a quiet, utterly safe blackness.

When she woke, it was very dark. The houses nearby were bursting with sounds of merriment: Roman candles whizzing, Victrolas playing, people chattering and laughing over the New Year's feasting in area homes. Perveen went out to her much-missed balcony, where she was surprised to find Grandfather Mistry's pet parrot, Lillian, sleeping in her large brass cage. Perveen opened the door, hoping Lillian would favor her with a rush of affection, but the bird pecked her hand, looking for food, and then sallied off. As the bird happily soared toward the garden, Perveen heard the door to the bedroom opening behind her. Camellia had come with a tray containing two cups of tea.

"Finally you are ready for tea," Camellia said. "I wanted you to get water inside you earlier."

Accepting her cup of the milky ginger-lemongrass brew, Perveen said, "I hope Lillian will return. Why is she on my balcony and not at Mistry House?"

Settling down on the swing, Camellia gave Perveen a sorrowful glance. "I know you've had your own concerns, but did you really forget about your grandfather?"

Perveen was taken aback by the gravity of her mother's words and demeanor. "I've never forgotten him. But what exactly do you mean?"

"Grandfather Mistry died in his sleep February twentieth. I wrote to you about it! The funeral was a month ago—the twenty-second."

Perveen's heart skipped a beat. "Oh my God, Mamma! I did not know. He passed away? It can't be true."

Camellia bowed her head. "Yes. He is in heaven now."

Tears pricked the corners of Perveen's eyes as she remembered the last time she'd seen her grandfather. It had been just before she'd traveled to Calcutta, when he'd spoken in strict tones about the importance of adjusting her behavior to the expectations of the in-laws. It was almost as if he'd known what would happen, just as he'd sensed the rotten core within the Sodawallas after hearing a description from Mustafa.

"He went without pain," Camellia said. "But it was a big sorrow for all of us."

"Why didn't I know?" Perveen asked, a sob breaking loose. "When did you write?"

Camellia put a light hand on the shoulder of her weeping daughter. "Pappa sent a telegram on the twentieth, and I sent letters afterward."

Perveen went rigid with anger. "During that part of February, I was in seclusion. I couldn't be downstairs to hear when the post came. Perhaps they didn't give me the telegram and letters because they didn't want me to go to the funeral."

"How would they know what was inside the letters?" Camellia asked.

"Because somebody opened the letters and read them—yet didn't say anything!" Perveen looked up, wiping tears from her eyes. She felt betrayed—even more so than when she'd realized her in-laws had solicited money from her parents.

"Could it have been Cyrus?" As she said his name, Camellia's mouth made a small expression of distaste.

"He was gone so much, I can't imagine it was he who kept the letters. It must have been Behnoush."

Camellia leaned forward in her chair and looked intently at Perveen. "Tell me who hit you. And how often did it happen?"

"It was Cyrus, not Behnoush. And it happened just once." Perveen explained how she'd rushed off to find Cyrus to ask if his family had been trying to get money from her parents. She spoke about the woman she'd seen in her husband's office and how he'd gone wild with rage when Perveen had confronted him.

Camellia held out her hand to Lillian, who had chosen to fly back. Stroking the bird gently, Camellia said, "He might have thought hitting you, and having other women, made him a strong man—but all his behavior has revealed weakness. But what exactly did you say that made him so angry?"

Perveen hesitated, not sure whether her mother could handle the final hard truth. It was something that was so sordid that it might make Camellia think Perveen didn't belong at home anymore. Slowly, she said, "He left another mark. He gave me a disease."

"A disease?" Camellia sounded taken aback. "You caught TB or—"

"It's what they call a venereal disease." Looking down in shame, she said, "I can't bear to say its name. I was treated early, so I will live, but the damage inside may be permanent. Not that it matters, as I won't be having children with Cyrus," she added sadly.

Camellia looked at her steadily. "I have heard of venereal illness, and I know just the female doctor, Cambridge trained, to make sure everything is cleared. I will get an appointment for you. How do you feel about my telling Pappa about all of this?"

Perveen was suddenly wary. "Do you think he'll want me to go back?"

"If he knows the full story, he most assuredly will not." Camellia's voice was acid.

"I wasn't sure how he felt when I saw him at the station. I don't want to be married anymore, Mamma! There is no point in trying."

Camellia stroked back the hair that had fallen across Perveen's brow. "What happens now shall be your choice, just as that marriage was."

"I love you so much, Mamma." Perveen wiped the tears that had come with news of her grandfather's death. "I don't deserve this after what I put you through last year."

Camellia took her hand away. She looked uneasy for a moment and then said, "I have my own confession to make. I did not share all your Calcutta letters with Pappa, because I thought he would be too vexed. I thought everything would resolve itself when Cyrus spoke up to his parents. He seemed such a pleasant, strong-minded young man—and I know how much you loved him."

Perveen nodded. "Once I started going into seclusion, we both changed. I was becoming sad and anxious—and he was spending that time apart from me drinking and, now I understand, carrying on with other women. I could have told Pappa this myself—but I did not want him to hear anything from Calcutta except good news. I wanted to make amends for the big disappointment I'd turned out to be."

"We were both trying to protect him," Camellia said, looking pensive. "But don't forget that he's one of Bombay's most successful lawyers. Now it's his turn to protect you."

The next morning, Jamshedji asked Perveen if she felt well enough to accompany him to the office.

"Gladly," Perveen said, putting down the knife she'd been using to butter a paratha. "But it's still Nowruz, and you always take a holiday."

"No clients are coming today," he said, stirring sugar into his tea. "This is a convenience that provides time to discuss your predicament."

As she watched her father drink his tea, Perveen had no idea what he had in mind. "Pappa, did Mamma tell you how I felt? That I wish to file for divorce?"

Jamshedji's face was studiedly calm. "She told me your intentions. I assure you that we both are against you returning to Calcutta, even though we received a ridiculous telegram from Bahram Sodawalla two days ago asking us to help restore the marriage."

Perveen almost choked on the paratha. After recovering, she said, "When you came to the train station, you didn't say that!"

"I would hardly wish to greet you with such news. And I was still very disappointed about your not coming to Grandfather's funeral. I wanted to hear your explanation for that." Looking soberly at her, he added, "Among all of us, too many things have gone unsaid."

"Yes," she agreed, feeling emotion swell inside her. "It can never be that way again."

Riding through Bombay with her father, Perveen could not get enough of the dear familiar sights. She'd forgotten what it felt like to have the warm wind ruffle her hair and to see the water shoot up from Flora Fountain, looking like a stream of diamonds. What a city she came from; it would be hard to ever leave it again.

When Mustafa opened the door to Mistry House, his graceful adab felt like an embrace. With a smile, he said, "Perveen-memsahib, is it really you?"

"I've missed you, Mustafa. How do you do?" Now that Grandfather Mistry was gone, Mustafa was the sole keeper of Mistry House. She imagined that it would feel lonely at times.

He nodded to her. "Regarding my health, it is very well, thanks be to Allah. I heard from your father that you were not permitted to come for your beloved grandfather's funeral. That must have been a sorrow. But he is here with us still. Just as large as he ever was." Mustafa gestured toward a towering portrait of her grandfather, a new addition to the hallway.

"That portrait certainly is a very grand likeness of my grandfather," Perveen said. "Who painted it?"

"Samuel Fyzee-Rahamin, who studied under John Singer Sargent," Mustafa said. "He accomplished it just in the month before your grandfather's passing."

"Then it's very special," Perveen said, regarding the stern expression on the subject's face. She would happily live with her grandfather's visage for the rest of her life, no longer taking it as a mark of criticism. She hoped he would watch out for her now, as he had when Cyrus has appeared.

While she'd been reflecting on the portrait, Jamshedji was already halfway up the stairs. "Chalo, Perveen! Mustafa, we shall take our tea in about thirty minutes."

In the office, everything was as she remembered it. The desks of her father's employees—the clerk, the solicitor, and the typist—were piled with work, but his own was spotlessly neat. It was a large partners' desk, although he used only one side of it. Ever since Perveen could remember, he'd said that he was keeping the other side open for the city's first woman lawyer.

"Sit." Jamshedji motioned her toward the desk's vacant side, where there was no chair. She fetched one from the other side of the room and sat down.

As if Jamshedji didn't know of her churning emotions, he said, "You'll see a row of texts I often use on the center of the desk. On the far left is a compendium of Parsi legal acts. It dates from 1865, but it's still the most recent accounting of Parsi family law."

"Yes, Pappa." Perveen located the slender red book and offered it to her father, but he didn't accept it.

"I know everything in those pages," he said with a shrug. "I want you to read the entire text of the Parsi Marriage and Divorce Act of 1865. Then you shall explain which, if any, points of the act favor your case."

It was almost just like law school, except she wasn't nervous. Perveen settled down and opened the book, keeping paper and pen at her side to jot down notes as they came to her. Section 31, "Grounds of Judicial Separation," would be the basis of the argument. Here was a discussion of divorces being granted for adultery or adultery with cruelty. But the definition of adultery was troubling.

"I have a question." Perveen looked up from the book at her father.

He raised his eyebrows. "Of course."

It was embarrassing to discuss sexuality with her father, but she had no choice. Clearing her throat, she said, "The law describes adultery as a married man's act with a married lady who's not a prostitute. It's called an act of fornication if the fellow takes up with an unmarried lady who's not a prostitute. What category does a prostitute fall under?"

"Do you think the lady you saw in Cyrus's office was a prostitute?"

"I'm not certain, but—possibly. Why is there no mention of prostitutes in the legal codes regarding men's behavior?" She pushed the text in front of her father and pointed at the pertinent paragraph.

Jamshedji read through it and then looked back at her. "According to Parsi law, a husband's engaging in relations with a prostitute is not cause for divorce or even legal separation."

Perveen felt disbelief. "But that's unconscionable."

He nodded. "It has been our law since the Parsi Marriage and Divorce Act was passed in 1865."

"What if a husband hits a woman? Couldn't that be grounds of divorce?" Perveen felt a surge of hope. "There were two witnesses in the room, and the tonga driver."

"Only if the violence is extremely severe," Jamshedji said, looking soberly at her. "And then, the court might allow you a judicial separation. But the fact is, you did not lose an eye; you were not stabbed; you didn't go to hospital. We can't begin to present such an argument."

Perveen swallowed hard, not wanting to believe what her father was saying. "But he hurt me badly. His friends pulled him off me before he could kill me!"

Looking grim, Jamshedji closed the book. "I don't approve of the regulations built into the Divorce Act. However, one blessing is that it's vague enough to be subject to many interpretations. We will think of something."

"I'm trapped," Perveen said, feeling hollow. "Just as if I were still lying on that metal cot in that stinking room."

"Come now! You must stop brooding about what cannot be and realize the challenge we have even with a request for separation." Perveen gaped at her father, who continued on in a businesslike manner. "If Cyrus complains you deserted him without lawful cause, he could sue for restitution of his conjugal rights!"

"I don't think he'll do that—" Perveen began.

"Why would he wish to be separated? He cannot ever remarry. You are a lost asset."

"What rot! You speak as if I am a jewelry set!" Perveen snapped.

Her father held up a cautionary finger. "Let me explain the worst possible outcome. If the court rules in favor of Cyrus, you could be ordered to return to him. If you don't go, it would mean a heavy financial fine or prison."

"But living with his family would be like going back to prison." Perveen leaped up from her chair so fast it fell backward with a crash on the floor. "Why would a Parsi judge rule in favor of a man who struck me, consorted with a prostitute, and gave me a venereal disease?"

Jamshedji closed his eyes tightly for a moment. Then, looking straight at her, he said, "Although a judge presides, the marriage court's cases are decided by juries of Parsi laymen. And remember, this case will be heard in Calcutta, where you married a man whose family is well-known in a small, tight-knit community."

Her father was practically promising they'd lose. Shakily, she said, "I can't go back. I'd rather take my life."

"Don't speak like that!"

Shaking her head, she said, "You already knew what was in the Act. Why did you force me to read it when you could have just told me the bad news straightaway?"

"You wouldn't have believed it, had I told you the only possibility is judicial separation," Jamshedji told her. "Of course, I will file for the separation, but I am anticipating they will file a countersuit demanding conjugal rights. We will have to convince them to let you live with us. And this is where I need your thoughts, Perveen. You know that family and what matters to them."

"All that mattered to them was that I'd bear children—and that I was well-off enough to provide money to them."

Jamshedji looked over the line of books at her. "If the Sodawallas read a doctor's letter stating that the infection Cyrus gave you had nullified your ability to bear a child, they might not want you back."

"True," Perveen said, feeling bleak at his casual prognosis. "But Cyrus can't remarry either."

"They are stuck. The whole marriage is a stalemate until he commits adultery," Jamshedji said with a faint smile. "We must keep our fingers crossed he will commit adultery with some foolish woman and provide us with grounds for a proper divorce."

"In Britain, if a married couple is unhappy, the husband goes off to a hotel with another woman, and a servant there provides testimony they shared a bed. Then they've got grounds for the divorce." She paused. "What about me? Could I do the same with a gentleman?"

"Absolutely not!" Jamshedji thundered. "Not only because it would ruin our family name, but also because there is no provision in Parsi law granting divorce to misbehaving wives."

"Never mind." She turned from that to the last possibility she could think of. "I've got another idea. Behnoush told her friends that you would be sharing in the costs of a new bottling plant for them. Was that true?"

His eyes flared. "They asked me to pay for everything, as if I were Lord Readymoney and not a simple city solicitor."

"What did you say to that request?"

"I never answered that letter."

"Could we get the divorce on grounds of their blackmailing us?" Perveen asked.

He broke out laughing. "You are certainly one who thinks of every angle. But once again, it's not part of Parsi marital law."

"I hate the law. It's unfair, and lawyers should advocate to have it changed."

Her father snorted. "You don't like the Parsi Marriage and Divorce Act? It's too bad you left law school. Only a Parsi lawyer who really cares about women's rights will push to change it."

She nodded. "Tell me, Pappa, what happens next? Will another lawyer represent me in the case for separation?"

"I'll prepare the case and hire a barrister in Calcutta to argue it before the court." He gave her a searching look. "Are you prepared for what this means? If you get the separation, we're willing to have you live in our home beyond our deaths. But you might never be able to remarry."

"The last thing I want is another marriage," she said with a dry laugh.

"What will you do with yourself, then?"

Perveen decided to tell him the idea that had slowly come to her during the long train ride from Calcutta to Bombay. "I passed the Oxford entrance examinations years ago. At the time I said I didn't want to go to England because I was afraid of seasickness and the long trip."

"You also stated you had no interest in spending time with the English," Jamshedji reminded her with a chuckle. "Even though I went myself, and you would have been part two in the Mistrys' Oxford legacy."

"I've reconsidered things." Taking a deep breath, she said, "Did you know that in the 1890s, a female student from Poona was admitted to Somerville College and read law? Miss Cornelia Sorabji works as a solicitor in Bengal and several of the princely kingdoms."

"Yes, I've heard something, but you are the one I'm concerned about. Why do you think studying law at Oxford would be easier for you than studying it in Bombay?" Jamshedji sounded skeptical.

"It will be hard. But as Grandfather Mistry would have said, every bead of my reputation is sold," Perveen said wryly. "I will be away in England for three years of study. Then I can return to Bombay as a working professional."

Jamshedji studied her for a long moment. "You've had a terrible time. Mamma and I want to hold you close to us and make sure you're all right. Do you really wish to leave?"

She wasn't excited to leave her beloved home. But if she became Bombay's first woman lawyer, that would string the beads back on the ruined necklace and turn them to diamonds.

1921

21

TALK BETWEEN MEN
Bombay, February 1921

*P*erveen had experienced enough blood and tears for the day. It was time to see Alice.

In the evening's darkness, the tall Palladian windows of the Hobson-Jones bungalow glowed golden and inviting. Arman pulled up to the gate, and half a dozen guards ran up to surround the car. This was a far cry from the fawning welcome the governor's car had received the day before.

A Scottish lance corporal demanded Perveen explain her business. In a cool voice, she gave her name and said she'd been invited by Alice. The Scot consulted a book provided by another one of the guards. Looking up, he grudgingly said, "Your name is here."

Perveen didn't answer. She was considering the fact that a day earlier, the property had only had four guards. She wondered whether the greater number of guards was tied to the events around the corner. Arman wasn't allowed to drive through the gates into the courtyard. They had a quick discussion about what to do and resolved that he would go back for her father but return for her at nine o'clock.

Perveen's suspicions were raised when she walked through the gates and saw, parked close to the house, a car marked with the insignia of the Bombay Police. Was an officer making a social call on Alice's parents, or was it about the trouble around the corner?

The household butler was a professional. The tall, elegant-looking Punjabi recognized Perveen from the previous day and ushered her in with the respect that had been missing from the guards. As she followed the butler down the hall, her nose caught the scent of tobacco, and she overheard the rumbling of men's voices from behind one of the closed doors.

In the vast, underfurnished drawing room, Alice sat on the carpet surrounded by several small cartons. Holding a record in her hands, she looked up at Perveen. "Good, you came! I'm looking through the records I brought. What do you fancy hearing?"

Alice sounded casually lighthearted; it was as if she were ignoring all that she'd learned about two hours earlier. Perveen wondered about this shift until she looked toward the veranda and saw a bit of blonde hair peeping over the back of a planter's chair. Lady Gwendolyn Hobson-Jones was within hearing distance.

"I should pay my respects to your mother," Perveen said, gesturing toward the veranda.

Alice winked. "At your own risk. She's in fine form tonight."

Perveen found Alice's mother nursing a half-finished drink and staring out into the dark garden.

"Good evening, Lady Hobson-Jones," Perveen said, trying to put warmth that she didn't feel into the formal greeting. "How was your first day with Alice?"

"Quite well, considering. Sit a moment, won't you?" The lady's tone was unusually mellow, perhaps due to the crystal tumbler in her hand. "I can't fathom why she stays inside on such a pleasant night."

"She's excited to unpack her records. What do you think of her collection? As my driver pulled up, I could hear it on the street."

"I'll listen to Cole Porter any day. Alice has some other records, though, with the most awful, scratchy, rough voices. Al Joneson—"

"Al Jolson, Mother. Honestly!" Alice called from the drawing room.

"And where is Sir David tonight?" Perveen asked. "Does he ever get a chance to truly relax and be at home in the evenings?"

"I wouldn't say he's the relaxing sort," Lady Hobson-Jones said. "Right now he's in his study dealing with some surprise visitors."

"Friends?" Perveen was fishing but trying not to seem like it.

"No. The police commissioner and his aide." Lady Hobson-Jones's tone was dismissive.

Perveen wanted to know why. "If they confer very often, they may yet become friends."

Lady Hobson-Jones sighed. "We knew the last police commissioner, Mr. Edwardes, very well. Of course, he was an ICS man. Commissioner Griffith is an imperial policeman who was promoted."

Her careful words made Perveen think that Griffith was not what she considered top-drawer.

Lady Hobson-Jones continued, "I can only hope Mr. Griffith's experience will enable him to suppress the city's dreadful crime wave. Today, a violent crime occurred around the corner in this very neighborhood!"

Perveen realized the conversational turn could put her in a difficult position if Alice said anything to her mother about Mistry Law's representation of the Farids. She could not possibly discuss the situation. "I'm very glad the police are with your husband. And it was nice to see you this evening, but I'll be—"

"Wait." Lady Hobson-Jones took a deep sip from the tumbler and then turned to Perveen. "You live in a Parsi-only colony, don't you?"

Perveen was not only annoyed to be delayed; she also didn't like being singled out for her religion. "Yes. In Bombay, religious communities tend to settle close to each other—not just Parsis, but Hindus and Muslims, too."

"What is the crime count in your neighborhood?"

"I don't think anyone's counting. But I can't think of any problems." Perveen looked at the woman who was now sitting up straight and looking alert.

"No murders, I'm sure!" she said with a light laugh. "I've been telling my husband, there is security in monotonous communities."

Homogenous, Perveen thought. That was the word Lady Hobson-Jones was reaching for. But homogeneity did breed monotony. Was Lady Hobson-Jones intimating that she wished Malabar Hill would once again become English only?

"Too many people die in India." The Englishwoman turned pensive. "One worries about disease first and foremost. Then there are the terrorists going into people's homes and shooting them. But our new crime is at a bungalow we can see from our windows. Remember, we showed you?"

Perveen nodded warily.

"My husband doubts it was a crime of religious hatred or politics. Nevertheless, I'm watching the back of the property tonight, because there aren't enough guards to properly cover all of it."

"The police and your husband will come up with a good security plan." Perveen tried to sound reassuring. She suspected that most of the woman's attitude was born from fear.

"Go to Alice," Lady Hobson-Jones said. "Tell her that she can't go about without a chaperone. This isn't Belgravia. She should behave with the same caution that you do."

Inside the drawing room, Perveen found Alice instructing two servants on carrying her Victrola upstairs.

"Take the last few records from the sofa," she said over her shoulder to Perveen. "And bring your drink. There's a gin-lime on the tray freshly made for you."

"Are we going to your room?" Perveen said, picking up the cold tumbler in one hand and three records in the other.

"No!" Alice said, huffing a bit as she climbed the stairs with her small load of records. "I've found an even better place just one floor up that I've decided to make my study."

This was a corner room with windows open on both sides up on the third floor. When Alice pulled the chain to turn on the overhead light and fans, an army of mosquitoes and moths began pounding at the wire-cloth screens. There were so many flying insects that it was like Victoria Terminus at rush hour.

"Come sit," Alice said. "I have lots to tell. But let's get the music started."

Perveen settled into a rattan lounge chair and looked around the room. Ever since her time in Calcutta, she'd had an instinctive dislike of small places. Alice's hideaway had some of the same elements of the Sodawallas' seclusion room: a small cot and table. But this retreat was soft. The bed was made up with a printed cotton quilt and embroidered cushions. Instead of a metal table there was a small rosewood desk holding a typewriter and a stack of mathematics books. A bookcase was being filled with records by one of the servants while the other set the record player on the floor.

"That's good, thanks." Alice waved off the two servants who had helped, then selected a record for the Victrola. Soon, Al Jolson's scratchy voice filled the room, but it sounded off.

Alice groaned. "The record looked warped—but I'd hoped it would be all right. I did so hope."

"It must have been those weeks on the ship," Perveen said. "My law books arrived looking like they'd grown coats of green fur."

"I'll just have to get another one," Alice said, going to the door to close it. "And how do you like the room?"

"It's very pretty but a lot warmer than your bedroom on the second floor. Do you have to keep the door closed?" Perveen asked.

Alice perched on the hard chair next to the desk. "I've something to tell you."

She'd already been through hot news in a hot place once that day. But Perveen sipped her cold drink with pleasure. Such announcements from Alice usually meant a good piece of gossip.

"Before you arrived, I had the records going because I wanted my parents to think I was listening to them in the drawing room."

"You weren't?" Perveen tried not to laugh. This type of scheme was so typical for her friend.

"Actually, I was curled up on the veranda just outside my father's study, listening to his conversation with some police bigwig. The man spoke about the Farids of twenty-two Sea View Road, so I thought of you!"

Alice had spied on the government—an act for which an Indian might go to jail. However, any tip could be helpful. Nodding at Alice, she said, "Your mother told me the commissioner was visiting your father downstairs."

"So that's who he is." Alice looked thoughtful. "I overheard a man with a Geordie accent talking about someone called Vaughan who'd requested permission to search the ladies' section of the bungalow."

Perveen felt a rush of anxiety, although she strove to keep her expression neutral. "Oh? You do have good ears."

Alice took a long sip of her gin-lime. "They also want to take fingerprints."

Recalling Sub-Inspector Singh's fascination with criminology, Perveen imagined he wanted fingerprint slips of all the women and children. He already had the silver letter opener, which was likely to have Amina's and Razia's prints.

"Perveen! You look as if your drink's too sour."

Perveen forced a smile. "It isn't. I was trying to understand why a routine murder investigation went beyond the detectives involved and all the way up to your father. I thought he was involved in land deals, not law and order."

"When the governor's away in Delhi, he designates my father to deal with pressing concerns," Alice said. "But my father's always been slow to act. That can be frustrating for people, let alone me."

Perveen didn't want the conversation to degenerate into Alice's objections about her father. "So what else was said?"

"Father asked some more about who might do the fingerprinting. The commissioner told him that the policeman holds the suspect's hand as the fingers are pressed into ink."

"I can understand your father's questioning," Perveen said, feeling a grudging respect. "A Muslim woman has legal grounds to refuse being touched by a man who is not her husband. She also cannot be ordered to appear in a court of law."

"But does that mean she lives subject to no laws?" Alice sounded incredulous.

"Of course not. In the case of a purdahnashin, a judge or another court official could record the testimony in her home, or an advocate who'd taken her sworn testimony at home could represent her in court." Perveen had thought this through earlier, knowing there was a chance Razia or any of the wives might become persons of interest. "But the pressing concern—excuse the pun—is that if a policeman touches the hands of Muslim gentlewomen, the community could take serious offense."

"Do you mean that Muslims might go to the police headquarters and complain?"

Perveen rested her drink on the chair's armrest while she put her thoughts in order. "Yes—and in Bombay, this could mean severe political unrest. We are talking about Muslims defending their women's honor and perhaps even sympathetic Hindus and Sikhs joining in their defense of the Indian female. Any chance to embarrass the government is a golden opportunity for the freedom movement."

"That must be the reason Father told the commissioner he should stay out of the zenana. He suggested instead that the police run extra checks for felons recently released from prison and make sure the press are aware of the effort."

Perveen didn't answer. It would be horrifying if some fellow with a checkered past was served up as the sacrificial lamb to make the police appear successful. At the same time, she worried about what might come up if the police searched the zenana.

"What is it, Perveen?"

Perveen smiled briefly and took another sip. "Just thinking."

"I wish you'd tell me whether you've got a suspicion about the crime. It's in everyone's interest for the killer to be put behind bars."

"I've already explained to you about my confidentiality situation." Perveen paused. "And please don't think I know what I'm doing. None of my law courses prepared me in the slightest for this afternoon."

Alice stood at the window, where a moth as large as a robin kept hitting itself against the wire cloth. "Just look at that big-winged fool trying to get inside."

"My parrot would enjoy making a meal of him," Perveen said.

"He makes me think of someone going after those secluded women. They're utterly trapped."

"Not exactly. It's their preference to keep away from men." Perveen recalled Gwendolyn Hobson-Jones's anxiety about mixed neighborhoods. "Consider your mother. Even though she's been here for many years, India is too full of people she considers frightening for her."

Alice wrinkled her nose. "My mother's hopeless—and she's got an army of servants and guards to protect her. The security around our bungalow's got even tighter, due to what happened around the corner. But I still wonder, are the Farid widows safe staying alone, given what the detectives think might have happened?"

Perveen went over to Alice, who was no longer fixated on moths and mosquitoes but gazing in the direction of the Farid bungalow. "My father convinced the detective to organize a police presence in the household tonight. Look, we can see the house has some lights on."

Alice squinted. "Is that it? I see two windows lit on the first floor, and on the ground floor, there's one."

Perveen wondered if the women were conferring downstairs and who was awake upstairs. Could it be a constable on patrol?

"How about another drink?"

Perveen was tempted but glanced at her watch out of duty. "Damnation! It's a few minutes past nine. I promised Arman I'd be at the gate for the ride home."

"You don't need to use your driver when we've got our own," Alice offered. "I can send the butler out to let him know you'll leave later in our car."

"I wouldn't dream of it. My father will be in the car, and I don't want to put him out." Perveen felt guilty about leaving Alice so quickly after arrival. "What about tomorrow evening? Perhaps we could meet at one of the cinema halls. There's a new film called *Shakuntala* based on Hindu mythology."

Alice brightened. "Oh, I've heard about it! But does it really star an American woman playing an Indian maharani?"

"Due to a labor shortage." Perveen rolled her eyes. "No Indian family would allow their daughter to be ogled onscreen."

"Really? Your family's allowing you to work in a men's world," Alice pointed out.

"Yes, but I'm still not allowed to present myself before a judge." Perveen stood up to go, smoothing her sari. "Whether in the cinema or real life, we ladies have a very long road ahead."

Perveen left her friend's hideout with the strains of the warped record accompanying her down the stairs. Tonight the recording of "Swanee" seemed a distant, distorted version of the one they'd played at St. Hilda's Hall.

Although she could strive to keep her old college friendship going, just like the record, it would play differently in Bombay.

The police car was no longer in the driveway when she went to stand by the gate. She didn't see the Daimler, which was initially a relief, because it meant that she couldn't be considered the late one. But when no cars drove by, and her watch read nine-fifteen, she began to worry. She stood at the gate, peering down Mount Pleasant Road. At last, the Scottish lance corporal lumbered out from the driveway to address her.

"You going or staying?" he asked in an accusatory manner.

"I'm hoping to go home in my family car," she answered sharply. "Have you seen that Daimler that brought me?"

He shrugged. "I stay inside the wall supervising. But I can tell you no cars are allowed to wait on the block."

Perveen suppressed her irritation and said, "What about the guards standing along the wall? Might they have seen a car?"

"Can't tell you. Ask yourself."

The first guard, an English soldier with a West country accent, was politer than the Scot. He confirmed that a Daimler with an Indian driver and Indian gentleman had arrived fifteen minutes earlier but had not been permitted to wait at the gate.

"Was there a message for me? Did you hear whether they intended to continue home or wait nearby?" Perveen asked the private. She could imagine her hot-tempered father going home and sending Arman back for her.

"Don't know. They could be farther along or around the corner on Sea View Road. That's where I'd wait, because it's closer," the private said, pointing in the blackness to where she imagined the cross street was.

"I'll walk there to see. Very likely, I'll come back." She didn't like the idea of lingering in an isolated neighborhood after dark.

"Apologies that I cannot escort you, madam, but I am on duty."

Perveen sighed and began her walk. Alice's street was darker than she liked, with the only lights coming from the gas lamps at household gates and the many stars above. There were no strolling people at all, but she imagined animals were afoot. Owls hooted ominously, and she wondered if they had their eyes out for mongooses and snakes.

She'd been listening carefully for footsteps, lest a stranger come up behind her. The sound that she heard, though, was the purr of a car. She stepped back, drawing herself close to a bungalow wall so she wouldn't get hit by the car. No driver could see her in such darkness.

And then she realized how strange it was that a car was coming up the road without lights on. It was as if the car didn't want to be seen.

The Bengali stranger and Cyrus collided in her imagination; and she saw Mukri's bloody body, too. Perveen felt panic rise within her. Where could she go? All the bungalows around her had their gates locked. She saw the sheltering bulk of a tree about five feet away and was in the process of running toward it when the car came upon her.

Its lights flashed on, illuminating her as she tried to climb the tree.

"Perveen, what in hell are you doing?" Jamshedji roared through a rolled-down window.

"Getting to safety. Why were you driving like that—no lights, no warning?" she shouted back. Her heart thumped from the sudden release from fear, and she slid down the three feet of tree trunk that she'd climbed.

Arman had already stopped and jumped out to open the car door. "So very sorry, memsahib. We were driving without lights to avoid the harassment of those ghelsappas guarding your friend's bungalow. They would not even let us wait!"

"There would have been no need to wait if Perveen had been outside looking for us," Jamshedji said tightly. "All because these English think themselves better than us."

"It's not like that with Alice," Perveen said.

"I don't want to hear another word about her," Jamshedji said curtly. "I've got a headache, and it's high time we get home."

22

BIRD ON THE VERANDA
Bombay, February 1921

Jamshedji's temper improved once the two of them arrived home. He answered Rustom's call to come into the parlor for a sherry. Soon the two men were laughing.

Perveen went to the kitchen and saw Gulnaz at the stove. She was tempering cumin seeds and onion, making the tadka that would top a pot of yellow dal Perveen's mother was stirring. "It smells good, but where's John?" Perveen asked.

"Since it's so late, we said to him, go, and we'll make the finishing touches," Camellia told her.

"I like cooking anyway," Gulnaz said with a shrug. "Why are you so late?"

"I was out at the Farid bungalow and then my friend Alice's house," Perveen said, pouring herself a glass of water. "Pappa came for me at nine, but we had a mix-up getting home. Sorry."

"You are spending all of your time with the English now!" Gulnaz spoke in a teasing tone, but it raised Perveen's hackles. Her relationship with Gulnaz had changed after the surprise of finding out Perveen's old schoolmate had been matched up with Rustom. Perveen was resentful that Gulnaz had such an easy, happy arranged marriage. Perveen imagined that Gulnaz might sometimes envy her three years in England followed by a career that took her out of the house daily. In any case, they chatted but never confided in each other the way they had during their time in the Elphinstone College ladies' lounge.

She knew it wasn't right—so she pushed herself to say something. "Alice and I want to go to the cinema tomorrow evening. Will you come?"

Gulnaz was silent for a spell. "I'm not sure. How can we sit with an English person? They've got their own section of the theater."

"Alice isn't that type. She will insist on sitting with us." Perveen paused. "Besides, weren't you the one who thought she'd be useful to know?"

"Yes, but . . ." Gulnaz didn't finish. Perveen knew her sister-in-law wasn't happy with the plan, but so be it.

Hanging up her apron, Camellia said, "No matter what you might do tomorrow, now is the time for washing hands. Supper is ready."

The meal was a good one: lamb curry with fenugreek and potatoes, coconut dal, a chicken and tomato curry, and a savory rice pulao. Perveen ate, keeping an eye on her father. She had a slight worry that he hadn't spoken to her in the car because he'd decided to take her off the case. He might have been counting up all the errors she'd made. The fact that she'd gone off walking Malabar Hill in the night could have tipped him over the edge.

But then, after supper was cleared, and Perveen was in the kitchen assembling a bowl of fruit and vegetable scraps for Lillian, he said he would join her on her balcony.

"God save the Queen!" Lillian squawked when they came out together. "Mataram!"

"You're hitting both sides of politics, aren't you?" Perveen said, smiling as she opened the cage.

"A clever bird indeed." Jamshedji settled down in one of the rattan lounge chairs and balanced a snifter of port on the wide armrest. "Tell me everything."

"All right. It's a long story."

Perveen explained how, after learning the facts, all three women had become hesitant to sign away their mahr, and then she recounted the terrible interruption of her talk with Mumtaz by Mukri. Hoping her father didn't think she'd been too naïve, she confided, "It was such a shock. I hadn't thought anyone could listen to us, and Mr. Mukri had told me he'd be away at work."

"Households with two sections might appear to have privacy, but it could be that they have the fewest secrets." Jamshedji sipped his port. "Precisely because of their walls and screens, people are curious to know everything."

Lillian flew the short distance from her cage to the back of Jamshedji's chair and pecked at his hair. He winced and batted at her until she flew off into the garden.

"Razia-begum managed to keep her role as the wakf's mutawalli secret from Sakina-begum," Perveen said. "That must have taken some doing. She said that she and her husband had agreed it was best."

Her father sighed. "Farid-sahib was a considerate man. It seems he was seeking balance, so each wife had something with which to occupy herself."

"I mentioned to you earlier that I talked with Razia-begum in the Daimler." Perveen detailed how the murder confession broke down after the direct questions about her clothing.

"You could be wrong. Might you be advocating for Razia-begum a bit too strongly?" Jamshedji asked, studying her.

"I think it's a classic case of a mother taking blame because she fears for her child. I must keep her away from the police until we know more. Right now, she's panicked."

Jamshedji nodded. "The need to defend Razia-begum may turn out to be moot, given the police have seized the durwan. Perhaps there will be evidence pointing to him."

"Actually, Commissioner Griffith would like to investigate the women."

At her father's raised eyebrows, Perveen said, "I learned from Alice that the police commissioner called on her father to discuss Mr. Mukri's death. The commissioner was interested in fingerprinting the women and searching the zenana."

Jamshedji looked at her intently. "What did the men decide?"

"Sir David told the commissioner not to do it. Instead he advised the police to round up men recently released from prison." Seeing her father's dubious expression, Perveen added, "I don't want to make life any harder on the widows, but I feel it would be dreadful if the police pinned the crime on an innocent. Certainly, if there is a homicidal person living at twenty-two Sea View Road, everyone is at risk. I'd want that individual to be caught."

"To be apprehended and have a fair treatment according to the law," Jamshedji corrected.

"Yes," Perveen said, taking in her father's serious expression.

"All right, then, I'll tell you what I learned tonight," Jamshedji said, taking another sip of his drink. "I went to Farid Fabrics' mills and was fortunate to find the acting director, Mr. Farid's cousin Muhammed, was still there. I told him about the demise of Faisal Mukri."

"What was his reaction?"

"He said all the right things, but it didn't seem as if he was heart-broken." Jamshedji gave her a sardonic look.

Just as there wasn't grief at 22 Sea View Road—just shock and fear that a savage act had taken place in the bungalow. Perveen asked, "Does he know where Mukri lived before the Farid home?"

"Apparently he had a rented room near the mill district, which he gave up when he had the chance to become household agent. But the office files had a record of his mother's address in Poona. Muhammed Farid was relieved I planned to go in person to tell them the bad news."

"I'm also glad you're going," Perveen said. "Did you ask him if there were any problems for Mukri within the company?"

"Muhammed said there was tremendous jealousy within the company about Farid-sahib giving such a perk to a minor accountant. Of course, I asked him why Farid-sahib hadn't asked him, a relative living in town, to do it. He answered that Farid-sahib was worried about the company's future and believed that for his cousin to do both jobs would be too much."

"I wouldn't be surprised if Mukri poisoned the relationship," Perveen cut in.

Jamshedji pointed a finger at her. "That is an ungrounded supposition. However, when I asked more questions about Mukri,

Muhammed brought in the accounting supervisor, Mr. Sharma. Sharma was surprised to hear of the death and offered condolences. When I pressed him, he said he regretted to speak ill of the dead, but in truth, Mukri was only a fair worker. Much of his work was done by underlings."

"Yet he managed to keep his job?"

"Mr. Sharma had heard a rumor that Mukri was a distant relative of Mr. Farid's. That's what Mukri told people all the time—that he was so close to Farid-sahib he'd surely become the mill director one day. It turned out he did get selected to be the household agent. Then he played this card to the greatest extent. When Mr. Farid fell ill, Mukri began going to work only two or three days a week, living in the bungalow and using the telephone and the occasional visit to connect with the company. Recently he'd been coming to work just once a week."

"Were you able to obtain information on the mill's financial state? I hear most of Bombay's mills aren't doing so well these days."

"True. In this case, Muhammed Farid blames the company's decline on a string of poor decisions pushed by Mukri during Omar Farid's illness. Apparently Mr. Mukri told management that Mr. Farid wished to produce new kinds of cloth now that khaki was in decline. The company began experimenting and invested in creating fabrics that haven't sold well."

"If Mr. Mukri was such a drain on the company and wasn't being fired, isn't there a chance one of his coworkers might have done him in?" She paused. "Perhaps Cousin Muhammed wished him ill."

Jamshedji shook his head. "Muhammed Farid confirmed he was at work all day. I did not cross-examine him because his behavior isn't for us to investigate. I went to him to get an address, and now I'm able to visit Mrs. Mukri to communicate my regrets, and to let her begin preparations for the funeral. I shall travel to Poona tomorrow."

"One of Mr. Farid's wives is from Poona," Perveen said. "Sakina Chivne. Do you have time to call on them? Sakina-begum might have concerned relatives who would hurry in to help her, despite what she thinks."

"Who would have thought, when I brought on my daughter, she'd be the one to direct my daily program?" Jamshedji said with a chuckle.

"If you can take care of two issues in one trip, isn't it better?" she answered with a smile. "Tomorrow I'll return to the Farids and see what other help they need."

Now that she and her father had talked and a plan was in place, it should have been easy to sleep. But Perveen was haunted by the thought that she had overstepped with Razia. And it was unjust that the family's durwan was in prison and could very likely be convicted through no fault of his own.

When she finally drifted off, she saw the Farids' house in her mind—not the cream-colored miniature palace of daylight, but at night, with a light burning in just one window. Whose room was it? As Perveen hastened toward the bungalow, the light went out, and she had an overpowering fear that someone else was in mortal danger.

23

A MISSING CHILD
Bombay, February 1921

"'*D*eath Returns to Malabar Hill Family.' This seems somehow familiar." Rustom put down the copy of the *Times of India* and turned his attention on Perveen. "Well, Perveen? Isn't this Farid family known to us?"

If Rustom had been an employee of Mistry Law, she could have told him plenty. But he was merely an annoying brother, so she would reveal the minimum. Yawning, she said, "Father represented Mr. Farid, who passed away in December."

"Of course!" Rustom said, spearing a piece of bacon. "Father asked me to come to Mr. Farid's funeral with him, but we were breaking ground on the flat building that morning. It says here in the paper that a household agent died on the premises."

"Will you go to this other man's funeral?" Gulnaz asked, taking the paper out of her husband's hands. She'd just come fresh from her bath, her damp hair hanging in a braid, although she was already dressed to go out in a yellow silk sari over a Chantilly lace blouse. She was the picture of youthful beauty; Perveen envied her.

"There can't be a funeral until the police are finished with their examination of his body," Perveen snapped. She was exhausted from bad dreams and long periods of being awake and worrying over the night. When she'd awoken, it had been late, and she'd learned her father had already gone off to the train station and Poona.

"I've always been interested in the spot where the Farid bungalow stands. I came across the plans some time ago in one of the office storage cabinets. We built that house in 1880." Rustom spoke in a manner that seemed both wistful and knowledgeable.

"You weren't born yet! It was your grandfather's doing," Camellia corrected with a gentle smile.

"All right, then, Mistry Construction built it," he acknowledged with an eye roll. "Father introduced me to Mr. Farid once when he'd come to sign papers at Mistry House. I advised the gentleman to consider taking down the old house and putting up a modern mansion block. If he had five floors, he could have lived on one with his family and taken revenue from the other four."

"The house is still standing, so he must have declined," Perveen said.

Rustom chuckled. "He declared, 'I have two wives and four children at present. There's a chance more will join. There would be no peace in one flat. For all of us to live in one flat would surely bring about suicide, if not murder.'"

"He must have been joking," Gulnaz said.

"Of course. Everybody laughed. I said that Grandfather built the house very well, so I could understand his continuing enjoyment."

"Good answer," Camellia said. "But now times have changed: will three secluded women do well staying on without a husband? Do they have friends and relatives nearby visiting them daily?" She looked across the snowy lace tablecloth toward Perveen. "And why are you so quiet about this?"

"Mamma, one of the widows is my client, so I'm maintaining confidentiality. But I will find a way for them all to have support." She would back them unequivocally, just as her mother had supported her.

A glint came into Rustom's eyes. "Now that the husband is gone, the wives are the ones who can decide about the bungalow. Ask the widows if they wish to profit in a booming market!"

"Are you saying this because you know of someone who's looking for land in Malabar Hill?" Perveen challenged him.

"I could find an offer for them before close of business today. Whenever they're ready," he added with an air of generosity.

"Please don't say anything to anyone about property coming available on Sea View Road," Perveen said. "It's putting the cart before the horse and would also place me in conflict of interest."

"Agreed," Camellia said smoothly. "Perveen, I wanted to mention that Pappa asked me to find out whether any new madrassas are being built in the city. Are you interested in the answer?"

"Naturally! What have you heard?"

"I spoke with two of the Muslim ladies in my Secondary Education Group. They said the only boys' madrassa being started is a school operated by Dawoodi Bhora Muslims," Camellia said.

"The Farids are Sunni Muslims. They probably wouldn't be involved." Perveen felt certain that Mr. Mukri's madrassa had been a fiction, and he'd wanted the wakf money to do something else.

A familiar tooting sound meant that Arman was back from taking her father to the train. It was time to go.

Half an hour later, the Daimler stopped at the locked iron gate of the Farid bungalow. Arman opened the car door for Perveen, who stepped out and went to the gate, looking through it for someone to help her. Feeling the attention of two durwans at a bungalow across the way, she decided to find out if they knew anything.

"Good morning! Are the police staying inside the bungalow?"

"What police?" The taller of the two guards snorted at her question. "Nobody's been there since the Sikh detective left yesterday. Little Zeid locked up the gate."

So the widows hadn't been secure. Immediately, she felt a surge of anxiety. "But I must see the begums."

"If you call, maybe the boy will come to the gate. He was crying earlier," the second guard said soberly.

"Mohsen is still away, then?" she asked.

"That liar?" the tall guard said with a grimace. "He told the police he was spending time with us on the street when he wasn't. We saw him go down the hill and come back. Perhaps this lie is the reason they took him away."

Sakina had sent Mohsen on an errand. Why hadn't he just said that? Feeling somewhat confused, she decided to ask the men more about the durwan. "What is your opinion of Mohsen, as a guard and as a man?"

The tall guard with the surly attitude shrugged. "He does his job the same as anyone. But he is not the happy sort. Doesn't talk much."

"He has a right to misery," the other guard opined. "To lose a wife and have to raise two children on so little money is hard."

"Everyone is paid too little," the taller guard said. There was an edge to his voice that was unnerving. What would the men say if they knew that she was a well-paid working woman?

Perveen thanked them and returned to the gate.

"Zeid, are you there?" After she'd called for a few minutes, the boy emerged down the driveway.

"Thank you for coming," she said, softening her voice. "I'm so sorry about your father still being gone."

"Why did they take him?" the boy whimpered.

"I told your sister that I'd try to find out. Will you please unbolt the gate?"

Zeid's face screwed up with effort as his tiny hands pulled back the iron bolt. Perveen walked on ahead with Zeid, Arman following in the car. The chauffeur parked outside the main entrance while Zeid opened the zenana entrance for her.

"What happened with the police yesterday?" she asked Zeid. She couldn't remember the details of her bad dream from the night before, but it had flickered back into her mind when she'd spoken with the two durwans.

"They stayed for a little bit. Some constables and the white officer took my father, and then the Sikh officer left." He looked up at her with wide eyes. "I'm glad they didn't take any more people. But why did they have to take Abba? He is the only one protecting the place."

"I agree that everyone needs protection. Zeid, perhaps you should stay at the gate to help if anyone comes?" Leaning closer to him, she said, "Don't let in newspapermen or curiosity seekers. Just the police, or people related to the begums, and others you know are trustworthy."

Zeid straightened up in the classic durwan-at-attention position he must have learned from his father. "Yes, I will be careful. Abba may come back today, Insha'Allah!"

Perveen heard footsteps and looked to see an elderly lady in a white sari coming downstairs carrying a baby. The nursemaid must not have expected to see Perveen, because she clutched the baby tightly, and her eyes widened in alarm.

"Are you Taiba-ayah? I'm the family's lawyer, Perveen Mistry."

"Eh?" the woman said as if she couldn't hear well.

When she'd reached the foot of the stairs, Perveen stepped forward and repeated the introduction and her question.

Taiba rolled her head sideways in agreement. "Yes, I care for the children. Are you the one who said I had to clean up the black dust and blood?"

Perveen wanted to say it hadn't been her idea—but shoving the blame on her father would be unprofessional. "I'm sorry. We could not think of anyone else, and I know it must have been awful. Your proper job is taking care of the little one. May I see him?"

"Look quickly." She adjusted the bundle so Perveen saw a fair-skinned baby wearing a crocheted cap and white muslin dress. His eyes were closed, but she could see that his nose and jaw had the same delicate lines as Sakina's.

"So this is Jum-Jum." Perveen studied the boy, who was gently snoring. She noticed that behind his ear, someone had marked a black dot of kohl. The protect-against-evil-eye mark was similar to the dots that Parsis drew on their children's head and feet, and the thick kohl eyeliner that adorned young Hindu children. She thought of Zeid, the little boy who had a true black mark. Zeid was healthy, but he had suffered misfortune.

As the Farids' only son, Jum-Jum was extremely precious. He would carry on the family name and would be the chief heir, inheriting 35 percent of everything. Each of the three daughters would get half his take—17.5 percent. Unfortunately, the wives would be granted far less. If Mr. Farid had had just one wife, she would have been allotted one-eighth; but because he'd had three, that share had to be divided, and each lady would receive just 4.17 percent. Knowing this was another reason she'd taken her time making sure the estate was in order. The widows should get every paisa due to them.

Taiba carried the child into the garden, where Nasreen and Shireen were playing a desultory game of ball rolling. Perveen realized to get anything more from the ayah, she'd have to follow. "How often are you outside of the zenana?" she asked.

"Now and again." She looked cautiously at Perveen.

"When I was in the main house yesterday, I thought it seemed Mukri-sahib used the former master bedroom. Is that right?"

Taiba-ayah spat out of the side of her mouth. "Yes. He moved in like he was the new burra sahib."

"Yesterday, I saw two glasses near the bed." She paused. "Do you know if anyone else slept there?"

"Eh?" The woman's face was a vision of confusion.

Slowly and clearly, she repeated, "I saw two drinking glasses in the bedchamber. Who stayed with him? Was it a lady from the outside or inside the house?"

Taiba-ayah shook her white head vigorously. "Don't ask me. I sleep with children."

"You sleep in the nursery with Jum-Jum, Shireen, and Nasreen. Not the older girls, Amina and Fatima." She paused, knowing her last question would be shocking. "Do you think he might have made them sleep with him?"

"Both are good girls! Who are you to say such things!" the ayah screeched and let loose some Marathi curses Perveen would not have expected her to know.

Perveen spoke hastily. "I was not blaming them—and I certainly hope for their own sake nothing happened. What about the widows?"

Taiba's rheumy eyes narrowed. "You are asking me that question in the house where they live? They are respectable ladies. You are rude."

Perveen raised her hands in surrender. "I'm sorry. Can you at least tell me whether you heard any shouting or screaming yesterday afternoon?"

"Of course! Jum-Jum was crying all afternoon. Bad tooth. Not even our Amina could calm him!"

Perveen seized on the revelation. "Did Amina stay with you in the nursery most of the afternoon?"

"She sang to Jum-Jum for a while, but he was still cross, so I let her go."

Perhaps this was when Amina had heard the cry. Watching Taiba-ayah squint into the distance, observing Nasreen and Shireen tussling over the ball, Perveen asked, "Do you believe the killer came from outside of the house?"

"From where else? It could not be Mohsen or our cook, Iqbal. Both were too afraid of Mukri to go near him."

"Why were they afraid?"

"Did you know he stopped all servants' payments, telling us that food and shelter was enough? We lost the six other staff we had when he did this. Only Iqbal and Mohsen and his children remained. I also stayed because it is a roof over my head, and I am too old to go anywhere."

"Did you speak to the police about this?"

Taiba-ayah broke into a hacking cough. At the end of it, she said, "They never asked. They only wished to know if I helped someone to get inside. The Sikh detective thought I was lying about not hearing sounds—when that baby was crying to the heavens, giving everyone headache."

And in the short conversation, Taiba-ayah had proven that she was hard of hearing. Perveen wanted to ask more, but Jum-Jum started bawling. A fly had landed on his face. Taiba-ayah swatted at it, making Jum-Jum cry more.

"It was very good of you to clean yesterday," Perveen said, giving the elderly lady a rupee that was accepted with a wide smile.

"It is good that you've come. The begums could use help because of Amina."

"Of course. There's much to get in order—" Perveen interrupted herself, because Taiba's sentence had ended strangely. "What about Amina?"

Shaking her head again, Taiba said, "She hid yesterday evening and hasn't come out."

"Are you sure she's hiding?" Perveen had an odd feeling: a tightness in her chest that she recognized as fear.

"Who knows? She thinks she's too old for me to supervise her. But then this happens—"

Perveen interrupted her. "Where are the begums right now?"

"Razia's room."

Perveen hurried upstairs, thinking that it was strange Taiba-ayah hadn't told her about Amina's disappearance immediately. Didn't the ayah fear Amina's disappearance following a violent crime might mean that whoever had killed Mukri had done away with the young girl? Or what if Amina had decided to leave the house and go to Perveen's office for help? But surely Mustafa would have admitted her and telephoned to say what had happened.

Rounding the corner into the hall where Razia's room lay, Perveen felt nothing but worry. Even if Amina turned out to be playing a hiding game, as the ayah thought, Perveen would be so relieved to see her that she wouldn't scold. If the girl was hiding, there had to be a solid reason for it.

Razia's door was open a crack, but Perveen knocked on it to alert the widows of her presence. Razia and Sakina, who'd been sitting silently at the partners' desk, turned quickly.

"Adab. May I come in?" Perveen asked.

"Please," Razia said, standing. She spoke shakily. "We're trying to manage a new trouble. My daughter is gone."

Coming forward to put a hand on Razia's shoulder, Perveen said, "Taiba-ayah just told me. We will find her."

"I telephoned last night at nine," Sakina said. "To the number on the card. But nobody answered."

Perveen felt sick. This was when she was at Alice's, and her father was away from the office. If only Sakina had called the number to the house.

"At first, we weren't very worried, because she has so many little hiding places where she reads and draws," Sakina said. "But then she never came out, not even for dinner."

"Why didn't you call the police?" Perveen demanded.

"They went away earlier," Razia said, her face a mask of misery. "We know they would not care. And then we found some objects were missing."

Perveen couldn't hide her apprehension. "How is this connected? The objects could have been stolen by whoever came for Mr. Mukri."

"No," Razia whispered. "Amina's clothing, her sketchbook, and satchel were gone."

"And tell her what you found later," Sakina interjected.

Razia sank down into her chair. "Also missing are my address book, a city guidebook, and twenty rupees from this desk."

Perveen's mind leaped to the obvious. "Do you think she left Malabar Hill?"

"Maybe." Razia sounded uncertain. "She is very fond of our relatives in Oudh. Two years ago, we went by train, and she took a great interest in the route. She might think she can make the journey herself."

"It is hard to think she would leave us at a time like this, but girls are emotional," Sakina said softly. "And the gate was unguarded. Perhaps she saw a chance."

Perveen thought it unlikely that Amina had taken advantage of lapsed security to explore the world. The only reason she would have fled would be to save her own life or possibly tell someone outside of the house that they needed help. "I don't understand why Amina wouldn't have left a note explaining what she'd done. How can a girl with no experience in the city make her way down from Malabar Hill and out to Victoria Terminus? And then she'd have to buy a long-distance train ticket at the window. If she tried that, it would have been noticed. We can tell the police to put out a watch for her. They can send a message out to constables and to the railways."

"No, no," Razia said with a moan. "No policemen. Not after yesterday!"

"But when people are looking out for a missing child, it improves the chance of her being found." Perveen had to struggle not to shake the woman, who knew so little about the world. "We can even offer a reward for her safe return."

"No." Razia shook her head decisively.

Perveen looked from her to Sakina.

"I think I can explain her feeling," Sakina said, patting Razia's hand. "If it's publicly known that Amina has wandered the city, her reputation will be ruined. We will never find a groom for her. We are praying for Allah's blessing on her travels to Oudh. After that, we would humbly request your assistance in returning her to Bombay."

Perveen knew all about ruined reputations, but wouldn't a mother wish to try everything to find a missing child? She looked imploringly to Razia to contradict Sakina, but the senior wife stayed silent.

And then Perveen recalled Razia's secret fear that Amina had killed Mr. Mukri.

What if Razia had sent off her daughter to avoid prosecution, not necessarily alone, but guided by someone whom she trusted? If that were the case—and Perveen called the police herself—she would potentially violate her attorney-client relationship with Razia and put Amina in jeopardy.

She couldn't do it. Sighing, she said, "I've told you what I consider the wisest course of action. I don't know what I can do to help you."

"There is something." Razia's anguished eyes fixed on Perveen. "Conditions are more old-fashioned in Oudh; my family house has no telephone. I will write a telegram—perhaps you can send it? I'd like my family to have my younger brother—he is Amina's favorite uncle—wait at the railway station."

"I'll do that." Perveen shifted her gaze to Sakina. "Please. I need to know more about Mohsen, because the police are still holding him."

"Why? I told you yesterday that I sent him to get me rose attar," Sakina said. "Did you not tell the police?"

"I told the sub-inspector about the errand, but it didn't make an impact. One of the problems was that Mohsen first gave the police a false story: that he was socializing with the neighboring durwans."

"I don't know why he'd say that," Razia said with a sigh. "But then, we don't know him at all."

Perveen wasn't sure that was true. "He runs errands often. How do you communicate with him when you're in purdah?"

Sakina shrugged, and her black chiffon sari slipped at the shoulder. "We speak to Fatima, and she brings him any of our requests. This time, I asked him to fetch rose attar from Mr. Attarwala's shop in Zaveri Bazaar. I did it right after Mukri-sahib threw you out."

"Why would you send him on an errand when so much was going on in the household?"

"Smelling roses calms my nerves," Sakina answered. "I have used it so much since our husband's passing. I realized that my bottle was empty. "

"The sub-inspector suggested that Mohsen could have been in the bungalow and killed Mukri-Sahib before he went off on your errand. What do you think of that?"

"I don't know," Razia said in a low voice. "I must not speak ill of someone who has only helped us in the past."

Hardly a vote of confidence. Perveen studied Sakina, who was fiddling with the edge of her sari, giving credence to her description of nervousness. "Mohsen came back yesterday evening and was stopped straightaway by the police. Sakina-begum, did you receive the attar?"

"No." Sakina put her hand to her mouth. "If the perfume isn't here, it might mean he didn't go to Zaveri Bazaar! That he did—that terrible thing."

"On the other hand, he might have given the attar to Fatima to pass on to you just before he was taken away. I shall ask her." Perveen paused. "Where is Mumtaz-begum?"

"We haven't seen her yet. She is always a late sleeper," Razia said with a hint of disapproval.

Perveen certainly hoped the widow was in her room sleeping. But she no longer thought that anyone could be safe at the Farid bungalow.

24

A WIFE'S SECRET JOY
Bombay, February 1921

Fatima was washing the carved marble baseboard running along the hallway when Perveen came out to visit Mumtaz's room. Bending down, Perveen said, "I'm on my way to see Mumtaz-begum, but I've got a question. Did your father leave anything with you before the police took him away?"

"No." Fatima put down the rag she'd been using. "What should he have given me?"

"I thought you might have the attar he bought for Sakina-begum. But never mind."

Fatima lowered her voice. "Did you hear Amina's missing?"

Perveen nodded. "Do you think she went to Oudh?"

Fatima picked up the rag again and squeezed it hard. "But how could she go? She's just a girl. And she was my friend. She wouldn't leave without saying goodbye."

"Is there a chance she's hiding?"

Fatima scrubbed away at the baseboard. "She hides because she listens to people—not because she's playing. Maybe she cannot be found because"—she took several deep breaths—"the killer came back."

"I pray that's not the case."

"It's so frightening now, with Abba away. Zeid and I were alone in our hut last night. We put a rice bag against the door, so we would hear if someone was coming for us. And Iqbal gave us a knife from the kitchen for our protection. Zeid said he'd use it to save the two of us, but he's so small!"

A voice moaned from the other side of Mumtaz's door. Perveen's first instinct was panic, but she controlled the reaction. "Is that Mumtaz?"

"Yes. She must have heard us," Fatima said, putting down the rag and standing up. "I'll go in with you. She's not well in the morning."

Fatima tiptoed ahead of Perveen into the dark room to touch Mumtaz on the shoulder.

"Sorry," Mumtaz murmured as she pulled herself up from the bed.

"No, I apologize for disturbing you again," Perveen said while the maidservant pulled open the long curtains covering the jalis.

"Mumtaz-begum, shall I bring your special tea?" Fatima asked. There was a note of tenderness in the girl's voice that showed her obvious affection for the outsider wife.

"Not yet." Mumtaz groped at the bedside table, knocking over a brass tumbler of water. Perveen rushed to pick up the tumbler as Mumtaz hurriedly used the previous day's sari to wipe at the spilled water. As Mumtaz moved, dressed in a blouse and petticoat, her rounded figure was revealed. Perveen looked away, trying to give the disheveled woman a bit of privacy as she covered up again with the sheet.

Mumtaz sleepily rubbed her eyes. "Is there any news of Amina?"

"The begums believe she went off to go to Razia's family home in Oudh. Does that strike you as likely?" Perveen added, "Whatever you tell me can remain private."

"Amina is so interested in going places; she's not fearful like the begums," Mumtaz commented. "Many times she has told me about her trips to Oudh. But this is not good. How could a child like that get out of our gate and know what to do?"

"I can't imagine it," Perveen agreed. "But if she had gone out, the neighboring durwans would probably have seen her—or someone else in the neighborhood would have told them."

"How would they know to recognize her? She's always stayed behind the property wall."

"You're right," Perveen said, feeling stupid.

"Bombay is a hard city for girls. Everywhere, there is a villain—oh!" Mumtaz put a hand over her mouth.

"Do you feel sick again?"

"The bucket—" Mumtaz gestured to the floor, and Perveen saw

a small bucket that she quickly grabbed and brought to Mumtaz. Mumtaz bent her head and vomited a watery stream into the bucket.

The sickly-sweet odor curled inside Perveen's nose, and she adjusted the fan's speed.

Putting the bucket aside, Mumtaz said, "Get Fatima again. This is too dirty for you."

"No, it is not."

Things were coming together in Perveen's mind. Mumtaz's weakness—her rounded figure. She had spent many months living with Omar Farid. Perveen would have thought him too weak for sexual activity—but she could be wrong.

"Have you seen a doctor recently?" Perveen asked.

"No, because it is still iddat." She paused. "If I tell you something, will you tell the others?"

"I promised your privacy," Perveen said, her suspicion growing.

Mumtaz gave a half smile. "I'm going to have a baby."

"That is a most blessed event." Perveen was shocked, trying to do the calculations in her head. "You must see a doctor. He can tell you when your baby will be born."

"I know that myself, based on when my husband and I came together," she said.

Perveen nodded, thinking again about the two glasses in Mr. Mukri's room. Perhaps Mr. Farid wasn't the father. "How many months until the birth?"

"Six months. Insha'Allah, my baby will be born during the rainy season."

So it was likely that Mr. Farid was the baby's father. She would not automatically doubt Mumtaz. On the other hand, Perveen remembered how Sakina had spoken dismissively of Mumtaz's knowing Mr. Mukri from Falkland Road. He could believe Mumtaz owed him something for introducing her to Omar Farid.

"What are you thinking? Are you displeased there will be another baby?" Mumtaz sounded aggrieved.

"I'm happy for you," Perveen said, trying to hide all the worries she felt. "I was only thinking you probably should tell Sakina-begum and Razia-begum, who may have guessed already. They were pregnant before. They know the signs, and they'll make you feel better."

Gingerly, she lay back down in bed. "I would fear that kind of assistance."

"Why?"

Lowering her voice to a whisper, Mumtaz put a hand on her stomach. "Imagine if I'm carrying the household's next son. Another heir. They will be jealous—Sakina-begum because she has a son and Razia-begum because she doesn't. They might say it's Mukri-sahib's child and throw me out."

She'd addressed what Perveen had been thinking about. Given Mukri's power, his abuse of any of the wives was a possibility. And Mumtaz was lowest in the hierarchy.

For now, Perveen would not jump to that assumption. Mumtaz had shared a bedroom with Omar Farid for the five months leading to his death. "Your husband was still alive ten weeks ago. If the baby comes in August, there should not be any doubt."

"It is many months until then. They could make my life very hard. I could lose the child or even my own life. How can I not feel endangered after the evil deed that occurred?"

Feeling a chill, Perveen pressed her arms around herself for comfort. If Faisal Mukri was the only one who could contradict Mumtaz's claim of impregnation by her husband, she'd had reason to kill him.

"You are looking so angry," Mumtaz said. "What are you thinking?"

Perveen loosened her grip on herself and forced a smile. "Sorry. I'm not angry; I'm thinking about many things. You have the worry for your growing baby. Razia has the sorrow of a missing child. And Sakina . . ." she trailed off, thinking. "Sakina is worried for everyone in the house. And her children are at risk, too."

"Things will change for everyone after iddat finishes," Mumtaz said. "Once the mourning time has passed, a widow can remarry. Probably both of them will do that. I shan't, because my son will keep me too busy. As long as I can stay in this house, I don't need a man's support. And that could make those two very angry."

Perveen tried to caution her. "You are just guessing that—"

"How will it be for Sakina, watching me all these months and wondering if I have a boy to compete with hers? And Razia-begum counts every paisa. There are four children now—a fifth would cause great expense. Better to get rid of me." Mumtaz pressed a hand to her brow as if she were a film actress showing great agony.

"They cannot throw you out," Perveen said. "Legally, you have the same rights as they do."

In a trembling voice, Mumtaz said, "I could fall down the stairs in a terrible accident. I might die from eating bad food. This is the reason I keep to myself. They know that Fatima tastes everything for me before I eat it."

"I offered to help you find a place to live when we spoke yesterday," Perveen said, feeling wary of Mumtaz's sudden show of desperation. "You fear for your life, but you want to remain here."

"If I leave, my child's claim on the estate becomes harder to prove; so I must endure." Mumtaz's voice was shaky. "I want him to grow up here, a Farid with wealth just like the others."

It seemed clear Mumtaz had a plan for the rest of her life and wouldn't be swayed. Perveen sighed. "Take care of yourself, Mumtaz-begum. I wasn't able to give you my card yesterday, but here it is now. Telephone if you need me."

The young wife nodded glumly. "I will do that. And I will make a prayer today for dear little Amina. May Allah protect her, just as I hope he protects me."

25

THE SCENT OF ROSE
Bombay, February 1921

*B*efore leaving, Perveen stopped in at the cooking hut to meet Iqbal, the elderly household cook. He had been at the market when the terrible event had occurred; he also had no idea about Amina's disappearance. He was anxious to know how he could buy food for the house now that Mukri wasn't providing any money. Perveen gave him ten rupees to cover the next few weeks' expenses, asking him to write down what was bought. He smiled at the money but did not offer any more information.

At her direction, Arman drove her down Malabar Hill and back into the heart of Bombay. Their first stop in town was the Telegraph Building, where she dictated the telegram for Razia and requested that it be delivered to her family estate in Oudh. Next, Arman drove to the Zaveri Bazaar. A. H. Attarwala's shop was one in a line selling attars: the alcohol-free essences of the most fragrant and healthful flowers, shrubs, and trees. Even though the vials and bottles were closed, the shop was heavy in scent. Perveen stopped breathing for a moment as she thought that these myriad fragrances, just like the secrets at the Farid house, couldn't be completely suppressed.

Mr. Attarwala, the shop owner, was a small man in his eighties who wore a tall, stiff tarboosh that made him eight inches taller. He had a genial air and listened carefully to what she said.

Perveen introduced herself as the Farid family's lawyer and asked about Mohsen.

"I know the fellow you speak of. His full name is Mohsen Dawai. He serves a gentleman who recently passed to paradise," said Mr. Attarwala, stroking his long, flowing white beard. "Farid-sahib was a righteous man with good wives. Over the years, Mohsen has come to buy attar for the household members."

"Did Mohsen shop here yesterday?"

"Yes, he arrived just after our late afternoon prayers. He purchased a vial of sandalwood attar."

Perveen recalled Sakina talking about needing a rose attar to calm her nerves. "Are you sure it wasn't rose oil? Rose is the attar that brings sleep and relieves anxiety, isn't it?"

"I am an old man with an imperfect memory. Let me check that." Mr. Attarwala invited her to follow him to a long counter crowded with bottles. From underneath, he brought up a large ledger book. "Here, here. Read it yourself."

He pointed to a line. He had sold sandalwood attar, one bottle for two annas. She could see listed next to it *Omar Farid, 22 Sea View Road.* Sighing, he said, "I will add this to the tally. Every month, I send a bill to the Farid house. Mohsen said that once a lawyer fixes the estate, the account will be paid."

Perveen went on alert. "Do you mean to say that Mohsen didn't pay you yesterday?"

"He has not paid in six months. He tells me to add the charge to the running household bill. He asked me if I could recommend a good jeweler, too; but I cannot imagine a jeweler would accept his promise of credit," the merchant added with a frown.

Mohsen's interest in jewelry was significant; what if he'd robbed Sakina? In any case, if he was taking attar without paying, it might mean that he'd pocketed the money Sakina had given him for the errand. If this type of behavior had gone on for months, and bills were coming to the house, surely Mr. Mukri had known. Perhaps he'd confronted Mohsen about it—and this had led to the killing. "What is the exact amount you're waiting for the Farid household to pay for all the past perfume expenses?"

"Let me go to the back of the book for that." He turned pages of the book until he reached the right place, stabbing a finger at a line. "Yes. Last payment to us was made in October. The household owes four rupees sixty paise. And not just for attar: for skin oils and incense, too. If you are able to pay today, I will be pleased to give a receipt."

Perveen looked down the line of expenses. There had been several bottles of rosewater attar purchased in the past, but it looked as if in the past six months the choice had been sandalwood—an oil more often used for erotic purposes.

Perveen opened her purse, examined what was left, and asked if he could please write a receipt for her in Hindi or English. Given the alacrity of his response, she suspected he might have been able to present a bill in German. She also requested him to write a statement detailing the time of Mohsen's visit the day before, which he signed with a flourish.

"I am grateful to you, madam. This is a small gift for your kindness." Mr. Attarwala put a tiny vial of pinkish liquid into her hand.

"What is it?"

"The rose scent. Once you smell it, I'm sure you will come back to buy more."

Perveen hadn't worn scent since she'd left her marriage—and that had been sandalwood. However, she thanked him for the attar and tucked it into her bag.

From the Zaveri Bazaar, it was only twenty minutes around the bay to the Malabar Hill Police Station on Ridge Road. The tile-roofed, yellow-stucco station looked very modern next to its elderly neighbor, a stone Jain temple dating from the early 1820s. A steady throng of barefoot Jains was coursing around the temple, not giving way for the constables. It was as if the fellows didn't even exist. Perveen couldn't help smiling at the sight.

Perveen stopped at the temple's bakery window and bought a box of caraway-butter biscuits. Namkeen biscuits would be a practical item to give Mohsen, because they wouldn't quickly spoil.

Perveen had visited different police stations around Bombay with her father, so she knew to go straight to the duty sergeant and present her business card. She opened her purse for it to be searched, as well as the small paper box of biscuits.

Taking one biscuit, the constable munched and swallowed before speaking. "He's in the cell block."

Perveen longed to tell the man to take his fat, ink-stained fingers out of the box, but she couldn't. The message was clear; she had to give him something in exchange for service.

All the prisoner cells were in the basement; Mohsen was in a hot, smelly chamber with four men of varying ages. He was the only one in a uniform; the others were in rags. The fact that the durwan still wore the long-sleeved green uniform—the symbol of respectability and the Farid household—struck her as poignant.

Perveen couldn't possibly speak to Mohsen in such an environment and in the presence of others. She made the point to the constable and a prison guard, who eventually agreed to allow Mohsen to accompany her to a nearby office room, which was better ventilated but had no amenities other than a table and two hard chairs.

As they sat down together, Mohsen looked uneasily at her. It was almost as if she'd come to the gate and he was once again hesitant to admit her.

"Do you remember me?" she asked. "I'm the Farids' lawyer."

"I know," he said gruffly. "Why have you come?"

"Your children are very worried. I wanted to tell them what happened to you." She handed him the box, which still had some biscuits in it. "You must be hungry."

Mohsen finished all that was within before he spoke again. "Thank you. They have only given me bread and water."

"What happened yesterday?" Perveen folded her arms on the table and settled in. There was no need to take notes yet; it might put Mohsen on edge.

"Sakina-begum needed attar from A. H. Attarwala's shop," he said in a monotone. "I did not wish to go, because the burra sahib had come home. But then I thought that he was inside for the evening. How would he know if I went off for such a short time? And the begums expect my services."

And he needed money badly because he was no longer paid. "How did you travel to the bazaar?"

"I walked downhill and then caught a tram."

"At Attarwala's, you purchased sandalwood oil costing two annas. Didn't Sakina-begum ask for rose attar?"

He shook his head vigorously. "She did not say the type, but I know what she wants. It is always sandalwood."

At times, Perveen could still smell the sandalwood oil from her wedding night. Shaking herself, she asked, "What amount of money did Sakina-begum give you?"

His face became guarded. "One rupee, but some was gone for the tram cost."

She suspected this was a partial truth. "Tell me—did you avoid telling the police about the errand at first because you wanted this trip to remain unknown?"

"Yes," he said, nodding with seeming relief. "When they met me at the gate, I thought that Mukri-sahib had complained to them about me. That is why I said I was just away down the street rather than farther away; he would not like me performing duties for the widows. Little did I know the other durwans would be asked and then contradict me."

"And what reason did the police give for arresting you?"

"They said because I lied about being with the durwans down the street, I must go with them to have my fingerprints checked. I said it was needless. The police made prints five years ago."

"In what situation were they taken?" she asked, wondering if he had been charged with a crime.

Looking warily at her, he said, "I'd been working at the docks, and Farid-sahib told me I could work at the house. When I started, the police came around and took the prints. Most durwans in Bombay have their prints recorded with the police."

Taking Mohsen here to be fingerprinted allowed the police to tell the press they had a suspect in custody. Furthermore, keeping him in the cell gave them the opportunity to force a confession if they never found anyone more suitable. "Did you ever tell the police you went to Zaveri Bazaar for Sakina-begum?"

"Yes, when I was questioned here. They looked at the attar I was carrying and said, 'This means nothing.'"

"What happened to it?"

He hesitated a moment. "They took everything from my pocket

and say they're keeping it for now. Probably it's gone," he added glumly.

Recalling the many inconsistencies, Perveen knew it was time to press on. "I visited Attarwala-sahib this morning. He remembers everything about your visit yesterday and wrote an affidavit. That is a sworn statement of the timing and so on."

"He said I was there?" A hopeful smile appeared on Mohsen's long face.

"He also shared this long list of purchases you made on behalf of the begums that weren't paid for with the petty cash they gave you," she said crisply. "At his request, I settled that bill."

"I wish I could pay," he mumbled. "But I cannot."

It was hard to maintain composure when she wanted to shout at him, demanding that he acknowledge his thieving. "You took money from Sakina-begum yesterday, and I know you have done the same with the others. What are you buying with the begums' money?"

"There is a lotion for skin—very expensive—made by a doctor. I've been putting it on Zeid for a year now. The mark is lightening, so perhaps he will find a paying position somewhere. We will have a better life, Insha'Allah."

Perveen opened her notebook now and made the notes on Mohsen's testimony that she had held back from making earlier, while he was talking. Then she read it all back to Mohsen, who nodded along with it.

"That is the truth," he pronounced gloomily.

"I know you asked Mr. Attarwala about a jeweler. Did you take any jewelry from the house?"

Now he looked incensed. "Certainly not. I am not a thief; I am a house guard!"

Perveen nodded, resolving to ask the women to look through their jewelry collections when she saw them. "Do you know anything about Mukri-sahib that might have led to his death?" She stared at Mohsen, looking for evidence of hesitation. "I know he tried to steal funds from the begums. What kinds of things did you notice?"

His eyes glittered with emotion. "He was a bad man. He only got his place at the factory because of being in the family. He did nothing to earn it."

This sounded similar to what her father had heard. "Do you know if he was into any type of business outside of work? Did strange men come around or . . . even ladies?"

He shook his head sharply. "Nobody came. He liked keeping that house for himself."

"Thank you, Mohsen." Perveen stood and slid her notebook back into her briefcase.

"Will you go back to the bungalow?"

She shook her head. "I've got other things to do first. I shall visit them tomorrow."

"Will the police allow me to place a call to the bungalow? I would like to speak with Sakina-begum."

She imagined that he'd make a plea for Sakina to tell the police about the errand. "I'll ask them. I will also show Mr. Attarwala's statement about your purchase to the police."

Mohsen had a spring in his step when the guard led him back to his cell. The same guard escorted Perveen upstairs. Taking a breath of good air, she tried to collect her thoughts. She had read Mohsen correctly as a disagreeable man from the minute she'd first pulled up in the car. Taking the money the begums gave him to buy items for them was an example of bad character. However, if it was true that he'd spent the begums' money on his son's skin cream, he had some kind of heart.

Upstairs in the Malabar Hill Station, Perveen approached the man she'd dubbed Sergeant Biscuit, who was now enjoying a cup of chai. "Sergeant, I need to speak with an officer," she said. "I have information regarding the prisoner I visited."

He smiled as if she were a child asking to see a busy elder. "It is not our investigation. That is the business of CID downtown."

"But the prisoner is being housed here. Which officer is responsible for him?"

Sergeant Biscuit looked at the closed door behind him. "Chief Fisher is holding a meeting. I don't know how long it will take."

She could hear a rumble of voices behind the door.

"I shall wait." Perveen seated herself on the edge of a wooden bench in the waiting area. She was among an assortment of depressed and anxious-looking people. She imagined many of them had relatives stuck in the cells below.

The door opened, and two Englishmen came out. One was middle-aged and plump, wearing a tight white uniform with some swags of braid across the chest. She guessed he was Chief Fisher. The red-faced, younger man was Inspector Vaughan from the day before. With them was Sub-Inspector Singh, who gaped at the sight of her.

"Good afternoon," she said, nodding at the group.

Inspector Vaughan's face was blank—as if he didn't recognize her. Well, she'd been sweaty and bedraggled the day before; now she felt fresh, in a starched green cotton sari with delicate chikankari stitching and a necklace, bangles, and earrings of Hyderabad pearls.

Chief Fisher gave her a dismissive glance. "If this is related to a family member, please speak with the public defender."

"No, thank you. I am a solicitor in private practice," she said crisply. "I have some information relating to the death yesterday at twenty-two Sea View Road."

At the words "Sea View," both white men looked at her sharply.

"Madam, who did you say you are?" Chief Fisher demanded.

"She is a lawyeress named Miss Perveen Mistry," Sub-Inspector Singh said quickly. "Her father represents the late Mr. Farid. The two Mistrys assisted us yesterday."

"Come into the office." The Malabar police chief's voice was curt.

After the door closed the four of them in, Fisher settled into a large chair upholstered in leather behind a wide mahogany desk. There were just two other chairs in the room: slant-backed campaign-style chairs. Vaughan took the one closest to Fisher. That left one chair for either Perveen or Singh. The Sikh glanced at Perveen and gestured for her to take the chair. While Perveen hadn't liked him calling her a lawyeress, she felt guilty taking the chair; his mannerism made her think he was used to being the one left standing.

"May I explain?" Perveen asked, giving her attention to Chief Fisher. After he nodded, she said, "I've spoken with two people regarding the activities of Mohsen Dawai, the Farids' durwan, who is in custody downstairs. What I've learned is important for you to know."

"We've reported the facts already," Vaughan said with a sneer. "First Mohsen said he was chatting with the boys down the street, and then he claimed he went shopping. What's the latest lie?"

Perveen would not respond to his slur. In a steady voice, she said, "I spoke to Mrs. Sakina Farid, who'd asked Mohsen to buy a vial of attar around three-thirty yesterday, which was the reason he was missing from his post. Just like you gentlemen, I had no reason to believe this was the truth. Therefore, I traveled to the shop in the Zaveri Bazaar where Sakina-begum had sent him. Mr. Attarwala confirmed Mohsen's arrival shortly after four-thirty and submitted an affidavit about the purchase and the time Mohsen was in the shop."

"A nice excuse for a trip to a perfume shop," Inspector Vaughan said with a laugh. "Did you get something for yourself?"

He was dismissing her, just like the men had at the Government Law School. Perveen felt anger rising but remembered how her father's smooth approach tended to serve him well. "My point is, Attarwala gave Mohsen the product he purchased. Mohsen said that the police who checked him in at this station removed his possessions for safekeeping. Do you still have the attar he bought, or did it somehow disappear?"

Chief Fisher spoke up. "I was the officer present when he was taken into custody. There was only the vial and a bag containing his other purchase."

Instead of saying what she really wanted to say—*why didn't you let him go?*—she asked, "What is it?"

The three men exchanged glances.

"Might it be a skin cream?" Perveen asked.

"Yes," Inspector Vaughan said.

"A medical treatment for his son. Mohsen had to go to the apothecary, also in the bazaar, for it. I'm sure you could check up on that, if you think it's necessary."

Inspector Vaughan cleared his throat. Roughly, he said, "Is there a reason you wish the fellow downstairs to be freed? I met your father, and he didn't mention anyone was representing the durwan."

"As the family's solicitors, we are invested in making sure that the household is protected by someone. My father and I left twenty-two Sea View Road yesterday with an assurance of round-the-clock police protection for three secluded widows and their small children. But the police left the place before night fell and still haven't returned."

"They didn't stay because I didn't put in a request," Inspector Vaughan said icily. "A suspect was taken into custody. There was no continuing threat."

"In any case, police are assigned duty at my discretion. The sub-inspector should never have told you there would be coverage without his superior's request to me." Chief Fisher glowered at Singh.

The fact that they'd left the women unprotected with a murderer on the loose caused Perveen's temper to spark.

"Perhaps you think this is trivial because it wasn't a European household that was attacked," she said. "The problem is, this is an Indian city. If you want law and order in the town, you need to protect all people."

If only she could tell them that their negligence had caused a young girl from the household to vanish.

Sub-Inspector Singh had such a look of tension on his face that Perveen almost wished she hadn't made the comment. She imagined he might agree with her, but in the hierarchy, he was powerless.

"Why would you want that watchman back? He's not much of a watchman if he wandered off and allowed a murderer to enter!" Inspector Vaughan said defensively.

"Just like your policemen, he had to respect a direct order."

Perveen gathered up the receipt and affidavit she'd placed on the desk. "Thank you for the chance to directly provide this information on the watchman's whereabouts. I shall not waste any more of my time."

Chief Fisher coughed. "Actually—before you go, let the sergeant make a copy of that affidavit."

Perveen paused, keeping the paper in hand. "I will certainly oblige, but in exchange, I was wondering if you might allow Mohsen Dawai to make a telephone call. He wishes to speak with Mrs. Sakina Farid."

Sub-Inspector Singh looked at his superior. "Sir, if the begum is on the telephone, we can speak to her as well. Perhaps we'll learn more than we did yesterday."

"All right, then." Vaughan shot Perveen a poisonous look. She had embarrassed him in front of his colleague.

"I have the number," Perveen said, writing it down. She was careful to keep her face expressionless, though she hardly felt that way. She was outraged the police would have kept Mohsen Dawai locked up without real evidence. And for the first time, she'd realized what her power as a lawyer really meant.

26

A WORD IN THE RIGHT EAR
Bombay, February 1921

*T*he police were efficient. Within minutes, Sergeant Biscuit had typed two copies of the statement and stamped them with the official seal. Inspector Vaughan took one and Chief Fisher the other while Perveen slid the original into her legal briefcase. Her meeting had seemed like a success, but she didn't know whether they'd release Mohsen. In the meantime, she needed to find a reliable temporary guard.

Arman was leaning against the Daimler, which was parked in the shade of a jacaranda tree. The chauffeur looked bored but brightened at the sight of her. "To the office, please." Perveen sank into the back seat. "You know everything about the city, Arman. Do you have an idea how to find a durwan to guard a house for a short time?"

"Everyone is wanting permanent work, memsahib. And durwans cannot simply leave one house to work at another place for a few days. The owners would not like it." He paused. "What about men with training as soldiers? The soldiers have come back from war, and not everyone has work."

"Perhaps." Hiring a veteran was a practical idea, and perhaps Razia would know of someone the wakf had helped who was nearby. But that would take time. Then she had it. "The docks! Jayanth knows many men there. I think Mohsen was a stevedore."

"But they are mainly Hindus at the docks," Arman said. "The begums may not like that."

"Perhaps the women won't mind. It's not as if they have to live together," she said, feeling irritated. The boundaries communities drew around themselves seemed to narrow their lives—whether it was women and men, Hindus and Muslims, or Parsis and everyone else.

"Perveen-memsahib, we are here."

Arman had driven all the way to Mistry House. However, she wasn't ready to go inside; her mind was too unsettled. "I'm going to take a short walk. Will you please bring the document case inside to Mustafa and have him take it upstairs?"

"Certainly. But where are you walking?"

"I'll just stroll over to the pier and back. I've a headache—this will make me feel better."

The wind buffeted Perveen as she walked toward Ballard Pier. After she was allowed through the gate, she gazed ahead at the sea filled with small cargo ships, the kind of vessels that Jayanth worked at loading or unloading every day.

A tall cargo ship was slowly steaming out of the harbor. Perveen stared at it, imagining the heat and rough conditions on board, so very different from the first-class quarters she'd occupied as she headed toward the unknown in England. In 1917, she'd not spent long thinking about the great expense her family had gone to to send her—or their belief that a failed law student in Bombay could succeed abroad. Would that investment prove sound?

As she walked along, she thought she recognized a small, wiry young man with a confident gait. She called out, and when he turned, she was pleased to see she'd been right.

Jayanth ran up, his sandals flapping hard on the stones. "Memsahib, why have you come?"

"I'm searching for someone who might like working as a household guard. Do tell me, though, how are things at your job?"

"I'm being careful," he said grimly. "My boss, Ravi, is always watching me with an angry face. He did not like giving the back pay. I am hoping he isn't planning to get rid of me."

Perveen tried to comfort him. "He must know that if he sacks you again, you would come straight to us."

"I do not mean sacking. I mean killing me off. From the way he looks at me and from how I hear him swearing about your father by name, I am concerned for the firm as well."

Perveen pondered his words and realized there might be some cases where the rule of law wasn't worth the consequences. "People say all kinds of things when they're upset. As lawyers, we don't worry for ourselves. But I worry for you. Although you have the right to work at the loading company—if you truly feel endangered, you should leave. In fact, I may have something for you in town, working as a house guard."

He looked dubious. "This family would hire someone who hasn't done such work before?"

"I would do the hiring. It could start—" She broke off, seeing a heavyset man approaching from the water. "Jayanth, do you know the man who's coming our way?"

The stevedore turned his head quickly. "It's Ravi. Please go! He may think I'm telling you tales!"

"All right, I'm on my way," Perveen said hastily.

Jayanth called after her, "Walk back through Ballard Estate. It's safer."

Jayanth was translating his own worry into overconcern for her. But as she walked through the elegant new office district, she recalled the Bengali stranger and the man who resembled Cyrus. So much had happened that she'd almost forgotten about them. She'd be glad if she never saw either man again.

Finally, Perveen turned into Bruce Street. The Silver Ghost was parked in front of Mistry House. This was unexpected. Perveen nodded at Sirjit, the Hobson-Joneses' Sikh chauffeur, who'd taken her home a few days ago. No passenger was in the car: Alice must have been admitted inside.

Mustafa opened the door to her and spoke in an undertone. "He's waiting for you in the parlor."

"Did Alice have any tea yet?" Perveen said, glancing at herself in the mirror in the entryway as she smoothed her windblown hair.

"No, he refused . . ." Mustafa's voice faded behind her as she stepped into the parlor and saw that her visitor wasn't Alice but Sir David.

"Good afternoon," he said, standing and extending his hand. He wore a crisp gray worsted suit with lapels that made his shoulders seem even larger than they were. "You had given me your card, so I decided to visit. What a pleasant base of operations."

Perveen had given Alice her card—but she decided she'd better not correct him. She doubted this was an ordinary visit. Either Alice had inadvertently spilled something to him about Perveen's representing the Farids, or he'd heard from the police.

Realizing he was looking expectantly at her, she belatedly put her hand in his. "How lovely to see you, Sir David. I hope you weren't waiting long."

"I've just been here about ten minutes," he said. "The manservant said your father is away, but you would be coming in sometime."

"If you don't mind, I'll order tea for us," she said, raising her eyebrows at Mustafa, who was standing silently in the doorway.

"That will be fine," Sir David said. "I hope I'm not keeping you from a client or another appointment?"

"Not at all. Since you've come for a visit, I am happy to show you around."

"I don't need a tour. I came because your name was mentioned by the CID."

"I left the Malabar Hill Police Station only about an hour ago. News travels quickly."

"Apparently you represent a family who owns a house in my neighborhood."

"That's true," Perveen said, nodding. "I shared with the police information that the Farid widows wished to communicate to them."

"Secluded communities of women are a concern. Some unfair and possibly illegal things happen that the government never knows about, because the women don't come out to tell what's going on."

She agreed with him, but she sensed there was more to come. She needed to maintain her guard. "Some traditions are slowly changing, while others will hold. We cannot force the women to come out into the wider world until they're ready."

"How long have you worked with the Farid widows?" Sir David

asked as Mustafa returned with the sterling silver tea service and Minton cups.

She hoped this question wasn't a trap. "Just since yesterday— although the family has been my father's client for more than a decade," Perveen added, pouring Sir David the first cup. "I went yesterday for an appointment to hear their wishes regarding the estate. Some hours later, the death of their household agent occurred."

He gave her a quizzical gaze. "Their wishes? Surely the estate settlement is determined by the deceased husband's will."

Perveen didn't think it wise to reveal that Mr. Farid had died without a will; nor did she wish to share that Mr. Mukri had demanded that the women abandon their assets. That could bring suspicion upon all three of them. "You're correct about set amounts going to each family member. However, it was necessary for the widows to understand what their existing assets are and what choices they'd like to make for the future."

Sir David eyed the tea but did not drink it. Either he didn't trust the water, or he was waiting for it to strengthen. "And their answer?"

"Answers," Perveen said with a smile. "They all have differences. And I'm afraid I cannot tell you what they said without violating attorney-client privilege."

The councillor smiled back just as pleasantly. "Of course. As the only female lawyer in Bombay, you hold a power that nobody else has."

"I don't think so," she said with a dismissive sigh. "After all, I cannot argue cases in court. I have to rely on my father for that side of the work."

Sir David leaned slightly forward across the tiny tea table, almost eclipsing it. "In light of your prior assistance to the widows, you seem ideally suited for a matter in which I could use some aid."

Perveen had the feeling it would be something she didn't want to do. She was on the verge of refusing when a soft chanting began outside the windows. It was a familiar incantation that she knew was a muezzin's call to prayer. The call reminded her of the Farid widows, who were likely on their knees, praying that God would assist them through the disruption they'd never expected. Perveen used the reassuring cadence to steady herself and then nodded at Sir David. "Tell me."

"Commissioner Griffith would be most obliged if you would assist the CID by taking the ladies' fingerprints. You see, it involves holding a person's hand—something that we both know goes against the traditional ways of Muslim women. Sub-Inspector Singh would be pleased to teach you."

The idea might have seemed sensible to them, but if she did such a thing, she could very well lead one of the widows into prison. Mr. Farid would not have wished it—but how could a young Indian woman refuse the request of an important government official? Her whole future—and perhaps that of Mistry Law—rested on her answer.

She reminded herself that Sir David Hobson-Jones was intelligent enough to grasp the reason she couldn't comply. Biting her lip, Perveen said, "Sir David, I wish I could, as criminology and fingerprinting are things I'd like to learn more about. However, to fingerprint these women would create a significant conflict of interest. Should the police charge one of the family, I could be in the dreadful position of giving evidence against someone I was trying to defend."

He gazed into his teacup and, having judged the tea was properly brown, finally picked it up and sipped. He smiled as if he'd gotten it just right. "You are getting ahead of yourself. The prints are needed for the process of elimination. If we know the familiar family member prints, we're better able to recognize the hand of an alien."

"I very much understand the CID's wish to be able to collect women's fingerprints. The police commissioner must begin hiring female constables—not ask lawyers to do it."

As she spoke, she felt her anxiety being replaced by the strength of knowing she had the law behind her. "I wish the police all the best in this investigation, but for me to fingerprint the widows would be such a violation of lawyers' conduct that I could be disbarred."

"Disbarred?" He paused significantly. "You're not yet a member of the Bombay Bar."

Realizing how neatly he'd used her own words against her, she struggled to keep her composure. "Once the Bombay Bar admits women lawyers, I shall be vetted not only on my knowledge of law but also on my past behavior as a solicitor."

The councillor took another sip of tea. Very likely, he was coming up with another objection. She had to turn the tables quickly.

"May I suggest one thing, Sir David? If you'd like to prevent another crime from happening while the investigation continues, it would be wise for the police to guard the bungalow. Without Mohsen, the widows and children are absolutely unprotected. What if the killer returns—or any other ruffian who hears about this unguarded house decides to try his luck?"

Sir David Hobson-Jones carefully put down his half-full teacup on the saucer. "I'll see what I can do about stationing a police detail at the house."

"That would be very helpful," Perveen said, knowing that this conversation was probably worth more than her heartfelt arguments to the police in their quarters.

"I've another request. If you could serve as a go-between in conversation with the widows, that would be within a lawyer's purview, wouldn't it?"

"Certainly—if each lady agrees to speak," Perveen added.

Five minutes later, the governor's councillor was gone. Perveen stood at the parlor window, watching the Silver Ghost pull away. She wondered if Sir David might say anything about Perveen's representing the Farids to Alice. What a sticky wicket!

Returning to the hall, she dialed the city operator and asked to be put through to the Hobson-Joneses' house. A manservant answered and told her to wait while he fetched the memsahib.

Two minutes of silence were finally broken by Alice's breathy, excited greeting. "Hello, Perveen! I wish I could have warned you that my father was going to visit. But I rang, and your butler said you weren't in."

Perveen felt taken aback. "Your father told you he was coming here?"

"Yes. He asked about your schedule, and I said you'd be working today." Alice's voice had a nervous edge. "Are you still speaking to me, or am I now persona non grata?"

"Don't worry about your father. He asked me to do some things to help the police, which I sadly cannot, due to conflict of interest."

"I doubt you're sad about it." Alice chuckled. "By the way, are we still on for going to the pictures tonight?"

Perveen had forgotten about the invitation she'd made. "Damnation! I wish I could go, but I've still got hours of work ahead. I don't see how I can go."

"That's a shame." Alice's voice sounded flat.

Feeling guilty, Perveen said, "I do want to spend time with you, Alice—"

"I'm sure you'd like that, if you had the time. You've got a career—you're always going to be busy. I've got to find something to do."

Perveen sighed, unable to keep from feeling irritated that a woman who'd been in India less than three days thought its people should have immediately come forward with a job for her. "Alice, I promise I'll help you find a teaching position. But I've got to keep going with my work tonight, and please know it will also take time for university administrators to respond."

"I see." Alice gave a dismissive laugh that was an echo of her mother's. "By the time that happens, my parents will have my engagement announcement in the *Times*."

Alice's comment was reminiscent of what Razia had said about Mr. Mukri's arranging a marriage for Amina. But the Farid women had faced a real threat, while Alice was engaging in hyperbole. And that was just another irritant. "Shut up, Alice. British common law protects you from that."

"Are you quite sure? Maybe I should retain your services," Alice said in a sneering tone. "On the payment clock seems to be the only way people can spend time with Perveen Mistry, Esquire."

"I'm not trying to avoid you—" Perveen began, but there was a sharp click.

She'd offended Alice—Alice, who hadn't listened to a word of her excuses. It wasn't fair.

Perveen felt the stern eyes of Grandfather Mistry upon her as she passed his portrait on her way upstairs. Did he disapprove of her attitude toward Alice, or was he trying to remind her that she was distracting herself from the case?

Pushing aside her superstitions, Perveen went to her desk, switching on the green-shaded lamp that was supposed to give the most concentrated form of light.

A pool of yellow light bathed a small mound of letters: two days' worth, since she'd been busy on Malabar Hill. On top was a letter from a client disputing the hours she'd billed and some documents that had been mailed from the High Court in regard of other cases. All of it seemed so petty and distracting with all she had going on. There was even a letter from the Petit Parsee General Hospital. Thankfully, it was not from the administration with some complaint but was signed by a prospective new client.

The name was Parsi: Siyamak Azman Patel. The man, who gave no particulars of his background, wished her to call on him in the hospital to assist in writing his will.

Perveen could only hope she'd have sorted the Farid case before the poor fellow died, but nothing was certain anymore. She resolved to pass the request to another law firm that could handle it immediately.

Once she'd dealt with the rest of the post, Perveen opened her briefcase and put all the Farid papers on the center of her blotter. Slowly she leafed through them, looking for something that would show a familial relationship between Omar Farid and Faisal Mukri. She had not dismissed her thought that someone within the family might have wished him dead for reasons of personal or professional gain. But there was nothing.

Annoyed, she continued leafing through the papers, seeing that they were out of order. Somehow the first pages of the widows' marriage contracts were all missing. This was unfortunate, as she knew those pages contained their fathers' names and home addresses. This would make it all the harder for her to follow up on finding relatives to help them.

Perveen gnawed on a fingernail, trying to remember the last time she'd looked at all these pages. It had been when she'd had the conferences with the women, before Mr. Mukri's death.

And then her briefcase had gone missing for a while. Had these first pages been removed? What was within them that could be damaging?

The situation was not irreparable. Copies of the marriage contracts probably were with their families as well as the Bombay High Court. But she wanted those papers now.

The sharp ring of the telephone interrupted her thoughts. Was Alice calling back to finish giving Perveen a piece of her mind? Perveen sat, letting it ring till it stopped.

In the silence, she turned back to the now dog-eared stack of Farid papers. Was there something there that might be a clue about Faisal Mukri's death?

The phone rang again, and this time, Perveen strode down the hall to pick it up.

"Hello?" she said.

There was a crackling pause, and then she heard three words spoken in a low, soft voice.

"Meri madad karo."

The caller had said, *Please help me.*

"Who is calling?" Perveen asked sharply in Hindi.

"Help!" the woman's voice repeated in accented English.

"Are you calling Mistry Law? Who is on the line? What has happened?" Perveen implored the caller. But within a moment, she heard the dull tone that meant the call was finished.

Perveen had no question about what to do next. She dialed the operator and asked to be put through to 22 Sea View Road. But the line was engaged. Either one of the widows was having a chat with someone—or the phone had been taken off the hook.

"Can't you interrupt the call?" Perveen asked. This kind of thing was common, given the impatience of the population.

"At this hour, it's not polite," the operator said.

"You must do it. This is urgent!"

There were some clicks, and then the operator said in her ear, "Nobody is there, madam."

"Then give me the Malabar Hill Police Station."

The phone was picked up by someone who sounded a lot like Sergeant Biscuit.

Perveen identified herself and described the call she suspected had come from 22 Sea View Road.

"But that is impossible. The house is secured," the sergeant told her.

"I have heard that time and time again. But this is an emergency!"

"I tell you, two of our men are on the gates, and there are two more inside. I am certain because three of us are taking extra shifts to make up for it."

She should have been reassured—but she could not forget the sound of the woman's voice. "I'm glad that your men are there, but there might still be trouble within the house. Could someone please request that the nursemaid check on the family members?"

"If anyone is calling out, the constables are surely hearing it," he said patronizingly.

"Maybe not, if they've called me." Perveen banged down the phone. It was a waste of time to continue—she'd have to go there herself.

Perveen hurried downstairs, calling for Mustafa. But he was out. Looking at her watch, she realized it was eight o'clock. He was off duty; perhaps he had gone to see one of his many friends.

Perveen gathered up the small purse she'd carried earlier in the day and stepped outside, looking for the Daimler. But the space where Arman always parked was filled with a slumbering brown buffalo.

"Arman?" she called out loudly as she scanned all of Bruce Street. Perhaps he hadn't been able to wake the animal and had stopped the car elsewhere. But she could not see him anywhere. Remembering her father's trip to Poona, she knew there was a possibility Arman had gone to fetch him at Victoria Terminus. This would mean he'd be dropped home before Arman came back for her.

She had to find another way.

Ramchandra the rickshaw-wallah was chatting with a few men at the only tea stall still open. As she approached him, he broke away and came forward.

Perveen spoke hesitantly, because she anticipated a refusal. "It's a bit far, but could you bring me to Malabar Hill?"

"Malabar Hill?" he repeated incredulously. "I'm not often taking my rickshaw outside Fort. That is far and steep."

The Farids did live very high up. Perveen understood the impossibility of the mission. She could go to a busier street and find a horse-drawn tonga, but it was dark, and traveling with an unknown driver was a huge risk.

"The Malabar Hill Police Station near the Jain temple. From there, I can insist the police bring me to the destination." She reached into her purse, looking at what money she had left. Recklessly, she said, "I'll pay a rupee if you can make it in forty minutes—and another rupee to cover your travel back. I'm sorry to ask you to pedal so far."

"Don't worry, madam," he said, turning toward the rickshaw stand. "It's been slow today—I have spent more time talking than cycling. And that sum is almost a week's take."

"Truly?" Perveen asked as she walked along, feeling bad that Ramchandra lived on so little.

"Yes. My friends will be envious when they hear."

As she climbed up into the familiar seat, Ramchandra poured oil into the small covered lanterns that hung on the rear of the carriage and the largest lantern, which was on his handlebars.

After all the lanterns were lit, the street seemed brighter, and Ramchandra set off cycling. Perveen leaned forward, wishing she could make the weight of the carriage and her own body disappear. The journey felt slow—and they'd barely started.

Turning off Bruce Street into a small lane, the rickshaw dragged even harder and then ground to a halt.

Ramchandra's voice floated back to her. "Sorry, memsahib. I must check the rickshaw. Something may be caught in a wheel."

What bad luck. How could there be a breakdown of his prized rickshaw on a night like this one?

Ramchandra had taken one of his lanterns to use while looking at the tires. She saw him bathed in the pool of yellow light, looking up at her with a grim expression.

"What is it?" she asked.

"Both my tires have punctures."

Perveen stepped down from the rickshaw and walked over to the tire he was studying. "Two flat tires? But how?"

Ramchandra's voice was mournful. "As I was just coming along Bruce Street, I felt something rough catch underneath. It's hard to see in the darkness, but I think something was there. I'm very sorry, memsahib. It will not be possible to fix these tires tonight."

Please help me. The urgency in the unknown woman's voice rang in her head. "But I've got to reach Malabar Hill."

"There is the tonga stand, but a lady should not ride alone—"

"I agree." Perveen had another idea. She would call the Hobson-Jones house and ask for Sir David. She hated to ask him for a favor so soon after refusing to do something he wanted. But she couldn't think of another option—and she knew he wouldn't want the widows to come to harm.

"I'll go back to the office and make a call to see if someone else can go to the police," she said. "Surely in the next half hour or so, Arman will return with the car. I'm so sorry about your tires. Take this rupee from me—no, you must accept it. You wouldn't have ruined tires if I hadn't called you into service."

Perveen ran off around the corner, realizing that she hadn't moved this fast since her days on the tennis court at Oxford. But this was no game. Someone could be dying just a few miles away.

It was dark, so she could not run at top speed. She also didn't want to stumble over whatever had damaged Ramchandra's tires.

Slowing slightly gave her a chance to hear more than the pounding of blood in her ears. She heard footsteps, fast ones, coming from behind her.

Instinctively, she moved to the side, but the fact that she stopped became her undoing. A rough cloth bag whisked over her head, and a thick, strong arm pushed her backward and hauled her upward. Perveen screamed, but her voice was lost in cloth as she felt herself lifted up as casually as a stevedore might carry a ten-pound box. She heard a male grunt as she kicked backward, trying to cause him to drop her.

Suddenly the telephone call for help and Ramchandra's ruined rickshaw came together. The call had been a ploy to get her outside, so she'd be vulnerable. All of it was planned.

Someone didn't like her meddling. She kicked again and again, hoping to put the man off balance, but all that happened was he paused, shifting the bag with her body in it up against a wall and punching her in the back.

Then all she knew was a slow dripping sound.

1917

27
THE JURY DECIDES
Calcutta, August 1917

Water beat Calcutta, turning the city into a lake. As Perveen stood in the portico of the Grand Hotel, she could hardly see across the drive. She'd already heard Chowringhee was three feet deep and rising. The summer monsoon rains fell loud and hard, refusing to break for anyone.

"Could the court close because of the rains?" she worried aloud to Jamshedji, who had been arguing with the doorman about why he couldn't get them a tonga.

"The weather is awful," her father agreed. "But since Parsi matrimonial court has a very limited number of hearings, the pressure is for the jury to decide."

Human-pulled rickshaws were the only vehicles capable of negotiating the flooded roads. Jamshedji spotted one making a passenger drop-off and agreed without question to the driver's fare. After a five-month wait, the Mistrys could not risk missing the scheduled trial. Perveen's freedom was dependent on it.

It was a bumpy, sloshy, and slow ride to the courthouse in Dalhousie Square. Perveen felt as if she couldn't wait for the journey to end—and then she was hit by the realization that what could happen in court might make her want to drown herself. The court could rule for her return to the Sodawalla house, and if she stood in contempt of that, she might be thrown in prison.

Perveen, Camellia, and Jamshedji left their sodden umbrellas in an overfilled stand and walked through the slippery marble halls to the designated court chamber. Perveen ignored the portraits of sober English gentlemen and scanned the benches packed with people. Did all of them have cases waiting? Perveen thought she recognized

Mrs. Banaji and her daughter, who were friends of the Sodawalla family. She'd probably come to collect a story for gossip. Still, the sight of those two wasn't as bad as the news Jamshedji brought when he came back from the bench.

"Our barrister, Mr. Pestonji, isn't here," he said, looking soberly at Camellia.

"Maybe he's caught in the rain," Perveen said. "He could arrive any moment."

Jamshedji shook his head. "His junior associate managed to get through the roads to tell me that Pestonji was double-booked for today and has given priority to another case."

"Oh dear. Does that mean we go with the junior—or that we must postpone?" Camellia asked in a low voice.

Perveen was too stunned to say anything. It was as if their lawyer had conspired with Cyrus's family to give her the worst possible outcome. Logically, she knew this couldn't be true—but it was a rotten hand to be dealt at the last minute.

Jamshedji grimaced. "I spent some time talking with the junior barrister and was not impressed. He isn't even a Parsi, so he won't be especially convincing to the Parsi delegates serving as the jury. I told him I'd rather represent you myself."

"Has your brain snapped?" Perveen asked, too shocked to be diplomatic.

"No," Jamshedji said flatly. "We will not delay. I was the one who prepared every detail of the case. The junior brought the file with all necessary papers—it's a bit damp, but I have what I need."

"It's good of you to offer, but how can you do that, when you're not recognized by the Calcutta Bar?" Camellia objected. Her voice was as soft as usual, but she had a tense expression Perveen wasn't accustomed to seeing.

"As you both know, I was called to the Bar at Lincoln's Inn. Having an English law credential gives me entry to any court in India. The largest challenge will be convincing one of the other lawyers to lend me a wig and gown."

"Oh my God. My father representing me, in borrowed clothes!"

Perveen moaned. "You will not only humiliate me, but we're bound to lose!"

"Hush, Perveen. Are you sure they'll let you, Jamshedji?" Camellia now had a sparkle in her eyes.

"I'll have to ask."

"Pappa, no!" Perveen's voice came out in a screech. "Postponement is what I want. And I'm the client!"

"How can you speak to your father like that? He's your hero," Camellia said, favoring her husband with a final smile as he departed to register himself as Perveen's advocate. "How many fathers can stand up for their daughters in such a manner?"

Camellia and Perveen settled together on a bench close to the front. She wanted to see the jury, who were filing into their special section that faced the judicial bench.

"I recognize a juror," she whispered to Camellia. "Mr. Sodawalla's friend who works at a bank. How can he possibly sit on a jury and be fair to me?"

"The delegates on any Parsi matrimonial court are pillars of the community," Camellia whispered back. "Very likely, every plaintiff in this room is connected somehow to at least one juror. The whole body listens to everyone's cases."

"What if the rain keeps the Sodawallas from coming?" Perveen asked. She'd kept careful watch on the courtroom and was convinced they hadn't arrived.

"I don't know," Camellia said, putting an arm around her. "Perhaps the jury would rule in your favor. But the judge might just wish to postpone."

The Sodawallas had not arrived by the time an English magistrate named Moody called the session to order with a bang of his gavel. Sad-looking plaintiffs hung their heads while their advocates detailed their grievances. As Perveen listened from her position between her parents, she realized all the other plaintiffs had filed for divorce after decades of misery, not six months. The only other plaintiff who looked close to Perveen's age was a recent bridegroom, whom she learned during the testimony was seeking a divorce due to his wife's inability to consummate the marriage.

Everyone's story was miserable. She listened to a tale about a businessman who'd moved a prostitute into his marital bedroom, forcing the wife to stay in the room's corner. Another woman complained that her husband of twenty years was having an affair with his cousin. The judge asked some questions, and the eleven-man jury sat stone-faced, listening to the responses.

In the middle of the third case, the Sodawallas arrived, thoroughly soaked from head to toe. The three of them walked up the aisle past Perveen and seated themselves. A man bustled over to sit down with them. He had to be their barrister, N. J. Wadia. Her father had found out that Mr. Wadia was a vakil, a lawyer with traditional Indian law training rather than a modern law school degree. N. J. Wadia was, in fact, representing clients in two other cases that day. When he left the Sodawallas to step forward and present the case of a woman trying to prove her husband had committed adultery with a neighbor lady, his accusations were pointed and powerful.

"Wadia knows this court," Jamshedji muttered to Camellia and Perveen. "But nobody will be as motivated to present a strong case as a father representing a daughter."

Perveen wished her father had been able to secure a Calcutta vakil for her. Surely that would make a better impression on the local jury. But nobody Jamshedji had spoken with would take the case.

Sodawalla v. Sodawalla was on the docket just after two o'clock. Perveen hadn't been able to eat during the lunch recess; now she realized that her empty stomach and dry throat were causing dizziness. She followed her father to the plaintiff's bench. He appeared eccentric in the black coat that was a bit too short and a wig that looked puffier than his own finely made one that sat on a wig stand in the Bombay office. A few people even snickered.

Perveen sat down, feeling the gaze of hundreds of eyes on the back of her head. Was it her imagination, or was Judge Moody looking contemptuously at her? Her father had already warned her not to look into the faces of the jury. Doing so would make her seem overly confident of success.

Using his best Oxbridge accent, Jamshedji Mistry introduced himself to the jury as a barrister-solicitor with twenty-five years' experience in Bombay now serving in place of Mr. Pestonji, who'd been unable to attend.

Mr. Wadia promptly pointed out that Jamshedji was father of the plaintiff, a revelation that resulted in a chorus of laughter and whispers.

"It is true that I bring the vantage point of lifelong knowledge of the plaintiff—of both her honesty and her tendencies to do what she believes is right, no matter the consequence."

Jamshedji went on to present a picture of Perveen being tricked into marriage by a stranger. He spoke of his opposition to the marriage but acquiescence due to his belief in the Sodawallas' enthusiasm for the two to unite. He'd trusted them and paid for the children's wedding in Calcutta. That trust was broken, he said, when the parents turned a blind eye as Cyrus indulged in prostitution.

It was an unusual strategy to bring the parents into the case. Perveen heard some disapproving mutters come from the gallery.

Mr. Wadia called out, "Objection. Councillor Mistry is new to Calcutta. Is he also new to the fact that Parsi marital law does not consider a husband's recreational behavior as justifiable cause for the dissolution of a marriage?"

"Your Honor, my point is to lead to section thirty-one. The sad fact is the defendant's behavior resulted in the transmission of a serious disease to his wife. I should not like to offend any sensitive ears with the name of this illness. But everything is here on paper."

Perveen longed for the rain to break through the ceiling and wash her away. She was aghast at what her father had introduced to hundreds of strangers.

"If it's true, why not speak it aloud?" challenged Mr. Wadia. "There is no fit reason to libel my client."

This was a clever action—if the disease was stated, it would label Perveen as damaged and unclean for the rest of her life. Perveen could barely watch as her father laid two papers in front of the judge—the medical diagnosis she'd received in Calcutta and the results of a follow-up with the physician who'd treated her in Bombay. Mr. Wadia leaned in to look as well. Then the papers were shown to the jury, whose expressions grew dour.

"To add insult to injury, the defendant, Mr. Sodawalla, continued his immoral activities," Jamshedji said after the rustling subsided. He closed his argument with a dramatic description of Perveen's visit to the Sodawallas' factory, her discovery of the prostitute in Cyrus's office, and Cyrus's ruthless physical attack—something that he called attempted murder.

"My daughter, Perveen, fled Calcutta in order to save her own life!" Jamshedji declared in his infamous rising tone. "Under section thirty-one, there are multiple reasons for this couple to be given a separation."

Perveen watched uneasily as Mr. Wadia asked the magistrate's permission to approach the bench. Immediately Mr. Wadia began peppering Jamshedji with questions. Where was his evidence of continued visits to prostitutes? Where was the prostitute he'd accused Cyrus of bringing into the factory? Who were the young men Perveen had said were witnesses to the prostitute's presence? What had become of the tonga driver who'd seen Perveen bleeding and taken her to Howrah Station?

The questions were difficult. Mr. Pestonji hadn't been able to find the tonga driver who'd helped Perveen. Cyrus's friends had refused to make any statements against him, just as no prostitutes in the chawl would say Cyrus Sodawalla had ever requested services. The only evidence exhibits were three photographs a detective had snapped of Cyrus in the Sonagachi red-light district—and that was hardly useful, since prostitution wasn't considered cause for divorce.

Mr. Wadia announced he would not cause the young wife embarrassment by bringing her to the stand but asked for his client, Mr. Cyrus Sodawalla, to answer a few questions about her.

Perveen stared at the tall, well-built man in a fine gray suit for whom she'd left Bombay. How had they come to this? He had loved her—and she him.

Cyrus answered a number of prompts that suggested Perveen's lack of interest in marital union, as well as her dislike of cooking and cleaning and typical wifely work. Perveen had constantly left their house without family permission. She'd come to his office and interrupted an important business meeting. He said the accused woman in his office had been only a poor maid who'd brought tea. His health was perfect; he had a letter from his own doctor that showed no evidence of any disease.

As his testimony rolled out, she could imagine what the delegates thought: Perveen was a spoiled young bride who had shunned her husband and then been upset when he turned to others for his marital entitlement. She shot a look at her father, silently begging him for the chance to speak for herself, but he shook his head. He had warned her about this ahead of time. A woman who chose to argue back against her husband would appear arrogant and lose the pity she needed. She was angry, embarrassed, humiliated—but she turned her eyes back toward her lap.

It seemed like forever until Jamshedji was offered the chance to question Cyrus. The vakil tried to dissuade Cyrus from allowing himself to be questioned by the opposing lawyer, but Cyrus shook his attorney's advice off and smiled benignly at Jamshedji. It was as if Cyrus thought Jamshedji was bound to fail.

Jamshedji began in a surprisingly casual fashion. "What do you think about all of this, my boy?"

"I don't know." Cyrus looked taken aback.

"Objection—" Mr. Wadia called.

"Objection rejected," said the judge.

"If you were asked to describe your marriage, what would you say?" Jamshedji asked in a friendly manner.

Looking startled, Cyrus said, "It's been unhappy. Perveen has been nothing but trouble to me and my parents."

Perveen should have been happy to hear these words of release; but instead, she felt a great sorrow that the one she'd believed was her kindred spirit had turned out to be such an ordinary, closed-minded man.

"She is the one who is trouble, yes?" As Cyrus nodded, Jamshedji gave him a mirthless smile. "You were almost twenty-eight when you approached Perveen; two broken engagements before you came to her. No family in Calcutta would accept you due to your reputation. Isn't that the reason you went fishing for a wife in Bombay?"

"Objection!" shrieked Wadia. "Irrelevant to any case for separation."

"Objection sustained," Moody said. "Strike from the record."

"So you got the girl you set your cap for—someone you thought was rich and glad hearted, and not terribly intelligent. That was what you wished for—but you accidentally got someone with a good head on her shoulders. Perveen demanded you account for your behavior. As Parsis know, our marital law doesn't permit every couple that doesn't get along to have a legal separation. Therefore, I'm curious to hear how you will manage your life if Perveen stays with you again."

Cyrus said nothing, and Perveen's heart ached. She was remembering the first night in their room together—the joy of a fulfilled dream and the certainty of an enchanted life ahead.

"Will you face her at breakfast and supper? Share the same bedroom suite and bath? Or will you ask your parents to make sure she's kept in a small prison away from your sight?"

The audience rustled, and Perveen wondered if their own households observed the custom of menstrual seclusion. Perhaps they'd have no sympathy.

"Many of you may know about these rooms," Jamshedji said, turning to address the room. "Binamazi—the Zoroastrian tradition of seclusion for women during menses—likely originated during the Yazdani era, twelve hundred years ago. Orthodox Parsis still practice this archaic custom to an extreme, forcing women to avoid cleansing themselves properly for the entire menstrual period, plus two more days."

"Objection! Vulgarity not suited for the jury's ears," Mr. Wadia called out. Perveen's face was hot with the embarrassment of the unmentionable being mentioned.

"Go on, Mr. Mistry," said Judge Moody, who was looking intrigued.

"Some people deny facts of modern medical knowledge and think that confining a bleeding woman prevents her from spreading fatal germs to the rest of the household," Jamshedji continued. "But not allowing a woman contact with others can lead to her own death. One female already has died during menstrual confinement at the Sodawalla home—yes, Mr. Sodawalla, I can see from your expression you already know who she is. Will you tell us her full name?"

Perveen felt an odd ringing in her ears.

"Azara," Cyrus croaked, his face white. Perveen had never seen him look so shocked.

"And were you living in the home at the time of Azara's death?" Jamshedji asked.

Cyrus nodded.

"And your age at the time of her death?"

Cyrus looked confused for a moment, then mumbled, "Twenty-five."

"Thank you." Jamshedji gave him a faint smile and turned to address the audience again. "We are speaking of Cyrus's younger sister, Azara Bahramji Sodawalla, born 1900 and deceased in 1914. The coroner's report lists the cause of death as natural causes. Azara had fever before her menses began—yet instead of the family seeking medical help as the fever rose, the child was left on a metal cot in an eight-by-twelve-foot room in a remote area of the house."

Perveen had always known Azara had struggled in that room. She thought back to the odd, melancholy presence that had accompanied her throughout her time in the little room: the faded marks of days. That must have been a calendar that Azara made.

"Objection," called out Mr. Wadia. "Opposing counsel is telling stories without any evidence."

"The Calcutta coroner's report is a public record," Jamshedji said, holding a paper aloft. "I have it here. As well as a letter of sworn testimony as to the nature of Azara's illness from Gita, former housemaid to the Sodawallas."

If Gita was being described as a former housemaid, it must have meant she'd been fired. Where was she now—and how had her testimony been obtained?

Perveen glanced toward the bench where the Sodawalla parents sat. Behnoush was slumped and had covered her face with a handkerchief. Despite Perveen's desire to hear the truth about Azara, the Sodawallas' naked pain was hard to witness.

"The maid has testified that water and food were provided at the door of the young girl's cell," Jamshedji said in a somber voice. "However, no family member went inside to make sure she took it. After several days, the maid went inside and reported the girl could not respond to her voice. Azara Sodawalla was in a state of coma when the ambulance arrived. She died one week later in hospital: an utterly needless death due to the family's lack of care."

"Objection!" screamed Mr. Wadia. "Another family member's death is unrelated to the marriage situation in question. Irrelevant!"

"Your Lordship, I plan to use this example to show that in addition to the physical harm Perveen has already undergone, there are reasonable grounds for anticipating continuing danger to both her life and liberty—chiefly, the death of another woman in the household. Perveen's husband, Cyrus Sodawalla, was in residence at the time and, despite the fact he was an adult, did nothing to help his sister—nor did his parents."

"Objection! A female's health is not a concern for a brother," Mr. Wadia shouted. "It is ladies' business only."

What her father had said was exactly what Perveen had been trying to say to the Sodawallas all along. She had gone stiff with anger, hearing her own argument used in reverse.

"Overruled," said Judge Moody, leaning forward slightly. "Please continue, Mr. Mistry."

"I seek to prove that Cyrus Sodawalla was negligent in caring for his sister. As section thirty-one states, such conduct that affords reasonable grounds for apprehending danger to life or of serious personal injury is entitlement for judicial separation."

Judge Moody frowned. "This is an interpretation of the act I've not heard before. Will you elaborate on your rationale?"

"Your Honor, it is entirely straightforward," Jamshedji said. "Already, Perveen's life has been ruined by her rash agreement to Mr. Sodawalla's proposal. She can never marry another, nor have children. Is that not enough punishment? Should she be forced back into this household, where she will be made again to lie on another woman's deathbed?" Jamshedji turned from the judge to look directly at Cyrus. "What do you think, Cyrus? Do you really long for your unhappy wife to return?"

He did not answer. The silence was filled with the rustling sounds of people in the benches, and she imagined they were craning their necks to look at him, to see the young man whose reputation had been ground into the gutter by his father-in-law.

"No." Cyrus's voice was barely audible.

Jamshedji nodded. "On behalf of the plaintiff, I rest my case."

The magistrate called a one-hour recess after the case. He gave the jurors this time to return verdicts on the nine cases that they had heard. This brief recess caused a flurry of movement in the court-room. Those whose cases hadn't yet been heard streamed out, complaining about having to come back.

"The jury has fewer than seven minutes to discuss each case. How can justice be done?" Camellia fretted.

"They will take longer if needed. Nothing to do now but relax." Jamshedji was flushed from the exertion of speaking, and Perveen saw rivulets of sweat running down from the edges of the wig. He'd presented a thoroughly ingenious argument while relatively unprepared, in a courtroom he didn't know. And he'd even gathered testimony from Gita.

One woman stopped by Perveen and put a hand on her arm. "I know what it is to be kept secluded. I hope you don't have to go back."

Perveen felt gratitude for this kindness. "Thank you. I—"

"The shamelessness of young women!"

Perveen recognized the scolding man who'd interrupted as an unpleasant member of the Sodawallas' agiary. Before she could respond, though, another woman had patted her arm.

"Very good to see a lawyer speak up for women's rights. All the better when he's her father." The friendly woman beamed at Jamshedji. "Give me your card. I've got plenty of business for you."

Jamshedji gave her a gracious half-bow. "You are most kind, madam; but my firm is based in Bombay. This will, I hope, be my sole court appearance in Calcutta."

When they had a bit of space, Perveen whispered, "You made a magnificent argument, but I didn't know what lengths you'd go to. I feel mortified."

Jamshedji looked soberly at her. "I'm sorry that I made you embarrassed. But I decided to follow my instinct. I needed to prove an existing danger to you in the marriage."

"How did you learn about Azara's cause of death?"

"I hired someone here to request the medical files for you and Cyrus. The hospital worker accidentally also brought the file for Cyrus's sister, as she was a family member at the same address. When I saw the doctor's report, I knew it would be vital to your defense, but there was the problem that the information was not obtained through proper channels."

"And that would make it inadmissible in court." Perveen paused, thinking. "But you spoke of a coroner's report."

"Yes. The coroner is a government official, and the Bengal Presidency has just as detailed records as the Bombay Presidency," he said with a satisfied smile. "I recalled you saying that your ayah was working in the household when Azara died. Our detective learned from Gita's mother, Pushpa, that the Sodawallas fired her for not stopping you from leaving. Since Gita had returned to her home village, she felt safe enough to provide the sworn testimony."

Perveen would never be able to thank Gita for what she'd done. How was it that she could speak the truth, and Cyrus had not?

"When I first met him, Cyrus lied to me about Azara's death being from cholera. I wonder why he thought he couldn't tell me the truth."

"Perhaps it was the family's agreed-upon story," Jamshedji said. "It was a risk to bring up Azara's death, but I believe it's now impossible for the delegates not to consider the possibility of continuing danger. Only when there is an actual death do people think twice."

"When you spoke so bluntly about it, that hurt the Sodawallas. They were in pain," Perveen said, remembering how she'd pitied the weeping Behnoush. "They hadn't faced up to their role in Azara's death. And now their community knows all about it."

"Maybe some of the orthodox will change their traditions," Camellia said, looking serious. "Some families will tell women to seclude themselves for one or two days, not eight. Pappa described a tragedy to everyone, but knowing about it might make a difference."

"Do you truly . . . ?" Perveen's sentence died as she saw Cyrus walking through the crowds toward them. She had no time to warn her parents before he was upon them.

"How could you do that? Shame my family—accuse us of killing my sister?" Cyrus shouted down into the face of Jamshedji, who was a few inches shorter than his six feet.

"You are the only one using those words," Jamshedji said tightly. They were becoming entertainment for anyone passing through the corridor. A knot of excited onlookers formed around the men, and Camellia put a protective arm around Perveen, who wished they were invisible.

"You bastard! You have brought up the sorrow my family has tried so hard to put behind us!" Cyrus shouted angrily, ignoring the constables hastening toward him.

"He didn't mean to insult you," Perveen said, her heart beating fast. "It's just an argument. What lawyers must do—"

"Perveen!" her father snapped. "Don't say anything more."

"Lawyers are the vilest creatures on earth—less than human," Cyrus said with a sneer. "Of course you wanted to be one, Perveen!"

Jamshedji tilted his head back to look fully at Cyrus as he spoke. "You testified on the stand that you were willing to have a separation. But all your vakil did was present a picture of a wife with bad housekeeping skills. No jury would permit the two of you to separate for such a small reason. You needed a stronger example—and I gave just that."

"You called my parents murderers." Cyrus was breathing hard, as if struggling to stay above water. "You said I was diseased. And you said I didn't care that Azara died—"

"If you don't care to be accountable for the past, think about your future," Jamshedji said between gritted teeth. "How delighted would you be to have my daughter living with you for the next forty or fifty years? Do you think you'll have one happy day within those decades?"

Cyrus answered him but kept his eyes on Perveen. "If the jury sends her back to stay with us, she will pay for every bit of filth you said in court today. And if she's granted a separation—it won't be a happy one. I'll make your lives hell."

A bell rang, signaling that the magistrate was ready to reconvene. The chief juror delivered a series of papers to Judge Moody, who read the decisions aloud and without expression. The wife whose husband had brought a prostitute into their bedroom was granted a separation with alimony. Divorce was granted to the woman whose husband had slept with his cousin. On the other hand, the jury granted an annulment to the man whose wife hadn't yet consummated. And then it was their turn.

"Sodawalla versus Sodawalla." Judge Moody squinted as if it was difficult to read the paper in his hand. Perveen felt an iciness flow through her, certain that the outcome was bad. "In this matter, the jury would like to state for the record its disapproval of the wife's intrusion into the husband's place of business. However, the Sodawallas' abuse of female seclusion—a respectable tradition if done with everyone's agreement—raised a reasonable doubt for the wife's safety. Six votes for the granting of judicial separation. No alimony."

The judge droned on, but Perveen did not hear the words. She'd heard "granting of judicial separation."

She had won. Although still married to Cyrus, she'd never have to see him again. Every day of the month would belong to her. Her life was her own again.

Shaking and sobbing, Perveen hugged her mother. She realized Camellia's face was also wet with tears.

"Yes," Jamshedji said, his own arms, strong as tree branches, going around the two women. "We have not lost her. Thank God."

Perveen could not let the delirium of joy overtake her. She remembered Cyrus's words during the break. "Pappa, can the separation be challenged?"

"It could—but they're not likely to do that," he said reassuringly. "Too much money and distress."

"But Cyrus threatened us." He had looked straight at her, and the hatred in his gaze had been clear.

Jamshedji took out his handkerchief to wipe Camellia's tears. "He can threaten all he wishes, but I suspect his energy for mischief will run dry during the three years you're studying in England."

"If I can get a place . . ."

"You earned it long ago," he reassured her. "And you've already got the necessary papers."

Her father had filed for her right to enter England right after she'd passed the Oxford examinations two years earlier. In fact, the document granting her that right was issued in the name Perveen Jamshedji Mistry, which was the name he told her to use for her university application. Nobody had ever heard of a married female studying at Oxford—to see if she'd be admitted as such was too great a risk. And using her maiden name wasn't quite a lie, given her legal separation.

Still, the challenge of presenting herself as a single woman dogged Perveen during the month that she and Camellia spent organizing her trunks. All the while, her father hunted for a booking for her on one of the few passenger steamships still operating between India and Europe. The seats were few, and he wound up having to pay for first class rather than second. Perveen felt guilty, knowing that most Indian students traveling to England had won full scholarships with travel and living stipends and were not imposing financial burdens on their families. She'd sold the jewelry her parents had given her for her wedding, but that would only cover one year's tuition.

"I can always raise my hourly billing rate," Jamshedji had joked when she'd expressed worry about all her expenses. "In any case, I expect to bring in a solicitor to raise the firm's revenue within the next few years."

Just four weeks after the separation was granted, Perveen stood on the first-class deck of the ferry that would take her to the *Dutch Emerald*. The sun was high, and she had to squint to see her parents and Rustom standing on Ballard Pier below. She could not see their expressions and could only hope they were smiling.

"Do you want a last look at someone?" a female voice said.

Perveen turned to see a very tall, blonde English girl proffering a pair of opera glasses.

"Oh. That's kind of you, but not necessary." It was embarrassing to have been caught on the verge of tears, and by a posh English person at that.

"Come on. They're really meant for performances, but they're still all right to use outdoors. Don't you want a parting glimpse?"

The girl seemed so sincere, Perveen didn't want to make her feel bad. "All right. Thank you." She took the glasses and adjusted the focus.

"Did you find your family?"

"Yes. My parents are crying. I can't stand to look anymore." She handed the glasses back to the stranger. Why was she leaving Bombay when she'd fought so hard to be with her own family again? Three years apart would feel endless.

The girl smiled wryly. "That's rather different from my own departure. I boarded in Ceylon, where my father's been working, and he, my mother, and I were arguing all the way up the gang-plank!"

"We argue, too. They say arguing is in Parsi blood," Perveen said. "I hope to hone my arguments to a professional level while in England."

The girl hooted. "Are you bound for Oxford? I saw a trunk labeled for St. Hilda's College. Was it yours?"

"Probably," she admitted, surprised her luggage had caught this stranger's eye.

"Well, it's your lucky day, because I'm a second year at St. Hilda's," the girl said, tilting her chin so she looked even taller. In a mock-confidential tone, she added, "I'll tell you everything you need to know."

"I'd like that," Perveen said, feeling a surge of relief that she wouldn't walk into the college like a complete know-nothing.

"I'm Alice Hobson-Jones," the young woman said, holding out her hand. "Born in Tamil Nadu, shipped back to London and Oxford, briefly moored in Ceylon, and who knows what's next?"

Perveen shook the girl's hand. "I'm delighted to meet you, Miss Hobson-Jones. I'm Perveen Mistry, Bombay born and bred."

"Do call me Alice," her companion said with a grin. "Fourteen days at sea is an overly long time to be formal, isn't it?"

The horn blew, signaling the ferry's departure. Perveen kept her eyes on her family until they blurred with the mass of other people around them. The lump in her throat was being replaced by something entirely different.

Anticipation.

1921

28

CAT OUT OF THE BAG
Bombay, February 1921

When Perveen awoke, her throat felt dry, although her body was soaked. She had sweated, maybe for hours. It was all because she was wrapped up in a thick, rough blanket. Reaching out a few inches, she tried to tug the cloth down; but it just pulled tighter around her curled-up form.

And then she remembered—Bruce Street, and the shock of a cloth sack coming down over her head. She had a memory of fighting against it and then being hit. She recalled a bumpy ride and being hauled out and hearing the sound of lapping water. She'd braced for the feeling of sinking like a stone into cold water. She would end her life in the Arabian Sea, the body of water her ancestors had crossed to build their new lives in India.

At the Calcutta High Court, Cyrus had sworn vengeance. The years between had been filled with the excitement of Oxford, returning to Bombay, and working as a full-fledged solicitor in her father's practice. Until the last few days, she had relinquished her fears.

The attack had caught her off guard, despite the warning signs. And the plan would come off without a hitch. Her parents didn't know about anything amiss, and enough time had passed so there would be no suspicion of the Sodawallas. And her death, once it was discovered, would allow Cyrus to marry a new wife.

A loud ship's horn interrupted her thoughts, reminding her of another possibility. She recalled the hulking figure of Jayanth's boss. Ravi had been furious about the changes Jayanth's victory had brought about for all the stevedores. As revenge against her father, Perveen, who'd shown her face at the docks, could have been abducted. She'd be left to die. Ravi would escape prosecution.

But there was also the Farid situation. Someone involved might worry she was getting close to the truth. The telephone call from a woman that had brought her out could have been a ploy; and the disabling of Ramchandra's rickshaw had been intentional. This, of course, pointed to the attacker being connected to the caller.

She'd been taken around eight in the evening. What time was it now? She slid her stiff right hand over her left forearm until she felt the rectangular face of her French wristwatch. She could not read time in the dark, but it was comforting to still have it. She wondered if she had anything else. Groping with both hands, she found her beaded purse trapped in a corner of the sack near her feet. How surprising that the assailant hadn't taken it. Perhaps it was meant to be an identifier after she was nothing more than a pile of bones.

The fact that she'd been left alive might mean somebody was nearby keeping guard. She wanted to know. Clearing her scratchy throat, she began shouting in Marathi. "What are you doing, sticking me in a bag like this? Kidnapping is a crime."

She shouted for five minutes, changing her language to Hindi and then English, steadily raising her level of profanity. Hearing nothing but silence, she gathered that she was alone.

If she truly was alone, she could try to escape the bag without interference. Feeling more determined than frightened, Perveen began exploring the scratchy sack. The top end was sewn straight across, but the end near her feet was drawn tightly together, as if it had been tied with a rope. She could not possibly untie something knotted on the outside. The only way out of the bag would be to tear the straight edge. Perveen searched through her small beaded purse, which contained a few coins, business cards, the vial of rose attar, and her mother-of-pearl fountain pen. She removed a metal hairpin from her braided coronet and tried to stab it through the cloth. The thin pin broke on her fifth attempt.

She needed a sharp bit of metal. She thought of the whalebones inside her brassiere, but she didn't have enough space to move her arms to unhook her blouse. Instead, she took the fountain pen and rubbed its nib against the sharp, broken hairpin. It took only a few minutes of industrious work to give the pen's nib a knifelike sharpness. She felt elated when she pushed the pen into the bag's fabric and it went through. Diligently, she stabbed the cloth until she'd made an opening of a few inches; and then, with her hands, she tore it open the rest of the way.

Squeezing herself out, she slowly released her arms and legs from the tight ball they'd been in. Her right foot throbbed with pain, and so did some spots on her back and one elbow. But she was free—in a short dark space that smelled of dust.

Groping around, she identified many more sacks around her. The crowding gave the impression she was in a storeroom: perhaps one of the many godowns built in rows near the harbor or at Ballard Pier itself.

Goods were held for months and sometimes years in such godowns. She remembered Rustom's frustration about a shipload of nails that should have been delivered to Mistry Construction but had been accidentally stored after the unloading and forever lost. That could be her plight.

She tried to think logically. If she'd been loaded into this place, there had to be a way to the outside. First, she searched the low ceiling, hoping to find the base of a chute. There was none—at least, not near her. She shifted her investigation to the cold cement walls around the sacks. But moving made her feel the impact of being in a windowless, doorless box. She was becoming frightened and realized that not knowing where she was in relation to the bag she'd broken out of made her feel lost.

Perveen said a silent prayer, and afterward, her mind was clear. If she'd been brought to a place already filled with goods, she'd probably been left close to the front of the space and whatever door existed. She crawled back to the spot where the destroyed bag lay. Then she sat down and felt everything around it. A raised edge on the wooden base below her caught her attention. When she touched it, she realized it was one edge of a large wooden square.

She was able to pry up the square and pushed one of her hands through. Her initial confusion was followed by the realization that she'd been loaded up onto a shelf in some kind of storage space. This was the reason for the very low ceiling above her head. The way out was to drop down to the next level—though how steep the fall would be, and what she'd land on, was unknown.

Sometimes people kept guard dogs in their storerooms. There even were rumors of certain merchants keeping snakes, which would dissuade both thieves and rats. She whistled to see if a dog might move below; there was no response.

Perveen slowly fit herself through the opening, feeling her way down with her feet. But then her tired arms couldn't hold her anymore. She slipped straight down, landing in a sitting position on another group of sacks. She sat there for a while, making sure no bones seemed to be broken—although when she gathered the strength to stand, she discovered a searing pain in her hip. Resolutely, she bumped her way around the room to the area where she saw some thin streaks of light.

A ventilated wooden door, she decided, after exploring it with her fingers. Unfortunately, it was locked from the outside. Pressing her eyes to the narrow bits of light, she realized the door was near an area with people. She heard the rumble of men's voices and, again, the blowing of a ship's horn.

She thought she must be at the harbor or very close by. And if she could hear voices, that also meant someone might hear her.

"Help me!" she called in English and then in Marathi.

She shouted again and again, but nobody heard; perhaps it was still too early or the storeroom was too distant.

Starting around seven, the dock became lively; but then there might be too much noise for a tiny cry to be heard from a godown. She had to draw attention to the door in the hopes that the earliest workers—the tea makers, the sweepers, and the dock loaders—might hear.

Perveen put her hand in her purse. She could write a note and push it through one of the ventilation holes—but the laborers reporting to work were mostly illiterate. Then she felt the cool glass of the vial of rose attar. If she spilled it, she'd create an overpowering aroma. An expensive, feminine scent that was unusual for the dock might draw men to the storeroom's door. And if she could push the anna and paisa coins through the ventilation holes, they might catch someone's eye.

Perveen opened the vial and spilled it along the open edges of the door. Then she pushed an anna coin through, hearing it clink as it hit cobblestones outside.

"Take the money!" she bellowed, feeling like a huckster at a circus. "Money! Money! Money!"

The light was brighter through the shafts, and her voice nearly gone, when she heard someone yell, "Look! There are coins."

"What a smell? Where are the roses?"

With her mouth close to the vents, she screamed, "Help me out, and you'll get more! Please, I tell you, help me!"

"Did you hear something?" one man said to another in Marathi.

"No, but that smell is making me sick."

"Sounded like a woman called out. But where?"

The last male voice sounded familiar.

"Jayanth-bhaiya?" Perveen shouted. "Jayanth-bhaiya, is that you?"

There was a long pause, then his shout. "Perveen-memsahib! Where are you?"

"Behind this door." She pounded it so hard her knuckles hurt. "The one that smells like roses."

"Get a lathi," Jayanth called out to someone. "And bring the harbor constable."

Ten minutes later, the men had forced open the door. Perveen emerged and, for the first time in hours, was able to straighten her back. She realized her sari had fallen away from her hair and the top of her body, so she wound it up rapidly. Jayanth moved forward protectively as she fixed the rest of her sari so it was presentable.

Some men in the cluster eyed the coins lying on the brick walk that ran along the godowns. As they brought the coins to her, she shook her head. "Please share it. You saved my life."

"My friend saw the coins," Jayanth told her.

"Where exactly are we?" Perveen looked around, trying to orient herself.

"Ballard Pier's section for godowns. Our work today is loading up a P&O cargo ship with tea. Please sit down, memsahib. You look weak."

Perveen sat down on a jute sack that he'd dragged out. She felt elated. She had been meant to die, yet she'd cut her way out of that fate and back to the world she loved. Taking a deep breath of the salty port air, she asked Jayanth whether the storage places were privately owned.

"They are property of the Bombay Port, but leased to various people," he said, bringing out another sack for her to rest her feet on.

"And your boss, Ravi—would he have a key to many of these places?"

Jayanth cocked his head to the side, as if he was considering all aspects of the issue. "I don't know for certain. I believe he can only obtain such a key the day that work is needed."

"But if work starts early in the morning, might the company needing assistance from stevedores deliver Ravi the key the night before?"

"Are you really thinking Ravi has done this?" Jayanth's voice dropped.

"It cannot be his doing," protested an anxious-looking stevedore standing nearby. "We did not come here yesterday, and it's not on the work plan for today. The door's number is wrong."

Perveen turned and looked at the door that was hanging askew. It had a number painted on it: 179. Nothing more.

"Does anyone have a torch?" she asked.

Jayanth shook his head. "The police will have such. Look, they are coming just now."

Two Indian constables were hastening toward them, followed by an English Imperial Police officer.

"What is the trouble here?" The Englishman frowned at Perveen's dishevelment. "I could not understand half of what the boy has told me. And there are complaints from the dock about men missing from work."

"These observant stevedores may have saved my life." Perveen looked at the ragtag group of workers with gratitude. "They are heroes."

"Who are you?" he asked, taking on a commanding air. "No civilian visitors allowed away from the area of passenger ships."

"My name is Perveen Mistry; I'm a solicitor with Mistry Law in Bruce Street. I was thrown in a sack last night and brought here by an assailant who locked me up."

But the officer seemed stuck on her opening statement. "You work for a salary, then? As a female legal secretary?"

"No," she said crisply. "I've been employed as a solicitor by Mistry Law for the last half year."

"Fetch the harbor master," the officer directed the smaller constable. "This will require a full investigation. Miss Mistry, are there others inside?"

"I didn't hear anyone."

"If it's white-slaving, there could be loads of ladies trapped inside."

"I'm not white," she protested. "I'm a Parsi. It might be that this is related to one of my cases—"

Ignoring her, the officer unclipped a battery torch from his belt and stepped into the storeroom, shining the torch around inside. Perveen stepped in close beside him, watching as the small beam of light ran over the room's sacks. The officer pulled a knife from a sheath at his belt and ran it carefully along the edge of one sack. Inside was a bolt of khaki cloth. The next sack he opened looked the same.

"On the outset, this looks all right. Just a lot of drill cloth," he said, turning to look at Perveen.

"Drill cloth?" she said.

Now she saw that the corner of each sack was stamped with English writing:

FARID FABRICS, GIRANGAON, BOMBAY.

29

AN UNEXPECTED SPACE
Bombay, February 1921

"Thanks to God and those wonderful stevedores you are home. But you must take what happened as a warning," Camellia Mistry said as she ushered Perveen onto the veranda and handed her a cup of her very best ginger and lemongrass milk tea.

She'd bathed, slipped into a fresh dressing gown and now was dipping a khari biscuit in the delicious tea. The anxiety she'd felt in the sack was a distant memory. "I was taken because I fell for a ruse. I've learned the hard way—just as before."

"There are ruses, and then there are traps. This was a bad trap," Jamshedji said from his lounge chair across the veranda. Perveen could hear the clattering of John in the kitchen making a large breakfast. The voices and sounds of her familiar household were the most beautiful music she'd ever heard.

"You can't fathom what it's been like since Mustafa realized you'd gone out at night on your own," Camellia continued. "We put our heads together and came up with so many different ideas of which way to turn."

Gulnaz slipped into a chair next to Perveen and patted her arm. "I remembered you planned to meet your English friend for the pictures. Mamma was anxious, so I rang up those Hobson-Joneses. What a chukoo, that mother! By the time she finished scolding me for calling her Mrs. instead of Lady, I was nervous to even ask for Alice, but she came on the line. Your friend is loyal. She wanted to come straight down to join us in the search, and when her parents wouldn't allow it, she said we should probably go to the Farid place."

"I must go there today. Did all of you go last night?" Perveen asked.

"No. Mamma stayed behind to be near the telephone. Pappa and

Rustom and I went over there. The constable told us nothing was wrong, but I insisted on going to the ladies' section. A servant girl let me in. I spoke to two widows who said you hadn't come by. When I said you were missing, they became worried, too."

"You probably saw Razia and Sakina," Perveen guessed. "What about the third wife?"

"I didn't ask to see her. I was only worried about you." Gulnaz looked anxiously at her. "We drove back along the Queen's Necklace and then every street in Ballard Estate and Fort. Arman was driving like a madman. He feels so guilty about being at Victoria Terminus when you needed him."

"If Arman had driven you last night, he'd have had had ruined tires," Rustom said, coming up behind Gulnaz to rub her shoulders. "Apparently after business was over yesterday, someone dropped nails and broken glass on both ends of Bruce Street. It took two hours this morning to clean up—the office workers and automobile drivers were quite put out."

"Did you see a face or have any inkling of your attacker?" Gulnaz's voice was urgent. "Was he a street type or a gentleman?"

"I didn't see his clothing, his face, not even the color of his skin," Perveen said. "As I told the police, the bags in the storeroom point to the involvement of the Farids, but it's not the only possibility."

"What else are you thinking?" Camellia pressed.

Perveen swallowed hard, then spoke the worry she'd been hesitant to divulge. "A few days ago, I saw a man who looked like Cyrus. I've been looking over my shoulder for him most of this week."

"Are you sure?" Gulnaz asked, her eyes widening.

"The bastard!" Rustom snapped. "He's no right to be near you."

Camellia's face sagged, and she sat down heavily in her chair. "I thought all of that was over."

"When was this incident?" Jamshedji asked quietly.

"Last Tuesday, I was in the Silver Ghost speeding along the Queen's Necklace. The man was waiting to buy food at a dhabba on Chowpatty Beach." She broke off. "Pappa, why are you looking like you know this?"

She'd expected Jamshedji to be shocked or angry. Instead, he had a knowing expression. "In all likelihood, you did see him."

"You knew he was here, and you kept it from me?" Perveen's calm was disintegrating like the biscuit she'd left dangling in her tea.

"Let me begin with the so-called Bengali stranger you were worried about. He's not strange to me. His name is Purshottam Ghosh."

"Is he your client?" Perveen was confused.

"He's the private detective based in Calcutta I hired to gather the medical records we used in *Sodawalla v. Sodawalla*. Remember?"

"I never met him. But of course I remember those files being used." Perveen's curiosity was mixed with irritation. Why hadn't her father said this straight out?

"I was pleased with Ghosh's initiative and have employed him since the trial ended to keep tabs on Cyrus."

"Mamma, did you know?" Perveen turned to Camellia, who shook her head.

"I had no idea," she said. "But I'm sure your father had his reasons."

"Perveen's safety comes first," Jamshedji said simply. "And if we could ever find proof of infidelity, it would mean a chance for the separation to become a divorce."

Perveen put down her cup. She was stunned by the lengths to which her father had gone. And if Cyrus discovered the surveillance, he'd have a valid grudge to pursue against her family. "Did Cyrus learn about this?"

"We're not sure," Jamshedji said after a disturbing pause. "But to recap the surveillance history, Ghosh wasn't following him daily—it was part-time observation done in conjunction with his other jobs. He's reported to me that Cyrus continued his activities, averaging twice a week with women of the professional variety, either in Sonagachi prostitution district or the slum near the bottling plant."

"Pappa, why didn't you tell me Cyrus was here in Bombay?" Perveen demanded.

Jamshedji raised a cautionary finger. "I didn't want to worry you unduly. At first, we thought it was a business trip. Or he might have been calling on his relatives the Vachhas. And then we got a surprise."

"I don't like surprises." Perveen felt sick with anxiety.

"Ghosh followed him to Petit General Hospital, where he walked in with a valise late on Tuesday and did not come out."

Rustom was angrily pacing the veranda. "What do you mean, 'didn't come out'? The velgard might have slipped out the back!"

"Or he is visiting a sick person or checked in himself as a patient," Camellia pointed out.

"The letter!" Perveen said, putting her teacup down so hard the saucer rattled. "This week I received a letter asking me to go to the hospital to see someone I didn't know. This man who wrote the letter wanted me to make his will. I can't recall the name, but it certainly wasn't Cyrus!"

"Why would Cyrus come to Bombay for medical treatment? Calcutta's full of doctors, isn't it?" Gulnaz asked.

"But there's no Parsi hospital in Calcutta," Camellia said. "I learned that when I was visiting there. Petit is a top-drawer hospital offering free and subsidized care to any Parsi. Might he have come for that, rather than to harass Perveen?"

Perveen took a deep breath. "I'd like to know. I'll go to the hospital."

"Don't let him speak to you!" Jamshedji said sharply. "A pitiful situation could be a ploy. I've seen this time and again with separated couples."

"Gulnaz and I are on the ladies' voluntary committee at the hospital. We'll find out whether he is a patient there before Perveen decides anything," Camellia said, pouring more tea in Perveen's cup. "Don't act without forethought."

Perveen was exasperated. "Why won't you let me go? It seems that I've escaped one prison to be kept in another."

"We are hardly imprisoning you," Camellia soothed. "We are only giving you a bit of time to settle and recover from a terrible attack. You haven't even had breakfast—and you're already raring to go both to the hospital and Malabar Hill! Frankly, I don't know which situation is more dangerous."

"I could tell you if I went. I'll go mad sitting here all day," Perveen said.

"Why not ring Alice?" Gulnaz asked brightly. "Perhaps she can drop by for a visit."

The thought of Alice was a comfort. Nodding at Gulnaz, Perveen asked Camellia if her friend could come over for lunch. It was high time for a chat, and Perveen knew there was a chance Alice had overheard more gossip about the government's interest in the Farids.

"We're happy to host Alice. I'll ask John to make it a special ladies' luncheon with a lot of sweets—unless you will also be staying, Rustom?"

Rustom yawned, putting a hand over his mouth too late. "I'd like to sleep a few more hours, but I'm needed at the construction office."

This gave Perveen another idea. "If you're going to your office, Rustom, may I ask you to do me a favor there?"

He gave her a searching look. "What?"

"You mentioned the architectural drawings for twenty-two Sea View Road are stored in a cabinet. I'd like to borrow them."

Rustom drank deeply from his coffee cup before answering. "I only saw the outside wrappings, and those plans are from Queen Victoria's time. They probably have deteriorated."

"Or the plans might be perfectly fine because of the care Grandfather took with wrapping them," Perveen said. "Will you please, please have one of the clerks look?"

"Haven't I done enough for you?" Rustom grumbled. "Why do you need them now? Too much is happening. I'm exhausted."

"Those plans offer a chance to understand the house's twists and turns," Jamshedji said. "It would be especially useful for me, as I can't go inside the zenana."

"All right, Pappa. I'll see what I can do," Rustom said.

Perveen smiled a silent *thank you* at Jamshedji. It often seemed she was in a contest with her father, but occasionally, they came to a draw.

Alice was pleased to get a call from Perveen. After hearing a summary of the events of the last day, including the rescue by stevedores, she accepted the invitation to join Perveen, Gulnaz, and Camellia for a Parsi lunch.

Alice arrived at one-thirty in a dark blue Crossley, rather than the Rolls. Still, the neighborhood's young cricketers stood gawking as the tall blonde Englishwoman strode up to the Mistrys' gate. Catching sight of the group, Alice wound up her arm and bowled an imaginary cricket ball straight at them. They broke apart laughing.

"Alice, come in!" Perveen said, coming outside when her friend didn't approach the door.

"It really is you!" Alice said, beaming at her. "I went to the wrong house first. They were too friendly—wanted me to come in for tea and started talking about wanting an English governess. I suppose it was my first job offer."

"Perveen, is that you?" Gwendolyn Hobson-Jones shielded her eyes from the sun with a hand as she peered from the car.

"Good afternoon, Lady Hobson-Jones," Perveen replied, her spirits sinking. She hadn't thought Alice's mother was coming.

Lady Hobson-Jones marched up the path and into the house, where she swiveled her head to take in the hall, parlor, and dining room. "I drove with Alice to ensure she arrived safely, given all that's happened in Bombay this week. Did you have some sort of trouble yesterday evening?"

Alice shot Perveen a glance that she interpreted to mean she shouldn't say much.

"It was a mix-up about where I was. As you can expect, my parents worry about me being out past dark, even though I'm twenty-three!" Perveen kept her tone light. "Won't you come in to meet my mother? And would you like to lunch with us?"

"Sorry. I'm off to a luncheon at the Bombay Gymkhana. Sirjit will return for Alice in about three hours."

"Sorry for the intrusion," Alice murmured to Perveen as the two watched the departing car. "She had some fears about what a Parsi home would be like. I think all the silver and mahogany put her to ease."

"Really? I thought she was the modern type." Perveen could never relax under Alice's mother's scrutiny. It was a good thing she hadn't been free for lunch.

"I like your neighborhood," Alice said, going into the parlor to look out the window at the street. "So many tall houses with pretty ironwork balconies—I'm sure they will stand the test of time. And it's practical to have so many small parks around for people to enjoy."

"My brother Rustom's head would swell if he heard your review," Perveen said with a chuckle. "He's building many of these homes, and while the trees in the parks and on streets are still small, he thinks this could become Bombay's greenest neighborhood in a few decades."

Camellia stepped into the hall to take Alice's hat. "How do you do, Miss Hobson-Jones? I'm Perveen's mother. She painted such a nice picture of you through all the letters she wrote from Oxford. I'm grateful that you were her first English friend."

"First and best friend," Perveen added. "In England and in India."

Alice bent awkwardly from the shoulders to address the petite woman at eye level. Holding out her hand, she said, "Mrs. Mistry, please call me Alice. And thanks very much for asking me to lunch. It's nice of you to have a guest when you are likely still getting over last evening's trouble."

"I am a bit weary; it's true," Camellia said with a warm smile. "And in India, we usually call our friends' mothers Aunty. I will be pleased to become your Camellia-aunty."

"Thank you, Camellia-aunty!" Alice said, beaming back at her.

Gulnaz drifted into the hallway toward their cordial cluster. Sounding very reserved, she said, "Miss Hobson-Jones, I'm Gulnaz. I'm Perveen's sister-in-law, but we've known each other since primary school."

"How intriguing that you married her brother," Alice said with a wink. "Do call me Alice, Gulnaz! Tell me, did you know Rustom when he was in short pants?"

Gulnaz blushed. "No. It was an arranged marriage."

"A blissful one," Perveen said, smiling at Gulnaz, who she suspected might have overheard her description of Alice as her best friend. "I can't tell you how much nicer my brother's become since Gulnaz's arrival. It's a terrific deal for all of us."

The young women had a few more minutes of pleasant small talk before Camellia called them to the table to eat fish, potato curry, chapatis, dal pulao, and kachumber.

"Do you eat like this every day?" Alice was already reaching for her fork and knife.

"Of course. Will you eat pomfret?" Camellia asked.

"Yes—but where is the fish?" Alice stared in amazement at the steaming banana-leaf package that John added to her plate.

"It's patra ni machhi, a Parsi specialty," Gulnaz said. "You don't eat the banana leaf. When you open it, you'll find a lovely fillet with a coconut spice paste on top."

"It's delicious," Alice said after a bite. "But did you leave off the chilies for me?"

"I thought chilies might hurt your stomach," Camellia said. "Am I wrong?"

"I was born in Madras and nursed by a Tamil. Bring the chilies!"

After lunch, Gulnaz decided she would take a rest. Perveen suspected Alice had overwhelmed her. Gulnaz had asked about the latest trends in England, and instead of talking about fashion and films, Alice had soliloquized on the recent triumphs of the suffrage movement, the future of women in mathematics, and Irish freedom.

The rich luncheon made Perveen slightly tired, too—but her mind was still reeling with thoughts about all that had happened over the last few days.

Perveen took Alice upstairs and through her airy bedroom out to the large balcony. Lillian was having a midday nap but woke readily at the sight of the saucer of chopped cucumber and tomato Alice fed her. After eating her lunch, the parrot sat on the Englishwoman's shoulder and stared at her blonde hair for a long time before making the first peck at it.

"Lillian, you mustn't bite people!" Perveen chided, and the parrot whooshed off to the garden. "You'd almost think she's ashamed of her behavior."

"No need to anthropomorphize," Alice said. "The bird is attracted to any source of light. She hoped that my hair was edible and went off because it wasn't."

"Oh, Alice," Perveen said with a sigh. "It's all so unbelievable, sitting here joking like nothing happened."

Alice reached out and closed her big hand over Perveen's small one. "When Gulnaz called, and I realized you weren't in the office doing papers, my first thought was you'd done another bunk. I thought you had wanted to go to the pictures without me."

"I invited you. Why would you think that?"

"I see the way people look at me as I go through the city. Yes, some of them are smiling and offering me namaste gestures, but I know they resent us. You probably had to lobby for me to be admitted to the lunch table!"

"As you know, I've wanted you to come since the day you arrived, and today's spontaneous luncheon was my sister-in-law's idea." Mischievously, she added, "I thoroughly enjoyed watching you sprinkle a few too many fresh green chilies on your fish."

"All the while your mother was explaining fish is called machhli, and chilies are called mirchi. Hindi is far too confusing."

Jaya, the housemaid, stepped onto the balcony with a long cedar box. "Memsahib, this was just delivered from Mistry Construction."

"Perfect timing." Perveen took the box into her lap and realized she was almost afraid to open it. Would the box have kept its contents well preserved, or was she going to find a nest of weevils and a few scraps of architectural plans?

"You're holding that thing like a baby. What is it?" Alice teased.

"I'll let you see when I open it up on my desk in the bedroom. The document is old, and I don't want anything to blow away in the wind."

"It's not a top-secret legal document I must not see?" Alice asked, following her in.

"Not at all. These are the architectural drawings for twenty-two Sea View Road."

Inside the box, a leather-bound folio held a series of drawings on thick stock that had yellowed and was brittle on the edges. But the plans hadn't been affected by damp or insects, and the ink markings were dark enough to see.

Perveen took extreme care as she opened the series of pages that showed exterior views and elevations of the bungalow. "What do you think? I suppose I should have my brother here pointing things out. It all looks very geometric."

Alice looked over Perveen's shoulder for a good minute before speaking. "If one counts up all my classes in public school and Oxford, I've studied geometry for five years. But one doesn't need a mathematics degree to see that the angles in these facades don't match the floor plans."

"What do you mean?" Perveen adjusted herself to see Alice, who was still gazing deeply at the building sketch.

"I can tell you what I think is strange, but it would be more significant if I knew about who's staying in which room."

Perveen thought she should wait to ask her father whether he'd approve of what she was about to do. But she wanted to hear from Alice, and she finally knew how she could bring her in.

"Just a minute." Perveen walked out to the balcony again and slid open the panel underneath the floor of Lillian's cage. She pulled out a tarnished sovereign, one of the few coins she had left from her time in England. Of course, keeping it outdoors for the last half year had resulted in its tarnishing, but it could always be polished. Returning to Alice, Perveen held out the coin.

"That is quite generous, but I'm more in need of rupees than a Queen Victoria sovereign," Alice said dryly.

"I gave away all my rupees and paise in the last twenty-four hours. This sovereign is a formal payment," Perveen said. "I'll write it up with a receipt. If you accept it, you'll become an employee of Mistry Law."

Alice looked cautiously at her. "You can offer me a job without your father's say?"

"A temporary job as geometry consultant," Perveen said with a grin.

"Geometry consultant? I never heard of such a thing."

"It's the only way I can stay within the letter of the law and tell you some important things about the Farids. I just hope that what you hear doesn't make you want to run back to England."

Alice shook her head. "The only ones with the power to put me on a boat are my parents—and you must believe I won't divulge a word of what you've got to say."

Perveen went to the bedroom door and looked out into the hall. She could hear her mother snoring down the hallway—and Gulnaz was likely doing the same on the other side of the duplex wall. Only after Perveen had locked the door and taken Alice back out to the balcony did she tell the whole story.

"I suspect the answer is in front of me, but I can't see it," she said at the end. "It feels as if I were on the beach, staring at a swimmer out at sea. I can't identify the black speck in the waves. Could be a man or a woman or an animal—"

"From the description of the murderer's style, I'd say animal," Alice said with a snort. "And when will it end? I'm not as confident as you seem to be that yesterday's call came from someone trying to get you into the street for kidnapping. It could have come from a woman who's no longer alive."

Perveen considered this. "Gulnaz said she spoke to two widows—I'm almost certain it was Sakina and Razia but not Mumtaz. What if one or both of them guessed she was pregnant?"

"You haven't yet calculated the estate payments due. There's still time for someone to reduce the number of inheritors and improve her situation." Restlessly, Alice picked up Perveen's mother's pen and tapped it on the table. "Remind me again of who's going to inherit?"

"Baby Jum-Jum is the largest inheritor, taking thirty-five percent. The daughters each get seventeen point five percent and the widows a touch more than four percent apiece. If Mumtaz's baby survives, the distribution percentages will change."

Alice shook her head. "I feel sorry for those widows. Except for Razia-begum, who owns the land, which the other wives don't have. Now her daughter's missing. Revenge, perhaps?"

"She might have been taken because she knows too much. Amina is such a smart little girl—and she is more outspoken than any of her elders. I'd think that we should have heard something from the relatives in Oudh if the theory about her journey was true." Perveen paused, feeling a stab of guilt at letting the widows keep her from sounding the alert about Amina.

"What are you thinking?" Alice looked at her soberly.

Alice could give her insight into the architectural plans, not Amina's fate. Sighing, Perveen asked, "What do you make of the bungalow's design?"

"Looking at the walls and windows, it appears there's no connection between men's and women's territories inside the house—but of course, there must be. How else would the husband visit the wives at night?"

Perveen explained about the brass jali door between the two sides. "Supposedly Mr. Farid held a key. It must be somewhere."

Sounding pensive, Alice asked, "Which room did Mukri sleep in? "

From her time observing Sub-Inspector Singh, Perveen could easily remember the orientation of the hall and the room where Mr. Murki appeared to have slept. She pointed on the drawing to answer Alice's query. "There appear to be five other bedrooms in that section of the bungalow, but for some reason, he chose this room."

"Because he saw himself as lord and master." Alice studied the plan a while longer. "On one side of the master bedroom, it looks like the wall is quite a bit thicker than the other walls. Do you see that?"

Perveen craned her neck. "It might not be a solid wall. It could be a storage area."

"It's strange to have this construction difference on just one side of the house. Other than this, the house is extremely symmetrical," Alice said.

Perveen tried to see the master bedroom again in her mind. She was walking through it, looking around. She'd put her hand on the bathroom doorknob when Singh had stopped her from going further. She studied the architectural drawing and recognized the bathroom and another door to its left.

"That can't be a closet," Alice said, following her gaze. "Unless it's the only closet in the bungalow."

"Indians use almirahs to hold their clothing and other possessions," Perveen said. "Of course, there are always storerooms within a bungalow."

"But those are clearly marked as very small rooms." Alice traced the lines on the paper with her finger. "If you look at the wives' rooms in the zenana, each of them has a door going into the same thicker exterior wall. And then, there are windows showing on the exterior wall—"

"What if there's a passage?" Perveen interrupted. "The fact is, the widows' rooms only have windows on the western side."

Alice stared at her. "I think you're right. Looking from my own bedroom window at the bungalow, I've seen those small windows."

Perveen felt gripped by excitement. "A passageway gives a husband access to various bedrooms in the zenana without his going down the main hallway and catching the notice of others. It allows discretion."

"And what about the converse?" Using her finger, Alice mapped a reverse journey. "The wives could have easily gone to the other side. They could have walked over, spent the night with their husband—or later on, Mr. Mukri—and nobody else would have known."

"I don't know that any of them would have willingly gone to Mukri," Perveen said with a shudder. But she could imagine any one of them using the passage to advantage—if she intended to commit murder.

30

THE SECOND ACT
Bombay, February 1921

*P*erveen woke at six-thirty the next morning and was too restless to stay in bed.

Her hip still ached slightly as she got out of bed and opened the doors to her balcony. The sky was slowly lifting its black veil. Something different was in the air: a feeling of something charged, almost electric.

Perveen stared at the changing sky, trying to think of all the small pieces of information she'd read and heard. The answer to Mukri's death was contained within a couple of pieces of this mosaic—and possibly, the answer to Amina's disappearance, too.

But although she and Alice had dwelled for more than two hours on the plans, they couldn't know anything more without going to the bungalow itself. That had been impossible, because Alice's mother expected her to attend a cards party, and Perveen had promised her father she'd stay home.

Lillian squawked from her cage, clearly aware of Perveen's presence.

"Go fly about the garden. There's plenty of food to find; look how busy the other birds are," Perveen scolded.

But Lillian remained, beating her wings to rise up a few inches and then come down hard on her perch bar. Over and over she did it, as if to irritate Perveen even further.

The bird wanted her breakfast in a dish because she'd never developed the skills to hunt grubs or pick fruit.

Perveen had once believed the Farid widows were similarly helpless, but she didn't anymore. It must have been maddening to have a household agent thrust into their world. Razia had the most powerful motivation against him: keeping her child from being married off. Sakina might have gone against Mukri because she hadn't liked the way he'd threatened Razia, and she might have feared for the future wellbeing of her own daughters. And Mumtaz would have wished him gone if there was a chance that he could claim parental rights to her child.

However, Perveen couldn't see how the women could have been involved in her kidnapping. They knew their home and its secret places but not the vastness of Bombay.

Thinking of this conundrum made her want to speak with her father, who had not arrived home by the time she'd fallen asleep. If she'd woken Lillian, she might as well wake her father.

Tying a wrapper over her nightdress, Perveen walked the short length of the hall to her parents' room. The door was ajar, and she saw her father was already dressed and standing in front of the mirrored almirah working on his cravat.

"Good morning!" he said, tugging at the edges of his bow tie. "You are awake early."

"And you are, too. When did you arrive home yesterday?"

"Well after you were asleep, and Mamma and I decided it was better to let you rest. Let us talk together while eating breakfast downstairs."

In the dining room, sun was slanting in from the eastern windows, casting a pattern across the mahogany table. As Perveen sat down, John brought coffee and toasted brun maska buns. This was a far cry from the large breakfast that would be served to the rest of the family at nine-thirty, but it was just right for the hour.

"What did you do yesterday?" Perveen yawned as she picked up her cup of coffee.

"I went to Sea View Road," he said casually. "I wished to check on the welfare of Mumtaz-begum, who wasn't observed by Gulnaz the other evening."

"And what about Amina?" Perveen asked. "Were you permitted to go to the jali screen to speak through it to Razia-begum?"

"Certainly," her father said, looking slightly affronted. It was surely a surprise to have her questioning his procedure. "Sub-Inspector

Singh was walking in, and I suggested that the two of us ask the young maid if all the women could come to their side of the jali screen for a conversation on the second floor. He didn't think they would—but when they heard I was your father, they agreed."

Perveen was too anxious to enjoy the pride she'd normally have felt in such a situation. "Did you mention Amina's disappearance in front of the sub-inspector? The family doesn't want a police investigation."

"I did not ask, although I am growing concerned that we should mention it. If the child has come to harm from a household member, I wouldn't wish to be charged with aiding and abetting."

Perveen's coffee went down the wrong way. Coughing out the fluid, she thought with horror about being charged for an offense when she'd thought she was in the right. Who knew? And say she wasn't charged—how could she live with herself if Amina died?

After looking at her reprovingly, Jamshedji spread more butter on his bun. "By the by, Mumtaz didn't come with the other two women to speak at the jali screen. Razia-begum said it was due to not feeling well—and remembering what you told me about her pregnancy, I suggested to Singh that we let her rest."

Again, Perveen was worried about her father's possible intrusion. "Please tell me you didn't mention the pregnancy—"

"Of course not!" he said briskly. "However, Singh stated concern that she should perhaps consult a doctor if she could not come to the window with the others. Razia-begum said she would call the doctor, although she could not promise Mumtaz-begum would be willing to be seen."

"What was it like speaking to them through a jali? Could you tell their voices apart?"

"Of course. Razia-begum's voice is lower and not as melodious as Sakina-begum's."

"What else did you learn in the conversation?"

"Singh questioned them about whether they had called you at Mistry House. Razia-begum said she hadn't and in fact did not have the business card any longer."

"If she looked for it, she might have thought of calling me."

"Sakina-begum denied ringing you. She and Razia agreed that Mumtaz was in her rooms all evening and did not call. This led to my asking whether they had any concerns for safety, and both agreed that they wished to have the durwan Mohsen continue guarding the gate."

"But will the police let him out?" Perveen asked.

"He'd been released and was on duty when I arrived."

So the police had acted on what she'd learned about Mohsen. He was reunited with his children, and the gate was secure. Perveen felt a small bit of pride for her part in this.

"You may recall that Farid Fabrics' office provided me the home address of Mrs. Mukri," Jamshedji continued, starting in on a bowl of sliced papaya. "Before going to catch the train for Poona, I checked your briefcase and found Sakina-begum's family address. I planned to call on both households during my day-trip. It wasn't until I was settled on the train and looking through the papers that I realized the addresses for Mrs. Mukri and Sakina-begum's father were the same. I would be making a condolence call—and an investigatory call—at the same compound."

"But that's remarkable! Are Faisal and Sakina-begum brother and sister?" Perveen was astonished.

Jamshedji dipped one corner of his brun maska in the coffee and ate at a leisurely pace. "No. The parents are siblings—which means Faisal Mukri and Sakina Chivne were first cousins. The house belongs to Sakina's grandparents, but when Mrs. Mukri became a widow in 1910, she and her children, including twelve-year-old Faisal, moved into the compound."

Perveen noted that her father had dropped the honorific for Sakina—he was scant on formality when they were in private conference. It felt as if the first important piece of the mysterious mosaic had emerged. The blood relationship was why Sakina had trusted Mr. Mukri so absolutely, no matter how unpleasant he might have been to everyone else.

"What was their relationship like as children?" Perveen asked

"Mrs. Mukri didn't say anything, and as she is mourning for

her son, I couldn't press her. Sakina's father, Mr. Chivne, said they became close as brother and sister, and Sakina missed him very much when he went away to school. When I stopped to speak with Sakina's younger brother Adnan, whom I met in the garden when I was leaving, I was able to learn a bit more."

Perveen had a number of burning questions, but she didn't want another pause, so she kept still.

"He said that when Faisal joined the household, he became the oldest boy in residence, and he attempted to gain the privileges that had been Adnan's."

"What kind of privileges?"

"Adnan chuckled about it—but I could tell, since he remembered so well, that it must have bothered him greatly," Jamshedji said in the relaxed tone he used when reading aloud. "Adnan Chivne said that after his cousin Faisal arrived, he received less choice pieces of chicken and lamb, and he no longer received many new clothes every season. Now Faisal got these things, because he was the oldest. Faisal also charmed Sakina, who favored him rather than her brother—to the point that their closeness became somewhat alarming to the family. Faisal officially left the zenana a year after he'd come to the household—but instead of staying on the other side of the house and going to school in town, he was sent to live at a madrassa."

"A religious boarding school!" Perveen said, thinking about the school Faisal Mukri had said he was going to build. Here was the root of his interest in such places.

"Sakina was heartbroken when Faisal went away. During school breaks, when Faisal returned to the bungalow, he was allowed to visit the zenana to see his mother—but wound up mostly with Sakina. Seeing that the affection between them was growing and might cause problems, Sakina's father accepted the proposal of a wealthy man he heard was looking for a second wife. This was Mr. Farid, who married her when he was thirty-nine and she was fifteen."

Perveen was trying to put together a timeline in her mind. "When was Faisal Mukri hired by Mr. Farid?"

"Three years after he'd married Sakina."

"Sakina-begum would have been eighteen—and she'd already delivered Nasreen and Shireen. Faisal Mukri would have been nineteen years old." Perveen thought some more about it. "I wonder if Sakina-begum suggested to her husband that he hire her cousin. It's an ordinary enough request."

"It's likely. As I've mentioned, the Farid Fabrics accounting supervisor thought Mukri was a relative of Mr. Farid's."

Perveen remembered Sakina's steadfast support of the proposition that she turn her personal wealth over to the wakf. Mukri could have promised her that in exchange they'd live their lives in luxury—and perhaps without the others. Mukri had the power to arrange marriages for the other widows; the household could have been stripped of everyone except for the two of them and Sakina's own children.

If Razia knew all of this, she might have realized Mukri was a threat to the household's existence. Would she feel the same way about Sakina—or would she continue to tolerate the second wife?

The only way Perveen could understand the truth of whether Razia had killed Mukri was by going directly to the women. "Pappa, I know you've been worried about me. I stayed home quietly yesterday and went to bed very early. I feel revived. I'd like to do some interviewing at the Farid bungalow today."

Jamshedji drained the last of his coffee and then looked at her. "I would be glad to accompany you, but I've got Mr. Reddy's trial today. Therefore, office work would be best for you today."

Perveen swallowed hard. After leaving Calcutta, she had pledged to herself not to disrespect her father. He'd taken her back without question, paid for her to study in England, and hired her as his employee when no other law firm in Bombay would. Jamshedji had delivered her second act.

But in her second act, she was a solicitor duty bound to do the best thing for her client, Razia Farid. Perveen looked her father in the eye. "While your work in Poona has brought out some great information, your experience speaking through a jali has not yielded information we need to ensure the widows' safety. I am the only one who can speak to Sakina privately about her relationship with Mr. Mukri and also to Razia and Mumtaz to determine if they knew about the family tie."

"That could be done another day, when I'm able to accompany you." Jamshedji laid his napkin aside, a subtle indication to Perveen that he was readying himself to move on to court. She was losing advantage.

"Another reason I wish to visit Sea View Road is to establish whether there's private access between the master bedroom and any of the wives' chambers. That's something that would be improper for you to try."

Jamshedji's gray eyebrows drew together in concern. "What is this about private access?"

Perveen decided to speak boldly, as if her actions of the day before were entirely natural. "Remember my request for the architectural drawings? I asked Alice to look at the plans with me. She noticed some inconsistencies and raised the possibility of a hidden passage—although it could also be a very thick wall."

"I wouldn't have expected you'd show Miss Hobson-Jones the drawings." Jamshedji's voice was stiff with disapproval.

"I contracted her services as a temporary employee." In response to her father's incredulous look, she said, "I paid her a sovereign and took a receipt. I knew Alice's mathematical acumen would be helpful with regard to the plans."

"Her father is the governor's councillor!" Jamshedji sputtered. "Didn't you think she might tell him about this and cause all manner of havoc?"

"Alice advised me she would not divulge a bit of it—and since she's our employee now, the court couldn't make her say anything."

Jamshedji was silent for a long moment. "As long as the police are still at the compound, you may visit. But don't go alone."

Perveen was flooded with relief—not just at being allowed to go, but also at his tacit suggestion that Alice be included. "Thank you very much for the permission, Pappa. And is there anything more I should know?"

"The autopsy was released. Sub-Inspector Singh informed me that Mukri's death was caused by a violent severing of his spinal cord."

"The back-of-the-neck wound," Perveen said, suppressing a brief rush of nausea as she recalled the scene. "I guessed that was the cause because of all the blood and the fact that the letter opener was still there."

"Ah, but the coroner didn't say the letter opener was the weapon. He suggested a stiletto-type item was used—although none was found on the scene."

Perveen thought this through. "Was the letter opener placed there after the fact?"

"No comment was made on that, but it surely must be the case." He put down his cup heavily. "For all we know, someone other than the killer came along after the deed was done and placed the letter opener there."

"It would be a way to throw suspicion on Razia-begum or Amina" Perveen was unable to sit any longer and got up to look out the window. "I feel we must investigate the past relationship between Sakina-begum and Faisal Mukri."

"You must be very careful when you speak to her—and any other of the wives," Jamshedji said. "Get the information, and get out."

Perveen hugged her father tightly at the door. He had given her his blessing to continue with the case. It was hard to express to him how happy that made her, even at a very difficult time.

Gruffly, he said, "This is a grand farewell for an ordinary morning in court."

"I'm only wishing you the best of luck. You are defending Mr. Reddy's sweetshop, which is one of my favorite places."

That brought a chuckle. "If we prevail, there won't be much of a fee—but I expect a big pan of boorelu."

"We will celebrate with sweets tonight," Perveen pledged, hoping that it would be a celebration of her work as well as his.

31

LEFT HANGING
Bombay, February 1921

"Hobson-Jones residence!" Alice answered cheerily on the second ring.

"It's Perveen. Are you up for work today?"

"Certainly. I've watched the telephone all morning hoping you'd call."

Perveen wasn't surprised that the energy that had woken her stretched all the way to Malabar Hill. "You can't imagine what I've learned from my father in the last half hour. I'm starting to put together the pieces—"

"I'd like to finish that puzzle we began at your house last night. One thousand pieces, wasn't it?" Alice spoke brightly, and Perveen suddenly realized that the councillor's telephone line was hardly confidential.

"Actually, I'd like to show you the Hanging Gardens. If it gets too hot, we can come back here and finish that puzzle."

"I'll come for you in the Crossley. No, it's not an imposition. Mummy has plans with Lady Lloyd and would much rather ride with her in the Silver Ghost."

Alice arrived in the elegant blue car shortly after nine. As Perveen entered the car, several neighborhood boys waved at the tall fair-haired visitor. Perveen ran past Camellia, explaining that she had to show Alice the Hanging Gardens before the midday sun rose.

"Good idea. She must not burn her skin. Take a parasol," Camellia said.

Perveen had not wanted to tell her mother about her visit to the Malabar Hill bungalow; while Jamshedji had authorized the trip, her mother would worry far too much.

Because the Hobson-Joneses' chauffeur, Sirjit, spoke excellent

English, she knew not to talk about anything in the car. She did ask for a stop at the Hanging Gardens. There, the two strolled far away from the memsahibs chatting together while ayahs trundled their babies. The two went through the little paths lined by roses and topiaries. At the park's far side, a stone wall bordered a steep drop. It was there that Perveen explained about the close relationship of Sakina and Faisal Mukri. Perveen also told Alice of her intent in exploring the passageway.

Alice's eyes glittered with excitement. "How shall we manage all of this? Do you think they'll just let us look?"

Perveen shook her head. "You shall be my decoy. What if you appeared at the door of the zenana hawking yourself as an English governess? Even if they say no, you can keep talking, and they'll not have the nerve to send an Englishwoman away."

"And where will you be?" Alice said as the two of them turned to walk back to the waiting car.

"Walking into the other side of the house and taking the exploratory route from Mr. Farid's room—or should I say, Mukri's lair?" she added with a grimace.

"But aren't there going to be police present?" Alice said as they passed through the garden's gateway to the street.

"I'm not sure because I heard Mohsen's back on the job. In any case, if the police are present, we'll tell them you're paying a social call, and they will think your mother sent you. They already know I'm the family lawyer and have good reason to be at the property."

Outside the bungalow wall, a young man carrying a notebook was arguing with a constable guarding the gate. Perveen guessed the young man was a reporter. She tried not to catch his eye as she spoke out the car window to the constable standing on guard.

"Are you from the Malabar Station?" Perveen asked politely in Marathi. "Thank you for coming. I'm Miss Mistry, the family's lawyer. I've come with the children's governess."

"You were at the station," the constable said, nodding in

recognition. "The inspector and sub-inspector are coming later this morning."

"I'm pleased to hear that. Thank you again," Perveen said.

"Who are you? What is this?" the reporter called out as the constable waved the car through.

"Good luck to both of us," Alice muttered after they'd both stepped out of the car. "Any new thoughts about our plan?"

Perveen glanced at Sirjit, who had been instructed to wait in the porte cochere close to the zenana entrance. He had already opened up a newspaper and settled in for the wait. "Let's divide and conquer as planned. You will knock on the zenana door and offer a free English lesson for the girls. It's really too bad Amina isn't here—she'd jump at the chance to speak with you. I will check if Mohsen's here and then get on with my search for the passageway."

"Do you have the plans?" Alice asked.

"Yes, they're in my bag, but I've got the layout more or less memorized."

"Then might I keep them in my satchel? Just because I don't know the bungalow at all."

Perveen gave them to her. "Let's meet at the car when each of us is done."

After they parted, Perveen made her first stop, at the garden hut. Right in front of it, Mohsen was lying on a charpoy. He was dressed just in a vest and pajamas and fast asleep. Zeid sat next to the charpoy, gazing adoringly at his father.

As Perveen approached, Zeid got up and ran to hug her. "You brought him back! Memsahib, thank you!"

Smiling, she said, "The police released him, not I. But I am glad for you."

The exchange had woken Mohsen. He lifted his head from under a blanket, grumbling at the children to quiet themselves. Then he turned and saw Perveen. Instead of giving her the smile she expected, he looked anxious. "You!"

"Good morning, Mohsen," Perveen said pleasantly. "When were you released?"

"A few hours after that telephone call they allowed to Sakina-begum. She convinced them."

It was hard to think she might be chatting with the man who'd abducted her. Carefully, she asked, "What is the situation with the household? Are the begums asking you to stay on?"

"Certainly." He looked at her with a hint of defiance. "I've done nothing wrong. I'm only resting here because the police are at the gate keeping away reporters."

She supposed the police wouldn't like it known that they'd released a suspect before taking a new one into custody.

Perveen told him she hoped he would be back on duty soon.

Feeling his eyes on her, she walked onward to the entrance to the main house. The front door was locked, and when she knocked, nobody came. This could only mean the police were clustered at the zenana. Alice would have to deal with them.

Perveen crept along the side of the house until she came to a side door that she remembered from the architectural plans. This was the servants' door, she realized after seeing a small pair of rough sandals next to it. It was unlocked. After a short walk down a hallway, she found the large, elegant reception room that she'd first visited. This time, she was well aware of the risks of being seen and heard through the pierced marble wall. Keeping her eyes on the jali panel, she slipped out of her shoes, but instead of putting them in the shoe case, she put them under a chair.

Tiptoeing upstairs, she began preparing an excuse in case Zeid or Fatima came upon her. She would tell them she was looking for papers connected to the estate in the upstairs study. The children didn't need to know she was looking for evidence connected to Mr. Mukri's death before she was certain of her suspicions.

They wouldn't like what she was presently thinking. Although Jamshedji had told her about Mohsen's release, she hadn't realized he'd been freed just hours before her abduction. All the widows had the street address for Mistry House on the business cards she'd given out. He could have been dispatched to get rid of her. And Mohsen knew the pier. Razia had mentioned that Mohsen's job, before he'd come to the house, had involved working for Farid Fabrics on the docks. Sakina might also have known.

Mohsen had wanted to know about a jewelry shop. Perhaps it wasn't because he intended to steal; Sakina could have promised him a portion of proceeds from selling her jewelry. Perveen caught her breath as she thought about the various things that might have been promised to the guard who performed household errands.

But how could such a conversation between a secluded woman and male servant have taken place?

Sakina had said she took care of the garden's flowers early in the morning.

In Omar Farid's old bedroom, a shaft of midday sun fell across the space, brightening it.

She was sure Mr. Farid would have kept the key to the locked door somewhere in the room.

First she checked the desk, but found only papers and money. She opened the double doors of a mahogany almirah. Gently, she moved her hands through stacks of folded men's shirts, pajama trousers, and sherwani coats. All were of average-quality cotton—the kind of clothing worn by an employee, not a boss. There was just one European suit, made from gray cotton and carrying the label of an ordinary Bombay tailor. The suit had a slight odor, as if had been put away without washing.

All of the clothing was free of dust; it had to belong to Mr. Mukri. He probably wore the suits only to work, or for special occasions. He had died wearing another suit; there had been so much blood, she could not remember its color.

But she did remember something else. It was a comment Sakina had made when Perveen had first asked the widows about what they'd done after hearing there was a wounded man lying on the other side of the brass jali.

Just because the man was dressed in an English suit, it didn't mean he was our household agent.

Perveen had long since ruled out that Amina was the one who discovered the body because she hadn't mentioned seeing it when Perveen questioned her. Sakina had said she didn't look, but she'd known what he was wearing.

A sharp lawyer would have recognized this incongruity the moment that the words had been uttered. But Perveen had been reeling with her own shock at seeing the body and the burden put on her by the police to get information from everyone. She had not registered what had been said until the moment she'd looked at the second suit in the almirah.

Perveen reminded herself of the task at hand. She finished checking the inside of the almirah and looked underneath and behind it for a hidden key. Nothing.

She realized ten minutes had already passed; she'd need to hurry up the search.

A box of matches was tucked in one bedside table drawer. The other one held a lady's hair comb, two hairpins, and a small vial of attar. She didn't need to open it to smell the scent of sandalwood, the attar used by couples.

Turning the hairpins over in her hand, she saw a long, lustrous black hair. Sakina had the prettiest hair of the three wives; it was very likely hers. But the hairpin gave Perveen an idea. She went to the locked door and slipped the pin inside the keyhole. She turned it this way and that until she heard a click.

The door opened with a creak of dry hinges, revealing a narrow, dusty marble passage. The hall was stamped with many footprints and couldn't have been more than two feet wide. It would have been horrifically claustrophobic if there hadn't been a row of clerestory windows close to the ceiling. The windows were closed, which made the passage stifling. There was also a faint smell that brought Perveen back to the little room in the Sodawallas' house.

Perveen walked the passage's length, arriving at the door on the left that she knew was Sakina's. But the footsteps in the dust didn't stop here; they continued around a left turn.

Was one of the other wives involved in the death?

Now she was in the second part of the *L*-shaped zenana hallway, where Razia's and Mumtaz's quarters lay. But her attention was no longer focused on the doors along its length. A dark bundle lay at the marble floor's end point.

Perveen rushed forward, the smell of old blood filling her nose, making her want to retch. As she reached the bundle, she jerked to a horrified stop. Black chiffon, stained brown with dried blood, had been wrapped all around a small body.

Perveen lifted the chiffon away and found a young girl curled up with her dark hair half covering her face. It was Amina.

Perveen felt tears starting. She should not have waited to report the disappearance. She should have carried out a house search with police assistance the moment she'd heard Amina had gone missing.

Her hand shaking, Perveen put it on Amina's forehead. It was still warm, although that might have been because of the heat of the passage. But as she moved the hair away from Amina's face, it seemed as if she saw the girl's nostrils move very slightly, as if she were taking in air. Her lips were dry and cracked.

Swiftly, Perveen reached under the chiffon and found Amina's arm. Sliding her fingers down to the inside of the girl's wrist, she felt a pulse. Amina was alive but unconscious—the result of the heat? Or drugging?

Perveen needed to get Amina to safety. Dehydration after three days was a serious matter. Cyrus's sister, Azara, had been neglected and had died after not taking in food and water. Perveen hoped it wasn't too late for Amina also.

As Perveen struggled to lift Amina's body, she thought about how only one of the widows wore black chiffon.

Perveen heard the sharp sound of a door opening. With a feeling of dread, she turned her head. Sakina had entered the passage.

32

A WIDOW'S LAMENT
Bombay, February 1921

*T*he veil had dropped.

Sakina rapidly advanced toward Perveen, who had nowhere left to go.

"Why are you here?" Sakina asked.

"I was interested in the passage." Perveen struggled to look composed. She thought of Alice, who was likely out at the car waiting for her. Even if Perveen screamed, Alice wouldn't hear her. The walls were too thick. Desperately, she said, "The police also have details about this place and my plan to inspect it."

Her second untruth of the day. But while Camellia had believed her, Sakina shook her head. "I don't think so. We've only got one constable, and he is gawking at the huge, ugly Englishwoman who would like to become our governess."

Perveen couldn't tell from Sakina's snide tone whether she believed Perveen and Alice were together. What she needed was to get Amina to safety; sorting out Sakina's suspicions could come later. Keeping her hand on Amina, Perveen said, "I'm amazed this girl is still alive after three days in such a stifling hot place. Will you help me carry her out?"

"But she is sleeping," Sakina said, sounding almost protective. "So tired, after all she drank."

"What do you think she drank?" Perveen almost said, *Was she poisoned?* but stopped herself just in time. She would not get far by accusing Sakina when there was so much she needed to learn. When Sakina didn't answer, Perveen said, "I must make clear I am not your lawyer. I have taken on that duty for Razia-begum."

"Of course you would help her—she gets everything," Sakina said, her resentment surfacing. "But her sweet-tooth daughter isn't as lucky. She drank falooda mixed with morphine."

"Did Mohsen buy the morphine?"

"No. It was left from my husband's illness. I found it in the room some weeks ago. At that time, I was only thinking about using it to take care of Mumtaz. But sleeping powder has a much greater effect on a small child's body."

Sakina had dropped two major revelations, but Perveen couldn't react with horror. She needed to calm the woman—and that meant letting Sakina feel understood. Softening her voice, she said, "You were worried about Amina."

"The girl was always watching and listening. I didn't know she had found this passage—maybe her mother told her it existed." Closing her eyes tightly, Sakina fell into a silence. Then the eyes opened, and she looked coolly at Perveen. "We must wait for her to awaken. When she has the ability to drink again, you will give her the medicine again, mixed with water. She trusts you."

Perveen felt her stomach turn. "We mustn't do that. You've known Amina since you married her father. She's been like a sister to your own daughters."

"It will be a loss for them. Just as I lost love—twice." As she spoke, Sakina's lovely features seemed to sharpen.

Perveen knew she had an opening. But how much could she say without pushing Sakina too far? Softly, she said, "Faisal lived with your family when you were young. You were so close. The best of friends."

Sakina looked at her for a long moment. "Who told you that?"

"Your family explained the situation to my father. They didn't want you to marry."

"They thought they knew better than us." Sakina's voice was wistful. "But I loved Faisal, and he loved me."

It was hard for Perveen to reconcile the unpleasant man she'd met with this lover that Sakina had pined for. But men could change their ways—Cyrus was proof of that. "Was Faisal going to marry you after iddat was over?"

"That was what he said at first." Sakina, who was leaning against the passage's wall just a few feet away, gave Perveen a pained look.

"But not after you visited—and we learned about what he could and could not do. Because of my questions, he became angry with me. He seemed to forget he would never have had a career in Bombay or a life in a mansion without me."

"Yes, in those early days when Faisal came to Bombay—you must have impressed your husband with information about him." Perveen strove to sound admiring. "After all, he later granted him the most important position, as household agent."

"Yes. I suggested he hire Faisal for the accounting department," Sakina said with a sad smile. "I told him about Faisal's degree, his good character, and that there were no opportunities for him in Poona. My husband took pity on him but thought it better for nobody to know that we were cousins. The other wives would have been jealous."

And they'd have been rightfully suspicious when he moved into the bungalow. Softly, Perveen said, "I saw the drinking glasses by his bed. You went to stay with him at night, didn't you, using this passage?"

"I gave him the privileges of a husband." Sakina rested her head against the wall. "And at first, I felt nothing but amazement at my turn of fortune. But then I began to see how Faisal had changed."

"Tell me," Perveen said, stroking Amina's hair as she spoke. She wanted to scoop up Amina and rush out—but the passageway wasn't wide enough for her to carry Amina and get past Sakina. She'd also noticed Sakina was keeping her right hand nestled in the folds of her sari, which could mean she was armed.

Sakina spoke in a rush, as if she had longed to unload her story on someone. "When we were young, he was so daring and funny. Now he was always cross. He could not easily understand the expenses of this household. But he promised me that after iddat was finished, we could marry and live very well."

"With the addition of everyone's mahr funds," Perveen said. "I don't think he planned to use anything for a boys' school. One thing I don't know is whether he would have let the other begums and Amina stay after your marriage." Perveen wasn't sure, but she thought she felt Amina stirring at her touch.

"No. He would have chosen their husbands—and one for Amina. But then, in the last few weeks, I realized it might be impossible to get them married." Looking soberly at Perveen, Sakina said, "Mumtaz was tired and smelled of sickness. I know what that means. Faisal must have planted the seed in her."

Perveen remembered Mumtaz's anxiety about Sakina finding out she was carrying a child. She'd been right about that fear. "How can you know she carries Faisal's child?"

"If I could not trust his intentions toward me, how could I trust him with anyone else?" She raised her eyes heavenward. "He had already seen her at that filthy place where she used to play music."

"We don't know the baby is his child," Perveen said, avoiding commentary on the Falkland Road lounge. "If the baby is born in August, it could very well be your husband's."

"I don't believe it." Sakina was trembling. "Her child taking a share of the inheritance? It's not fair."

Perveen thought carefully about how to sound like an ally. "Seeing the baby, once he or she is born, will tell us the truth. We cannot guess at it now."

Sakina looked back the way Perveen had traveled, as if remembering her own past journeys. "In the month just after my husband passed, I believed all that Faisal said. But when you spoke to me and showed me the papers and spoke about Razia, I realized that he could not use funds as he said." A tight grimace twisted Sakina's beautiful face. "We would have lost our security. He deserved to die for taking everyone's money."

When Perveen had rushed to see Cyrus at the bottling plant, she had felt as if she were being carried in a dark, furious cloud. Nobody could have stopped her from getting to him. "Sakina, I know the pain of betrayal. Is that how you felt? Is that why you killed him?"

The passion must have come through in her voice, because Sakina looked at her with a hint of surprise in her eyes. "Yes. When you drove away that afternoon, I made up my mind that I had to rid us of Faisal. I sent Mohsen off to buy something so he would be away from the gate, and everyone would think a criminal had slipped in. I had this already. It is a family piece that I keep in my safe for protection." Now she brought her right hand out so Perveen could see the long silver dagger. The weapon had an elegantly worked handle and was highly polished; it looked like a relic from the Mughal period, something that should have been in a museum.

Thinking of the ugly cuts Sakina's beautiful dagger had made a few days earlier, Perveen swallowed hard. "If you wanted to make it look like an outsider had killed Faisal, why did you leave Razia-begum's letter opener in the back of his neck?"

"Razia shouldn't have had the wakf!" Each word was a bitter jab. "I did it to teach her that I could speak out and blame her at any moment. She understands that I've become the family's head."

Sakina's style of vengeance revealed something about her. She was filled with emotion—not just the pain she felt at being betrayed by a boy who'd grown into a tyrant, but also resentment of the other two women who'd treated her like their middle sister. Perveen would work with this understanding. "Nobody knew how intelligent you were. In fact, it is likely that Mumtaz-begum doesn't know this passage exists, because your husband didn't use it to visit her. He stayed in her room all the time, didn't he?"

"Mumtaz doesn't know about the passage." Sakina sounded contemptuous. "Of course, Razia knows it exists—but she will not say a word about it, lest she be accused of using it herself. Because Faisal tried to take Razia's precious wakf, and then her daughter, anyone would think she'd be the one who killed him."

"I see. Did you go through the passage to surprise him in his room?"

"Yes, as I had done many times before." Sakina sighed. "When I saw him, I began crying about how Razia controlled the wakf. He took me in his arms, never seeing what was in my hand."

"Did he fight?" Perveen asked, remembering the many wounds.

"He screamed, and he did try—but he was already too injured to do much. I didn't enjoy it," she said, looking sadly at Perveen. "He wept as he died, as if he could not believe what I'd done. And I felt the same."

The sight of Mr. Mukri's bloodied body would be in Perveen's memory forever, like a curse. Trying not to let the image rattle her, she said, "But you didn't confess."

"No, of course not! I needed to save our family. I took everything off and cleaned myself in his bath. I was afraid to bring the sari into my own room, so I left it in the passage. Nobody would have known if it hadn't been for Amina."

At the sound of her name, Amina shifted. Perveen gave the girl a warning pat, willing her not to move again. "Did Amina speak to you about it?"

"No. I found her looking at my ruined sari. I did not know for certain if she'd guessed, but I told her that we would have a glass of falooda together in my room and she could ask me anything she liked—that I would just tell her, because she was more clever and brave than anyone. After half a glass, she fell unconscious. It was no trouble to pull her right back into the passageway."

"And then you took her belongings so it appeared she might have run away." Perveen spoke in a soothing tone. "Just as you made it look as if I were kidnapped by a common criminal. You had Mohsen grab me, didn't you?."

"He was allowed to use the telephone from the station to speak to me," Sakina sounded defiant. "He said you were investigating everything. I told him to get rid of you; he said he had a key hidden at the docks to a place where nobody would ever find you."

"He did this all for you because you promised him a share of the sales of your jewelry," Perveen ventured.

"He told you that?" Sakina looked panicked. "I'll have to sack him."

As Sakina spoke, Perveen thought she heard something. Had it been a turning doorknob? If Mohsen was coming into the passageway, both she and Amina were done for.

Now there were footsteps. In the moment that Sakina turned to look toward the corner, Perveen shot up from her kneeling position and flung herself at the small widow. As she knocked Sakina to the ground, the woman struggled against her. Silk tore as Perveen used her superior weight to hold Sakina down, all the while trying to keep track of where the dagger was.

"You ruined everything!" Sakina screamed. Perveen dug her nails hard into the woman's right hand, and the knife finally clattered out.

With Alice leading them, Sub-Inspector Singh and the constable came rapidly around the corner. Everyone stopped short at the sight of Perveen atop Sakina.

"The knife," Perveen said. "Take it!"

Alice dragged a wrinkled handkerchief out of her pocket and used it to pick up the dagger while the sub-inspector and constable surrounded Sakina. Perveen could barely get past them in the narrow passage to reach Amina, who was trying to pull herself up but had flopped back down.

"Am I dreaming still?" Amina asked in a slurred voice. "I had such a bad dream. It was about Sakina-khala—"

"Thank God she's all right. How long has she been here?" demanded Alice, who was still holding the knife.

"Sakina-begum gave Amina morphine the evening of Mukri's death. The child has been lying here with no food or water for more than three days!" Perveen looked gratefully at her friend. "I'm so glad it was you."

"I knew you were going to explore the passage—when Sakina-begum went off and didn't return, I became nervous. I asked Razia-begum if she knew about the passage. She said she didn't, but when I showed her the architectural drawing, she admitted she had heard of it. She said that if I went inside there, I'd better bring the police."

"I'm glad you came," Perveen said to Sub-Inspector Singh. "I'd also like to state that I am representing Razia-begum in this matter—not Sakina-begum."

His head swiveled from Sakina to her. "So you will answer all my questions?"

"I'd rather speak with you than Inspector Vaughan," Perveen said shortly. "But could we have the interview later? Amina must get to her mother, and then a doctor should be called. I don't know what effect the morphine might have—"

"Put your hands behind your back, Sakina-begum," Sub-Inspector Singh said in formal Hindi. He was trying not to look into Sakina's tear-stained face, as if the fact he had to arrest her was profoundly embarrassing. Perveen thought it unlikely he'd ever arrested a woman—let alone a purdahnashin.

"But I am a respectable woman—you must not touch me," Sakina pleaded as the constable awkwardly fitted handcuffs around her wrists.

"Gentlemen—just a moment." Perveen gently lifted the end of Sakina's sari and let it fall so it covered her face. It was a small thing to do, but it preserved her dignity.

"Thank you," Sakina whispered. "Tell them I will go to their prison. And to please not touch me again."

33

A WANING LIFE
Bombay, March 1921

"*I* believe I owe you an apology."

From the depths of the plush armchair, Perveen regarded the man seated behind a highly polished mahogany desk. It was a week after the incident and she'd come in expecting the worst, especially since Alice had been on the scene when the police apprehended Sakina. "But Sir David—whatever for? You have been nothing but kind."

"I am speaking of your effort to work with those women within the house. The police would probably never have been able to gather the necessary evidence and confession that you could behind the curtain."

Perveen felt herself stiffen. "I'm not trying to be the police's helper. My concern has always been for the family's safety. In the end that meant looking carefully at all three women, as well as others within the house."

He nodded. "I accept that. How is the little girl doing?"

"The doctor says she must continue treatment at Cama Hospital for a few more days, but she's chattering happily. Her mother is with her every day, and you must know that Alice has been teaching geometry to Amina and accounting principles to Razia-begum."

"Speaking of my daughter, she has informed me that she has taken on a part-time consultancy at the law firm. I'd like to know more about that."

Here was the reason for the conference. "My father and I both think the world of Alice. I know that helping us is not the ideal career for an Oxford-trained mathematician. The thing is, Alice is not confident you'd approve of her becoming a lecturer at a local college."

After a pause, Sir David said, "I'm not against it, as it would keep her in India at least."

"You should tell her," Perveen advised, thinking how much his support would mean to Alice. "And at least until she's found a position, we would be grateful for her assistance. Her mathematical acumen can be put to use in calculating inheritances and other matters."

"As long as she's not going about Bombay alone. But her mother is understandably anxious about the dangers that are inherent in this city."

"Is Lady Hobson-Jones relieved two suspects were caught and taken away?"

Sakina had spent one night in the ladies' cell. She'd been released on bail into the care of her parents at their home in Poona. Her trials would take place in a few months' time: the first for murder of Faisal Mukri and the second for attempted murder of Amina. Mohsen faced charges for abduction of Perveen. He would not be allowed out of prison before the trial.

"She's not just relieved, but has now taken it upon herself to set up a fund for widows with young children. But tell me, what is the situation with the other two widows? I understand the house isn't occupied."

"Razia is staying in my home, and we are engineering ways for her to spend the last few weeks of iddat without running into my father and brother," Perveen said. "Mumtaz has gone to stay at a maternity hospital, where she's being pampered and feels much better. The two widows are thinking of selling the property, but that cannot be done until Sakina's trial is done and Mumtaz's baby is born."

"I imagine you're waiting to see if it's a boy or girl," he said.

Sinking a bit deeper in the overstuffed chair, Perveen said, "In either case, the child will inherit something."

Studying her, Sir David said, "Muslim law is all about mathematical fractions—Alice will be a champion with such numbers. Is it true that Parsi estate law is even more complicated?"

Perveen chuckled. "While I feel there are still a few regrettable aspects of Parsi law, one of the best parts is the long-standing vast distribution of inheritance. A deceased's wealth is shared with so many relatives that it's allowed many in our community to become financially stable."

Sir David gave her a wry half smile. "And you Parsis have stabilized Bombay as well—building hospitals and schools, projects that my people overlooked."

There were so many things she could say about what the British should do, starting with granting Indians self-rule. But she sensed she would have Sir David's ear again. "Good thoughts, good words, good deeds is the Parsi credo; however, there is no monopoly on it."

"Goodbye, Miss Mistry," he said, putting a hand out to her. "Although I'm certain it's not for long."

Two days later, Perveen climbed into the Daimler with Gulnaz, reflecting on what Alice's father had said about Parsi philanthropy. She was on her way to one of these laudable places that Parsis had built: the B. D. Petit Parsee General Hospital.

Gulnaz had checked with the hotel registrar and confirmed that a thirty-two-year-old man named Siyamak Azman Patel was staying in the ward for incurables. She had insisted on going along to help Perveen overcome any red tape.

The car rolled along, passing a young girl in a ragged sari picking through a small mountain of rubbish for pieces of glass. The ragged urchin made Perveen think of Fatima, whose fate might have brought her to the same place. But the widows had kept her and Zeid.

Perveen had visited Mr. Farid's bank and, using her legal authority, paid out every rupee of the mahr due to Razia and Mumtaz. Taiba-ayah's and the cook's salaries were once again being paid—with a bonus for the months they'd served without pay. With the widows and children away from the house, Fatima's and Zeid's duties had lightened, and the two were even able to attend a community school several half days per week.

"I looked up the meaning of the patient's first and middle names in the Persian name book," Gulnaz said, interrupting Perveen's warm thoughts about Mohsen's children.

Perveen turned to her. "What is it?"

"Siyamak means 'alone in the world.' And Azman means 'infinite.' Quite mysterious, isn't it?"

Cyrus had told her at Bandra how lonely he felt in his world. She was sure this was another message.

At the hospital, Gulnaz breezed through reception and into the critical care ward. The head nurse, though, was not as accommodating as the receptionist. The nurse said they could not see the patient, who was too weak to see visitors.

"But he asked for me." Perveen held out the letter that she'd had the foresight to bring.

The nurse's eyes lit up. "Ah, very good. I posted the letter some days ago. We had almost given up hope."

"Is Mr. Patel close to death?" Perveen was suddenly anxious that she'd missed her chance to know the truth.

"Time will tell. He can speak, although he suffers from confusion." As the two young women looked inquiringly at her, the nurse shook her head. "I am not at liberty to give information about his diagnosis, just as I cannot admit anyone to see him except for the solicitor he requested: Miss Perveen Mistry."

"At least let me stay outside the door," Gulnaz pleaded. "He could do something terrible!"

The nurse looked at Gulnaz as if she were insane. "Mr. Patel is a very weak man. He needs your prayers, not your fear."

Gulnaz took a seat in the hallway while Perveen followed the nurse into a patient room that smelled heavily of disinfectant. There were two beds in the room. One contained a teenaged boy and the other a hideous man speckled with red spots and lesions. "This is Mr. Patel," the nurse murmured to Perveen. In a louder voice, she said, "Mr. Patel, the lawyer you wrote to has come."

A stranger bearing no resemblance to the man she'd loved. Perveen chided herself for assuming the letter writer had to be connected to what Mr. Ghosh and her father had learned about

Cyrus. But because she'd shown up, he'd expect her to help with the will.

The head nurse drew a curtain between the two beds, giving Perveen and the spotted man privacy from the boy.

"Miss Mistry is here," the nurse said loudly.

The man's eyes fluttered and then opened fully. Perveen caught her breath, because now she saw the hazel eyes were just like those of Cyrus.

"My wife." The man spoke between wheezes. "Perveen."

Perveen felt blood pounding in her ears. The sick man had Cyrus's voice, but she saw no trace of his former beauty: just a body covered in pockmarks.

Perveen shot a look at the nurse, who was gaping. "This is a lawyer-client meeting," Perveen said. "It requires privacy."

The nurse's expression was indignant. "But my patient—"

"I shall call if he needs you."

After the nurse had stiffly exited, Perveen asked, "Why are you calling yourself by another name?"

"So you wouldn't stay away," he rasped.

Softly she said, "I should not write a will for you. I am still considered a family member; it would be a conflict of interest."

"So be it." He sighed. "I am glad to see you again. I wanted to see you one more time."

"Do your parents know you're so ill?"

"Yes. My father told me to stop work. They wished me to have treatment far from Calcutta, so people won't know. "

"Do you have smallpox?" she ventured.

"I've got syphilis. Do you know what that is?"

"I do." It was the most terrible venereal disease. Swallowing hard, she asked, "Is there a treatment?"

"First, I was injected with malarial blood. But the fever I had didn't kill the disease. Now they are giving me medicine with arsenic."

Cyrus fell into a coughing spell. Noticing a pitcher and glass on the bedside table, Perveen poured a glass of water.

After drinking a small amount, he gave her back the glass and spoke in a stronger voice. "The doctors say the arsenic may cure me; but it could also fail."

"Imagine yourself becoming well, and the strength will pull you through." She was stunned to hear herself saying words of encouragement. She'd spent so many years thinking of him as a threat—when the only one he'd harmed in the end was himself.

"Maybe the medicine will work, but what is the point? All my life, I have run after false gold. You were the only treasure I ever had—and then I lost you."

Perveen was startled to hear him sound as sentimental as in their courting days. "How long have you been following me?"

"Last October, my cousin sent me the *Bombay Samachar* article about you. It wasn't till this year I fell very ill. And then I came here. I only wrote about the will to get you to the hospital. I want you to help me."

"How so?" she asked apprehensively. If he asked her to come back to nurse him, she would refuse. No matter how selfish it would be, she couldn't bear to go back. Or perhaps he thought the Mistrys should take him into their home. There was no end to the responsibilities a wife owed a dying husband—

"Help me," he croaked, interrupting her panicked thoughts. "Just a bit more medicine, and I will sleep forever."

Perveen felt relieved by the simplicity of his request. "I shouldn't give you medicine; I don't know the dosing. I'll call for your nurse."

"No. I want you to give me all the medicine in the bottle right now. When I die, it will make you free."

As the meaning of his request hit, Perveen felt faint. "You wish me to poison you with arsenic?"

"Please," he said in a wheedling tone. "If I could reach from the bed to where the nurse has put the bottle, I would do it myself."

Perveen's initial shock was turning into suspicion. He'd asked her to commit an act for which she could go to prison. A young man lay on the other side of the curtain; if he had awoken and heard all of this, he'd be a witness against her.

Standing, she looked down at Cyrus. Once he'd been so charming; he had commanded her unquestioning love. And he was trying to tempt her, to give her the idea of forthcoming freedom that could cause her to hang for murder.

"Won't you do it?" he wheezed.

"I will not," she said, hearing the shakiness in her voice. "You must speak to your doctor. He might be able to adjust your medicines so you don't feel as desperate. The journey to recovery could be a long one. But if you hold on to your life, you can change it."

"And if I die?" he asked pitifully.

Trying to sound dispassionate, she said, "Under Parsi law, if you die intestate, your assets will be dispersed to your family members in set amounts. For this reason, you might wish to write a will with a solicitor and leave me out of it. I want nothing."

"But Perveen, I owe you everything."

Was this his true thought, or just another lie? She'd never be sure. He was so ruined that it was hard to hold on to the anger that had consumed her for the last four years. "I'm sorry that I cannot help you with what you asked for. You will be in my prayers."

Perveen left the room, knowing it would be forever.

34
A COCKTAIL AT THE TAJ
Bombay, September 1921

*I*t was a pleasant day in late rainy season when Perveen went to meet Razia and Mumtaz at the Taj Mahal Palace. As she'd walked in from the garden, she'd parked her umbrella in the long rack in the reception area but kept her briefcase in hand. It was light because all she had inside were a few checks and papers.

She had reserved a table in the same dining room where her family had met the Sodawallas. But she told herself she wasn't going to think about Cyrus, who wasn't in Bombay.

Gulnaz had found out that Cyrus left the hospital against doctor's advice two weeks after seeing Perveen and, accompanied by a servant, taken the train home to Calcutta. She imagined that he might end his life there or perhaps was faring better than expected and would survive. Purshottam Ghosh was keeping an eye on things and had promised to report to Jamshedji if Cyrus died.

"Your life will become a new book once you become a widow," Jamshedji had said, sounding hopeful. "Marriage is once again a possibility. Who knows? You might bring me grandchildren before Rustom does."

She had nobody in her sights for a remarriage, though, and hardly wanted her parents to look. As she'd said to Gulnaz, she was looking forward to being an aunt.

Perveen's speculations ended as the maître d' brought her through the dining room to the corner table where Mumtaz and Razia were already seated. Mumtaz wore a lovely orange-and-cream paisley-printed silk sari, and Razia was elegant in a soft blue sari shot through with silver embroidery. The saris covered their hair, just as Perveen's did; a sign of modesty that crossed both their cultures.

Smiling at the two of them, she apologized for making them

wait. "You both look very well. I am especially thrilled you were able to come, Mumtaz. How is baby Aisha?"

"She cries like a singer, even though she's only six weeks old! Good thing Taiba-ayah's hard of hearing. But I can't be away too long—she will wake and want my milk in a few hours." Mumtaz gave a happy giggle. "You know, I don't mind at all that she isn't a boy. Everything has turned out so well."

Rustom had found an apartment for Mumtaz in an immaculate modern building on Nepean Sea Road. Her sister Tanvier often came to visit—but as Mumtaz said, there was no reason for her sister to move in when Taiba-ayah was living with her and doing such good work. Fatima and Zeid slept in the apartment, too, helping out in small ways after they'd finished their school day.

After the ladies had ordered the day's lunch special—veal with mushrooms, rice pilaf, and ice cream—Perveen opened her briefcase. She handed each of them the papers outlining their disbursements from the Farid estate. Razia silently read the English document Perveen had given her, but Mumtaz looked anxiously at Perveen.

"Will you please tell me what it says?" Mumtaz asked.

"First, it says that I paid off all outstanding bills to the household's creditors, so there's nothing more to worry about," Perveen said. "As far as your inheritances, you and Razia each are receiving seven thousand three hundred rupees. Both of you are entitled to a small percentage of residual profits from Farid Fabrics, if it begins to do well again."

"By the way, I don't wish to try to claim the land and factories for myself," Razia said. "I wish to build a future for all the children."

"I understand that," Perveen said. "But if you wish for your daughter to be secure, we should put the land in your name and allow the company to pay you something for rent each year. The separation of land value and mill value is important. If the mills ever close, you can sell the land for your and Amina's benefit."

Razia pondered Perveen's words, and then nodded. "We could also use such a profit to help the wakf. It seems sensible. Will you file the papers for me?"

"I'll do it tomorrow." She turned her attention back to Mumtaz. "The largest asset isn't yet dispersed. That is the bungalow. You and Razia-begum share its ownership along with Jum-Jum and the girls. Sakina-begum is due a portion as well."

Razia grimaced. "To think of sharing anything with her is dreadful; and I feel the judge's punishment of just one year in prison is very mild. I do not mourn the death of Mukri, but I cannot forgive her plan to kill my only daughter."

Perveen paused, thinking about how Sakina's world had crumbled—and with it, all her common sense. Now she would likely live the rest of her life with her parents—unless they could find a groom who didn't mind a bride with a murder conviction.

"What do you hear about Nasreen, Shireen, and Jum-Jum?" Mumtaz asked. "I cannot forget them. They became my family."

"They're in good health and being raised by their grandparents," Perveen said.

"If it's allowed, I will visit with Aisha. I would like her to know her half sisters," Mumtaz said.

"They will be delighted to see both of you." Perveen had visited twice already, just to make sure the girls weren't miserable. "Returning to the matter of the bungalow, what do you wish to do with it?"

"I think we should sell," Razia said. "Mumtaz agrees that there are too many bad memories for us to ever go back."

"And why would we stay behind all the jali windows?" Mumtaz added with a shudder. "I don't ever want to live without a clear window again."

"As you know, because of inheritance law, the property is chiefly owned by the children," Perveen said. "Your children and Sakina's are collectively entitled to more than eighty percent of its value. For you to sell the bungalow now, rather than wait years for the children to become old enough to fully participate in the decision, requires an exemption of sorts."

"What is an exemption?" Mumtaz looked anxious.

"It means that a judge will allow a rule to be broken, if there's good cause," she explained. "To get an exemption to sell the property now requires authorization by a male relative. I've met your late husband's cousin, Muhammed, who is running Farid Fabrics. Based on several conversations, I think he'd make a trustworthy and kind estate executor."

"But do you really think he will let us keep the money?" Mumtaz looked skeptically at Perveen. "He could do the same thing as Mr. Mukri."

Razia smiled gently at Mumtaz. "We shall meet him and ask that before we permit Perveen-bibi to make him executor. In fact, we could demand he set down his intentions in writing."

"Goodness! You have the makings of a lawyer," Perveen said, impressed.

Mumtaz blinked. "I think it's a clever idea. Razia, will you really go with me to meet him?"

"Certainly. It's not been as difficult to leave purdah life as I thought it would be," Razia said, looking around the busy dining room with a confident air. "Amina is enjoying taking me to her school and showing me the sights of the city. Nobody has bothered us. I believe everyone must know that I'm a mother, because I am treated with respect."

"As it should be," Perveen said.

"I've enjoyed staying in your home, but I'd like to take a flat in the same building as Mumtaz," Razia said, putting her hand lightly over the other widow's.

"We will have each other as friends—and our daughters can live as sisters," Mumtaz said, her face finally relaxing into a warm smile.

"I'm sure it will be easy to find a number of buyers to make offers on the house," Perveen said, already thinking of Rustom's connections. "But would you be sad if it is knocked down? That is the pattern with everything in Malabar Hill now."

Razia gave Perveen a serious look. "It is best for the house to be removed. Only then will the tragedy be erased."

"I should not like to see that house again," Mumtaz added with a shudder.

Razia lowered her voice. "By the way, even if I move into Mumtaz's building now, I might be moving on in a year. I received a letter recently containing a proposal."

"You left such a surprise until now?" Perveen said with a laugh. "Tell me!"

"Captain Ali, of course," Razia said.

After the widows' iddat period had ended, Captain Ali had asked Razia's permission to call on her at the Mistrys' home. The Indian Army officer had turned out to be a gentleman with regal bearing and kind eyes. He had been most courteous to everyone and had insisted on Perveen and Jamshedji remaining in the room whilst he chatted with Razia as they sat in chairs placed exactly five feet apart.

Perveen noticed that the two of them, who had maintained a long correspondence over the last four years and spoken twice before on opposite sides of a screen, had plenty to say to each other. The next visit included Amina, who had recovered well and was attending the same girls' school that Perveen had.

"If Ammi marries Captain Ali, we will travel all over the place," Amina had confided to Perveen. "We could go to New Delhi or Peshawar, Burma or Mandalay. That is how life is for an army family. One is stationed and must adjust. One must learn the languages and see everything!"

"You wouldn't miss Bombay too much?" Perveen had asked.

"We can always come back. Do you realize we could see all of India using the rail passes for Indian Army families? I do hope he proposes."

Now it turned out that he had.

"What will you do, Razia-begum?" Perveen asked.

"I would like to see him a few more times before deciding." Razia sighed. "I don't need to marry. But it might be very nice. And of course, I would have my own home to stay in whenever I wished."

After a convivial meal, Perveen presented each lady with her check from the estate, and Mumtaz and Razia agreed to accept a ride in the Mistrys' car to the bank.

"We don't need you to come with us. We have bank accounts

now, and I can help Mumtaz if needed," Razia insisted as they stood at the hotel's entrance, waiting for Arman to pull forward in the Daimler.

Perveen was going to protest, but then she realized that they truly wanted to be independent. She had to let them try. "That's a good idea. Afterward, ask Arman to take Mumtaz-begum straight to her flat. Why don't you come back here, Razia-begum, and we'll go back to Dadar Parsi Colony together? I'll tell Arman to wait right outside for you while you're there."

After seeing off the widows, Perveen glanced across toward the hotel's outdoor Palm Lounge and the sea. The sea-facing veranda was fully occupied by British and Indian ladies enjoying themselves with tea and cocktails. She thought she recognized a head of wind-swept blonde hair.

She went over and saw it was indeed Alice.

"Glorious to see you, darling." Alice stretched out her arms and enveloped Perveen in an embrace. "It's not too early for a whiskey-soda, is it? I tried to order one, but the waiter brought me tea."

"Must be a language problem." Perveen fluttered her hand to a young waiter, who came over to take the order. "One gin-lime and a whiskey-soda, please. And nuts—"

"The hotel does not serve single ladies alcohol," he said in an officious tone.

"But not men, hmm?" Perveen commented in Hindi. "Tell me why this is."

He twisted his hands nervously. "The ladies who come here to drink tea wouldn't like it."

"I think the danger is the tea-drinkers might join us. And then you'd have a very loud, boisterous group of aunties!" Alice said with a smirk.

Perveen reached into her bag and handed him a business card. "Perhaps you didn't know, but I'm a solicitor in practice. Will you bring the maître d'hôtel, please?"

Two minutes later the officious-looking Anglo-Indian was frowning at her. "Miss Mistry, what is this hubbub about? We have our rules."

Smiling at him, she said, "I've just a few questions. I've heard this magnificent hotel was founded to allow equal hospitality to Indians and foreigners. Is that really true?"

He nodded. "It most certainly is."

"To allow male guests alcohol—but not the female guests—runs against the idea of equal hospitality, doesn't it?"

"Well, I—you don't say, but—" He had no further words.

Five minutes later, Perveen had a frosty gin-lime in front of her, and Alice had her whiskey-soda.

"To the power of women!" Alice toasted.

"The power of women," Perveen answered as their glasses clinked.

The End

GLOSSARY

Abba: father (Urdu, Arabic)

Agiary: house of worship for Zoroastrians only; also can be referred to as a fire temple

Ahriman: the devil in Zoroastrianism

Ahura Mazda: the creator and sole God of Zoroastrianism

Almirah: cabinet often used for clothes (Urdu, Hindi, and other languages)

Anna: unit of money equal to four paise or one-sixteenth of one rupee (Hindi and other languages)

Arre marere: oh my! (Parsi Gujarati)

Bapawa: grandfather in Parsi Gujarati

Bhabhi: son's wife (Gujarati, Hindi and Urdu)

Badmash: bad guy (Urdu)

Bhaiya: friendly term of address for a man you don't know well who is not your social superior (Hindi/Marathi and other languages)

Bibi: respectful honorific for an unmarried woman (Urdu)

Binamazi: Zoroastrian/Parsi term for menstrual period

Chalo: let's go! (Hindi and other languages)

Chukoo: silly show-off (Parsi Gujarati)

Dagli: white suit worn by Zoroastrian men to the fire temple and for ceremonial occasions

Dal: lentil dish (Hindi and many languages)

Dhabba: roadside café (Hindi and many languages)

Dhansak: stew made with dal, many spices, and meat (Parsi Gujarati)

Dhoti: long, full loincloth (Hindi, Bengali, and other languages)

Durga: Hindu goddess believed to be mother of the universe; a divine representation of female power (Sanskrit, Hindi, and other languages)

Falooda: sweet milk shake often flavored with rose syrup and basil seeds (Urdu)

Fetah: traditional hat worn by Zoroastrian men

Ghelsappa: crazy moron (Parsi Gujarati)

Insha'Allah: if God wills (Urdu)

Jaan: dear (Urdu and Parsi Gujarati)

Khala: aunt (Hindi, Gujarati, Urdu)

Khastegari: in Zoroastrian tradition, a formal meeting between a man and the parents of a woman he'd like to marry

Kid ghosht: lamb-and-rice dish

Kumkum: red cosmetic paste used to adorn the forehead (Hindi and other languages)

Kem cho: hello (Gujarati)

Kurta pajama: male costume of tunic and trousers (Urdu)

Kusti: woven cord of wool worn around the waist as a sign of religious devotion and used in prayer by Parsis who've completed their navjote

Lathi: stick used for fighting (Hindi and other languages)

Lungi: short loincloth (Hindi and other languages)

Madrassa: school teaching Islamic education (Urdu)

Masala: mixture of spices (Hindi and other languages)

Meethi papdi: semisweet fried chickpea wafer (Gujarati and other languages)

Mohammedan: English term for a Muslim

Mihrab: special ornamental niche used for worship in a Muslim home or mosque

Mutawalli: the administrator in charge of a wakf or Muslim charitable foundation

Navjote: coming-of-age ceremony for Parsi boys and girls

Nowruz: Celebration of the Spring Equinox in Iran; the Zoroastrian new year

Pandal: an artistic temporary structure set up to honor a Hindu god or goddess

Pagri: a tall, lacquered hat with a tapered top worn by Parsi men for special occasions

Paisa: small coin equal to one sixty-fourth of a rupee (Hindi and other languages)

Parsi: Indian-born Zoroastrian; "a person of Persia"

Rotli: round bread (Parsi Gujarati)

Sali boti: slow-cooked lamb curry topped with crisp strands of potato (Parsi Gujarati)

Salwar kameez: woman's tunic and trousers traditionally worn by Muslims (Urdu)

Solar topi: pith helmet often worn by light-skinned people to guard against the sun (Hindi and other languages)

Sudreh: thin linen undershirt worn by Parsi men and women after their navjote ceremony

Taro: white bull urine used as an antiseptic in some Zoroastrian rites

Vakil: authorized public pleader to the Indian court (Hindi and other languages)

Vande Mataram: hail to Mother India; freedom cry in India; also the name of a famous poem (Hindi and other languages)

Velgard: vagabond or bum (Persian)

Yazata: angel in Zoroastrianism

Zoroastrian: member of the monotheistic faith Zoroastrianism, which predates Islam and Christianity; Zarathustra, also called Zoroaster, is the religion's prophet

ACKNOWLEDGMENTS

$\mathcal{P}$erveen Mistry was inspired by India's earliest women lawyers: Cornelia Sorabji of Poona, the first woman to read law at Oxford and the first woman to sit the British law exam in 1892, and Mithan Tata Lam of Bombay, who also read law at Oxford and was the first woman admitted to the Bombay Bar in 1923. Cornelia's memoirs, *India Calling* and *India Recalled*, paint a fascinating picture of what it was like to work as a female solicitor in British India and the princely states. I also enjoyed reading *Opening Doors: The Untold Story of Cornelia Sorabji*, a biography by her nephew, Richard Sorabji. Mithan Tata Lam shared memories of her education and work in her memoir, *Autumn Leaves*. Mithan was a key player in drafting legislation for Indian women's voting rights and also expanding people's freedom to divorce in the amended Parsi Marriage and Divorce Act of 1936.

One of my most important sources was *Law and Identity in Colonial South Asia: Parsi Legal Culture, 1772–1947* by Mitra Sharafi, a legal historian and associate professor at the University of Wisconsin Law School. Dr. Sharafi was astonishingly generous in answering my queries about Perveen's complicated legal situation. I also learned about common law and a lawyer's professional responsibilities from Robert Rubinson, professor of law at the University of Baltimore School of Law.

I'm indebted to my stepfather, Bharat Parekh, for encouraging me to explore the heart of old Bombay. Bharat connected me with his close relatives, Chetan, Sonal, Gopika, and Raj Parekh, who made my research trips a real pleasure. I'm always glad for advice from my mother, Karin Parekh, who knows the what, where, and when of everything in Bombay. Thanks to my father, Subir Kumar Banerjee, for his encouragement and reading suggestions, and my stepmother, Manju Parikh, for sharing her vast political science knowledge and introducing me to one of India's eminent historians, Usha Thakkar, director of the Mani Bhavan Gandhi Museum.

Usha Thakkar brought me into contact with her niece, Neeyati Shethia, an alumna of the Government Law College (formerly the Government Law School) and expert on Malabar Hill. As longtime residents of this special neighborhood, Usha and Neeyati revealed charming old sections of their neighborhood and provided an insider's tour of The Asiatic Society and Ballard Estate.

A number of erudite Zoroastrians generously shared their magnificent culture with me. Mehernaaz Wadia, a lawyer and contributor to the website Parsikhabar.net, showed me the Bombay High Court, the Ripon Club, and the Cama Institute. I appreciated tips given to me by the historian Simin Patel, whose website, Bombaywalla. org, is a treasure chest of information on Bombay's heritage. Simin's father, Jehangir Patel, editor of *Parsiana* magazine and its website, Parsiana.com, offered insights and some historical book recommendations. Perzen Patel, a chef and food writer with the food-centric Bawibride.com website, fed my hunger for information about Parsi cooking and wedding customs and was also gracious enough to read through the manuscript. A discussion about traditions with Perzen's mother, Shernaz Petigara, was the icing on the cake.

The screenwriter and director Sooni Taraporevala is well known for her films, but her side project—an anthology of Parsi slang and idioms, *Parsi Bol 1&2*, co-edited with Meher Marfatia—proved invaluable. Just as precious to me was the time spent with Sooni and her husband, Firdaus.

More Parsi slang and insights came to me from Rayo Noble; I also appreciated quick answers on family naming that came from Leeya Mehta, a Bombay expat living and writing in Washington, DC.

Other Bombayites who aided my research include Nisha Dhage, a public relations officer at the Taj Mahal Palace Hotel, an august institution that knows the value of keeping old menus and other institutional history. Hussaina Hatim Matcheswala, a retired professor from the University of Mumbai, gave me a specialized tour of historic Fort through the Mumbai Magic tour group.

Outside of Mumbai, I learned about South Asian Muslim family traditions from Shabnam Mahmood. The mystery novelist A. X. Ahmad connected me with his parents, Naseen and Ameer Ahmad of Calcutta, who offered gracious hospitality and stories of the past.

Both Hussaina Matcheswala and Mehernaaz Wadia brought me in different years to Yazdani Bakery, a traditional Irani bakery in a heritage building that dates to the early twentieth century. In homage to this gem, I've given almost the same name to my fictitious bakery on Bruce Street. If you want to try biscuits and tea at the real Yazdani, it's on Cawasji Patel Road!

More dining adventures and insights into the city came with Avantika Akerkar, the Bombay-born actress and writer. Rajendra B. Aklekar, a writer and authority on India's railway history, helped me learn the railway lines with his book *Halt Station India*. He also was kind enough to answer many questions about railway routes and stations in 1920s Bombay.

Anyone might wonder how I managed to meet so many people during my research trips. All was made possible by my steadfast and good-hearted driver Namdev Shinde and the travel agent who matched us, Bhavin Toprani of Travelite in Mumbai.

Big hugs to my indefatigable agent, Vicky Bijur, for bringing my idea for a new series set in 1920s India to the excellent editor Juliet Grames and the rest of the outstanding team at Soho Press. I also owe much to Ambar Chatterjee, my editor at Penguin Random House India, for his thoughtful notes and ongoing support of my historical fiction.

Loads of kisses for the Masseys of Baltimore. My husband, Anthony Massey, was the one who said, "Why not a legal mystery?" Tony endures my absences for work and keeps the home fires burning without complaint. My children, Pia and Neel, have grown in taking on responsibility when I'm away doing research. Yes, I've noticed!

If I've forgotten to name anyone else who's helped, please accept my deep apology, and know how grateful I am for your help in bringing this project from daydream to print.